DEATH IS THE NEW BLACK

Dominic Piper

© Dominic Piper 2017

Published by Opium Den Publishing

Dominic Piper has asserted his rights under the Copyright, Design and Patents Act, 1988, to be identified as the author of this work.

All rights reserved. No part of this publication may be reproduced, distributed, or transmitted in any form or by any means, including photocopying, recording, or other electronic or mechanical methods, without the prior written permission of the publisher, except in the case of brief quotations embodied in critical reviews and certain other noncommercial uses permitted by copyright law.

All characters in this publication are fictitious and any resemblance to real persons, living or dead, is purely coincidental.

Books by Dominic Piper

Kiss Me When I'm Dead

Death is the New Black

Femme Fatale

1

THE GIRL WITH THE CATWALK STROLL

I can spot a dipshit a hundred yards off and this guy certainly qualifies.

He's about thirty, noticeably short, wears a smart black suit, aggressively speed walks and has a black cloud hanging over his head that looks like it's about to be spitting lightning any time now. Whatever it is he's so pissed about, he's taking it out on one pedestrian after another.

He's already jostled a middle-aged woman carrying a couple of bags of shopping and barges past a besuited businessman, almost knocking him into the traffic. The businessman says something. The dipshit stops, swears at him, and pokes him in the chest a few times before continuing on his ill-tempered way.

By the time he's half a dozen yards away from me, he's had a brief, fractious interval with a construction worker whom he almost knocks to the ground and has pushed his way through two office girls that were walking and talking together, angrily gripping the upper arm of one of them to shove her out of his way.

And now he's coming straight towards me. Normally, I'd give someone like this a wide berth, but feel compelled to stand my ground, if only on behalf of the others whose lunchtimes he's just polluted by his sullen, bullying existence.

I brace myself just before his shoulder rams mine and at the last possible second yield to his force, so his own momentum makes him stagger forward a few feet and almost fall flat on his face.

Outraged and furious, he turns to look at me. I can tell immediately that this isn't some local worker in a sulk; this is some sort of professional psychopath who isn't used to being fucked with. Well, that makes two of us. He looks confused, as if he doesn't quite realise what has happened, but is going to have a go at me about it anyway.

'You watch where you're going, mate.' This is a command, not a complaint.

'Why? What are you going to do about it, shortass?'

I've nothing against short people, you understand. I was short myself once. I'm just trying to rile him. It worked. He's apoplectic – vibrating with righteous fury, rage and indignation. He bunches his fists. They're big fists. He grimaces. He's got bad teeth. He has some sort of serpentine tattoo up the left side of his neck.

'What did you fucking say to me?'

'You heard. How's the weather down there, girlfriend?'

Well that's done it. He's quicker than I thought. He grabs the lapel of my jacket to keep me in place, then pulls back his fist in readiness to administer the first of many punches to my face.

During the one second he's hyping himself up, I twist his other hand around so his little finger is facing upwards, push it into my chest and press downwards. The pain instantly takes him to his knees.

While he's down there, I change my grip on his hand to something a tad more painful, turn hard to my left, whack him on the triceps to get him prostrate and he's soon snacking on the paving stone he's just been forcibly slammed into.

We're right outside a Greek restaurant and diners are now looking out of the window. I hope no one thinks I'm mugging the poor little guy. While I'm holding him in place I wonder what to do next. The problem is solved by the hurried arrival of the two office girls that he'd bulldozed past a minute earlier. They start kicking him in the head and hitting him with their bags. Another couple of women join in for solidarity's sake. They're more vicious than the first two. I have to say he looks rather stunned.

'Well done,' one of them says to me. She's pretty. Great legs. Full lips. I'm only sorry I can't hang around and hit on her.

'You little bastard. You little knob jockey,' says the other, kicking him repeatedly in the side of the thigh. They all lay into him. I'm reminded of sharks in a feeding frenzy.

Well, that's London for you. I manage to disappear just as a crowd is forming around this urban fracas and continue on my way, wondering what the hell the problem was with that asshole. Ah well: I'll probably never know.

As Marylebone High Street morphs into Thayer Street, I start looking for the address I've been given and then I find it; Hinde Street, a small road with maybe a dozen or so tightly packed four-storey, eighteenth century houses, part of which leads into leafy Manchester Square.

On one side of the road there's a long row of hire bikes and EVs, while my side is filled with clothing shops and permit-only parking. High up, there's a blue plaque on the wall for a writer called Rose Macaulay. I locate number 16 and press the buzzer. It's loud. The sound drills through my head like a sonic pickaxe. My fault. Last night I had one of those evenings that are best forgotten if you could remember them in the first place. No: I don't understand that, either.

I've got an appointment to see Sara Holt. She's the chief designer and creative director at Maccanti, an independent UK fashion house and one of the few that mean anything on the international scene.

Although it sounds like it should be an Italian company, the founder, Terzo Maccanti, was actually born in the UK and when he died of an AIDS-related illness sometime in the 1990s, his position as chief designer was taken by a series of successors, Ms Holt being the latest.

This wasn't general knowledge for me. I happened to mention Sara's name to a female acquaintance last night and she, well, *shrieked*.

The upshot of the shriek was that Sara Holt was hot – her designs sexy, arty, feminine and extremely expensive. Her collections are regular hits at the big four twice-yearly fashion weeks (New York, London, Milan and Paris, if you're interested) and any woman who could genuinely call herself a woman would crawl over broken glass to own one of her creations.

After I'm buzzed in, I take the lift up to the third floor and wonder what the problem can be. When she rang me up a couple of days ago, she said that I'd been recommended to her by a woman called Gracie Short, who was the editor/owner of an online fashion journal.

I remember Mrs Short well. She was having suspicions about her husband who turned out to be married to not one, but two other women, using fake identities and financing the whole mess with a trust fund his wife didn't even know existed. I'm pretty sure that her army of lawyers are still gouging him for everything he's got at this very moment.

Perhaps this is a similar thing, though you never can tell. People have many reasons for hiring a private investigator and few of them are predictable.

Somehow, though, I already like the sound of this job without really knowing what it's all about. It's probably because of all the connotations that the fashion industry has for me – glamour, beauty, sex and models – though not in that order.

I took a look at Sara Holt's Wikipedia page before I came out this morning, but it was all work-related stuff and contained no details about her personal life or any decent photographs. All I know about her is that she's twenty-nine and was born in Hurst Green in Surrey. I've never heard of Hurst Green.

When the lift doors open, I get a little light-headed with disorientation. I don't know what I'd expected to see, but I think I'd anticipated something a little more homely, perhaps smaller, judging from the outside of the building and the quaint wrought iron gates on the ground floor.

But this is big, white, bright and ultra-modern, seemingly extending into the building next door and maybe further. The whole back wall is lit up with some sort of slow-moving digital mural of snow-covered trees in a white forest. In front of that are four black and white, egg-shaped Koop chairs and centre stage is a big lit-up leaf green reception desk, behind which sits a strikingly beautiful girl of, I would guess, nineteen or twenty years old.

She's got straight, light brown, shoulder-length hair and is wearing a dark green cotton t-shirt which looks like it's been painted on the nothing that she's wearing underneath and I'm jealous of whoever did the painting.

When she sees me come in, she stands, smiles, leans over and shakes my hand. She's petite with a lissom, athletic figure and it's only now I notice the amber eyes. The whole effect is so spellbindingly and exotically sensual that I decide that whatever happens with Sara Holt, I'm going to…

'Hello. You must be Daniel Beckett. I'm Sara Holt. I'm so pleased to meet you. Shall we go in my office?'

My mouth opens but nothing comes out. I follow her down a long, busy, white corridor and take in the tiny waist, skinny black Levi's and three-inch heels.

She has a lazy, hip-swivelling walk and her arms swing loosely at her side. It's almost a catwalk stroll and it's making my mouth go dry. As she holds open a door for me, she turns and assaults me with another dazzling smile.

'You thought I was a receptionist, didn't you? Go on, admit it.'

She's caught me. I have to laugh. I should have noticed the white gold Rolex Datejust Lady 31 on her slim wrist. You couldn't afford a watch like that on a receptionist's salary.

'You were sitting behind the reception desk. That's usually an indicator.'

'Well, some detective *you* are.'

'I'll have to give you a discount.'

Her perfume is light and flowery. I can't identify it.

'The receptionist is still at lunch. I just needed to use her computer for something. I can see you're wondering what's going on with this place. We own the third and fourth floor for three of the houses in a row. We had them knocked through two years ago. You wouldn't believe the hassle with the authorities. Luckily, none of them were listed buildings, so it could have been worse. My office is just down here.'

She has a charming, cut-glass home counties accent with maybe a hint of American in there somewhere. Her voice has a soft, seductive tone that you could listen to for hours without actually hearing what was being said.

She's a little twitchy, though. She's under some sort of stress and she's trying hard to hide it. It could be work or it could be the reason she wants to see me. It could be both. It might be neither.

'You lead, I'll follow,' I say, stupidly. Beautiful women distract me and shut down parts of my brain that should be switched on. I've already forgotten what year it is and who my parents were.

I'd somehow imagined that the office of a top fashion designer would be full of clothes rails, huge swatches of expensive fabrics and perhaps a drawing board or two, but this is nothing like that at all. It's a big room, but the walls are almost completely obliterated by bookshelves, so it looks more like a library than anything else.

But it's an enormous wooden table that dominates the room. It's maybe ten by fifteen feet and is covered in books, piled three or four high in some cases. A casual glance reveals it to be mainly art books, with a smattering of photography. I spot thick tomes by Doisneau, Atget and Cartier-Bresson, among others. There's a little area down the far end where work is maybe done, judging from the notepads and pens.

'Would you like a coffee? I can stick the kettle on.'

'Yes please. Black with a dash of milk, No sugar.'

I get mine in a yellow Pantone mug. We both sit and look at each other. I get the impression that she's looking at my clothes with a critical eye, but that may be understandable paranoia on my part. She slowly rubs a hand across her collarbone and smiles. I just hope she doesn't have some rat of a partner who's cheating on her; I may be forced to take action. I can hear what sounds like tinny 1960s French pop music playing quietly in the background.

'You don't look like a private detective. You don't dress like one, either. If someone told me you were a graphic designer or something in television, I'd believe them.'

'Should I get a trench coat or change jobs?'

She laughs. It's a sexy one, as I feared it would be. 'A deerstalker and a trench coat together would be a good look.'

'I'll look into it.' I take a sip of my coffee. 'What can I help you with, Ms Holt?'

'Call me Sara.' She looks downwards and fiddles with a fingernail. 'I don't know where to start, really.'

A heavy-set blonde woman raps on the door as she strides in and hands Sara a big Jiffy bag with something heavy in. 'Y-3 FW15,' she says, mysteriously. As she leaves, another woman takes her place and starts looking for something on one of the bookshelves. She finds it and leaves. Sara smiles politely at both of them, hiding her impatience gracefully. At this rate, I don't think she's going to start at all.

She takes a deep breath, but just as she's about to start talking again, the door opens and possibly the tallest black guy I've ever seen in my life comes through the door. He actually has to duck to avoid hitting his head on the lintel. He's wearing a Ren & Stimpy t-shirt and royal blue cargo shorts with fluorescent yellow trainers. I doubt whether I could get away with that look. He looks at me and grins.

'Sorry. Sorry, Sara. I've just had Larry on the phone about the mock-ups for CR? I can't find Isolda anywhere?'

'Have you tried her mobile?'

'Switched off.'

'She was having lunch with her bf. Probably having a row.'

'Makes a change,' he says, rolling his eyes and raising his eyebrows.

Sara sighs. 'OK. Don't worry, Gaige. Tell Larry I'll speak to him later. Tell him I'll call him at exactly five o' clock. Tell him you spoke to me and I said that. I'm going out for a bit. Can I give you this?'

She tosses her mobile phone at Gaige who catches it, slips it in a pocket, grins apologetically and walks backwards out of the door. 'I'm sorry,' she says to me. 'I should have known we wouldn't be able to talk here. Have you had lunch? I haven't had a chance for anything yet today. There's the Wallace Collection just around the corner. The restaurant will be quiet about now and they have great food. We can talk there without any risk of eavesdropping or interruption and get something to drink if you like.' She grins briefly and her eyes widen. 'I think I'll need something even if you don't.'

The twitchiness appears once more in her voice and I wonder what's wrong. She smiles at me and slips on a short orange and red fluffy jacket.

'That's fine by me,' I say. 'And no – I haven't had lunch.'

'Great. Sorry again.'

We leave her office and head down a staircase I hadn't noticed. I think she wants to avoid going through reception and being seen with me. Doesn't bother me; I'm sure she has her reasons.

Just as she takes the first step down the stairs, something happens and she falls forward. I grab the waist of her jeans and her upper arm and hoist her back into position. She thanks me and laughs nervously, blaming her Burberry heels. I haven't been this close to her before and I can see now that her pupils are looking a little dilated.

Perhaps she's under more stress than I imagined.

2

NEW YORK & MILAN

It takes us two minutes to walk to the Wallace Collection. For those of you who don't know, it's a world-renowned museum stuffed with Old Master paintings, suits of armour, furniture and porcelain; and that's just for starters.

I can't have been here for at least a decade, but it hasn't changed much. The courtyard restaurant has changed, though. What used to be a glorified snack bar is now a rather classy and expensive French-style brasserie with planters containing real trees, vases containing fresh flowers and friendly white-clad waiting staff.

There are about thirty tables, but only four of them are occupied. I think you're meant to book for lunch, but one of the waiters smiles at Sara and waves his hand to indicate she can sit wherever she wants. I suspect she's a regular here and they know she's important.

We sit at the back, far from the serving area and the other diners, and stare at the menu for a few minutes. While we're staring, Sara orders a glass of white wine and I have a Miss Saigon, just for the hell of it. The waiter looks amused at my choice.

She takes a sip of her wine and looks up. 'I love this place. It's like you're outside, but it's still warm. It doesn't even matter if it rains. In fact, it's better if it does.'

This is true. Technically we *are* outside, but a glass roof was built over the courtyard some time ago to protect diners from the elements and to make the restaurant into more of a going concern than it had been.

She eventually decides on pâté de campagne while I have the crab salad on toast. I decide to make small talk while we're waiting for the food to arrive. She's still a little jittery despite the white wine and I want whatever it is to flow naturally.

'So what are you working on at the moment?'

She reaches in her bag and produces an iPad Mini, pats it delicately for a second and hands it to me. I flick through a series of brightly coloured modernistic paintings; jagged, abstract, scary, many with scrawled words, almost like graffiti. I don't recognise the artist.

'It's Jean-Michel Basquiat,' says Sara, smiling. 'It's 1980s American art. I don't copy stuff, but I like to have things around for inspiration for my collections and this is what I've chosen this time. I want the feel, not the actual style. Does that sound mad? I never steal from people, so please don't think that.'

I continue to flick through image after image.

'Green is pretty predominant here.'

'Green is the new black. Or it will be when I've finished with it. I'm doing two shows at the same time this year. Two different collections. No one else has done this. I'm doing Milan and New York virtually simultaneously in the autumn.'

'Sounds like a lot of work,' I say, smiling. It might be, it might not be. I have no idea.

'It is, but I wanted the challenge. I just wanted to be the first. It's a Big Thing, you know? It'd be stressful enough without all that's been going on, but…'

'I can't wait to see them. The collections, I mean. This is great stuff. Exciting and colourful. These would make good prints.'

She laughs. 'Pretty good mouse mats, too!'

'Or even fridge magnets for the true connoisseur.'

The food arrives.

After a few mouthfuls, she looks up. 'What I'm about to tell you, well, I've already told the police. I spoke to two detectives and they've been to my flat twice and couldn't find anything. I've been to the police station and made a statement.'

For a second, it looks as if she might cry, then she composes herself.

'There's no evidence that anything I've experienced has actually happened. There have never been any witnesses. I think they thought I was a bit crazy, to be honest. The police, that is. I think if I wasn't, well, who I *am* – does that sound awful? – they, the police, wouldn't have made any effort at all.'

She sighs and rubs the palms of her hands together. 'That might be being too hard on them, the police, I don't know. But, no evidence, no witnesses, just my word for it, well; you can imagine what it's been like.'

I have no idea what she's talking about, but nod my head sympathetically. I'm good at this and practise it regularly in the mirror. Sometimes I even convince myself that I'm a sympathetic guy; it's that good.

'It's all been so complicated and sinister and strange and frightening that I don't even know where to start.'

Now there are tears starting to well up in her eyes. I've got to say something to calm her down so we can get on with whatever this is. Also, I get viscerally upset when women are crying in front of me. I can't help it and don't know whether it's a weakness or not.

'It's OK. Don't worry. Whatever it is, we'll sort it out. Can you just give me a fuckin' clue, please?'

This makes her laugh. She sniffs, wipes her eyes and takes another sip of her wine.

'Well, there's no other word that I can use here. I think I'm being stalked. I'm being stalked by more than one person. At least that's what I think it is. It's been going on for just under a month. At least, I *think* it has. Does that sound vague? After I went to the police it stopped for three or four days – sometimes it's hard to tell if it's happening or not – and then it started again. I'm not suggesting that it stopped *because* I went to the police. It's always been erratic.'

'What form is this stalking taking?'

'Well, for a start – and this isn't in chronological order or anything – someone's been breaking into my flat and moving things around.'

'What sort of things?'

'Just – I'll come back from work and go into the kitchen to make a coffee or something and I'll just *know* that the coffee mug wasn't on that shelf when I went out to work that morning. I live alone, by the way, so the blame can't be put on anyone else.

'I have a lady who cleans and irons, but she only comes on Saturday mornings and I let her in; she doesn't have a key. I was burgled a few times in the past – not in my current place, mind you – and I didn't like it. If I'm away on a Saturday for some reason or other, then the flat doesn't get her attentions and I'll clean and iron myself. It's a small price to pay for security and peace of mind.

'The people who maintain the building do a cleaning service if you want it, but they'd have to have a spare key or keys and I didn't like the idea. If you rent, the landlord or whatever might have a key or a master key, but not if you own, which I do. I pay a small maintenance charge, but that's for the appearance of the grounds, reception staff, security, cleaners, gardeners and all that sort of stuff.'

'So you're the only key holder.'

'Yes. I have the ones on my key chain and spares that I keep in work for emergencies.'

'Who knows about those spares?'

'No one. I keep them taped to the back page of one of my books.'

'OK. Give me another example.'

'In my bedroom, there's a small chest of drawers with jewellery in it. I came back one day and one of the drawers, the middle one, was wide open. I'm really fastidious and tidy. I know it's a fault of mine. And I would never, ever go out leaving a drawer open like that. I always close them when I'm finished with them. It's just a habit. I'm not anally retentive or anything. At least I don't think I am. Maybe I am.'

'Had anything been taken? Any of the jewellery?'

'Not as far as I could tell. There was another instance that I wasn't sure about. My stereo was switched on when I got home from work one day. That's another thing I never do – forget to switch it off when I've finished using it. Someone I knew had their house burn down from leaving a stereo on in their kitchen while they were on holiday. I've never forgotten that, so I always make a point of turning electrical things off, apart from things like the fridge, obviously.'

'OK. And these things only happen when you're at work?'

She wipes away some sweat that's gathered on her upper lip. She's displaying lots of physical signs of stress. I don't think she's making all of this up, but you never know. The unreal can seem real to some people and the symptoms are the same.

'No. That's when it started to really get me rattled. One morning when I woke up and went into the living room, there was a neat bunch of magazines on the sofa. I *couldn't* have put them there. I knew that the last time I saw them they were on a coffee table by the window. It's just something that I would never do. It was when that happened that I called the police. I mean – they could have actually been in my bedroom, watching me sleep.'

This sounds really sinister. Someone's letting her know that they've got access to her flat by doing things that just *might* be the result of an overactive imagination or plain forgetfulness. The sort of things that would play on your mind the whole time. The sort of things that would make you sound a bit mad if you spoke about them to anybody.

No wonder the police were dubious. At the moment, I have to admit that I'm dubious, too, though just the thought of something like that happening to me gives me shivers up my spine. At least with a real burglary the motive is clear.

'So you think someone's been in your flat on three occasions; coffee mug in the wrong place, drawer left open and magazines moved.'

'I know how silly that sounds, but I *know* it wasn't me. Any one of those events on their own I might have shrugged off, but *three* of them…'

'Is it possible that this has happened more times than you're aware of and that you just occasionally missed some of the signs?'

'I suppose so. I hadn't thought of that.' She laughs. 'Why did you say that? That makes it worse!'

'And the police found no signs of forced entry?'

'None at all. I'm on the eleventh floor. There's no way that anyone could get through any of the windows from the outside unless they had a helicopter, but they checked them anyway. There's a front reception area with two full time staff always on duty. They know everyone who lives there by name and by sight. There's someone there twenty-four hours a day. You have an electronic passkey to get past a turnstile gate before you even get to reception. They'd challenge anyone who tried to vault it, for example; at least I hope they would!

'Apart from that, there's CCTV surveillance. They keep records for a month before erasing them. The police looked at the images and there was no unusual activity on the night that the magazines were moved. The magazine thing was the only definite, specific date and time I could give them. I don't want you to think I've got anything against the police, by the way. By hiring you, I mean. My dad was a policeman.'

'What type?'

'Detective. With the Met.'

It's not impossible to get past that sort of security in a residential block like the one she's describing. I've done it many times. But to go to that sort of trouble just to move a coffee cup around is something else altogether. A highly motivated professional criminal could do this, but only if there was something for them at the end of it. No. This is being done purely to freak her out. I'll have to see this place for myself.

'Tell me what else has been happening.'

'I was on my way home, um, about two weeks ago this

was, and two guys were walking towards me. They intentionally blocked my path. When I tried to get past them, they kept getting in my way. They were laughing and sneering. I was quite frightened. One of them tried to grab my bottom and the other made comments about my tits. He was blowing kisses and saying not to be shy, while the other one sniggered.'

'How long did this go on for?'

'Not long. Perhaps thirty seconds at the top. But it wasn't an accident, you know? It wasn't *opportunistic* is what I mean. This was intentional. I saw them coming and they were both looking at me before they switched on that behaviour. It was as if they'd planned it in advance. It was as if they'd rehearsed it. I know that sounds like I'm paranoid, but it's the truth. I was about five minutes away from my flat.'

'What sort of people were they? What did the one who spoke to you sound like? How old were they?'

'Casually dressed but not scruffy. Both medium height. Not six foot; not as tall as you, say. One of them had a dark blue suit on, with a buttoned-up shirt and no tie. Shiny leather brown shoes. The other one was wearing smart black jeans and a dark green turtle neck sweater. Light grey suede-effect trainers. Not cheap, not expensive.

'The one in the dark blue suit was the one who spoke. London accent. Nasty voice. Harsh. Not too bright, I would guess. He asked if he could have a feel. I'm not a very good judge of men's ages, but I would say they were in their forties, maybe late forties. Both had short dark hair. The one who spoke was greying.'

'Did you ever see them again?'

'No. A similar thing happened, but with only one guy.

I'd been looking at the shops in Bond Street and South Molton Street. This was late afternoon on a Saturday. Every time I tried to get out of his way he kept stepping in front of me. He was very close and it was really intimidating. He wasn't having a laugh about it, you know? This guy's face was hard and serious. I thought that perhaps he was a little mad. I felt that if I'd tried to push past him he'd have hit me. I finally got away from him, but I turned around and he was still there, following me. He was laughing. Then he was gone.'

'What else?'

'I was coming out of a restaurant at about eleven at night. I'd been to a birthday dinner for someone in the business. This was, er, eleven days ago. I was walking down Heddon Street on my own. I left a little early as I had a stomach upset. I was going to head into Regent Street and pick up a cab to go home. This guy came out of nowhere, walked up towards me, jostled me hard in the shoulder and called me a bitch. That was it. He almost knocked me down. He spat the word out like he really meant it. It was chilling. He was grinning. That one really hurt. When I was getting dressed the next morning, I noticed a bruise where he'd jostled me.'

'This was another guy entirely?'

'Yes. It's never been the same people twice, or if it has, I wasn't aware of it.'

'What did this one look like?'

'Too old to be doing something like that, unless he was a crazy. Short, grey hair, grey sports jacket, white shirt, blue silk tie and a very lined, lived-in face. Hard looking, if you know what I mean. Like a TV criminal. Would have been at least mid-sixties, I think but I'm only going on the hair colour and lined face. Bit of a fat gut. It was a shock to hear him use the word *bitch*, for some reason. His age, maybe.'

The waiter reappears and takes our plates. I order another two drinks.

'OK. This birthday dinner. Was it in the public domain at all? Could someone have read about it in a magazine and have known you were going to be there?'

'Yes. Yes they could. It was Jessica Tan's birthday.'

'Jessica Tan the model?'

I know her. Looks seven foot tall, severely beautiful, outraged eyes, Chinese/Danish ancestry and cheekbones you could damage yourself on if you were very lucky. Things are looking up. I wonder if I'll somehow end up meeting her.

'That's right. It's the sort of thing that could appear in gossip columns and the like. Or fashion blogs. At one point a photographer appeared and was asked to leave. A birthday thing like that could probably be leaked by her people on Twitter. That wouldn't surprise me at all. She's very nice, but, you know…

'These are just a few instances. There are more. My car was scratched pretty badly last week. It was as if someone had run a key all down the side. They rang me with the estimate yesterday. You wouldn't believe it. The guy said it was something bigger than a key. He thought it might have been a chisel or a screwdriver.'

'Where was this done?'

'Just outside the office. It would have to have been done in broad daylight. It must have happened sometime between ten and a little past midday. One of the secretaries noticed it.'

Someone took a risk because they thought it was worth it. We're dealing with cocky bastards.

'Nobody witnessed this guy calling you a bitch or any of the other stuff?'

'No. It's as if they're waiting until I'm alone or there's a lull in the crowds. I'm aware that this sounds like I could be making the whole thing up and sometimes I wonder if I am.'

'*Are* you a bitch? I have to check. It could be important.'

This gets a laugh. 'Yes. I'm a bitch.'

'I knew it. You said this has been going on for just under a month. How many incidents like this have there been, when you've been directly shoved, hassled, insulted or assaulted?'

'Maybe nine or ten. You know what it's like in London. A few of them could have been genuine wankers, but I can't be totally sure.'

She laughs nervously at her own joke.

'Give me a couple of possible genuine wanker incidents.'

'Er, a guy sitting opposite me on the tube, leering in a menacing way. When I stood up to get off, he stood up as if he was going to follow me. Like it wasn't really his stop, you know? He gave me a really bad look; moronic, lustful, stupid, open-mouthed, simple. But then the doors closed and he was inside the train. He didn't get off after all. I turned and saw him through the window, laughing and rubbing his crotch.

'Then another guy shouted at me to come and talk to him. This was near Leicester Square. I started walking away but he followed me. Eventually I had to run and went in a shop. I told them what had happened. I called for a taxi and two of the staff escorted me to the door when it arrived. That rattled me, actually, but I couldn't tell if it was like the others, though in that case, the guy slightly resembled one of the ones who got in my way near my flat, so who knows?'

'So some of these could have been events you were attending that someone could have heard about, while others could only be the result of you being followed from work or home, if, indeed, they were connected.'

'Yes. But as I said, it's been hard for me to tell which of these things might have happened anyway, do you know what I mean? The ones I've described to you are the most strikingly scary where there could be no doubt that they were aggressive acts towards me personally. It wasn't just like it was because I was a female; it was because it was *me*.'

We both sit in silence for a while. This is a big, nebulous series of events, but I have to start somewhere.

'How many months have you got left before the two shows you're doing?'

'Six months.'

'Will that be enough?'

'It would be tight, but I know I can do it. On the other hand, I hadn't reckoned on all of this crap happening. It's in my thoughts all of the time, particularly the stuff to do with my flat. It's distracting me. One of them would be bad enough, but…' The tears start appearing in her eyes again. 'I had such high hopes for this and now I don't think I can cope with it. But at the same time, part of me is determined to overcome it. Sometimes I feel like a victim because of it; other times I feel more stubborn. I'm not going to let it stop me going out, I'm not going to let it stop my work and I'm not going to let it frighten me out of my home.'

'I take it that it's occurred to you to move into a hotel

or something until we find out what's going on?'

'That was the first thing that came to mind. Then I thought *why should I?*'

'Is the fact that you're doing this work for these two shows common knowledge in the fashion industry?'

'There was an article in *Vogue* about it six weeks ago. After that, it was common knowledge. Before that, only a few people in the company knew. I told my mum.'

'Is there anyone at all who would come to mind as a possible culprit for all of this? Rivals in the industry, for example?'

'No. It's not the way people in fashion work.' She laughs. 'If someone was trying to wipe you out, they'd do it with a whispering campaign or bitchy tweets.'

'OK. How about an ex-boyfriend?'

'I split up with my last boyfriend just over eighteen months ago. First of all, he wasn't the type and if he was, he wouldn't wait almost two years before acting.'

'Maybe he's been brooding about you and it's just come to a head.'

'Unlikely. He got married to a model. Do you know Edina Balogh?'

'Not intimately. Not anymore. Our work schedules were incompatible.'

'Well it was her. They got married in Kecskemét eight months ago.'

'What a coincidence. I own property in Kecskemét.'

'Are you always this witty?'

'Only when I'm on the pull.'

This cracks her up and she almost chokes on her wine.

'What about your mother?' I ask, while she's recovering.

'My mother? I don't think so. Besides, she lives in New York.'

'So the whole thing is completely baffling to you.'

'Yes. Sorry. No clues at all.'

'But they do know where you live. I'm assuming that the street hassle people are connected to whoever broke into your flat, at least for the moment. How easy would it be to get hold of your home address?'

'I don't know. There are online things where you can look up someone, aren't there. My flat was bought under my own name. I've never made any effort to hide where I live. Why should I? I'm not really a celebrity. I'm not Stella McCartney or anyone. There's no interest in me like there would be in someone like that. I don't go to parties any more than I have to. I'm not photographed a great deal. I have stuff delivered sometimes by couriers. I've got an Amazon account. That photographer at Jessica Tan's, for example. He wouldn't have wanted pictures of me. He probably wouldn't have known who I was.'

'When was the last time anything happened?'

'The day before yesterday. About two in the afternoon. I was walking down Margaret Street. I'd just been to see some fabrics. A guy across the road just shouted my surname. I thought I was imagining it because of the traffic noise. I only saw him for a brief instant and he was grinning to himself. Some cars and lorries went by and he was gone. He was medium height, wearing a dark green suit, black shoes and was maybe thirty.'

'OK. First, I want a list of all your appointments over the next two weeks and I want to know which ones are in the public domain and which ones aren't. Second, I want to take a look at your flat. When can I do that?'

'How about tomorrow morning? I'm not going into work until after lunch. I have a few things to do at home. I have to go out at around nine for about an hour or so. How about eleven?'

'That'll be fine.'

'We can go back to Hinde Street now and I'll get my MTA1 to give you all the info you need about the next two weeks.'

'Sorry – your *what*?'

'MTA1. Most Trusted Assistant. Sorry – fashion's full of obscure acronyms. Her name's Isolda Jennison. I have a strange feeling you'll like her. Just call it female intuition.'

'I'll look forward to meeting her. What are you taking?'

'What?'

'Pills. What pills are you taking?'

She looks shocked that I can tell. Her eyes dart nervously from left to right.

'Diazepam. The doctor said…'

'Give them to me.'

She hesitates, then rummages around in her bag and hands me a small plastic container. It's a low dose, which is something. I put the container in my pocket.

'You don't want your mind fogged. You'll need all the concentration you can get for your work. You won't need these anymore.'

I don't know if that's true or not, but fuck it. It's all part of the service and makes the client feel better and have confidence in you.

I think, from her expression, that she's a little glad someone's taken her in hand. We discuss my fee, pay the bill and head back to the office. It's starting to spot with rain and I can hear thunder in the distance.

As we walk back, something makes me jerk my head over my left shoulder. I sometimes get a slight skin-crawl if someone's attention is on me and it just happened then. But it's nothing. Manchester Square is empty, apart from an elderly woman on a bicycle and two obvious tourists getting out of a black cab. Maybe it's me that needs the diazepam.

3

MTA1

The words 'holy' and 'shit' are the first to invade my brain the moment Isolda Jennison oozes into Sara Holt's office.

Sara's MTA1 is a ravishingly beautiful woman of about twenty-five. She's tall, extremely desirable, excessively voluptuous and for a moment I think she must be one of those plus size models that the fashion houses have been favouring for the last decade, except she's not quite plus-sized enough. Pretty close, though. Then I decide she's a little too carnal for modelling; maybe much too carnal.

She's been poured into a black silk sleeveless dress that cuts off a little above the knee and flaunts delectably wide hips and a lethal cleavage. Both these attributes are accentuated by a wide, studded silver belt around her waist that just stops short of being fetish wear.

If all of this wasn't bad enough, she has full, moist lips, exquisitely pretty dark brown eyes and a gorgeous mane of expensively coiffed black hair that seems to reach all the way down her back. I just hope Sara is going to say something, because I've temporarily lost the power of speech.

'Oh. Hi, Isolda. This is Daniel Beckett. He's the private detective. He'd like to have a talk with you about my itinerary. Daniel, this is Isolda Jennison, my MTA1. She'll give you everything you need.'

A less sophisticated guy than me would be thinking 'I should be so lucky' at this point. It's a good job I'm so smooth and urbane.

Isolda steps forward and shakes my hand. Now I can smell her perfume, which is heady, musky and catches at the back of my throat. I think I may need to sit down. I just hope my mouth isn't hanging open; I wouldn't want any flies to think they'd found a home.

'Pleased to meet you,' says Isolda. It's a classless, London accent with a hint of Hertfordshire or maybe Essex. Her grip is firm and dry and lingers for a second too long. She's very close; another foot and one of her breasts would be touching my forearm. My mouth dries up as I visualise this. 'Shall we go into my office? Sara doesn't have a computer in here.'

'That's fine by me,' I say, as nonchalantly as possible. I turn to Sara. 'I'll come back and have a quick chat when we've finished.'

Sara nods and smiles, already engaged in something else that involves a pink fluorescent Magic Marker. Despite my efforts to suppress them, the contrasting physical beauty of both women is putting scenarios in my head that are best eradicated, and fast. I have to concentrate, not fantasise. As soon as I think that, the scenarios return with a brutish, salacious vengeance. I need therapy.

I follow Isolda down a corridor to her office and I can hear her nylons swish together as she walks. That sound: it's a bastard. She knows my eyes are on her curves and I guess she's probably used to it. I look at the zip on the back of her dress and imagine slowly pulling it down.

I try to imagine the sort of lingerie she favours and my imagination kindly supplies me with a few distracting adjectives – *black, provocative, indecent, revealing, tight, evil.* As if reading my thoughts, she turns and flashes me a knowing smile. 'Come inside.'

We turn into her office. It's smaller than Sara's and less cluttered. There are three shelves of books and a couple of small tables groaning with magazines, but her desk is tidy, with only a computer, a notepad and some pens.

There are prints on the wall; something by Weguelin and Andromeda by Poynter. She picks up a spare swivel chair and places it next to hers. We both sit down. She crosses her legs, looks at me and smiles. Her eyes are a little red, like she's been crying recently.

She runs a hand through her hair and shakes her head quickly from left to right. This releases more of her perfume into the atmosphere and, far worse, causes her breasts to wobble slightly. It's the 'slightly' bit that causes me to swallow and lick my lips, like a schoolboy nervously flicking through his first girly magazine.

'You were my idea, you know,' she says, pursing her lips in a knowing half-smile. 'Sara's told me everything about what's been going on. I said that she should get a bodyguard. I was half-kidding, but…'

'Well, I'm not quite that,' I say. 'To have someone shadowing her twenty-four-seven would be impractical and much too expensive. And you'd need more people than just me. Also, if we're going to catch the perpetrators and make all of this stop, we want to make them think that it's business as usual for her. I don't want to scare them off. Not yet.'

'So what do you want to know?' She uncrosses her legs, and then crosses them the other way. Her skirt is now higher and I can see black metal suspender clips gripping her stocking tops. Her thighs are heavy, white and firm. I must focus.

'On a couple of occasions, she's been hassled after leaving events or dinners that someone could find out about by reading magazines or checking the net. If this is some sort of stalker who's following her, perhaps someone who's obsessed with her in some way, then I'd like to know what she's doing socially over the next couple of weeks if that's possible. As much detail as you can give me.'

As I'm talking, Isolda is slowly running a hand up and down her bare arm. Whether it's intentional or not, and I think it is, she's giving herself goose pimples. This is a clear message and I'm intrigued and stimulated.

'Of course,' she says. 'I'll just get her social diary up on the screen.'

I watch her as she taps away on the keyboard. She's a fast typist. I notice that her nail varnish is silver, matching her belt, shoes, necklace and earrings. The necklace and earrings are genuine silver. I wonder who bought her those.

She's wearing heels, but they're only about two, maybe three inches. Any more than that and she'd be too intimidating for most people. She has great legs and nice ankles. Her toenails are silver, too.

'OK. Here we are.' She points at a load of lines and words on the screen. 'This is two weeks' worth. If you like, I can highlight the stuff that anyone could find out about and leave the rest as it is. Then I can print off a copy for you.'

'That would be great. That's exactly what I want.'

She uses the mouse and the keyboard together and I watch her lick her lips as she concentrates. I've already forgotten what it is she's doing and why I'm in her office. It's that bad. I close my eyes and inhale her perfume, only paying attention again when I hear the printer clatter into life.

'She's actually got something tomorrow night at The Royal Academy of Arts. It's a magazine launch. Do you know Dania Gamble?'

'Not anymore. Big falling out.'

She laughs. Good.

'Well, it's her. She's American. Used to be a stylist for *Vogue Japan*. She's been working on this new magazine that's about five inches thick and only comes out four times a year. It's called *Mode*. That's 'fashion' in French. Clever, eh? Mainly photographs by top photographers, beautiful ads and the odd interview. Expensive. Heavy to lift. *Vogue* need fear nothing.'

I don't say anything. I just stare at her mouth.

'This party is the UK version of one they had in NY last week. Sara got to go to that one, too, as she was over there at the time for a lightning visit, so I think she's already got a proof copy of the magazine. If she gets two we can use them for weight training.

'They've invited a load of fashion bloggers, online fashionistas, stylists, editors, suits and designers. The first issue has got a spread that strongly features work from Sara's last Paris collection. There's an online version that you're meant to be getting on your iPad, but they've been having trouble with it. Something to do with the sheer bulk of the material. They've tried to be clever and have animated bits like *Vogue* do now, but something got overloaded, it crashed and they can't get it back up. I'm sorry – would you like a coffee?'

'Thanks. Black with a dash of milk. No sugar.'

I watch her as she walks over to a coffee area. She has an awesome, ample ass. She has the same cafetière as Sara, except hers is black where Sara's was white. When she returns with the coffees, she seems a little more relaxed. We stare at one another, both trying to think of something to say. She holds my gaze for about ten seconds, flicks her hair back with her hand, then slowly rubs the side of her neck.

'So what does an MTA1 do, exactly?' I say, trying hard to look at her face and not her body.

She starts to speak, stops herself, then takes a deep breath. I wish she wouldn't do that. 'It's a difficult job to describe and it's different for every assistant. It depends on who the designer is, too. With Sara, most of my work involves helping her with the colours and patterns that she'll be using for whatever collection she's working on. I do a lot of research on the themes that we'll be dealing with.'

'Sounds like you'd be pretty busy most of the time.'

'Well, not all of the time. You have to keep some space for yourself.'

I get a seriously meaningful flash from those dark, dark eyes. It's so blatant that I wonder if I've imagined it.

'I also help with the sourcing of fabrics and things like that. But that's only a small part. I'll also do technical sketches for the manufacturers, work out trend boards and have to be continually plugged in to whatever's going on in fashion all over the world and with every designer. You have to live and breathe it. It's just wonderful. I couldn't imagine doing anything else and working with Sara is a dream.'

She flicks her hair back again and licks her lips.

'So you have to be as creative as she is, in some ways,'

I say. 'Did you go to college to be able to do all of this?' My interest in her education isn't as intense as it may seem to her. I just want to keep this going and listen to her voice, which is pretty damn sexy. It's the sort of breathless tone that most women reserve for the bedroom. I wonder if it's an effort for her to keep it up all day long.

'Well, I got a BA from Central Saint Martin's. It's the only place to go in the UK if you want to work in fashion. I mean – there are other ways in, but Saint Martin's is still the best.' She looks down and slowly rubs the inside of her wrist. 'But what about you? How on earth did you become a detective? Were you in the police? I've never met a private investigator before. It's quite exciting.'

'I just downloaded an app with a load of multiple choice questions and started the next day.'

She laughs at this. 'Everything's so easy nowadays, isn't it!'

'I've asked Sara this, but I'll ask you as well. What the hell's going on? Could she have made enemies who'd be doing this to her? Could she have a deeply disturbed fan?'

She purses her lips and her expression darkens. 'I just can't imagine what's going on and I've thought about it a lot. The first thing I thought was that it was some guy who'd seen her in a magazine or something. It's just possible, isn't it? Someone flicking through *Vogue* in the dentist or something and there's a photograph with her name underneath and she's a beautiful woman and they get obsessed with her and then all the rest.'

She leans forward. I wish she wouldn't. I keep my eyes firmly focussed on hers. 'But the thing that frightens me is that stuff with people moving things around in her flat.

Like, just to let her know they've been there? Isn't that the creepiest thing you've ever heard?

'If it's true, if she's not imagining it, then it's downright scary and I'm amazed the police haven't been taking it more seriously than they have. And the fact that it wasn't just when she was at work, it was while she was in the flat, asleep. I'll tell you, if that was me – and I live alone, too – I'd be sleeping with a fucking huge knife under my pillow, or a gun, if I could get hold of one. I don't know how she can stay there, to be honest.'

'I think she thinks she can stay there because she's not sure whether it's really happening or not. Also, she's a bit stubborn, as I'm sure you already know. But you're right; it may not be safe. I might discuss that with her tomorrow. Tomorrow is officially Day One of the investigation.'

'So you're not doing anything else for the rest of the day?'

'Not officially, no. But there's someone I want to talk to about this when I leave here, if they're available.'

'Do you work in the evenings?'

'If necessary, yes.'

'But you're not working this evening.'

'Why do you ask?'

'Do you know where William IV Street is?'

'Yes, I do.'

It's conveniently and pleasingly close to where I live. I know what's coming. Welcome to my parlour, as they say.

'Well, Gaige was raving about a new Vietnamese Restaurant that he and his crew went to the other night. It's called The Perfume River. It sounded great. I just wondered, without being too forward, if you'd care to escort me there this evening. Unless you're too busy with detective things, of course. The food's meant to be gorgeous.'

'Are you asking me out for dinner?'

'I don't know. What do you think?'

'I think you might be.'

'I hope you don't think I'm being too presumptuous. I've always been a bit impulsive. It's a weakness.' She smiles sexily. 'Back away in terror if you want. I won't mind. I'll be terribly hurt, that's all. If you want that on your conscience that's fine. Anyway, I'm sure I can find someone else if you're not interested.'

I have to laugh at this. She laughs, too.

'There's a bar called The Korova across the road from it,' I say. 'I'll meet you in there at eight.'

She looks like the cat that got the cream. 'Good. I'll book a table for eighty-thirty.' She leans forward again, her hand on my knee. 'I've *really* wanted to go. I'm a bit of a foodie.'

'I'll look forward to it,' I say, smiling at her.

'Me too. Thank you.'

Before I leave, I check in with Sara once more. She looks up when she hears me enter her office.

'Did you get everything you needed from Isolda?'

'I think so. Maybe a little more.'

She grins like she knows what's been happening. 'Good. She'll always be available for you if you need her.'

'No comment. Just one small thing. You said you had a couple of spare keys in your office. Can I see them?'

'Of course.'

She drags a cane dining chair close to one of the bookshelves, stands on it and takes a book from one of the upper shelves. It's a battered hardback copy of a book called *The Makioka Sisters*. She opens the back cover and hands it to me. There's a shiny mortice lock key and a Yale key, both attached to the cover with a single strip of Sellotape. The tape is firmly attached, doesn't look new, and hasn't obviously been removed or tampered with. There's a fair amount of dust on the top of the book. No one has touched this for quite a while. So much for that theory, then.

'OK. I have to go now,' I say. 'I'll see you tomorrow at eleven. And don't worry. We'll get to the bottom of this.'

She smiles, but I can tell she's not quite sure yet. I'll have to make her sure. We shake hands and I get the lift down to the ground floor and walk out into the street.

It's raining a little more heavily, so I get a cab and tell the driver Seymour Street Police Station. I get inside and give DI Bream a brief warning call.

4

POLICE INTERVIEW

Detective Inspector Olivia Bream is a useful contact for someone like me. I met her on a previous case when she was only a DS. I like to think that I was in some way responsible for her promotion, but I'm sure she'd have got there by herself in the end.

Still, handing her the clean-up of a case that involved multiple manslaughter, attempted murder, torture, serious assault, unauthorised weaponry and grievous bodily harm must have tipped the scales in her favour a little.

Of course, this would never mean that she'd give me access to police files, confidential information or anything like that. She's as by-the-book as you can get, which is fine by me. It means she doesn't have to create smokescreens which might push me in the wrong direction.

She answers my call after two rings.

'Well, well. Mr Beckett. To what do I owe this unexpected pleasure?'

She has an attractive, husky voice with a hint of Yorkshire.

'So I'm on your mobile now,' I say. 'Things are looking up. Would you like a caller ID photograph? I can text you one when this call is over if you like.'

'I think I'll be OK. What can I do for you?'

'Well, I'm in a cab on my way to see you. I'm probably about three minutes away. Are you free? It'll only take a short while. I just need to pick your brains about something.'

'Luckily for you I'm in my office.'

'We can do it out in the street if you don't want your colleagues to know what's going on between us.'

'No need for that. I have no shame.'

She clicks off. I have a little bit of a problem with DI Bream. She's a very attractive woman with a beautiful smile, amazing eyes and ravishingly shaped breasts and there's certainly a suppressed mutual attraction between us. But she's a police officer, and if I was her and I was seeing someone like me, even if it was just for a night, I'd want to know more about me and I'm not very comfortable with that.

When I arrive at Seymour Street, I walk straight in and she's waiting for me in the foyer. She still wears her customary blue jeans, but there's something about her appearance to suggest she's smartened herself up since getting promoted. Her hair is shorter, too, and she has on a touch of makeup where before there was none. Still looks good enough to eat, though, and the shorter hair suits her face. We shake hands. She smiles with her eyes and purses her lips in a humorous little moue.

'D'you want to come in my office? I can only spare you a few minutes. I've a meeting to go to. It's all I seem to be doing nowadays.'

'That'll be fine. It's just that something's come up and I'm a little unsure about the crime I'm dealing with. I'm also going to ask you to look something up on your computer which is to do with another officer's case, just so you can say no, because I like the way you use that word.'

'I'll look forward to that. Saying *no*, I mean.'

'The hairs on the back of my neck just stood on end.'

I follow her down a cold corridor and we go into her office. It looks like no one uses it, but I think she's just a tidy person. There's a half-dead spider plant by the window, one pale grey filing cabinet and a desk with a computer screen and keyboard but no CPU. Presumably they use mainframe computers in the police.

'Coffee?'

'Please.'

She fills a coffee maker up with water, spoons some grains into a paper filter and switches it on. While it starts to drizzle coffee into the jug, she sits down across from me and smiles, self-consciously running a hand through her brown hair.

'So what's it about?'

'Have you heard of Sara Holt?'

'The fashion designer? Yes. Her clothes are a little out of my price range, but I've seen photographs of them. Very colourful and sexy. She's at Maccanti. Quite young for a chief designer or whatever it's called.'

'She's got a stalker or stalkers. At least I think that's what it is.'

'Has she been to the police?'

'Yes. But it's all a bit nebulous. I can't say for sure, but I would think that the police might think she's making it all up. Maybe that's someone's intention, I don't know yet. There's no hard evidence and there have been no witnesses when people have hassled her in the street. They pick their moment. It's possible that all of the events she's described to me might be connected, but it's equally possible that they may not.'

As she pours two coffees into dark blue Metropolitan Police mugs, I run through all of the incidents that I can remember.

'And what did the bloody useless police say about all of this?'

Our eyes meet. She looks away.

'Well, she had two detectives visit her flat twice. DS Marshall and DC Knowles, I think it was. Do you know them? It would be really handy if you could pull up their report on the computer.'

'And tell you exactly what's in it.'

'Basically.'

'I don't know them, and I'm afraid I can't look at their files. They'd be password protected. The only way I could access them would be if I knew the password or knew someone capable of hacking into the Met's database.'

I look straight into her eyes and raise my eyebrows innocently.

'And, of course, I would not be acquainted with anyone capable of doing something like *that*. Or, at least, I hope I wouldn't.' She takes a sip from her coffee mug and peers at me inquisitively.

'So what do you think?' I say. 'From what I've told you so far.'

'Well, strictly speaking, what you've been describing here is not stalking. Not really. There's an element of stalking, sure, but it doesn't quite tick all the boxes.'

'Why do you say that?'

'Stalking is usually the work of a single individual. They don't ask for help from their mates, you know? And this seems like more than one person was involved, perhaps quite a few if we can believe what we're being told.'

She takes a sip from her coffee then stretches back in her seat, both of her hands clasped behind her neck, stretching the fabric of her blouse against her body, immediately drawing the eye to her breasts. I try to focus on what she's saying.

'Stalkers are not particularly well known for delegating their activities,' she continues. 'That's not what it's about. They get too much of a kick out of doing it themselves, and getting other people to help would mean taking those other people into their confidence, which would be too much of a risk on many levels. The stalker is usually a solitary.

'Having said all of that, there are definitely stalker-type events going on here, from what you've said. The vandalism with the car, for a start; that would be the sort of thing a stalker might do. But stalkers tend to communicate directly with their victim. They'll threaten them, they'll physically attack them, though the physical attacks are intended to frighten rather than hurt or injure.

'They might use the telephone, or at least leave sinister messages on an answering service. They may even communicate through social media, but that's cyber stalking, which doesn't seem to be happening here.'

'So this isn't some deranged individual who's obsessed with her, as far as your intuition can tell,' I say.

'It doesn't sound like it. Technically, stalking is, and I quote, "A constellation of behaviours which an individual inflicts upon another with repeated unwanted intrusions and communications".'

I let that sink in and rub a hand across my mouth. 'Hm. I see what you mean. That doesn't really fit this.'

'But it would certainly come under The Violence Against Women Act of 2005.'

'You'll have to refresh my memory, officer.'

'Conduct that would make a woman fear for her safety and inflict demonstrable emotional distress. Something like that, anyway.'

'Well, she's got the emotional distress. She's taking diazepam, she's twitchy, stressed and is often close to tears. So what's going on?'

'Off the top of my head? I think she's the target of a campaign of psychological harassment. I think all the things that she's described are connected, if only because they happened in the same short space of time.'

'Could this be to do with the stuff she's working on? She said that no one in the fashion business would do anything like that to her, but at the moment, it seems the most likely scenario.'

She finishes her coffee. 'It certainly looks that way, doesn't it? The thing about psychological harassment is that it's *specifically* designed to leave no evidence other than the complaints of the victim. That seems to fit this situation to a T.

'She's being tormented with the possible intention of lowering her self-esteem and, in this case, her focus. I mean, she's a designer. Presumably, she has to have nothing else on her mind while she's creating. And those guys who were getting in her way and calling her a bitch and all the rest of it – that can be classified as engineered intimidation. Just *one* of those incidents would be enough to prey on a woman's mind for weeks afterwards; even months.'

'This has been great. Thanks.'

'All *you* have to do is find out whether it's all really

been happening or not. I don't know anything about her mental state, obviously, but if none of it is *true*, it might be something she's created to excuse herself from possible failure at what she's trying to do. In a way, hiring you would make the whole thing more real for her, if it was all in her head. She may be giving herself permission to fail. That's just my cod psychology interpretation. No extra charge.'

'And the fact that your colleagues found no sign of forced entry into her flat…'

'They're not my colleagues. I don't know them. Well, yes. You can make of that what you will. I can fully understand why their attitude seemed lacklustre. Not professional and very sloppy, but still understandable.

'There's a phrase: 'likelihood of solvability'. In cases like this, that likelihood seems pretty low. But you don't let the victim know that. You always give the victim hope and the impression that you'll be doing your best. You don't snigger and exchange amused glances in front of the victim. That pisses me off. Marshall and Knowles, you said. I'll find out who their boss is and have a word when I've got some time. Leave a little stain on their records. Bastards.'

'OK.' I stand to leave. 'I must pay you back for this. I'll take you out to dinner sometime soon. If you're free that is.'

'I'm free tonight.'

'I'm not. Got a date. Sorry.'

'Oh, really? What's she like?'

I look upwards and to my left, pondering my reply. 'Tall, beautiful, impossibly glamorous, full-figured, obscenely busty, hair down to her coccyx – bit of a plain Jane, really. I just hope we can find something to talk about so the evening's not a total waste of time for me.'

This makes her laugh. She's beautiful when she laughs. I laugh too. She escorts me down the corridor to the exit.

'Well maybe another time, then. *Enjoy your evening,*' she says archly.

I laugh at her implied bitchiness. She's funny.

'Do I detect a hint of jealousy, DI Bream?'

'On the contrary, Mr Beckett. I rather like the idea of you spending the night with a sexy, beautiful woman, it's…I can't think of the right word.'

'Amusing?'

'Exciting. Have a nice evening.'

She turns on her heel and walks back to her office. As I walk down the steps into Seymour Street, I can feel the small hairs on the back of my neck standing up, for real this time.

5

FEMME FATALE

I get my cab to drop me off outside the McDonalds in St Martin's Lane, which is currently like an obstacle course of road works, on the pavements as well as in the actual road. It's noisy with drills and hammering and the smell of exhaust fumes seems to be worse than usual, so much so that I can taste the acidity on my tongue.

I live in Exeter Street in Covent Garden, but never take a cab directly there. I prefer to walk back from maybe half a dozen streets away, maybe more, using the most convoluted route I can manage and using reflections from shop windows and vehicles to make sure no one's following me. I repeatedly tell myself that I'm just keeping my hand in for old times' sake.

After a few yards I have to cross over the road and negotiate a big throng of tourists hanging around outside the Nöel Coward Theatre. I like it when it's crowded like this and I like crowds. By the time I reach the National Portrait Gallery I cross over to the side of the street I started on and head past The Chandos pub and down William IV Street.

I noticed the Vietnamese restaurant that Isolda mentioned about two weeks ago and made a mental note to check it out the next time I was taking a woman out for a meal. From the outside, at least, it's an amazing looking place and stands out from the other restaurants in the street.

It has an impressive grey slate front with two gigantic pots of black bamboo parked either side of the wrought iron doors and the name, The Perfume River, in black stone letters above the lintel. You can't see inside, but I'll bet anything the bill will be a killer.

I glance across the road to make sure The Korova bar is still there and head back home.

As I'm walking down Charing Cross Road, I feel like I've got eyes on me again. I do a couple of checks in the reflections of shop windows, but I don't notice anyone. There's a group of nine tourists about ten feet to my left; Korean, as that's the language their tour guide is speaking.

There are two local female workers walking and eating directly behind me. One of them has just torn a French bread sandwich apart and handed the smaller bit to her friend. A besuited guy of about forty barges past a couple of Asian teenagers, who are too busy texting to notice. Three middle-aged French women are pointing at the display outside one of the theatres. Shoppers, tourists, office workers; there's no one standing out, at least not yet.

I cross over the road as if I'm going to the National Portrait Gallery. This gives me a chance to get a good look to my left and right. I almost get winged by a fluorescent cyclist, but that's OK as it gives me an excuse to do a quick, worried-looking scan in all directions and still look like I'm behaving naturally. Still nothing. If there is someone keeping a tail on me, then they're hard to spot, but that's because they've got the advantage of the crowds and the traffic.

I walk down into Trafalgar Square and sit next to one

of the fountains, pretending to look at my texts, but actually keeping an eye on the whole area. I notice one guy in particular. He's tall, smartly dressed, in his fifties and is loitering just across the way from the National Gallery. He looks at his watch, then he looks left and right as if he's waiting for someone who's late, but I think he's faking.

I keep him in my peripheral vision for a couple of minutes and then smile as he insinuates himself through a group of dozen American tourists, lifts a purse and a wallet and continues on his way. Very smooth technique and obviously a pro.

To my right, a cab is emptying its occupants. I wait until they've paid, then quickly get inside and tell the driver to take me to the Novello Theatre in Catherine Street. If I am being tailed, they'll almost certainly be on foot, and if I notice another cab in pursuit, I'll bribe the driver to take evasive action. They always enjoy doing that, especially when there's money involved.

After five minutes, whether the threat was real or not, I know that I'm clean, and head back to my flat.

Exeter Street is one of those roads that're about as Central London as you can get, but still manage to look like an uninhabited no man's land. People who work in the area walk past it every day and don't give it a second glance. Two minutes' walk and you're in Covent Garden Market, a minute's walk in the other direction and you're in The Strand. It's not a road where someone would live, which is probably why I live there.

I've always been finicky about my security, which is why I had two enhanced Yale cylinder locks fitted to the front door of my flat, to make it difficult for potential burglars. You have to open them simultaneously with the correct keys. You can't pick the lock on one and then go to work on the other, as the first one would click back to its original locked position after five seconds. Only a very skilled and talented burglar would be able to get past them and I'm hoping there are few of those about who would be interested in burglarising me.

Once I'm inside, I walk down the short hallway and step carefully across my nightingale floor, avoiding the noisy parts. This was built for me shortly after I bought the place. Nightingale floors are a squeaky security device, and make such a racket when you walk on them that it would awaken the deepest or most intoxicated sleeper. Invented in Japan in the seventeenth century, they were meant to be a defence against ninjas, though I'm not sure how many of them lurk around twenty-first-century Covent Garden.

I turn the heating on, fire up the computer and load my Siemens coffee maker with Bugishu coffee beans. That brief meeting with Olivia Bream has planted a few doubts in my mind about Sara Holt's story. What if she really is making the whole thing up? She's obviously an intelligent woman and seemed pretty together to me, but you never can tell.

Her stress and anxiety seemed real, as did the tears welling up in her eyes from time to time, but those could be the symptoms of something else altogether.

It may be that a few disturbing, isolated occurrences increased her paranoia, so that she couldn't tell which were real, aggressive acts and which were ordinary London stuff. As I take my jacket off, I hear a slight rattling noise and remember that I've got her diazepam. Was that too cruel? I don't think so.

I sit down at the kitchen table with a coffee and start a

more in depth search for information about Sara Holt. After ten minutes I'm still no wiser than I was this morning, then come across something called *Victoria Ferguson's Style Blog & Website* and there's an interview with Sara from fourteen months ago, if the date at the top can be believed.

There's a photograph of Sara to accompany the piece and I stare at it for a while. She's still just as pretty and looks even younger than she did this afternoon when I mistook her for someone in their late teens. It's impossible to know when this photograph was taken, of course, but there's a little more weight in her face and her lips look fuller and more sensual.

Her hair is longer and looks darker, though that could be to do with poor image replication. The photograph's in black and white, so you don't get the impact of those lovely amber eyes, but I can quite imagine some guy coming across this article by accident, seeing Sara and thinking *wow*.

Of course, I'm still in the mind-set of Sara having a proper stalker, which DI Bream disagreed with, for various logical reasons. Still, I think it's worth keeping in mind that there are images of her on the net, but when you Google her name for images, you generally get photographs of catwalk models wearing her clothing lines.

The interview deals mainly with her work. There's something about it that makes me think that it wasn't done face to face. The questions are all a little nebulous and non-specific and I'm guessing that all interviewees are sent the same list of queries by email, which they then fill in and email back. I read the whole thing, though. I'm looking for something, but I'm not sure what it is.

She mentions that her father died when she was nine years old. Her mother remarried six years later and they relocated to New York City. I can't begin to imagine the culture shock that would inflict on a fifteen-year-old girl, travelling from leafy Surrey to the Big Apple, but it doesn't appear to have been particularly traumatic for her and she seems to have enjoyed it.

This, of course, would explain the slight American accent I detected in her voice. She doesn't mention whether her stepfather was an American or not, but I'm assuming he was.

When she was eighteen, she did a bachelor's degree in liberal arts at Brown University. I have to look this place up as I've never heard of it. It turns out to be a private Ivy League university in Providence, Rhode Island, established in the eighteenth century, one of the most prestigious in the country and very selective about whom it accepts. I check it on a map, not very far from New York, really. Just up the road.

When she finished at Brown's, she returned to the UK to do a master's degree in fashion at Central Saint Martin's. That's where Isolda went for her bachelor's. I wonder if they knew each other. Unlikely, I would think, though they might just have overlapped.

But after a term at Saint Martin's, she had what sounds like a nervous breakdown and had to take some time out. No particular reason is given for this. In her interview, she just said that she'd bitten off more than she could chew, and that could be true. Brown's looks like a place that leaves you to your own devices, so she may have found Saint Martin's more stressful than she imagined it would be.

The MA in fashion at Central Saint Martin's lasts for

one year and two terms. Unless she went on further courses that aren't mentioned here, that means that it took her about five years to get where she is today, which I think could be described as meteoric, to say the least.

The tone of her interview is light and playful, no signs of paranoia or anything that might lead to my thinking that she'd imagined her recent harassment issues, but the nervous breakdown thing is still interesting, if only mildly so.

I stretch back in my seat, close my eyes and think about Isolda. Considering the clothing she favours for a day at work, I can't imagine what she'd choose to wear for a date, if that's what this is. Then I remember Sara saying earlier that Isolda was probably having a row with her boyfriend and Gaige rolling his eyes and saying that it made a change, so perhaps this is some sort of revenge date for her, of which I'm the beneficiary.

Still, I should care. When you have the opportunity to take out a woman who quite literally makes your mouth water when you think about her, then her relationship problems don't matter a shit. Besides, I've been on quite a few revenge dates in my time and they always turn out to be pretty stimulating to say the least.

I finish the cold remnants of my coffee, get undressed and take a long, hot shower.

*

I arrive at The Korova approximately ten minutes before I'm meant to meet Isolda. I somehow expect her to be late; she seems the type. The place is fairly crowded, so I sit at the bar, sip a double vodka and soda and stare at my reflection through the bottles on the wall. I'm thinking of nothing, but then get a little alarm bell ringing in my head. Something's not right. It's the bar noise. It's as if someone just turned the volume right down.

Instinctively, I turn my head towards the entrance and then see what's caused the sudden silence. It's Isolda. Her appearance is so arrestingly and deviantly exotic and sexual that everyone in the bar, men and women, are staring at her open-mouthed.

I'll start with the provocative, figure-enhancing, black under-bust corset, shall I? Made from thick, ridged leather with five burnished silver clasps down the busk, this pinches her waist in such a way that not only draws the eyes to her spectacular bust, but also weaponises her breathtakingly wide hips. Under it, she wears a plain, white, thick cotton shirt with the top four buttons undone. This doesn't actually expose a huge amount of cleavage, but you feel it might if she moved in the right way.

She's moving in the right way.

At a glance, it's impossible to tell whether she's wearing any sort of bra or not, but I'm already past the point of caring about trifling details such as that.

Her skirt is black, short, perhaps twelve inches above the knee and the look is completed by sheer black stockings and four-inch heels. She's done something with her hair which makes it seem, well, *bigger*, and it's glistening with some sort of treatment or other. Add to that a slash of bright red lipstick and a touch of green eye shadow and the overall effect is stunning, deeply sensual and worryingly overpowering.

Slightly dizzy with sensory overload, I have to put a hand on the bar to push myself up to a standing position. We kiss each other on both cheeks and I get a blast of that musky perfume again. In those heels, she's almost as tall as I am. I briefly rest a hand on one of her hips. Our mouths are about six inches apart and I can smell mint on her breath.

'You look absolutely amazing.'

'Thank you, kind sir. I thought if I was going to have dinner with a genuine private detective I'd better look the part.'

'You're a real femme fatale.'

Did I just say that? I do believe I did. She looks pleased and grins.

'Thank you!'

I let her walk in front of me so I can watch that hair cascade down her back, glance at the tight lacing and see the effect that the tightness of the corset is having on her rear. The result is uncompromisingly intoxicating, and I feel an involuntary twitch in my hand, like my mind is suggesting I give her ass a hard slap – a very hard slap.

We sit down at the bar. I order another double vodka and soda (I need it) and Isolda asks for a Bitter Crush. She crosses her legs as she takes the first sip of her cocktail. She's wearing hold-ups with a black and red lace top, not that I'm looking.

The bar noise has gone back to normal now everyone's had a good look. The perfume she's wearing is something else; notes of lily of the valley, cloves, myrrh, orange blossom and cedar wood. It makes the air around us sparkle. The bar guy can't take his eyes off her. I can't remember why I'm here. I must say something.

'I've got to ask you, Isolda. Who tightened and tied up the back of your corset?'

She laughs. 'I might have just slipped into it for all you know.'

'I have my doubts about that.'

'I asked the cab driver to do it on the way over here.'

'Was that his tip? I'm in the wrong job.'

'I had no idea detectives were so droll.'

'I'm the only one like that. It's a gift. And a curse.'

'I got a friend of mine to come around and help me with it. Her name's Kitty. She's a freelance stylist for a couple of fashion magazines. She managed to force me into it so that all the bumps were in the right places. It's quite a skill. You don't think it's too much, do you? This is the first time I've worn it out anywhere.'

'Of course not. I'll probably be all right in a few days. I can't speak for everyone else in the bar, though.' Even though everyone's chatting again, the number of sly glances I've spotted in the last minute must run into hundreds.

'I'll let you into a secret,' she says, conspiratorially. 'It was a freebie. I went to a shoot with a friend of mine about a year ago. It was for some high-end fetish wear catalogue. Some of the companies sent two or three different sizes for each garment. As you've probably realised, I take quite a large size in most things and this was much too big for the model they were using, but fitted me perfectly. They said I could have it, which was *amazing* of them. I could never have afforded it. It would have been well over three thousand pounds if you bought it in a shop.'

'It looks great on you.'

'Thank you! I know it pushes my boobs up and makes my ass stick out and it's a bit outrageous, but it just feels so great having it tight against my body. I couldn't really wear a bra with it, but I don't think it really matters with this shirt.

'I always used to wonder what the fuss was about corsets, you know? The sexual thing about them? Now I can see. They make you feel, like submissively restrained but powerful and assertive at the same time. Both those feelings together make you feel, well, *wow*, you know?'

I take a sip of my drink to kill the dryness that's suddenly taken over the inside of my mouth. 'I couldn't imagine anywhere except Central London where you could go out wearing something like that,' I say, uselessly.

She leans towards me and places a hand on my knee. Her long fingernails are blood red. 'I *know*. I barely got a second glance when I came in here. It was as if I was *invisible*.' She laughs at her own gag. It's a throaty, dirty laugh. She looks at her watch. 'Shall we have another one and then go over to the restaurant? I'm starting to feel ravenous.'

Me too.

6

THE PERFUME RIVER

The Perfume River is fabulous and the food delicious. For her main course, Isolda has some sort of highly spiced shrimp kebab, but with lemongrass skewers instead of wooden ones. I have a grilled eel dish which is unexpectedly fiery and makes me perspire after one mouthful.

More small dishes start appearing, as if we'd inadvertently ordered something by mistake, but we eat it all anyway. As she eats, I watch her mouth. I can imagine kissing that mouth, devouring it and devouring her. Making her gasp and cry out; finishing her off, making her submit, enslaving her.

We have a break before ordering any sort of dessert and order a couple of Absolut Bellinis. I don't normally drink cocktails, but they seem to go well with the exotic, colourful food that we've been eating. Isolda's hand has found its way across the table and is resting on top of mine.

'I have *got* to come here again. This is just incredible,' she says, stroking my hand slowly. 'And these cocktails are delish, too. I'm afraid I'm beginning to lose track of how much I've drunk this evening. If it goes on like this, you're going to be taking advantage of me. I've read enough detective novels to know what you're all like.

We're all just *dames* to you, aren't we. There to be ruthlessly ravished and tossed aside the following morning.'

'That's not true. You'd be gone well before the morning.'

'Mmmm. That might be the sort of bad guy treatment that turns us dames on. Maybe we *like* to be used and discarded. Maybe that's our thing. Maybe it makes us feel good. Maybe it makes us feel sizzling *hot*.'

She breathes the last word, jokingly purses her lips, pushes her shoulders forward to accentuate her cleavage and dramatically flicks her hair back. To be honest, her cleavage doesn't need any accentuating, but I let her do it anyway. One of the waiters catches my eye and winks.

I rest my chin on my hand and peer across at her through half closed eyes. 'Her name was Isolda. She had a mouth made for the worse sort of sin and a body that made decent, churchgoing men dream about pushing their wives and children off a cliff.'

'I can see I must wear this corset more often!' She leans towards me and whispers, 'You wouldn't believe what it looks like without the shirt.'

'You've tried it?'

'Oh yes.'

Oh God.

She laughs wickedly and takes another sip from her cocktail. I put that image out of my mind, but it's hard in more ways than one. I've been waiting for her to talk about Sara without me forcing it. I want the moment to be natural, so she doesn't think I'm mixing work with pleasure, which, of course, I am.

'Are you ready to order a dessert yet?' I say. She shakes her head. 'OK. No pressure. I don't really feel like one myself. I ate lunch pretty late today when I went to the Wallace Collection with your boss.'

I bring us towards the subject of Sara. Now I swerve away from it.

'I've never been there before. That's a pretty amazing restaurant they've got. Fantastic food. It's one of those places that're in the centre of London that a lot of people don't know about. The Laughing Cavalier's there, did you know? And if you're a fan of eighteenth-century French musical clocks, you need look no further.'

She laughs, looks downward and runs a finger around the rim of her cocktail glass. 'Yes, I've been there with Sara a few times. It's handy and usually quiet in the daytime.' She looks up and looks me straight in the eye. 'So what's your take on the Sara problem so far? Oh, I'm sorry. You probably can't talk about it. Forget I asked. Client confidentially and all of that.'

For a second, I wonder if she's playing the same game as me. I push the topic away, but not too much. 'Well I haven't got anything to talk about yet. I don't really start work on it all properly until tomorrow. We'll see what happens. It's often useful to have some time to let the facts sink in to your brain. Sometimes a solution will reveal itself quite early on if you're incredibly lucky.'

I take a slug from my glass and look to my left as a group of six women come in, looking for a table. There isn't one and they leave, disappointed. It's a shame; two of the women look fabulous, both wearing low-cut backless maxi-dresses. I presume they're going on somewhere later and I wonder where. Maybe I should ask. A place where women like that hang out might be worth a visit.

So now I change the subject entirely. 'This is a really

popular place. I'm glad we booked in advance.' One of the waiters is hovering and asks us if we'd like to order a dessert. He's been hovering since we sat down; such is the Isolda effect. 'No, thanks,' I say, pointing at our empty glasses. 'But could we have two more of these?'

The waiter smiles, nods, takes a last grinning look at Isolda and heads for the bar. She flashes me a look of mock concern.

'Are you trying to get me drunk?'

'Any decent man would do the same.'

'Are you a decent man?'

'Not the last time I checked.'

'Mm. I may have to put that to the test.'

'I'll look forward to it.'

'My tests are pretty exhaustive.'

'I just hope I can stay the course.'

'I have ways of testing *that*, too.'

She looks straight into my eyes. I feel my stomach turn to water.

And now back to the story. 'I guess you're worried about her, are you?' I say, casually checking out the six disappointed woman as they leave.

She raises her eyebrows and takes a sip of her cocktail. 'It's just – I don't know how to put this without it seeming that I'm a real cow.'

'Go on.'

'Well, sometimes first impressions are the ones you have to go with, d'you know what I mean? When Sara told me that she'd gone home after work one night and that coffee mug wasn't where it should have been, I just thought, well, things like that just *happen*, you know? I mean, I'm always losing things that I'm absolutely one hundred percent positive should be where I left them before I couldn't find them again.'

She giggles. 'Did that come out like a normal sentence?'

'Don't worry. I know what you mean.'

'Example: I'd been reading a book for about a week and last Thursday, just before I was going to work, I couldn't find it anywhere. It was missing for about three days. It was *The Butcher* by Alina Reyes; do you know it?'

'I do.'

'I was sure I'd put it next to my bag, but it seemed to have disappeared into thin air. I eventually found it under a couple of magazines in the kitchen. I couldn't imagine why I'd put it there as I usually don't take my book or my bag into the kitchen. I *never* take books into the kitchen, you know?

'But it would never have occurred to me that someone had come into my flat and moved it; do you see what I mean? Even if something like that happened half a dozen times, my first thought would still not be that someone was coming in my flat to move things around just to annoy me or whatever. Sometimes you do things and you forget about them.'

'So you think she may be imagining it all?'

'Well, not all of it, perhaps. Maybe she's been hassled in the street a couple of times. It happens to all of us. I mean, you've seen her, she's very pretty, she's got a sexy figure and she's the sort of woman that people notice.'

'So you're saying that a few street incidents have helped to hype her up to the degree where she's imagining lots of other things.'

'Well, it's possible, isn't it? To be honest, I think she's wasting your time and she's wasting her money. I know that sounds awful, but no one's seen any of these things happen. She wasn't even sure *herself* if some of them were connected to what she thinks has been going on. Did *that* sentence make sense? I think I've been drinking too much.'

'But what about the fact that all these things only seem to have been happening over a four-week period? Might not that give them a common source?'

She frowns. 'I hadn't thought of that. But at the same time, isn't it possible that there had been some things happening before that four weeks and she just hadn't noticed them?'

'That's possible, yes.'

The waiter brings our drinks and hands us the dessert menu. 'No pressure!' he says, smiling at Isolda's breasts.

'The reason,' she continues, 'that I half-jokingly suggested her getting a bodyguard was that if these things *were* happening, then she'd at least have an independent witness. Then she'd know for sure and the bodyguard could tell the police and they might take it a bit more seriously. I *think* that's what I was thinking, anyway. I didn't expect her to take it seriously and get an *actual* private detective involved.'

'But at the same time,' I say, 'the presence of a bodyguard might make her harassers, if that's what they are, back off. Whoever it is might wait until she dismissed the bodyguard and then start all over again.'

She takes a sip of her drink and licks her lips. 'Oh, I don't know, then. It just seems a bit funny that there are no witnesses to any of this and the police couldn't see any signs of a break-in at her flat. That's what she told *me*, anyway. I *so* want her to do Milan and New York. It'll be such a great thing for her and it'll be a real boost for Maccanti. The publicity it'll get – *well*. Also the parties, of course! And if it leads to her getting her own label, she'll hopefully drag yours truly along with her!'

She takes another drink and holds both of my hands in hers. 'It did occur to me that it might be someone from a rival fashion house, you know? But people in fashion aren't like that. A lot of them are superficial, controlling, narcissistic and catty, but they don't call each other *bitch* on the street or break into each other's houses.'

'I read somewhere that Sara had some sort of nervous breakdown a few years back. Is that true?'

She looks surprised that I know about this. 'Oh. Oh, yes. But I don't think you can really bring that to bear on this situation, can you? I think that was to do with pressure of work when she was a student. She's always pushed herself really hard.'

'Like she's doing now, you could argue,' I say, with a fake expression of sympathy on my face. 'And – just speculating – if we're talking about someone in the fashion industry trying to put her off her stride, they would probably know about that breakdown, wouldn't they. It's in the public domain.'

'Hm. Well I suppose so. But she's always been a teeny bit paranoid, as well. I suppose you could even say she had a bit of a persecution complex. She's always been worried about people pinching her ideas and so on. I even heard her say that Anneliese Orie would hack into her computer and steal her designs if she could find someone who could do it for her.'

'Who's Anneliese Orie?'

'She's the chief designer at Fanucci.' She laughs, then adds a disdainful tone to her voice. 'Do you know *nothing*, Daniel?'

'I'm beginning to think that might be the case.'

'I may have to teach you a few things.'

'I hope you're not too strict.'

'Only if you want me to be.'

That's enough of Sara for now, but it's given me more stuff to think about. When she was talking to me this afternoon, I took the whole thing on face value, but Olivia Bream's comments changed the emphasis a little for me and now Isolda is doing the same. I'm not making judgements, just keeping everything in mind.

What was it Olivia said? All I had to do was find out whether it's all really been happening or not. Well that seems like common sense to me. That's the key that will start to unlock the mystery and give me somewhere to begin.

We take a look at the dessert menu. After staring blankly at the huge variety of stuff on offer, I finally choose the chocolate-filled dumplings with sweet green cream, while Isolda plumps for the Vietnamese coffee jelly with roasted sesame seeds and shredded coconut.

'So where do you live, Daniel? In some rundown hotel in Soho with only vodka in your fridge and a gun under your pillow?'

'It's a sawn-off shotgun. And it's the vodka that's under the pillow.'

'I should have known.'

'I live in Exeter Street, WC2.'

'You're *kidding*. Really? God! That's only about ten minutes' walk from here. That's amazing. Joe Allen's is just around the corner. I *love* Joe Allen's. We should have gone *there*!'

'Maybe another time.'

'Maybe, indeed.'

Our waiter places the desserts in front of us. I order

two more drinks.

'I had no idea people actually *lived* in Covent Garden.' she says.

'That's what they all say.'

'And you're right next to the Lyceum.'

'I go to see *The Lion King* every night. I can't get enough of it.'

'That's so cool. Not *The Lion King* bit. What sort of place is it?'

'It used to be a wood storage place for a local carpentry firm. That was in the 1940s. I've got the entire floor. It runs across two of the original houses. The carpentry people had the walls knocked through. Had to do a lot of work on it, but it was worth it.'

Is this how ordinary people talk? I really must look into it.

'It sounds incredible. I'd love to see it.'

'Strictly appointments only.'

'What sort of notice do I have to give?'

'Five minutes.'

'I'll have to check my diary.'

'How's your dessert?'

She licks her lips slowly and deliberately, holding my gaze the whole time. 'Very, very moist.'

And then we're walking, a little unsteadily, it has to be said, down the pedestrianised section of Adelaide Street. We haven't spoken since we left the restaurant. I'm holding her hand. She's looking downwards, intentionally avoiding my gaze. As we walk past a freshly whitewashed office building, I swing her around and push her hard against the wall, pinning her there by her shoulders. It makes her gasp with shock, then her arms are around my neck and we're kissing. Her kisses are hungry and abandoned. She tastes good; alcohol, lipstick and spices, and the scent of her perfume, sweat and arousal is exhilarating.

She presses her body hard against mine and adjusts to allow my knee to insinuate itself between her thighs. She's grinding her hips a little and her eyes are becoming unfocussed. 'Can you imagine?' she whispers. 'Doing it here? Now? Like this? With people watching?'

She moans. It's a low, guttural, animal noise. 'Oh, Jesus Christ, Daniel.'

For the second time today, the words 'holy' and 'shit' invade my brain. They're getting to be regular visitors.

7

PSYCHIATRIST'S COUCH

My alarm clock goes off a few seconds after I wake up and I give it a quick slap to silence it. It's seven o' clock now and I can remember glancing at the display after Isolda and I had finally finished with each other. It said 4.19 am.

My mouth is so dry I can hardly open it, and as I lick my lips I can taste garlic. Isolda is lying next to me, still asleep, and the whole room smells of her perfume and her sex. I turn so I'm lying on my back and try to focus on what I have to do today. I've got a very slight headache, but I can't truly say that I'm feeling hungover, just a little dehydrated, though I'm experiencing varying degrees of muscle-ache.

Usually, this is always a good time of day for me to think things over, but this morning I'm having problems bringing things into focus. This is Day One, and the first thing I'm going to do is check out Sara's flat. But there's another call I want to make before that, even though, for various reasons, I'm a little reluctant to do it.

While I'm lying there thinking, Isolda starts to wake up. She groans and stretches, and in the same moment, rolls over so she's lying on top of me, her breasts squashed against my chest, her arms snaking around my back. I can think of worse ways to start the day.

After five minutes, she suddenly sits up and runs a hand through her hair. She looks into my eyes, the expression on her face amused, curious. 'I thought you'd be bad, but I didn't realise you'd be *that* bad,' she says, gently stroking the hair out of my eyes.

I hold her waist firmly in both of my hands. 'Well, you know what us detectives are like. You're just *dames* to us, there to be used.'

'Maybe I like being used.'

'Maybe you do.'

'Maybe you like doing the using.'

'Anything's possible.'

She laughs and gets up, heading towards the bathroom. She looks over her shoulder, catching me staring at her ass. 'If you were a gentleman, you'd make me a coffee.'

'You still think I'm a gentleman after last night?'

She narrows her eyes. 'I'll make the coffee.'

I laugh. 'Don't worry. I'll do it. I need to see if I can still walk.'

I go into the kitchen, load the Siemens with Black Ivory coffee beans and start it up. I'm just about to look for a couple of big cups, when I feel Isolda behind me, her arms around my waist, her breasts against my back and her chin resting on my shoulder. I should have heard her approach, but I didn't, and feel mildly annoyed with myself.

'What do *you* want?'

'Well,' she purrs, 'coffee will do for a start.'

'Then what?'

She pulls back and slowly drags her fingernails down my back. 'Then maybe something to eat.'

'I'll see what I can find.'

'You do that.'

She sits down at the kitchen table and looks around. 'This is such a cool looking place. Why have you got bars on all of the windows?'

'To stop people escaping.'

'I should have known. And what about the squeaky floor in the hallway? That's some sort of old-fashioned security thing, isn't it.'

I stick four plain croissants in the oven. 'Well spotted. It's called a nightingale floor. In the unlikely event of a burglar being able to pick my door locks without me noticing, they'd find it difficult to sneak through the hallway without making a terrible racket.'

'You're obviously very security conscious.'

'Or I don't want people running away in the middle of the night. It works both ways.'

'Does that happen often?'

'All of the time.'

'I'm going to have to get back and change before I go into work. Got to look a bit more respectable today. I'm having lunch with my dad.'

'Well, it's still early. What time do you have to be in?'

'Ten.'

'And where do you live?'

'Farringdon.'

'Well, that's only a twenty-minute cab ride from here.'

'Plenty of time, then.'

'For what?'

'What did you have in mind?'

When everything's ready, we eat and drink for a while in silence, both of glancing at each other's bodies. Naked, Isolda is just as I imagined she would be. Her breasts are very large but pleasingly firm, and the rest of her body fashioned with dangerous curves that are luscious and captivating.

Her movements are precise and provocative; she keeps raising an arm to rub her neck or fiddle with her hair, she leans forward, she crosses her legs, she runs a hand down one of her thighs. The effect on me is enormously predictable, but she makes a point of ignoring it.

'So what are you going to do today, Daniel? I can't imagine where I'd even start, trying to sort something like this out.' She grins. 'Won't it be very, very hard?'

'I don't know. There're a few things I want to check out and they're mainly to do with verifying Sara's story. It would be unfortunate for many reasons if all of this was in her mind, but if it *was*, I wouldn't want to keep charging her for my services. It wouldn't be fair.'

'So what are you going to do first?'

'The main thing that concerns me is that someone is breaking into her flat. If that's true, and the police can't find any evidence that it's happened, then it could be we're dealing with professionals of some sort, and I'd like to know which type of professional they are, why they're doing it and how they can be stopped.'

'So you don't think it's some solitary unhinged individual?'

'I honestly don't know. There seems to be more than one person involved, but whether a single individual is responsible for orchestrating it all, I can't tell. At the moment I'm open to all possibilities.'

'You must tell me what you find. I'm so worried about her. It's awful when something like this is going on and you can do nothing about it. Me and the rest of the designer posse – we're more like a family than business associates. Something like this affects us all emotionally.'

'Sure.'

She sits up and stretches, running her hands down the side of her body. This is killing me, but it's not disagreeable. 'I'd really like to see you tonight, Daniel,' she murmurs. 'I really must. I'm not even sure I'll be able to get through the day.'

'I don't know what I'm doing tonight, yet. I'll give you a call.'

'Are you playing hard to get, you bastard?'

'Yes.'

She gets up and walks towards the bedroom, glancing over her shoulder at me as she leaves. To demonstrate my admirable self-control, I hesitate a full two seconds before I follow.

*

By the time I'm walking up Wimpole Street, it's almost nine-fifteen. The road is already very busy and noisy work on a lot of the buildings has already started. As there are so many medical practices here, I wonder how they cope with this racket. Perhaps they don't.

All the parking places are already occupied, too. If it isn't three-ton flatbacks laden with scaffolding, it's Rolls Royces and Mercedes with smoking chauffeurs leaning against them, slagging off their rich employers to each other. All the chauffeurs, I notice, have really big, expensive-looking watches. Perhaps it's one of the perks of the job.

This visit may be a total waste of time or it may be useful in some way that I can't appreciate yet. Attempting to visit the private practice of a top Wimpole Street psychiatrist without an appointment has its risks, but if I called in advance, there'd be a chance that I wouldn't be seen at all, maybe with good reason in this case.

Dr Aziza Elserafie is a former client of mine. She hired me about six months ago when she suspected that her husband was having an affair. She was right, but it was a little more complex than that. He actually had two separate families that she didn't know existed, as well as an 'ordinary' mistress. All of these franchises were financed by bank accounts she had no knowledge of, two of them under false names, one of them in Liechtenstein.

Her husband was a pretty smart guy – he was a high-profile hedge fund manager – and had covered his tracks with some skill, but eventually I managed to get enough evidence for her to sue for divorce. She didn't want the money; she just wanted to ruin him, which she succeeded in doing in spectacular fashion, with the help of her attack dog lawyers. He'd been so careful. He truly didn't know what had hit him.

Aziza's case was strangely similar to that of Gracie Short, who'd recommended me to Sara Holt. Intelligent, attractive women with good careers and jackass husbands who had secret alternative marriages, families and money. I can't imagine expending the energy and subterfuge skills for something like that. Why not just leave the original wife in the first place? Fear? Insecurity? Love?

When Aziza's case was complete, we started seeing each other intermittently for about three months until it had to fizzle out. She wasn't too pleased about this, but I was pretty sure she'd get over it. I just figured she needed some relief after the trauma of finding out about her husband's behaviour and she had to agree.

I'm just crossing the road at some traffic lights when I suddenly get the feeling I'm being watched again. When this happens, you tend to assume it's connected with the case you're on, but that's not always true. Whatever the cause, you have to treat it with the same diligence.

I spot a middle-aged man and his wife examining the contents of an M&S shopping bag. I smile, approach them, point at my watch, tell them that it's failed and ask them if they have the correct time. This gives me an excuse to alter my position in relation to the road and take a quick glance in the direction I just came from.

There's a heavily made-up young Arabic woman in a tight black top, khaki cargo shorts and pink high heels, two men in dark blue overalls unloading scaffolding from a lorry and a well-dressed woman in a silver fox fur coat waving at someone on the third floor of one of the houses. She's left-handed. Everything looks fine.

It may be nothing, of course, but if it is, they're keeping their distance, which means my not noticing is important to them in one way or another. This is usually the sign of a professional, which always has to be of concern, but I'm also aware that I might be imagining things. When any degree of counter surveillance is hot-wired into your brain, you do get the occasional false alarm.

On the other hand, that's three times in less than twenty-four hours that I've got the surveillance shivers and I'm not usually wrong. Ah well.

Aziza's practice is in a solid-looking nineteenth century town house, sandwiched in between two more modern buildings, just after the intersection with Queen Anne Street. The exterior of the ground floor is painted white and festooned with colourful hanging baskets.

Presumably you don't want things to look too dreary and unwelcoming if you're a psychiatrist.

I check the brass plaque and there she is: Dr A. Elserafie MBChB MRCPsych FRCPsych. I press the buzzer.

'Hello?'

'Good morning. I have an appointment with Dr Elserafie.'

I'm buzzed in without question and approach the elderly lady sitting at the reception desk. She looks up and smiles, waiting for my details.

'Sorry. I don't really have an appointment. Could you just buzz her and tell here that Daniel Beckett is here? I'll just go and wait in there. Thanks very much indeed.'

I give her my best grin and disappear into the waiting room before she can say anything. As this is a medical place, I'm depending on them being nice and understanding.

I sit down, pick up an old copy of *Condé Nast Traveller* and wonder what I'm going to say to Aziza, if I can get a word in. I'm alone in here, which is good. If she's got any patients who urgently need their wallets emptying, they obviously haven't arrived yet.

I can tell she's come into the room without looking up. Firstly, she has a strong presence and secondly, she wears Amber Mystique by Estée Lauder, a distinctive, woody perfume with an unmistakable aroma.

Aziza is about fifty-five, Egyptian, alluringly and strikingly attractive, with jet black hair flecked with grey tied into a tight bun, beautiful soft olive skin, great cheekbones, big brown eyes shadowed with green and a full, sensual mouth painted with dark red lipstick which is presently pursed into a sour expression of indignation.

She stands with her arms folded and stares at me. She's wearing a crimson and purple long-sleeved velvet blouse buttoned up to the neck, a black pencil skirt, black stockings and black court shoes. Even in this straitlaced work attire you can tell she has a knockout figure. For a second, I remember what it was like being with her; the way her face changed, the unexpected intensity, the brazen snarl of lust on her lips, then I put it all out of my mind: this is business.

'What the *fuck* do you want, Daniel?'

I stand and put my hand out for her to shake. I know it's a waste of time, but I couldn't think of anything else to do. A kiss on the mouth would be out of the question, I'm guessing. I can see the receptionist craning her head to see what's going on. The room smells of furniture polish. Aziza keeps her arms folded. Oh well.

'I need to have just five minutes of your time, Aziza. I'm working on a case where a woman seems to be the victim of a campaign of psychological harassment…'

'Seems?'

'That's why I wanted to speak to you. I just wanted to run a few examples past you and get a quick opinion. I want to see if this is worth continuing with before I start looking into it in detail.'

She stares at me in silence for about ten seconds. Her eyes are boring into my skull. 'Who is this woman?'

'You know I can't tell you that.'

'Come into my consulting room.'

We walk past reception and I follow her up to the first floor. Her consulting room is a tidy, sparse place; beige walls, beige carpet, two bookshelves filled with psychiatry books, a sideboard with a small stereo on the top, two large black leather sofas facing each other, two chairs, a couple of side tables and not much else. I'd expected to see a psychiatrist's couch, but maybe they don't use those anymore. By the window there's a large desk with a green leather top and on it, a banker's lamp with an orange shade.

On the wall there are four framed certificates, and three inconsequential paintings of the countryside. Aziza points to one of the sofas, so I sit down. She sits on the one opposite, still staring at me with pursed lips, her posture straight-backed, tense and uncomfortable.

Her hands are clasped tightly together and I notice she still wears all her gemstone rings – malachite and lapis lazuli on the left hand, black tourmaline, sapphire and pink topaz on the right. She isn't saying anything, so I take that as a cue for me to start. Typical psychiatrist's ploy; they can't help themselves.

'OK. First, nothing I've been told by this client can be corroborated. There are no witnesses to any of the events that I'll describe and no hard evidence of any sort. I only have her word for any of this. Whatever, the stress of it drove to her to get a prescription of diazepam, which I've since taken off her as a confidence builder.'

'Go on.'

'The only connecting factor to all the events is that they've taken place over a four-week period, as far as my client can tell. There may have been events before this, but if there were, she was not aware of them and/or didn't connect them to the harassment she's been experiencing more recently.

'Some of the events may just be coincidentally similar and not connected to any theoretical campaign of harassment. She is taking on a large amount of important and stressful work and this became public knowledge about six weeks ago. On the face of it, it could seem as if the events I'll describe are a concerted effort to put her off her stride, though, once again, there is no proof of this.'

She fiddles with the malachite ring. She looks downwards to the left. She quickly smiles to herself and then raises an eyebrow.

'You have ruined me for other men, Daniel. I just thought I'd better tell you. I'm not saying this to make you feel guilty. Yes I am. I am saying it to make you feel guilty and to make myself feel guilty by saying it. I want to punish you. God knows I have tried to find satisfaction by other means, but it's not enough. It's never enough.'

I knew this wouldn't be easy. I guess I'll just have to plough through it, insensitive as it may seem, and hope some of it piques her interest. 'I'll give you the most interesting example. She thinks that someone has been breaking into her flat. They have not been stealing things and she has not seen or heard them, but they are moving small items around. Things are not where they should be. She is positive that she is not imagining these events.'

'Has this been happening when she is actually in the flat?'

'It's usually when she is out, though on one occasion it seemed as if someone had intruded while she slept and moved some magazines around in one of the rooms. The police have found no evidence whatsoever of a break-in and nothing showed up on the reception CCTV for that particular night-time visit, if it really happened.'

'Why have you not called me? It's been over six months. Am I not appealing to you anymore? Am I too old for you? Is that what it is? I don't seem to recall you being too concerned about my age during the times we were together. You said you liked it. You said I had the eagerness and drive of a thirty-one-year-old. You said that my age excited you.'

I take a deep breath. 'You had been through a major upheaval in your life, Aziza. I thought you would now need time to rebuild things…'

'To find out who I really am? Is that what you're going to say? What utter bullshit, Daniel. That's the sort of lunacy that psychiatrists come up with. I know who I am and I know what I want; what I *need*.'

'I…'

'What else is happening to her?'

'People are accosting her in the street. They are obstructing her way, they are calling her by name and insulting her, they are jostling her in the shoulder. It's a huge variety of deniable actions from a variety of people. She's never seen the same person twice, at least she thinks not.'

Aziza looks down at her hands and fiddles with another of her rings. 'I see. My first thought is that she is suffering from some type of persecutory delusion,' she says, not looking up. 'It is the fact that none of it can be corroborated that makes me think that is the case. If a single instance could be seen to be real, then that thesis would instantly collapse.

'The person thinks that something bad is going to happen to them, or is already happening. They think that a person or persons is intending to cause them harm. They think that people are spying on them. They think they're being followed or ridiculed. This is common in schizophrenia. Does she strike you as being schizophrenic, Daniel?'

'Give me three symptoms that I may have noticed.'

'Disordered speech, flat facial expression, lack of motivation…'

'No. Nothing like that. She's lively, garrulous, obviously smart, enthusiastic and confident.'

'You find her attractive.'

'Why do you say that?'

'Your facial expression changed slightly when you spoke about her. Your eyes lit up. A *wry smile* flickered across your mouth. You readjusted your seating position. You used wide movements of your hands as you spoke of her.

'Have you slept with her? Tell me what it was like. Tell me if she pleased you like I did. Tell me the things she said. Did she say the sort of things that I did? Was she that crude? That uninhibited? That vulgar?'

I take a deep breath. 'No I have not slept with her. She's a client.'

'I was a client of yours once. You told me you wanted to sleep with me as soon as you saw me. How old is she?'

'Late twenties.'

'Is that what you like now? Young flesh?'

'She had some sort of nervous breakdown when she was a student. I don't know if that would help with your diagnosis.'

She shrugs. 'That term means nothing, really. I'd need to know the symptoms, causes and what was done about it. What is her body like? Is she slim? Do you fantasise about caressing her body? Do you casually daydream about taking her?'

'Listen, Aziza. I'm not one of your bloody patients.'

'I'm sorry.'

'Someone scratched her car pretty badly with a chisel or something.'

'She could have done that herself. Perhaps all of this is to draw attention to herself in some way. In a sexual way.

To draw attention to her suppressed desires. Does she have a lover or lovers? Perhaps she fantasises about a man, a burglar, breaking into her apartment and ravishing her.

'Whatever her work is, perhaps she is trying to give herself permission to fail. Perhaps the stress of her work is too much for her and she's looking for a way out. Stories, none of them checkable, piling up one on top of the other, and she even goes as far as damaging her own car and hiring a private detective.

'I think about you every single night before I go to sleep. Do you understand what I'm saying to you, Daniel? Do you? Can you imagine what those thoughts are like? Do you want me to tell you? Do you want me to be brutally explicit?'

'So you think there's a good chance that she's imagining it all.'

'I can never give an accurate assessment without actually meeting her, but the lack of corroboration, the big stressful project on the horizon, a previous nervous breakdown – unless you can prove otherwise, that will have to be my assessment.'

'That's very helpful, Aziza.'

This is very similar to DI Bream's theory, which is interesting.

It might be something she's created to excuse herself from possible failure at what she's trying to do.

Aziza fiddles with the pins holding her hair in a bun. It falls loosely to her shoulders. Now what?

'Have you any idea how much an initial consultation with me costs, Daniel?'

'Um…'

'Three hundred and fifty pounds.'

She stands up, glides over to the door and locks it. I look at my watch. Nine thirty-five.

'That seems pretty reasonable.'

'I've been ready from the moment I saw you in the waiting room. I hate it that I'm like this. My body is rebelling against my mind. My id is at war with my super-ego. I am like an animal, ready for a mindless rutting, controlled by desires that I cannot understand or control.'

She pushes a button and speaks, I assume, to the receptionist downstairs.

'Joyce? It's Aziza. Hello. Yes. Is my ten o' clock there yet? OK. When he arrives, can you move him forward half an hour? Tell him to go and get a coffee or something? Better still; tell him he made a mistake. I'm seeing him for paraphrenia, after all. I'm not to be disturbed. Thank you.'

She looks away from me, starts to unbutton her blouse and I wonder if I've avoided the three hundred and fifty pounds initial consultation charge. I think I probably have.

8

BURGLARPROOF

I get out of my cab near St John's Wood tube station and head up Abbey Road. Already, there are about half a dozen tourists hanging around the graffiti-covered white walls of the famous recording studio and several more taking selfies while jaywalking on the nearby zebra crossing. Sara Holt lives in Satterfield Court, which is about half a mile further north.

It's an attractive, modern block, perhaps built in the 1980s, though it's been designed to match the character of the surrounding buildings which are certainly a few decades older. There's neat shrubbery and a well-stocked garden outside. This is a pretty well-heeled area and you'd be spotted loitering straight away. Even in the thirty seconds I've been standing here staring at the building, I've attracted several suspicious glances, one of them coming from inside the reception area.

I count the floors so I can locate the eleventh, where Sara lives. The walls appear to be flat red brick and would be impossible to scale. Even if you could do it, in the daytime you'd be spotted immediately and in the night you'd be illuminated by the powerful spots that I can see dotted around the entrance and behind the hedges. Too high and too dangerous to bother, especially if you weren't going to steal anything.

I decide to take a more detailed look at the outside later if I think it's necessary. For now, I'm just going to head inside, before the concerned security staff call the police.

As soon as you push your way through the heavy, spring-loaded glass doors, it's obvious that you couldn't slip in here without anyone noticing.

The first thing you encounter is a burnished steel security barrier with two solid-looking turnstiles. You'd need the electronic passkey to get through these, as Sara mentioned yesterday. The height wouldn't stop you vaulting it, but the width would; you'd need a run-up of fifteen to twenty feet and there simply isn't that sort of distance between the barrier and the entrance.

There are five security cameras aimed directly at the entrance and two more on the ceiling that slowly rotate. If by some miracle you got past the security barrier, you're then faced with the reception desk and its vigilant staff.

There are three people here – two sitting, one standing. The standing guy looks like a typical security heavy. He's about fifty, heavy set and his deportment tells you he doesn't take shit. He's talking and laughing with a female receptionist but has pinned me immediately and doesn't take his eyes off me.

The female receptionist sees me and smiles. Sitting next to her is a guy in his twenties. He looks up, and then continues with whatever he's doing on a computer screen. Despite this, he's watching me too; his eyes flick upwards every couple of seconds and he keeps glancing at the security heavy. It's a scene you'd normally encounter in a hotel, albeit with a little less vigilance.

'Can I help you, sir?' says the receptionist.

She smiles, stands up and walks towards the security gate. Maybe she thinks I'm delivering something.

'My name's Daniel Beckett. I'm here to see Sara Holt in 11a. She's expecting me.'

'Just one moment, sir.'

The young guy is already calling up. After a second or two, he nods to the woman, a green light appears on the turnstile and I walk through.

She walks over with me to the lift and presses a button on the wall. She's blonde, petite, has a cute wiggle and looks undeniably foxy in her grey uniform. I wonder what it would be like to sleep with her. 'Eleventh floor. Turn left when you get out.'

'Thanks.'

I see her staring at me as the lift doors close. I decide to give her my card when I leave, if I get an opportunity. You never know.

'Come in, Daniel. Dead on time, I see!'

She's wearing pale blue jeans and a yellow sweat top which is slightly too large for her. Beautiful without makeup, shorter as she's not wearing shoes and her pupil size is back to normal. She seems pleased to see me.

'Would you like a coffee?'

I nod and we make out way into her kitchen. This is a big, big place and must have cost a packet. At a glance, there're no carpets; everything is pine floors. Slightly more difficult for an intruder to remain silent, particularly at night. You'd have to take your shoes off or wear crêpe soles. Big purple abstract prints in the wide, white hallway and a long glass table with a few pieces of junk mail on top.

The kitchen is to our immediate left. I sit down at a big wooden table and watch her as she prepares the coffee things. I realise that I'm observing her in a different way after the theories I've heard about her possible mental state and finding out about the breakdown.

It's cruel, but I'm now watching for signs of mental instability. When we met yesterday, I had no doubt at all she was telling the truth. Now I wonder if she was just telling the truth as she perceived it.

She stops in mid preparation and turns her head to the left, sniffing once.

'Is that you?'

'Is *what* me?'

'That smell; Taif Rose, Pink Pepper – is it Amber Mystique?'

I have to laugh. 'You've caught me out. But very good.'

She sits across from me and places the coffee cups on a couple of flowery William Morris coasters. 'Eventually I'm hoping to create my own perfume brand, just like Coco Chanel. Well, she chose it rather than created it, but you know what I mean. I've been on a couple of courses, so I recognise all the individual notes in well-known brands. Why do you wear it?'

I'm speechless for a couple of seconds, then laugh out loud. 'I don't wear it.'

'Ah. I see. Sorry. A lady friend, I assume.'

'No. I just hang around Selfridge's perfume department a lot. I can't resist the free samples.'

She giggles and holds her coffee cup in both hands and takes a small sip. 'So what do you want to do? What do you want to look at?'

'I'd like a tour of this place and I'd like you to tell me what the police said when they were here.'

'They said that there was no sign whatsoever that anyone could have broken in.'

'Did they check outside?'

'No. They said there was no need to. There were no signs of forced entry on any of the windows. The only door is the one you just came in through and they said that seemed fine.'

'Did they check for fingerprints?'

'Yes. The only ones they found were mine.'

'And what about the things that you said had been moved?'

'No prints on them either. Just mine, though I had washed the coffee cup I was telling you about before the police came. I wasn't thinking straight. It was only my prints which appeared on the drawer in my bedroom and there were poor quality prints on one of the magazines, but still identifiable as mine.' For a moment, the brightness disappears from her face. 'I'm not lying about this, you know. I realise that it looks bad for me.'

You can say that again. 'Don't worry yourself about that. OK. The police are making a couple of assumptions here, which may not be correct. Firstly, they're assuming that the only way into this building is by passing through the reception area, something we know didn't happen during the night-time visit because of the CCTV footage and the statements of reception security staff.

'Secondly, they are then logically assuming that the only way of gaining access to your flat would be through the windows, which they couldn't find evidence of, and would, in any case, require astounding burglarising skills by whoever did it. Someone of that calibre would not be doing it to leave a drawer open.'

I'm thinking there has to be an easier way of getting in

here, but I can't imagine what it could be. I've got a headache. I start thinking of last night and Isolda. I take another sip of coffee.

'Right, Miss Holt,' I say, brightly. 'Let's commence the tour. Which room do you want to start with?'

'Let's have a look in the living area,' she says, downing her coffee in one.

This is a large, pine-floored room with a single white sofa in front of a fireplace that's never used, with big black stereo speakers on the right and left. CDs scattered on the floor; Björk, Diana Krall, Louie Bellson, Annette Peacock. Above the fireplace is a large print of Avenue de l'Observatoire by Brassaï. I'm slightly surprised she has well-known stuff on the walls in print form. I somehow imagined she'd always be buying originals.

The wide, high window overlooks the street. There isn't an inch of the windowsill that isn't covered in piles of books. Even if you managed to scale the wall outside, coming in through a window like this would be a nightmare, even for a professional. There are white venetian blinds, but they're pulled up.

'Is this window always locked?'

'Yes. I never open it, mainly because those books are in the way. There are three parts to it with three different keys. I think I've opened these windows once since I've been here. It took me and the police ten minutes to get all of those books out of the way so they could take a detailed look at the windows and the locks.'

It's the same story with the kitchen and bathroom. These have windows which are opened from time to time, but, once again, they are usually locked and the keys in envelopes in a kitchen drawer. Like the living area, all of them have windowsills that are covered with stuff that you'd knock over if you entered this place through the window. In the bathroom it's shampoo, bath oils and feminine stuff and in the kitchen it's indoor plants, potted herbs, framed photographs and a Hawaiian Munny.

You could, of course, put these items back if you knocked them over, but it would be unlikely they'd be in the right place and/or position and someone as bright as Sara would notice the change immediately. Plus, it would be too obvious and not creepy enough.

Sara's bedroom is another large room, very cool in black and white with a king-size bed and a wall-sized wardrobe, but unlike the others I've seen, the window is on the side of the block, overlooking the enormous, forest-like back garden of the house next door. I check all of the windows and they're secure.

Sara tells me that she does open these windows from time to time in the spring and summer, but usually they're closed and locked. There aren't any curtains, but there are four big sections of black metal venetian blind which are worked by a remote control I can see on the bedside table.

Any burglar would make a hell of a noise negotiating these, but that wouldn't necessarily matter in the daytime when she wasn't here. I get her to open one of the windows for me so that I can look down.

The drop is well over a hundred feet and, like the front, there are no drainpipes or anything similar that anyone could scale up, even if they had the skill, motivation and nerve. Besides, it's concrete at the bottom; you slip this high up and you're more than likely dead.

The blinds are left half open, and I wonder for a moment if anyone has a direct view of Sara's bedroom, perhaps some solitary perv with a pair of binoculars watching her getting undressed, but nothing overlooks this section of the flat and the tall evergreens growing next door prevent all direct views.

'How many flats on each floor here?'

'Two. When you get out of the lift you turn left to get to me and right to get to my neighbour.'

'Who's your neighbour?'

'An old lady. Mrs Antúnez. She's a widow. I don't know her, really. Rarely see her.'

There's a large, airy, second bedroom immediately next to Sara's, filled with piles of magazines, half a dozen racks of shoes and huge wardrobes. There's a large bed, which doesn't look as though it's ever been slept in. Prints on the wall; Braque, Matisse and a couple I don't recognise. I do the same checks on that one, once again getting her to open the window so I can look down. Same result. No way up, no way in.

A professional mountaineer might be able to climb up here using the gaps in between the bricks as a gripping aid, but that would be an insane amount of risk and effort just to move some magazines around, it would take a long time, and once again you'd be noticed.

If I was trying to break in to somewhere lower down, say the second or third floors, I might use a grappling hook if I was confident that it would fasten itself on a window ledge effectively enough that I could pull myself up. But even then, there'd be the problem of getting through a locked window without leaving a trace.

There's another large room, which I suppose is a work area, except it has comfy-looking velvet sofas, a wide screen television and another big stereo. The walls are all bookshelves except for one gap where there are a couple of Paul Klee prints.

In stylistic contrast to everything else in here, there's an enormous glass and metal desk, which is piled high with yet more books. I spot two about Basquiat that have been left open and have pink Post-it notes stuck to the pages. This room also has windows on the same side as the bedroom, but the story's still the same – securely locked and no access from outside.

I start thinking about my perv with the binoculars theory again, and it makes me go back into the living area/room and look out of the window.

Across the road is a church, and either side of it are two four-storey buildings; one of them modern flats and the other discreet offices. Nothing that can be seen from here is high enough to get a good view into the flat so I discount the idea that someone creepy is observing her.

I close my eyes and try to think how I would get into this place without passing through the reception area and without scaling the walls. Well, if they didn't or couldn't come in through the windows, the only possible alternative is through the front door, so I'll check that now, just so I get a feel for how easy it would be.

Sara follows me as I take a look at the inside of the door. There's a security chain, a mortice lock and a rim cylinder lock. Let's deal with the security chain first. Obviously, it's not going to be on when she's at work, but what about when she's here?

'Do you put this security chain on at night?'

'Yes. Always.'

'You never forget?'

'No. I told you. Once you've been burgled you become a little obsessive about these things.'

'And this chain was definitely on the night that

someone came in here and moved those magazines?'

She shivers a little as she remembers and crosses her arms across her chest. 'I told the police. Yes, the chain was on. I think that's when they started to have doubts about my story. They said you couldn't get past a security chain like that without someone opening it from the inside or maybe kicking the door down.'

'Not necessarily true, madam. Do have any string? Dental floss will do if you haven't got any.'

She looks baffled, as well she might. 'I've got some string in the kitchen. How much do you need?'

'Four or five feet.'

'Hold on.'

I can't remember the last time I did this, but I'm assuming I haven't lost the knack or the speed. It isn't really showing off, it's just making a point, for me as well as her. Sara returns with the string and hands it to me.

'OK. I'm just going to deal with this one first. I'm going to go outside and I want you to put the chain on. Don't do anything with the other two locks. When I knock, I want you to open up but keep the chain in place, OK? Then walk five paces away and turn your back on the door.'

She frowns slightly, but humours me anyway. As soon as I'm outside, I quickly make a small noose on the end of the string and then knock on the door. I hear the rim cylinder lock turning and the door opens. It's tight. There's maybe three inches to play with, but that'll do. As quietly as I can, I slide my hand through the gap, hook the noose over the end of the chain and pull it tight. I can see Sara standing several feet away as requested.

I feel with my fingers to make sure the noose is secure on the chain, then loop the string over the top of the doorframe and pull it slowly and carefully to my right. There's no noise, but I can feel the chain sliding across the track and when there's nowhere left for it to go, I stick my hand through the gap and catch it, so it doesn't clatter against the door. I open the door wide, take a few paces forward and tap Sara on the shoulder. She jumps.

'Jesus!' She turns to look at me in amazement, then laughs.

'That took about twenty seconds. How much noise was there?'

'Nothing. Well – a few small noises. Nothing you could identify.'

'Would that have woken you up if you'd been asleep in your bedroom?'

'Definitely not. That was amazing. But you'd have to be able to get past those other two locks to be able to do that in the first place, wouldn't you?'

'You've got a Chubb 3g114 mortice lock here. It's one of the best for preventing forced attacks. That means someone trying to kick the door down wouldn't have much success with this model. The lever pack inside makes it problematic to pick, but a professional could do it in a couple of minutes, even if you'd locked it from the inside.

'The cylinder lock – the Yale you stick your key in when you come home – is even easier. You could do it with a tension wrench and a paper clip in about thirty seconds, maybe less. A professional burglar would probably carry a tension wrench on his key ring; it's just a thin strip of metal, as thin as a hacksaw blade.

'The whole process, from arriving outside the door here to undoing the security chain and coming inside would be a job lasting under five minutes, a little longer if you were trying to limit the noise.'

Sara goes pale. 'It's *that* easy? Oh my God. Is that what happened here, do you think?'

'I don't know. There are small scratches around the exterior of both locks, but those could have been caused by you and your keys. The only way I could check to see if someone had picked these would be to take them apart and look for unusual damage inside, but I'd need special tools and a magnifying glass. But we don't have to do that. I think it just makes the point that even though no one could have come through the windows, as far as I can see, they *could* have come through your front door.

'This door can't be seen from your neighbour's place. If she came out unexpectedly, or the lift was ascending, anyone working on these locks could just walk to the end of the corridor, open that fire door and go down the stairs.

'As you said yesterday, you'd need a helicopter to get up this high, and I think that would attract a little bit of attention. Any intruder would have to have come through your front door. Now all we have to find out is how they got past reception. Can I just ask you one thing? The coffee cup you said had moved. Can you just show me where it was and where it should have been? I'd just like to see an example of their handiwork.'

We walk into the kitchen. On one side there's two sinks, a dishwasher, fridge and all the rest of it, and on the other side cupboards, food preparation areas and a bookshelf crammed with cookery books.

'OK,' she says, stretching her fingers out. 'First of all, I have to tell you that I'm very organised and relatively tidy. I can't stand things not being where they should be. You saw my study and I know it looked a bit of a mess, but I still know exactly where everything is.'

She produces a dark orange Pantone mug from one of the cupboards opposite the dishwasher. 'This is the mug I was telling you about. The famous moving mug. The poltergeist mug. I make coffee over there by the kettle. That's the only place I make it. It's where all the coffee things are.

'I drink coffee in a variety of places; I drink it in the bedroom, I drink it in my study, I even drink it in the bath, but wherever I've been drinking it, when I've finished, I always rinse the grounds out in the sink straight away and stick it in the dishwasher. Always. I never leave things hanging around the place making clutter. Never.'

'OK. So…'

'So once the dishwasher has enough stuff in it, I stick a dishwasher tab in it and turn it on. When it's finished, I open the door for five minutes to let the steam dissipate, then I put all the clean things back where they came from. I do it all in one go. I don't leave some stuff and then do the rest later, OK?'

'OK. And the coffee cup in question would have gone straight into that cupboard.'

'Exactly. That shelf in there is the coffee mug shelf. Nothing else goes on it. There's no coffee mug halfway house that it would have rested in before going in that cupboard and onto that shelf.'

'And where did this coffee mug turn up that time you came back from work?'

She takes my wrist in her hand and quickly walks me over to the far side of the kitchen. There are three pine shelves attached to the wall. The top one has a couple of plants, the middle one has a traditional and never-used

Chinese teapot in dark grey clay and the bottom one has various bottles of herbs and spices in a neat row. She takes the coffee mug and places it carefully next to the teapot.

'That's where it was. There is no way on *earth* that I would have taken *that* coffee mug out of the dishwasher and put it there. *Absolutely* no way.'

'OK. Come with me. You're going to tell reception that I'm a nice guy and can be trusted.'

'Don't worry. I'm a convincing liar.'

9

GOT YOU

As we leave Sara's flat and she closes the door behind us, I take a quick look down the corridor. I was wondering if there were security cameras here, but there are none. That's not unusual. Nobody wants to be under surveillance the whole time, especially when there seems to be no real need for it, and if you bought a place here, you'd be reassured enough by the measures taken at reception. There aren't any cameras in the lift either, probably for the same reasons.

When Sara and I get out of the lift on the ground floor, the reception staff are friendly and accommodating. They all seem to like her. This could be because of her looks and personality, it could be because they know who she is, or it could be that they're embarrassed about possibly cocking up with security and having the police here asking questions.

On the way down, Sara told me that when they found out about her intruder problem, the head of the building's security told her that he and his colleagues would be doubling their routine checks on all of the floors. It was the least they could do. I don't know what they thought about it all, but it seems like they took it seriously and on face value. Maybe they had to, or maybe it wasn't their job to speculate on other possible causes.

'Hello, John,' says Sara to the security heavy I saw earlier. 'This is Daniel Beckett. He's a private investigator working for me and he'd like to ask you a few questions, if that's OK.' John stares at me and immediately wishes me dead. 'Daniel, this is John Kimmons. He's in charge of security for the block and was the person the police spoke to.'

John Kimmons and I shake hands. Like many men before him, he attempts a bone-crusher, but I let him get away with it. I don't want to alienate him quite yet.

Sara returns to the lift. The blonde receptionist smiles at me and I smile back. The young guy notices the smile between the receptionist and me and looks downwards, his lip curling slightly and his left eye twitching. John Kimmons beckons me and I follow him to a small office to the left of the reception area.

We sit down opposite each other and I attempt to get a quick reading on him. He's closer to sixty-five than the fifty I'd guessed at earlier. Close-cropped white hair and a pristine uniform that's trying not to look like a uniform. He's suspicious, surly and looking down his nose at me. His eyes are dead, humourless and even though he's looking at my face, I can tell he's taking in everything about me. He's almost certainly ex-police, which could be useful.

'So what can I do for you, Mr Beckett?'

'I'm sure you know that Miss Holt has reported several instances of intrusion. I'm sure you also know that the police have been here and have found no evidence of a break-in of any sort.'

He snorts. He's definitely ex-police and contemptuous of the two detectives that looked into this.

'Those two wouldn't have found anything if her front door had been hanging off its hinges.'

'You used to be a police officer.'

He looks shocked. 'How the hell did you know that?'

'The same way you know I wasn't one.'

'Fair enough.'

'Tell me how reception here works.'

He rolls his eyes and takes a deep breath. 'Two staff on twenty-four-seven, receptionist here nine to five, a different receptionist at weekends. The receptionist deals mainly with maintenance requests, contacting contractors and admin work of all types. There are three security shifts, ten pm to six am, six am to two pm, two pm to ten pm. The desk out there is never left unattended.'

'What about if one of you goes to the toilet?'

This gets an almost-grimace out of him. 'Then they do it as fast as possible, Mr Beckett.'

'So generally speaking there are at least two people on reception all of the time.'

'That is correct. Toilet breaks allowing, of course.'

'And if one of you gets sick or goes on holiday?'

'Since I've been here, we've usually been able to get one of the others to cover. The overtime's good, particularly for unsociable hours. If that wasn't possible, we'd go to a reputable agency.'

'When was the last time someone was off sick or on holiday and you had to do that?'

'Not since I've been here.'

'And how long have you been here?'

'Five years, three months, sixteen days.'

'And this is the only way into the block.'

'There's a room at the side for maintenance equipment storage which is locked all the time. Even if you got in there, it doesn't go anywhere. It's a dead end. Designed that way when they built the place. This block was built in 1979 and they made sure that it was secure. The architects knew all the tricks. You probably noticed the sheer walls and lack of obvious drainpipes. Believe me; no burglar could scale those walls. Reception is the only way in.'

'What happens if someone loses the electronic pass key that gets them past the reception turnstile?'

'We get them another. The code on the old one is nullified on our computer system straight away, so if someone finds it they can't use it. There's no clue on the passkey as to where it came from, anyway. Until a new one arrives, we buzz them in manually. When people move in here, we take two photographs of them and those are on the reception computer. As soon as someone uses the passkey on the turnstile, their photographs pop up on the screen.

'There are some people you don't see very often; they might use their flat as a pied-à-terre, for example, so it's useful to have a photographic record of what they look like. We take new photographs every two years; people dye their hair, grow beards, get fat.'

'When was the last time someone lost a pass key?'

He purses his lips and looks up to his left. 'Probably three, three and a half years ago? Something like that. Doesn't happen often.'

'Do you have some sort of master key to the flats here that the owners don't know about?'

His eyes widen. 'Absolutely not. There'd be trouble if we did and they found out about it. Hell to pay. Women, in particular, don't like the idea of someone being able to gain access to their flat, however benevolent their intentions. These are property owners, not tenants.'

'What would happen if one of the flats caught fire?'

'Then the fire brigade would smash down the windows and doors and attempt to put the fire out with water from hoses, Mr Beckett.'

I can tell he's getting impatient with me. 'How are the windows cleaned?'

'We have a contractor do that. Four times a year. Trusted company. Rope access from the roof. There are pulley locks which are in my safe, so unauthorised people can't use the gear. If they did, we'd know immediately. It's quite noisy. At night it would be bloody impossible. It's quite a skill. An amateur could end up killing themselves.'

I rest my head on my hand. I was hoping to get a coffee out of this, but I don't think that will happen. 'Would you say, then, from your past experience in the police force and from your experience of working here, that it was *impossible* (I leave a little dramatic pause here) for anyone to have broken into Miss Holt's flat?'

I can tell he doesn't like dealing in such certainties and watch his eyes as he mulls this over for a few seconds. He takes a deep breath. 'I wouldn't say anything was *impossible*, Mr Beckett; just very, very, very unlikely.'

'What would you think of the idea that this was all in her mind?'

I'm taking a gamble asking him this, but I think it's worth it. If nothing else, his facial reaction will tell me what he thinks. I continue to keep my eyes on his. He looks up and to the left. He's not going to give me a quick reply.

'I'm not a psychiatrist,' he says, finally. 'I don't know or understand the ins and outs of why someone might report crimes that hadn't happened. Having said that, I have come across it. Usually, it's because the person who reports the imagined crime is trying to cause trouble for someone else, trying to pin something on them if you get my meaning. People occasionally report crimes that haven't happened for financial gain, though I can't see how that would work in this case.'

'From the times you've had any contact with her, and I know they would have been brief, would you say, in your opinion, that Miss Holt was a candidate for that sort of behaviour?'

He thinks about this for about ten seconds, as if he's collating all the encounters he's had with her. 'Seems sensible enough. Sunny disposition, though that can mean nothing. If she can afford a flat in a place like this then she's doing well, as far as I can make out. She's some sort of clothes designer so Helen tells me.'

'Helen?'

'Receptionist. So an arty type. Seems a little brittle, maybe a tad neurotic, no boyfriends that I've ever seen, though that can mean nothing. No visitors of any type, in fact. No family as far as I can make out. Of course, I'm not here all the time.'

'Could I have a look round the outside of the building with you, if you're not too busy?'

'If you think it'll help. Not much point, though.'

We stand outside the front of the building. Mr Kimmons points up at Sara's flat on the eleventh floor. 'See, for a start, most burglars would never even *think* about breaking into a flat that high up. Too much personal risk, too great a chance of being caught, too much skill required.

'If you're up that high and someone points at you and shouts, where the hell are you going to go? Are you going to jump? I don't think so. Most burglaries happen on the ground floor and on the first floor of a building. Basement flats are favourite, too.'

'What about cat burglars?'

He snorts. 'Don't really exist anymore. Each generation of buildings are constructed while keeping that sort of thing in mind, so your cat burglar has sort of died out as anti-burglary architecture and design improved. I'm sure there are still some around somewhere, but I was in the Met for thirty years and I never once heard of one being apprehended.'

'Let's say I was really motivated to get up there. Let's say there were five million in diamonds up there or something.'

'From here? From the front? No way. Quite apart from the fact you'd be lit up by the spotlights, or, in the daytime, detected by security or spotted by passers-by, there is nowhere for you to get a grip. The whole frontage looks very ornate, but it's actually very flat and it's made that way on purpose, as I told you earlier. OK – you could probably use pitons and hammer them into the grouting like you were some bloody mountaineer or something, but now we're in the realms of fantasy, and bloody noisy, conspicuous and time-consuming fantasy at that.

'While we're fantasising, the only other thing that springs to mind would be a grappling hook, fired from a crossbow or whatever and powerful enough to land on the roof, but then this is reality, not Batman.'

'And to add to that,' I say, 'I couldn't see any evidence at all that someone had come in through the windows. Can we go around the side here?'

This is the side of the building that Sara's bedroom

looks out onto. At this stage, I'm not really looking for someone being able to break in through the windows. Not anymore. I'm looking for another way in. If I wanted to get into Sara's flat through her front door, it would be easy, whether she was inside with the security chain on or whether she was at work. The problem now is how you would get inside without going past reception and would it be possible at all. If it doesn't seem possible, then I may have to think the worst about Sara's story, at least about this part of it.

Mr Kimmons points upwards. 'These are generally the bedrooms on this side, though not in all cases. Some people don't like their bedrooms overlooking the garden next door and have their main bedroom where Miss Holt has her living room, even though most of the rooms at the front have a bloody great fireplace in them. Also, each one of these flats is laid out slightly differently. Don't ask me why.'

Once again, the brickwork is the same as at the front; impossible to scale and even though you wouldn't be seen by the occupants of the house next door, you'd have to walk past reception to get down here and your movement down this side of the building would trigger three bright motion sensor security lights, according to Mr Kimmons.

'Are these security lights checked regularly?'

'Every Tuesday. Bulbs replaced every six months whether they need to be or not. All the motion sensor lights are linked to our computer system. If one of them comes on, the computer behind the reception desk shows a little triangle sign and makes a bleeping noise that you can't miss. Bloody annoying it is. The security lights used to come on if a bloody cat went past, so we had them adjusted.'

'So to get round here,' I say, 'you'd have to walk directly towards the main entrance, as there are walls and shrubs either side of the path. Presumably you'd be seen by one of the reception staff.'

'Little bit more to it than that. Keep it under your hat, but there are three pressure sensors under the concrete. Every time someone walks down that path, we get another little warning noise in reception. It happened when you arrived, for example, though I'd already seen you hanging around outside.'

'Is it the same for the other side of the block?'

'Exactly the same. No access except by approaching the main entrance and turning left. You'd have to walk over the same pressure sensors and if you went down the side, you'd get the same number of security lights coming on, unless you were a cat.'

'Can I look round there anyway?'

'If you must.'

My neck is starting to ache from looking upwards. This side of the block is much the same as the other.

'These windows would generally be the bedroom windows of the people on the other side of the block, like Miss Holt's neighbour,' I say.

'Correct. Though for some reason, the flats on the left side of the block are not a mirror image of the ones on the right, if you see what I mean. For example, their bathrooms and toilet windows are on the back of the building, whereas Miss Holt's bathroom window looks out onto the garden of next door's house.'

I couldn't see a way to the back of the building on the other side. It just seemed to end in an enormous brick wall, definitely unscalable and about forty feet high. Here, however, there's a very sturdy-looking metal security gate.

It has tough steel bars about six inches apart and a solid grey metal grill behind the bars. The top of the gate is crowned by a row of nasty-looking metal spikes which curve outwards and there's an unbreakable-looking rim gate lock keeping it shut.

This would not be impossible to get past. If it were me, I'd save myself the trouble of getting impaled on the spikes and attack the lock. With the right tools, you could open it in two minutes. The only problem would be the fact that you wouldn't be able to get down here in the first place without someone noticing.

'Can we go through here?'

'Nothing to see, really. Just a big metal fence and behind that is a service road for the ordinary houses on this side. It's where you put your bins out if you live in one of them.' He smiles. 'I don't mean that you live in the bins. Ours are collected from the front so there's no access to the road from this property. The reason there's a gate in the first place is because of the electric stuff around the back. Once or twice I've had to allow an electrician access. The last time was eight months ago.'

'And you would accompany the electrician.'

'Always. Me or one of my colleagues.'

He produces an enormous bunch of keys from somewhere and unlocks the gate. I notice he has an Alberto Vargas key ring. As we walk around the back of the block, it becomes dramatically darker and quieter. There's a thick layer of bright green moss growing on the floor and that's probably what's causing the earthy damp smell.

The fence in between the block and the service road is tall, but it's not that tall, perhaps eight or nine feet. This means that the flats, which start on the first floor, don't have their view hampered. The gap between the fence and the back of the building is about seven feet. Like the security gate, the fence has vicious outward facing metal spikes to prevent anyone climbing over from the service road.

Down the opposite end of the building from where we're standing, there's an old-looking brick wall covered in moss, lichens and ivy. That would belong to the house next door. It's higher than the security fence at the back, but not by much.

At the base of the building, there's a big, dirty, grey box covered in electrical hazard signs. Emanating from this box is a network of white plastic cable coverings. These are firmly fastened to the brickwork every fifteen inches by four small screws or rivets.

One of them travels vertically up the wall in a straight line and stops three feet below and a little to the left of what must be a bathroom window on the first floor. The coverings then continue horizontally to the left and right, forming an irregular T shape. Then, they just terminate, presumably at a point where the electrical cables enter the building directly and don't need further protection from the elements.

These cable coverings are five inches wide and two inches deep, and the plastic is smooth and shiny. They'd be difficult to get a grip on, but not impossible, as long as you didn't have to do it for too long. I feel my fingers twitch involuntarily as I imagine what it would be like to scale this wall using only these plastic coverings for support.

I look down and to my left. There's a barely discernible area near the cable box where the layer of moss has been repeatedly and haphazardly disturbed in

several places, revealing the rich black soil beneath.
Got you.

10

BREAKING AND ENTERING

John Kimmons nods his head up and down and allows himself the luxury of a quick chortle. He's never been so vindicated in his life.

'Those two clowns didn't even think it was worth looking out here. I asked them if they wanted a tour of the grounds and they just laughed, condescending little pricks. It was bad enough in the old days, but they still don't take women seriously, do they. I bet they were having a good laugh on the way back to the station.'

'To be fair, they did make two visits.'

'They probably fancied her.'

'Maybe they had more important work to deal with.'

'No. They were looking at it the wrong way. They were too focussed on her flat and how you might break into it from the outside or the inside. Getting past reception was a no-no, so, then, was getting in through her windows. Case closed, let's go down the pub. What do you think happened?'

'I think whoever it was did a recce from that service road. I'll bet you anything there's probably some sort of door or gate going into the back garden of the house next door, and one you could easily break into if you were a pro. From what I saw, their garden's like a jungle, so they wouldn't have seen anyone come into their garden from the house. Once they were through the gate it was a matter of getting over that wall down the end there. Maybe they had a ladder or stood on something, I don't know.'

'And getting back over it? It's pretty high.'

'It's high, but not that high. You could probably do it with a good run-up, if you were fit enough, and there are plenty of spaces in the grouting to get a grip with your hands or feet, if you knew what you were doing. The light isn't too good here even in the day, but I reckon if you did a close examination of this area and next door's wall, you'd see plenty of signs that someone had been here.'

'And you think that someone could get up those cable covers and get into that bathroom?'

'That's what I'm about to find out. Who lives in that flat?'

'Er, that would be, er, Mr Nuttal. He's one of the ones I mentioned that use these flats for their pied-à-terre. I have no idea what he does. Rarely see him. D'you think…'

'I think our burglar had a bit of luck.'

I put my key ring and one of my metal business cards in my back pocket, take my jacket off and hand it to Mr Kimmons. 'I'd get out of the way, if I were you. If I fall on you and we're found dead here, people'll get the wrong idea.'

I wipe my hands against my shirt to get the sweat off and do a test grip against the first section of cable coverings. It'll be difficult to hang onto this, but that's mainly because of the narrow width and depth. The second problem I'll encounter will be that my weight might be too much for the screws attaching these covers to the wall and I'll pull the whole lot down.

I console myself with the thought that someone has already done this before me, so it can't be that difficult. It'll have to be quick; I don't think something this weak will tolerate anyone's weight on it for more than a few seconds.

I place a foot on the grey box, grab two sections of the cable cover and launch myself upwards, so that my feet are flat against the wall and I'm hanging on to two sections of the cover. So far so good; the whole thing hasn't been ripped from the wall, it isn't as slippery as I thought it would be, but it still feels flimsy, the plastic bending inwards slightly with the force of my grip.

The initial pain is in my fingers, forearms and shoulder muscles, with my calves and back not far behind. With the confidence of someone who's just scaled an amazing two feet of a sheer brick wall, I continue upwards, one painful hand-over-hand at a time. I don't look down or up, because I don't want to see how badly I'm doing. I just keep my eyes on my hands, watching the muscles and tendons straining and my knuckles whitening.

I start to stare at details in the bricks; little chips that have come off the sides, random slime and dirt, pale green and bright yellow lichens. I consider telling Mr Kimmons that that whole wall needs to be hydro blasted and re-grouted. I feel a vibration in my left pocket; someone's just texted me. I wonder who it is. Isolda? Maybe she wants to meet for lunch. No. She's meeting her father.

This seems to be taking a long time, but I know that's an illusion. To keep my feet pressed firmly against the wall, I have to pull hard at the coverings to get the balance just right. The pain in my thighs is considerable.

This activity is attacking muscle groups that rarely see action.

'You're doing well, son!' shouts Mr Kimmons from below.

'Thank you,' I manage.

Then, suddenly, the vertical cable coverings stop and spread out into the T shape. I stretch a hand out to grab the section to my right, but it's slippery and my hand slides off, grazing the wall, so for a moment I'm just hanging on by one hand.

I push my feet harder into the wall, even though I know that won't correct things. I can feel myself leaning backwards at a bad angle. In a panic, I increase my grip and scrape my knuckles against the brick surface as the covering bends inwards. I get a huge surge of adrenalin and can just hear Mr Kimmons hiss, 'God Almighty!'

But I recover, and manage to pull myself up using the left side of the T bar. Now I can reach up and grab the windowsill and get one foot on the cable cover. I have to be careful not to put too much weight on this as I can tell it won't take it. Looking down, I can see several finger marks on the dark algae covering that section. It doesn't look like there are fingerprints, so my predecessor was using gloves.

I'm in quite a bit of pain now, so I've got to get this over quickly. I don't want to fall down and have to start this all over again. I don't want to fall down, period.

The window doesn't have a handle on the outside. After all, why should it? But I can see the interior handle and I have to assume it's unlocked or there's no lock at all. There's been a lot of activity around here; dirt and algae are smudged against the frame and there are big smears on the brickwork below. Whoever did this made no attempt to tidy up after themselves; either too cocky or they weren't bothered one way or the other.

I switch hands so my left is hanging onto the windowsill, and fish one of my business cards out of my back pocket. It's made from a thin, silvery metal and is ideal for this sort of thing. I slide it in between the lock and the strike plate until I feel the latch bolt pop back, then grab the window frame and pull. It opens so easily, it almost knocks me off and I drop my card.

'Got it!' I hear Mr Kimmons say.

With the window wide open, I jam both of my elbows onto the ledge and slowly pull myself up and into the bathroom. The windowsill inside is clear, so I don't knock anything off. My stomach muscles and armpits hurt and I'm panting like I've just sprinted half a mile.

I'm on my hands and knees and remain there for a few moments to get my breath back. That seemed like it took about fifteen minutes, but I think it was closer to four. I get up, lean my head out of the window and wave to Kimmons. He gets the message and heads back to the reception area.

I stand on the tiles, stretch the pain out of my muscles, massage my fingers and then close my eyes, listening and trying to pick up on any human presence. There's no one here. In fact, it feels and smells as if there's been no one here for some time; the air is dead and there's a very slight smell of mould.

I take a quick look around the bathroom. There's no sign that anyone has broken in; nothing knocked on the floor, no footprints, no dirt and the inside of the bathroom window is clean. Whoever did this made sure there was no mess, at least not on the inside.

As I push open the bathroom door and step into the

hallway, I make another attempt to get my head around this. What sort of person are we dealing with here? Is this teenagers or opportunistic burglars? Unlikely. It doesn't necessarily have to be a career burglar, though. It could just be someone with good climbing skills who has been asked to do this for reason or reasons unknown.

But whoever it was, they'd be comfortable with acting outside the law and would have little fear of being caught. Whatever you want to call these intrusions into Sara's flat (and the one I'm currently standing in), I'm sure they break a shitload of laws, burglary with intent being the least of them, not to mention trespass.

The hallway is the same as the one inside Sara's place. I feel momentarily dizzy as I walk down it, as always happens when I'm invading someone else's premises for the first time. I must look into that one day.

There's no problem with opening the front door. There's a security chain, a rim cylinder lock, but no mortice lock to deal with. I open it, close it quietly behind me and a minute later I'm in the lift heading up to the eleventh floor.

*

When I tell Sara what I've discovered, she runs a hand through her hair and breathes a sigh of relief. For a moment, she doesn't seem to know what to do or what to say, then she puts a hand on my shoulder and kisses me on the cheek.

'Thank you. You – you can't imagine what it's like when something like this has been happening and when you talk to people about it you can see in their eyes that they don't really believe you.'

'You can't really blame people for that. Not really. It's a difficult thing to believe. Breaking and entering without any theft involved. Who would do that and why? It sounds crazy, particularly when all of the things that have been going on in your flat are things that you could easily have done yourself.'

'But why would people think I'd be doing that?'

'I'll be honest with you – I don't know what's going on yet, but you're on the receiving end of a campaign of psychological harassment. Things like the jostling in the street and the moving of stuff in your flat; these things are designed to leave no evidence apart from your complaints. The stuff in the street, calling you bitch and so on are classed as engineered intimidation.'

Tears start to appear in her eyes.

'Start crying and I quit this job.'

This makes her laugh. Good.

'So who do you think is doing this?' she says, sniffing. 'Shall we go in the kitchen? I can make you another coffee.'

'Sure. Well, my instinct is to assume that it's somehow connected to a rival fashion house. It can't be coincidence that it's all started since you announced your plans for New York and Milan. Whoever it is has got money. From what you've told me, they must have hired anything up to half a dozen people so far, assuming that everything is connected, which I think it is, and in the case of your intruder, you're looking at someone with a fairly high level of burglarising skill, probably a professional. There are a fair amount of people like that around and their services can be bought.'

Sara shakes her head. 'It's just so *unlikely*. I've run it over in my mind again and again and I still can't think of anyone who might do something like this.'

I sit down at the kitchen table while she prepares the coffee things. I'm afraid I start looking at her bottom.

'This might sound like an odd question, and we've been over it before, but have you got any enemies at *all?* People from the past, perhaps? Someone who really hates your guts, possibly for reasons unconnected to your job? Someone whose boyfriend you once stole? Something like that? Anything?'

'I'm not that sort of person. Not yet, anyway. I'm always nice to people. I don't use people to get what I want. I always treat the people I work with fairly. All I've ever done is to work hard at what I wanted to do.

'I've had a few relationships suffer from it in the past. Guys who thought I was not paying enough attention to them in one way or another. But there was nothing big and dramatic, if you know what I mean. No big blow-ups. No words of vengeance. No promises of retribution. That would make it all more clear cut, wouldn't it; something like that, I mean.'

She hands me a coffee in a cup with 'Euromoka' written on the side in brown script.

'Thanks.'

She turns to face me. Her eyes don't leave mine. 'So what happens now? Anything?'

'I can always get in touch with the police and tell them that I've found a way of getting into your flat and have found evidence that someone managed it before me. That might spur them into a more thorough investigation.'

She sits down across from me, takes a sip of her coffee and frowns. 'The police were condescending towards me and made me feel like I was wasting their time. They kept looking at each other with amused expressions that they couldn't conceal. I'm not giving them a second chance. I want you to sort this out. What are you going to do? Are you all right? You look tired.'

'I'm fine. Well, as neither of us have a clue as to who's behind this, we need to speak to one of the perpetrators and find out who is.'

'What if they don't want to tell you?'

'They'll tell me.'

'Should I change the locks?'

'No need. I'll get Mr Kimmons to take down the cable coverings at the back of the block. Without those, they won't have access to the building. That's the only possible way they could have got in. It may not be necessary or useful, but I'll lock the bathroom window of that flat downstairs on my way out.

'And another thing, Sara, from now on, you keep whatever happens to yourself, starting with what I've done here this morning. You don't talk to anyone about it, OK?'

'OK.'

'Isolda told me that you're at the Royal Academy of Arts tonight. Some magazine launch?'

'That's right. Dania Gamble's. Her people have hired the John Madejski Fine Rooms from seven until eleven.'

'How many people?'

'Over three hundred.'

'Anyone there you know or work with?'

'Gaige is going. He did some freelance work as a stylist on the first issue. There'll doubtless be lots of people I'm on air-kissing terms with.'

'Have you been there before?'

'To a reception? Yes. Maybe half a dozen times.'

'What's the security like?'

'Effective. It has to be. No one gets in without an invitation. They're always very strict because the rooms are seventeenth century and have works of art in them – Hockney, Constable, Gainsborough. There are always loads of huge shaven-headed guys in suits with earpieces.'

'What's the hassle like when you leave?'

'What do you mean?'

'Coats, cloakrooms, queues.'

'Fairly quick. Big cloakroom area, usually six or seven staff.'

'So from the moment you say you're leaving to the point where you're standing on the pavement in Piccadilly looking for a cab. How long would that be?'

'Exchanging cards, air-kissing, getting your coat; I would say ten minutes.'

'OK. When that process starts, text me. Just one word will do. I'll know what it's about. Don't forget.'

'Do you think something'll happen?'

'No idea, but I have to start somewhere. You've had a couple of days without incident, so you're due for a spot of engineered intimidation, I would say.'

'Oh God.'

'Don't worry. It'll all be OK.'

We both jump when there's a knock at the door. It's Kimmons. He's brought my jacket and business card. He looks embarrassed and apologetic, staring over my shoulder at Sara.

'I take full responsibility for this, Miss Holt. It won't happen again.'

He looks at me. 'I'm going to take all of those plastic casings off the electric cables at the back there and have a word with the people in the house next door. I'll check their back gate for them and give them suitable advice –

put the frighteners on them so they act quickly. I'll get that wall re-grouted on our side and suggest they do the same on theirs. I've already rung the electrical contractors and told them what's happened. They're sending someone over here at two o' clock. They sounded like they were shitting themselves and so they should be.'

'That sounds fine.' I had considered leaving everything in place at one point, but that would be putting Sara at too much risk. Kimmons grins at her and points at me.

'It took him a quarter of an hour to work out what those detectives couldn't manage in two separate visits. I'm not a big fan of the private sector, but I would stick with this bloke, if I were you.'

She smiles at him. 'Thanks, John. I will.'

He pokes me in the chest. 'Don't fuck this up, private fucking detective.'

11

BLUE CRYSTAL NECKLACE

Green Park station is only three stops away from St John's Wood on the Jubilee Line and after an eleven-minute tube ride I'm standing in Piccadilly.

I head towards Piccadilly Circus with The Ritz on my right, then turn left into Dover Street and go inside The Clarence pub, which is much quieter than I'd expected for the time of day. I get a double vodka and soda and, as I'm feeling in a sophisticated mood, order scampi and chips with tartare sauce.

I sit down and start to think about whatever it is that's going on with Sara Holt. If it were a spiteful ex-colleague, bitchy acquaintance or something similar, they'd have to have some pretty dodgy contacts to pull off something like this.

They'd also have to have a fair amount of time on their hands to organise it all and a good amount of disposable income to pay the perpetrators, who, for the moment, I have to assume aren't doing this for free.

Let's take the intrusions into her flat first. If I were organising this campaign I'd have to find out where she lived. Then I'd have to find someone who had the skill to break into her apartment block undetected. Someone who was smart enough to scope the place out without being noticed. Someone who was able to get themselves into next door's garden, scale the adjoining wall, climb up those cable coverings, break into Mr Nuttal's deserted pied-à-terre (a lucky break if ever there was one) and get past Sara's locks even when she had her security chain on. Someone who knew to wear gloves so there were no fingerprints. The question is: how would I know someone like that?

Also, there would have to be a discussion about what happened once this person was in Sara's flat. The sort of things they would do, things that a third party would find hard to believe, things that would disturb or frighten her, things that could give the impression that she was making it all up, things that would leave the police incredulous.

Then there would be other contingencies to discuss. What was to happen if Sara woke up while the intruder was in her flat at night? Attack her? Knock her out? Who would these things be discussed with? Who would have the knowledge, experience and maybe even the imagination to discuss them? The more I think about it, the more it seems that this has to be the work of a professional criminal or criminals.

A smiling girl wearing a red kitchen apron and a grey t-shirt places my meal in front of me and asks if there's anything else I need. I tell her no. She smiles at me. 'Are you sure?'

'Yes, thank you.'

'Are you a tourist?'

She has a strong Swedish accent, pretty Scandinavian looks, enormous blonde curly hair, a remarkable bust and she's glowing slightly, probably from the heat of the kitchens. The combined aromas of her perfume and her sweat lash at my senses and I make a mental note to discover her working hours and come back here, though not as a customer. I smile at her.

'No, I live in London. I've just been to a meeting around the corner.'

She unwraps my cutlery from a paper napkin, leans over, and as she places the knife and fork on the table our eyes meet. Her mouth is about a foot away from mine.

'Important meeting?'

'We discovered how to see through people's clothing.'

Her eyes widen and she jokingly crosses her arms across her breasts. 'Oh! Now I feel embarrassed.'

I smile at her. 'I'm sure there's no need to be in your case.' Was that too corny? It seems not. It was, though. I'm going to cringe whenever I think about it, probably forever. How old am I? Fifteen?

'You are *bad*.'

'It's worse than you think.'

She wiggles off, glancing at me over her shoulder and smiling before disappearing into the kitchens. Is *women sweating* a thing for me, I wonder? I must look it up when I get home. I'm sure there'll be an article on it somewhere.

*

I start to eat while having a think about the street guys. From what Sara told me we have three definite semi-assaults here, could be more. If we take the three she describes as strikingly scary, they involved four different men. They were older men, which is fairly interesting, though not necessarily significant.

These guys would also have to be paid and briefed, one assumes. Make it frightening but make it quick. Make it deniable. Make it seem playful. Make it seem sinister.

Make it seem accidental. Make it seem intentional. Once again, these incidents leave no evidence other than victim complaints.

The scratch down the side of her car was real enough, I guess, even though I haven't had a look at it yet. That could be classed as criminal damage, but once again, it's one of those things that could happen to anyone, particularly in the West End of London. It's the sort of thing a kid might do on a whim, if they were carrying a chisel or a screwdriver.

I have to get something tangible to work on here, preferably a human being. I ask for my bill, pay and head up the street to look at the Royal Academy of Arts and its environs. Just as I'm about to stick my receipt in my wallet, I notice something written on the back. It says 'Klementina. 07002690444. Please call. I like Chinese food! ☺'.

I've decided to take a look at Burlington House, where the Royal Academy of Arts is situated, adjacent to a load of other societies, most of them scientific. I can see the colourful banners advertising the latest exhibitions about half a mile up the road, but I cross over, wanting to get the feel of the surrounding area.

I want to put myself in the position of someone who's looking out for Sara Holt leaving a magazine launch at a little past eleven pm. There's a good chance that nothing will happen here tonight, but I still feel compelled to check it out.

In the space of a minute, I walk past half a dozen cafés with seating outside. I check the opening times where they're visible in the windows and consign them to memory. About half will be still serving food and drinks late into the evening. There are no pubs, at least not on the main road. Lots of souvenir shops, which may or may not be open late, but the two I go inside are too small to loiter in without being noticed and hassled by the staff.

As usual, there's a lot of work being done on the buildings here, and there's scaffolding of one sort or another every hundred yards or so. There's constant drilling, dust in the air and an all-pervasive, caustic burning smell; sometimes it's like tar, other times like cheap diesel.

There are many places where someone could conceal themselves without being noticed, but if you tried it under the scaffolding, you'd just get in people's way.

Traffic is busy; lots of black cabs, cars, cyclists and buses. It'll be better late at night, but not by much; just the proportions will change. It's thick with tourists and it's unlikely that'll calm down until well after midnight. It's always busy in Piccadilly, no matter what time of day it is.

The Piccadilly Arcade is full of high-end clothing retailers, photography galleries, jewellers and art bookshops, most of which close at five-thirty or six. If you walk down the far end, you come out in Jermyn Street, to be greeted by a statue of Beau Brummell.

But even when the twenty-odd shops here are closed, they'll still be lit up for window-shopping, so you could saunter here without drawing undue attention to yourself. I imagine the big ceiling lights are kept on all night to encourage casual browsers and discourage thieves.

As I look in the windows and check out the closing times, I remember the text message I received while scaling the wall. It's from Isolda and it's refreshingly obscene. I text something even worse back and await her response with interest. Probably won't be for a while if she's having lunch with her dad. When I arrive back at the Piccadilly end of the arcade, I stop and take a look at the other side of the road.

There's an almost direct view of the entrance to Burlington House. If I wanted to look out for people leaving without them seeing me, this would be a good place. Directly across from the entrance are two black telephone kiosks, a lamppost and a few black roadside cabinets, probably with electrical stuff inside. You could hang around there, but the shop lights directly behind you would illuminate you. The telephone kiosks would be worth remembering though, particularly if the person you were observing didn't know what you looked like.

The road markings are mainly double yellows with a few areas telling lorry drivers that they can't even unload or load. I run across Duke Street St James's and take a look in Fortnum & Mason's window. Fortnum's closes at eight, though you can bet there'll be people ogling the attractive window displays well after that.

I keep walking. More shops, more crowds, more coffee bars and another arcade. I cross over the road and turn back the way I came. There's a Pret A Manger and that doesn't close until eleven. There's a fast-food place next door that closes at nine, then a couple more telephone kiosks and more shops. If it was me waiting for Sara to emerge, I could easily and inconspicuously kill time around here while keeping an eye on Burlington House.

Another hundred yards and I'm at the main entrance. Straight ahead of me, across two hundred yards of paved courtyard, is the Royal Academy building. A gigantic banner advertising a *Rubens and His Legacy* exhibition hangs down over most of the first and second floors.

On my left is the Society of Antiquaries and on my right the Royal Society of Chemistry. By the Royal Academy entrance, there's a statue of Sir Joshua Reynolds, holding a paintbrush in one hand and a palette in the other. I wonder what he was painting.

This is a big, wide area and there are a lot of people walking around, looking at the buildings, the statues and the keystone heads. I decide to take a look inside. No need to buy a ticket, as I'm not going into any of the special exhibitions. I do go into one of the shops, however, and buy Isolda a Ken Howard blue crystal necklace.

I wander around looking for info. The place closes at six, and that's when public access to the courtyard stops for the general public. This means that no one other than the magazine launch folk will be making that walk from the entrance to the main building across the big courtyard. Well, that's one headache out of the way.

I wanted to have a look at the John Madejski Fine Rooms where tonight's event will be taking place, but the young guy I asked said they were closed to the public. Oh well. It doesn't seem to matter that much. If anyone's going to try anything with Sara tonight, I don't think it'll be in here. Besides, from the way she described her assailants, I think they'd look and sound out of place if they tried to gate-crash, and also she won't be on her own.

Of course, all of this may be a waste of time, but it only took me half an hour and may come in useful for something else one day. Who knows – I may even visit the place for pleasure.

I've started to notice a lot of muscular aches and pains in the last few minutes, probably as a result of the climb that got me into Sara's place, so decide to go back to Exeter Street for a hot bath.

I head down towards Piccadilly Circus and I'm considering walking back, then someone gets out of a black cab right next to me, so I hop in that one and tell the driver to take me to Kean Street, Covent Garden, so I can take my usual random, tortuous route home.

Once I'm back, I run a bath, pour some Thymes Goldleaf bubble bath into the water, go into the kitchen and start up the coffee machine. The bedroom still smells of Isolda, the sheets are still dishevelled and both pillows are on the bedroom floor where we left them this morning.

I take the necklace I bought her out of my jacket pocket and place it on the kitchen table next to the coffee maker. I hope she likes it. I get out of my clothes, dump them on the bed, then get in the bath, turning the cold tap off, but keeping the hot one running slowly until I can stand it no longer. Then I lie there, sweating from the heat, sipping my coffee and thinking.

I decide to give Sara a call. She answers straight away.

'Hi. Have you solved it yet?'

She sounds a little more happy and relaxed now, probably the effect of having her story believed at last, or at least part of it.

'Just give me another five minutes. Where are you now?'

'At Maccanti's. I left about half an hour after you did.'

'Are you going to this launch tonight straight from work?'

'Yes. I'm going to stay late and then get a cab down. I've got something to change into in my office, so I won't be going home again until it's over.'

'Tell me what you'll be wearing.'//
'You sound like a pervert.'
'I am. Tell me.'
'It's one of my own creations. It's like a short, sleeveless, over-the-shoulder prom dress. One shoulder bare, the other with a bow. Elastic satin; light turquoise. I'll be wearing lime green pumps and carrying a matching clutch bag.' She pauses, then laughs. 'No bra.'

'Stop that right now.'

'Is this turning into phone sex?'

'Why do you think I rang you in the first place?'

'You were lonely?'

'A guy like me is never lonely, honey.'

She giggles. 'I go crazy when I think of you with other women. I want to kill all of them.'

'OK. Just do me a favour and book a cab to pick you up right outside the office, just until I can get this sorted out. Don't walk around hailing one. Pick a company you haven't used before.'

'Sure. If that's what you want. Gaige will know of one.'

'And make sure you get out right outside Burlington House. Try to limit your walking time. And when you get inside, forget all about this. Just have a good time. And remember to text me ten minutes before you leave.'

'I won't forget.'

I click her off. Well, at least she sounds a little more playful now. Just as I put my mobile on the side of the bath, it starts buzzing, the vibrations almost tipping it into the water. It's Isolda.

'Who were you talking to?'

'Your boss.'

'Did you tell her about us?'

'Right down to the last detail.'

'I bloody hope not! Listen – are you busy at the moment? Where are you? Are you at your place?'

'I'm having a bath.'

'You mean I'm talking to a naked man?'

'A first for you, I'm sure.'

'Ha. I'm finishing here in a few minutes. Just have to courier some stuff. Can I get a cab to your place? I'd really like to see you. I was going to suggest we have dinner again, but I don't think I can wait that long. I've been thinking about you all day.'

'Sure. There's a buzzer on the street level door.'

'OK. Mwah!'

I try to work out how long it's going to take her to get here. I would say about fifteen to twenty minutes. That gives me another ten minutes soaking time. Whatever she has in mind, I'm going to have to extricate myself from her at some point so that I can get down to Piccadilly to check on Sara.

I am aware that I've put myself in a difficult position as regards confidentiality here, but then it was Isolda's suggestion that Sara contact someone like me in the first place. Still, it isn't good business to let a third party know what's been going on under *any* circumstances, so I'm going to have to be diplomatic, which'll involve lying, which I'm very good at. I close my eyes, feel the sweat drip down my face and the pain slowly leave the muscles in my back and shoulders.

12

A HANDS-ON PERSON

I'm still in my robe when I hear the buzzer, and push the button in the kitchen to let her up. When I open the door I think it's a different woman. Her long hair is tied back off her face, making those gorgeous eyes and plump lips more noticeable. She's wearing a navy blue jacket with wide shoulders over a black low-cut t-shirt that narrowly avoids showing any cleavage but accentuates the broad swell of her breasts.

She's wearing a short, black skirt, but this time it's patterned with interlaced gold and is a little longer than the one she had on last night, reaching maybe three inches above the knee. High heels once again – black, suede, five-inch stilettos that make her almost as tall as me.

I grab her by the waist and push her against the wall. She moans as I kiss her neck and stops me as I lean across her to close the door, which is wide open.

'Keep it open,' she whispers, her voice hoarse.

'Are you sure?'

'Yes.'

'There are people downstairs.'

'I don't care.'

In between kisses, she removes my robe and lets it drop to the floor. When I start to undress her, she shakes her head. 'No. Like this.'

Her lovemaking is intense, crude and demanding. Her body responds with enthusiasm, though her eyes are unfocussed, clouded over, as if her mind is elsewhere.

When we finally get into the bedroom, she looks disorientated, but her craving is even more urgent, until she loses herself completely, her demands profane and violently coarse.

During what can only be described as a brief interlude, she stands up and finally strips off her work clothing. Her body is flushed and moist, the sweat streaming from her skin and hair, livid red lines where bra straps and garter belts have dug into the pale flesh.

She crawls up the bed, leans over me and runs a hand up my chest. 'I've been waiting for this all day. Don't think I've finished with you yet.'

I grab her hair tightly in both hands and flip her over onto her back. 'So how's your day been? Any interesting developments?'

She presents herself to me with cupped hands.

'Busy. I've been sourcing materials from a couple of new suppliers for Sara's new designs. It's all going according to plan with that side of things, anyway. Sara came in this afternoon and she seemed a little more up. Having you around has changed things. Something's being done about all of this now. I'm so glad.'

She clasps her hands behind her neck and arches her back, grinning wickedly as she sees where my eyes are going. I try to stop myself holding her waist just below the ribs, but it's impossible. 'It's a tricky case; difficult to penetrate.'

'Mmm. It sounds frustrating. Have you been to her flat?'

'I had a look this morning.'

She places her hands on the back of mine, slides them about six inches up her body, closes her eyes and gasps. 'Did you see anything the police had missed? Anything you wanted to grab onto? Any big theories you felt compelled to embrace?'

'There were a couple of things that interested me.'

'I'm sure you're a hands-on person.'

'I'm starting to run out of innuendo.'

'Doesn't seem that way to *me*! How secure was her flat? It still freaks me out, thinking about someone creeping around the place.'

'I couldn't see a way in through the windows. Even if she had easily openable window locks, which she didn't, the walls of her block are pretty sheer. A professional mountaineer could do it, but they'd be noticed. Besides, you can't really approach that building without someone noticing and the security team are pretty hot.'

Still gripping the backs of my hands, she slides herself directly beneath me, raising her legs. 'So it looks like the intrusions into her flat might be all in her mind after all, unless there's something that even *you* are missing. Are you alright?'

'Making a full recovery. You?'

'Mm. Never felt better. A little restless now, perhaps; all this talk of penetration and intrusion, particularly the intrusion.'

'I'm sorry. I didn't want to cause you any discomfort.'

Once again, her eyes meet mine. 'You won't. I'm used to discomfort.'

'So how did lunch go?'

Her expression changes very slightly; a tiny crease in between her eyebrows, a miniscule pout on those full lips.

Something not right here – an argument with her dad?

'It was fine. We went to a Romanian restaurant.' The pout disappears and she's smiling again. 'Now you've got me feeling hungry, talking about food. Have you got anything here?'

'Go and have a look in the kitchen.'

I watch her as she gets up, runs a hand through her hair and leaves the room. I take a look at my watch. There's still plenty of time to get to Piccadilly in time for Sara, but I don't know what Isolda's plans are for the rest of the evening. I don't want to make it seem like I'm trying to get rid of her, but at the same time, I try to keep the number of people who know what I'm doing on a job to a minimum, even if they're kind of involved, like I guess Isolda is. *Need to know*, as it used to be called in the old days.

As soon as I can hear her making identifiable kitchen noises, I lean over the edge of the bed and pat the floor looking for my mobile, finally finding it under her black vest. I scroll down my contacts list, find what I'm looking for and start texting.

'Can we open one of these bottles of champagne?'

'Sure. Do you need any help?'

'I think I can manage, thank you, Daniel. Where are the…oh, it's OK. I've found them.'

I finish what I'm doing just as she comes in with two glasses, handing me one as she wriggles next to me, her hair falling against my shoulder and her thigh pressing against mine.

'Cheers,' she says, kissing me briefly on the lips before we both drink. I notice that her lipstick will have to be reapplied.

'What are we going to be eating?' I say, running a

fingernail down her back and casually groping her bottom. It's that old cliché: I can't keep my hands off her. The memory that she has a boyfriend briefly echoes, like a cloud passing across the sun.

'Stop that or we won't be eating anything. You've got such a lot of stuff in your fridge, haven't you?'

'You never know when you're going to need it.'

'Do you cook a lot of Italian food? You've got loads of Italian ingredients. I'm making meatballs in tomato and garlic sauce with melted Parmesan on toasted focaccia.'

'Sounds wonderful.'

'I'll cut the bread up so we can just use forks. Sound OK?'

'Fantastic.'

She returns to the kitchen and keeps at it. I lie on the bed and let the combined aromas of Isolda's perfume and frying garlic waft over me. My left forearm still hurts from my climb this morning. I try not to think of what I've got to do later on, but it keeps nagging at me. Part of me knows that it'll probably be a waste of time. Sara will come out of Burlington House about ten past eleven, she'll get into a cab and she'll be driven home and that'll be it.

But there's a slim chance that someone might try hassling her when she comes out, so I feel obliged to be around, not just to prevent it happening, but also to try to get to the bottom of what's going on.

If I could just grab one of the people who're doing all the harassment, it would be extremely useful; otherwise, I can't really see a way in. Of course, the potential grabee may not want to talk, but there are ways of getting around that. I can be very persuasive under the right circumstances.

Isolda comes in with the food and we start to eat, while watching a documentary about white tigers with the sound turned off. She's still interested in knowing how I became an investigator in the first place, and I fob her off with the usual convincing-sounding stuff about insurance investigation and all the rest of it.

I can make it sound interesting, plausible and mildly boring all at the same time. Sometimes I almost believe it myself, which is the best way of making lies sound authentic. I can also push you to change the subject without you realising you've been pushed.

She's interested that I worked in Milan for a couple of years, and we compare notes on the place. She went to both Milan Fashion Weeks last year and managed to see a lot of the city whenever there was time.

'I was so annoyed that the McDonald's in The Galleria had gone! Did you know? There's another Prada there now. McDonald's sued Milan for millions and gave away free food to thousands of people just before they closed for the last time. Can you imagine that happening here? There'd be riots!'

'Was Sara with you?'

'Yeah, both times. And Thai Hunter while she was with us.'

'Who's that?'

'Thai was Sara's MTA2. Melody, who you probably haven't met, is MTA2 now. Thai was lovely. Lots of fun and great at socialising, but you have to be on the ball with tiny details in that job and she screwed up one too many times and had to be let go.'

'When was that?'

'I can't remember now, but Melody has been with us for three months, so it must have been something like that.'

'What's Thai doing now?'

'She went to work for Jigsaw. Not sure what she does. Once people leave, you tend not to see them again unless you bump into them at some event or other. It's just the way it is. I can't imagine Thai would get involved in something like this, though.'

'Why not?'

'I don't think she'd be smart enough. Or rather, her mind wouldn't work that way. What will you do if you can't make any progress on this? Just give up and return Sara's money?'

'I never give up. It wouldn't be good for my reputation.'

'You have a reputation?'

'Hard to believe, isn't it.'

'You might *have* to give up at some point.'

'No. I'll sort it. Things like this are always solvable eventually. You're only dealing with people, and the sort of people who would do something like this are nearly always weak and/or stupid individuals. They'll crumble.'

She laughs. 'I wish *I* could be that confident about things!'

Thai Hunter. Well, there's another little thread. Isolda collects our plates and takes them into the kitchen. When she returns, she picks up the empty champagne glasses, places them carefully on the windowsill in front of the fixed metal bars, leans against the wall, tosses her hair back and fixes me with one of her libidinous, X-rated grins.

*

When my mobile starts ringing, I know that it's precisely nine-fourteen pm. I'd intended this as an alarm call as well as my cover story, so I'm glad when it's Isolda that picks it up.

'Good evening. This is Mr Beckett's executive secretary, concubine, slave and mistress. How can I help you?'

I can just about hear the fake confusion on the other end. Male voice. North London accent.

'Sorry? What? Is, er, is Daniel there now? Who are you?'

'I'm afraid Mr Beckett is in a terminal post-coital coma at present. Can he call you back?'

'Who *is* this?'

She giggles and hands the mobile to me, moving close, almost with her ear against it, so she can listen to the conversation. I run my hand down the inside of her thigh and dig my fingernails into the soft skin.

'Yes, Ashley, what is it? I'm in an important meeting so make it quick.'

'Important meeting my arse. Listen. Can you come over? It's Millie. She was out with some of her mates and she's taken something or someone's given her something without her realising it. I don't know. But she's fuckin' off her tits. I don't know what to do.'

I roll my eyes at Isolda and take a deep, impatient breath. Isolda bites my neck and grinds herself against me. 'What – what's she doing?'

'She's lying on the floor. She's already been sick once on the bed. She swears she only had three drinks. She came home early. She got a cab 'cause she wasn't feeling so good. Her pulse rate is really high and she's sweating like a fuckin' pig. Can you…?'

'OK. Listen. Get her onto her side. If she's been sick she might be again and we don't want her to choke on it. Get her something to drink like orange juice. Stay with her. Don't leave her alone, understand? I'll get over as soon as I can.'

'Cheers, mate. I owe you one for this.'

'Yeah, yeah, yeah.'

I click the mobile off and stare at the ceiling.

'What was all that about?' says Isolda, with genuine concern in her voice.

'It's a friend of mine. His girlfriend has a history of, er, *issues*. This has happened before. He's a bit hopeless in situations like this. I'm going to have to get over there and see what the hell's going on this time. I'll have a shower and get a cab. I'm sorry.'

'That's OK, babe. I think I might need an early night tonight, anyway.'

'Are you sure you're not pissed off?'

'Of course not. I've had a great time. Three or four great times. When you're ready I'll walk with you while you're looking for a cab. I'll get one after you've got one.'

I kiss her on the mouth and head for the bathroom.

Of course, there's no such person as Ashley. This is a service I discovered about a year ago. It's expensive, but very professional and very, very convincing. You have a contract with them so they know who you are from your number.

You send them a text including the time you want the call, what the call will be about, the relationship of the caller to you and the caller's name. They do all the rest, including the improvised dialogue.

Some bright spark set it up so people could extricate themselves from bad dates, boring business meetings and family Sunday lunches, but I found it had uses that I could employ professionally.

Fifteen minutes later, Isolda and I are walking along The Strand, looking for cabs. When I finally flag one down, I say 'Clissold Park' to the driver, kiss Isolda one more time and off I go. When we've been driving for a couple of minutes I tell him I've changed my mind and ask him to take me to Piccadilly Circus. He tuts impatiently and rolls his eyes. Prick.

13

PICCADILLY AT NIGHT

I sit outside one of the coffee places that I noticed this afternoon, order a big one and watch the crowds. It's probably as busy here as it was this afternoon, but the people are different; fewer kids, fewer shoppers, more dressed-up girls, more big noisy groups of guys. It's dark now, and the street lamps, car headlamps, hotels, bars and shops are doing most of the illuminating.

I can see Burlington House on the other side of the road. It's maybe six or seven hundred yards away. It's lit up and looks good for it. There's a lot of taxi activity outside. I can't tell whether it's people leaving early, people arriving late or nothing to do with the event inside at all.

Occasionally, I can spot security guys moving in and out of the courtyard, but they're casual, laughing and smoking, not expecting any trouble. All they'll have to do now is smile politely to exiting partygoers when the Dania Gamble function finishes at eleven.

Someone sends me a text, and for a moment I think it's from Sara, but it turns out to be from Isolda, wishing me luck with Ashley's problem, which I'd already forgotten about.

After ten minutes of pinning people, I idly classify them into a loose number of groups; people looking for restaurants, people looking for clubs/pubs, ordinary sightseers, local workers, late shoppers and people who want to stroll down Piccadilly because it's Piccadilly.

Any left over, I classify as 'others'; solitary people walking quickly but going nowhere, creepy, unaccompanied guys pretending to look in shop windows while really looking at girls, older men having suspicious trysts with much younger women, edgy, fucked-looking strangers trying to make eye contact. I get a feel for the clothing that they're all wearing and I get a feel for the way they're walking, noting when they stop, why they stop and how long they stop for.

After a while, I start to notice a few sub-classes. There's a subtle bit of drug dealing going on here; inconspicuous but largely effective, as far as I can tell. Crafty-eyed, sharp-suited, smiley-faced dealers approaching likely customers, speedy exchanges of money and packets, quickly flitting out of sight and impatiently moving on to the next mark whenever they get a negative reaction.

There's also a fair amount of prostitution, both male and female. Middle-aged businessmen having quick, awkward conversations with tough-looking teenage boys or almost-classy women, their knuckles turning white against their briefcase handles as they look guiltily from side to side as if their wives are about to appear and give them a major bollocking.

As if on cue, one of the almost-classy women sits down at the table adjacent to mine without ordering anything. Business must be slow in Mayfair tonight. She looks at me and smiles. She's somewhere in her twenties, dyed chestnut hair, smart black suit and some good-looking jewellery.

Pretty in a wholesome, countrified way, but her eyes are frosty and she looks tired. I smile back and give her a brief shake of my head; just enough to let her know that she's wasting her time and can try someone else. She nods her thanks, gets up and crosses the road. Great legs and doubtless worth whatever she's charging, if you can put up with her yawning.

Two coffees later, I pay the bill and take a slow walk up the south side. When I'm opposite Burlington House, I don't look across the road, but allow my peripheral vision to do the work for me. Two cabs, one limo, and a group of five people milling about who look like they're something to do with the event inside. There's a solo security guy nervously chatting up a tall girl with great silver and purple hair.

I keep watching the crowds until the night-time population of Piccadilly becomes an organic whole. I try to think of nothing as I walk along, hoping that my subconscious will alert me to any anomalies.

I look at my watch to check the time. It's still a little early for Sara's event to have finished, so I cross the road and even consider popping into The Clarence to see if Klementina's there, but then realise that it's pretty unlikely she'd be on this late if she was working the lunchtime shift and she probably doesn't hang out there in her spare time; they never do.

As I approach Green Park tube station, I can see a police car parked up on the pavement with its blue lights flashing, and like a good Londoner, I walk a little faster so I can get a good look at what's going on.

There's a man lying on the pavement with blood oozing out of a nasty gash on his forehead and one of the police officers is holding a thin, struggling guy in his twenties in an arm lock. He's spaced and laughing. Nothing particularly interesting to look at, so I cross the road and head back the way I came.

Just as I'm walking past The Ritz and admiring their window displays, my mobile makes its text noise. It's from Sara and it just says 'now'. That gives me ten minutes or thereabouts before she comes out, which I decided to spend sauntering rather than standing or sitting at some fixed point. I check my watch. It's ten forty-four.

Still keeping to the south side of the road, I pass Burlington House and keep going, once again not looking directly at the entrance. I plan to walk all the way down to Piccadilly Circus and then walk back on the north side until Sara appears. The crowds here have increased a little, but nothing too dramatic.

There's a big pack of tourists milling around someone demonstrating a glow-in-the-dark novelty of some sort. I weave along the pavement, sink into my Zen-like trance once more and see if my subconscious picks up on anything.

I stop to look in Fortnum's window, mainly because it gives me an excuse to stand next to a statuesque, expensively dressed, black-haired woman in her late forties/early fifties. I look at her reflection in the glass while pretending to look at the spectacular flower display inside. She's wearing a midnight blue dress with three strings of grey pearls. Heavy makeup, tanned, lines around the eyes, but giving off an erotic charge you could cut with a knife. Probably on her way somewhere to meet someone. Great mouth. She turns to look at me and smiles.

'It must take them a long time to do these wonderful displays.'

Low, husky voice. Can't place the accent. Somewhere in southern Europe. Spanish? Portuguese?

'I think it's worth it, though. It makes you want to go inside, doesn't it.'

'It's such a shame it is closed now. I may pop in tomorrow and have a look around. I am here with my husband. He has business here for ten days, but he isn't interested in shops. You know what men are like.'

'I've heard they're terrible. I'm glad *I'm* not one.'

'You look like one to me.'

'I was just attempting to be witty to impress you.'

'Why would you want to impress me?'

'I can't help it. I'm compelled to suck up to remarkably beautiful women. It's an affliction, really. A scourge.'

This gets a laugh. 'I hear they serve afternoon tea in the Diamond Jubilee Tea Salon. I may come in and see what they have; tea at Fortnum's is very *chic,* I have heard. I may be there around three tomorrow.'

And then I see him.

I can feel in the pit of my stomach that this is my guy. I don't turn around but keep checking him out in the reflection of my window. He's almost directly opposite on the other side of the road, trying to be as inconspicuous as I am, but not nearly as successfully.

There are a million interesting windows to look in down this road, but he's chosen to be intensely interested in a small jeweller's which has had the window display removed for the night and a thick metal grill drawn over the glass. His clothes aren't right and his facial expression is uncomfortable and tense.

He keeps looking to his left, in the direction of

Burlington House. He walks away from the jeweller's, then, as if he'd decided it was much more interesting than he'd realised, walks back to it. A couple of policemen stroll past him and he automatically scratches his head in an almost quaint attempt at innocent nonchalance.

'Are you staying in a hotel round here?' I say.

Suddenly, this woman has become useful in a way she can't imagine. She smiles smugly to herself before she replies, pleased that she's got my interest and basking in the flirtation. I can smell her perfume now. Intense and spicy.

'Yes. I'm staying at the Hotel Café Royal. Do you know it?'

'A few minutes from here, I believe. Regent Street, isn't it?'

'That's correct.'

He's in his late sixties with receding short grey hair, a fat gut and a rough-looking face with deep lines down the cheeks and around the eyes. *Lived-in. Hard-looking.* This is almost certainly the guy that called Sara a bitch. Are they, whoever they are, running out of staff?

He's wearing a black suit with a white shirt open at the neck and a handkerchief poking out of the top pocket of his jacket. Sara's description of him was pretty good, but she missed one thing: his build. This guy is muscle and no monkey suit can disguise it.

'Have you got a suite or a room?'

'A suite. We wanted the Empire Suite, but it was fully booked. We're in the Celestine Suite. My husband wasn't that bothered, really. He's in Edinburgh for five days from tomorrow, but I do like the Empire. My name's Doroteia, by the way. Doroteia Vasconselos. Mrs Doroteia Vasconselos.'

'I'm Daniel Beckett. Please to meet you, Doroteia.'

'It is my pleasure, Daniel.'

We shake hands. I keep eyes on my man, who's still loitering uncertainly. He's at a disadvantage in that he doesn't know the precise time that Sara will appear, and doesn't want to wander far in case he misses her. He looks around innocently, but his acting is poor. For a second, he's looking directly at me, but looks away again. Nothing to see, just a man and a woman talking in front of Fortnum's.

'Well, we may bump into each other tomorrow, Doroteia. I often come here at around three.'

'I hope so. I would like that. I have booked a fitting at Rigby & Peller later in the afternoon. Perhaps you could accompany me. It can be useful to have a man's opinion when one is buying undergarments.'

'That's so true. Well, let's hope our visits here tomorrow coincide.'

'Yes. Let us hope they do. I must leave now. My husband will be wondering where I am.'

'Tomorrow, then.'

'Yes. Good evening, Mr Beckett.'

'Good evening, Mrs Vasconselos.'

I watch her as she strolls slowly towards Piccadilly Circus. Her ass is swaying a little more than might be usual and she slowly runs a hand through her hair. Well, that should be interesting if I can get here.

When I look across the road at the jeweller's again, my man is gone and I get a brief surge of adrenalin, but then I spot him walking past the entrance of Burlington House and as he passes it he takes a conspicuous look into the courtyard. Fuckin' amateur.

I remain on my side of the road and track him,

keeping about thirty feet back. He turns into the Burlington Arcade and pretends to look at some of the shops, all the while looking over his shoulder in the direction he's just come from. It's close on eleven now and he's unsure what to do. He doesn't want to get too far away, but at the same time he doesn't want to loiter directly outside.

He crosses the road and strolls past Piccadilly Arcade, stopping, lighting a cigarette and keeping his eyes on Burlington House. I walk straight past him without giving him a glance and stop about half a dozen shops away, looking at some souvenirs while keeping him in my peripheral vision.

He's still not moving and I suspect he's just waiting now. I'd identified the entrance to Piccadilly Arcade as being a good observation point when I was here this afternoon and he obviously feels the same way.

I feel uncomfortable standing still, so I keep moving, cross over Arlington Street and walk past The Ritz once more. I'm getting bored with this now, so I cross over to the north side yet again and slowly walk towards the Burlington House entrance, where I hope to see Sara at any moment, unless there's been a major frenzy at the cloakroom.

My guy is focussed on spotting Sara and I'm betting he's not switched on enough to notice me, even if he was looking.

A hundred yards ahead of me, about eight or nine people come out of the Burlington House entrance. They're all laughing and talking and in the middle of them I see Sara in the light turquoise dress she described. In one hand she's holding a clutch bag and in the other a kind of black wrap. I slow down and watch.

My man has seen her, too. He throws his cigarette into the gutter and walks towards Fortnum's, never taking his eyes off her and her little crowd. The expression on his face is stern and full of concentration, rather like some predator that's waiting for the weakest antelope to get separated from the herd. I've never seen Sara in high heels and get momentarily distracted by the sight and the effect they have on her bottom.

I can see Gaige, who towers above everyone else. He laughs at something, wags his finger at one of the other women and walks into the road to flag down a cab. When it stops, he and three others get in, leaving Sara a little more exposed on the pavement. She looks around nervously. Is she looking for me, I wonder?

Now there's Sara, two older looking women and a guy in a yellow ochre suit. There's a lot of hugging and air kissing. Yellow Suit runs across the road, is almost mown down by a cyclist and narrowly misses bumping into my man. I can see now that Sara is holding a brightly coloured bag with something big and rectangular inside. Presumably, this is a copy of Dania Gamble's hefty magazine.

She hands this bag to the taller of the two women, who says something and laughs, kissing Sara on both cheeks. Sara, of course, would already have a copy of this from the US launch party and is doubtless giving hers to this woman. After another monumental session of kisses and hugs, these two women turn and start walking towards me.

I don't look at them as they pass by and keep my eyes on Sara. She looks from left to right as if she's looking for a cab, then decides to walk down towards Piccadilly Circus. She slings her wrap over the bare shoulder that doesn't have the bow on it. It's a little chillier now and I can feel a cool wind on my face. It's suddenly much busier on this side of the road.

I'm probably a hundred yards behind her, but there's a big crowd of people milling around and sometimes my view of her is blocked. I quicken my pace and keep my eyes on my guy, who has just crossed the road and dropped in behind Sara. I wonder what he's going to do?

He's keeping about ten feet behind her and is looking around, checking out what sort of people are nearby and how near they are to her. She has two guys in their twenties walking fairly close behind her. They're looking at her body and talking about her.

It would be a mistake for him to try anything while they're around as they'd probably do something about it, particularly as they look a bit pissed. He keeps following her and I keep following him.

I'm also keeping an eye out for an accomplice, even though I'm pretty sure he's working alone. As we cross over Sackville Street, the two guys cross over the road and are gone.

I'm keeping a small group of tourists between my guy and myself as I close in on him. He looks quickly over his shoulder, but his gaze is on the tourists, not me; I'm making myself invisible.

He takes a look across the road as we approach Swallow Street, glances over his shoulder once more, then moves in for the kill. He's about four feet behind Sara before he starts talking to her. She doesn't react at first; presumably thinking he's talking to someone else.

'Hey! Darlin'! Aren't you a bit far away from Shepherd Market?'

This is a well-known upmarket prostitute hangout

about half a mile away. He's calling her a prostitute, in effect. Not a very nice introductory gambit and one that might offend if you were hoping to ask her on a date and then get married and raise a family.

'Hey! You fuckin' tart. Look at me.'

He's right up behind her now. He rams his shoulder into her back, making her stagger forward. She turns to look at him and recognises him, alarm appearing on her face. The tourists are still in front of me, but they're oblivious, looking at the sights and laughing at something.

He grabs the back of her dress.

'What sort of fuckin' thing d'you call this? What's this?'

He pulls her black wrap away and grabs the bow on her right shoulder. I've no idea how designs like this work, and I'm wondering if the bow is a real one and will undo the dress if it's pulled hard enough. I suspect that's what he's trying to do. I remember she said she wasn't wearing a bra with it.

We're feet away from a small alley called Piccadilly Place. It leads into Vine Street, which is a sort of nowhere area. Sara tries to grab his hand. She sounds frightened when she speaks.

'What are you doing? What are you *doing*? Get *away* from me.'

'You fuckin', stinking whore.'

He tugs at the bow and laughs. The road is suddenly filled with taxis. Lots of diesel engine noise. Car horns. Kids screaming and laughing somewhere. Thumping music from a club. I pass through the family of tourists and I'm right behind him.

This has to be fast. I grab his shirt and jacket collar in one hand and tug down. Just as his balance is going and he starts to fall backwards, I spin around to face him and hit him hard in the base of the windpipe with a fast, powerful, open hand punch.

I can see the panic in his eyes as he realises he can't breathe and the pain has made his eyes bloodshot. His mouth is open and he croaks as he attempts to inhale. He looks stupid. I smile quickly at Sara to reassure her that it's me, then drag him into Piccadilly Place, out of sight of the public.

He's still choking as I push him against the bricks and administer the first of two swift punches to his nose, breaking it and spattering his face in a fair amount of blood. I just hope Sara didn't hear the splinter of cartilage and bone. I give him a testicle-crusher with my knee, belt him just once in the guts and let him drop to the floor. Sara is standing on the pavement in shock.

'Listen. Sara. It's OK now. This guy was on his own. I'm going to have to get a cab straight away. You get the next one and take it right to your front door. I'll arrange for you to be met when you arrive. I'll give you a call as soon as I can.'

She nods dumbly and tries to look behind me at what's happened. She looks incredibly sexy in that dress and those heels. I flag down a cab and explain to the driver that my dad's been mugged and I need to get him home as soon as possible.

He's dubious at first, but after I've hit him with the facts that tonight was my dad's seventieth and that he's been boozing and that he used to play for Stoke City and that I'm a male nurse and can look after him and here's a hundred for the fare, he agrees, and I go in the alley, get this fucker up to his feet and push him in the back of the cab. His face is red, he looks like shit, his breathing is ragged and he's shaking. Fuckin', stinking whore indeed.

I manhandle him into the back seat and close the door. He moans. Through the back window I can see Sara getting into another cab.

'Where to, mate?'

'Alaska Street, Waterloo.'

The meter goes on and off we go.

14

FOOTBALLER DAD

'On his fuckin' birthday, as well,' says the driver, as we head along the Victoria Embankment on our way to Waterloo Bridge. He's a tad younger than my Footballer Dad and has a strong Glaswegian accent. 'How many of them were there?'

'He said there were four. It happened really fast. We were in the pub and he wanted to go outside and have a fag. He'd only been out there for about a minute when I heard all this noise and went to have a look and they'd already done it and were running away. I only saw two of them, mind. I wish I'd got my fuckin' hands on them, but I had to see he was alright.'

'How much did they get?'

'Well, we'd been in the boozer all night so it can't have been that much. A tenner, maybe? Ridiculous, innit.'

'Jesus. What position did he play?'

'What?'

'Your dad. In Stoke City.'

'Left wing.'

'If he's seventy, he must have known Stanley Matthews during his comeback days. He might have even played with him! Bloody hell!'

My Footballer Dad starts to moan. He's coming round, which I don't want.

'Are you OK, Dad? We'll be home soon.'

I take his head in my hands as if I'm examining him, and with the ring finger of my left hand, press a point just below the ear, near the angle of the jaw. He passes out in two seconds. Next, I text John Kimmons and ask him to get someone to wait for Sara outside the entrance to the flats and to accompany her inside.

'I think he may have been lucky he'd had a skinful,' says the driver. 'Numbs the pain a bit. He'll feel it all when he wakes up tomorrow morning, though.'

'I'm sure you're right, mate.'

'I got mugged in 1986. Three of the bastards. I can still remember it like it was yesterday.'

'Yeah?'

Kimmons returns my text. He's not on duty, but has called someone called Kevin Jenkins who is. Kevin is, as we text, waiting outside the entrance to the block for Sara's cab to arrive and will personally see that she gets to her room OK. I text Sara with the news and tell her I'll give her a call tomorrow morning. She texts back: 'bLoOdY hElL!!'. Well, at least her spirits are high.

We arrive at our destination and after another bout of sports banter with the driver, I help my Footballer Dad out of the cab and onto the pavement. He's a heavy bastard and is difficult to manipulate, but he looks like a convincing drunk/mugging victim. The cab driver is looking around for a house, but he won't find one, and luckily Alaska Street is blocked to traffic by half a dozen sturdy metal bollards.

This is a crowded area, directly beneath a low railway bridge that runs from Waterloo Station and it's become home to a number of restaurants and pubs as gentrification creeps in.

The combination of railway noise and milling crowds make it an easy and inconspicuous place to manhandle someone like Footballer Dad and I'm lucky I don't have to go too far, as I don't think I have the strength. I chat encouragingly to Footballer Dad to avoid causing suspicion. He doesn't respond.

After a few yards, I turn right into Brad Street. On one side there are a load of garages belonging to the houses on the next street along and on the side I'm staggering along, there's a long sequence of railway arches that have been converted into a variety of formats; there's a rehearsal studio, two car repair shops, a small wholesaler of shop mannequins, a gym, a club and four lock-up garages, one of which is mine.

Driving around in London actually slows you down, particularly in my line of work. There's never anywhere to park and whenever there is, there's a queue. It's much quicker and less stressful to take the tube, take a cab or take to the pavement; sometimes a combination of all three.

I do have a car, though. It's a 2001 black Maserati Coupé that I acquired about five years ago. It has a V8 fuel injection engine (built by Ferrari), does 0 – 60 in 4.9 seconds and has a top speed of 177 mph. I know all of this thanks to Mr Ralph Blake, who owns the lock-up garage next to mine.

When Mr Blake first saw me reverse the Maserati into my lock-up, I had a friend for life. He's about eighty and is an Italian car nut. He currently owns a Rococo Red Alfa Romeo Giulietta and a blue and white Bugatti Veyron Vitesse. Needless to say, the security he has is the best, as is mine. It's also a plus that he spends most of his time here, fiddling with the engines of both cars. Luckily, he's never here this late.

I press the password codes on two separate keypads before I hear the heavy, grinding clicks that tell me both inertia tube locks are open. I push the door with my shoulder, drag Footballer Dad in with me and close it behind us.

I'm greeted by the familiar smell of petrol, oil, plastic, leather and cold concrete. Straight away, I notice I'm shivering slightly. This place never catches the sun, so it always feels like it's winter in here. I turn a switch and the neon strips flicker into life. My Footballer Dad groans.

To my left is the Maserati, protected by a dark blue made-to-measure car cover. On the right is a small metal table and some rusty metal shelves, which are home to a half empty tin of oil, a few basic car tools and spares, a kettle, two mugs, coffee stuff and a battery charger. There's a sink with hot and cold taps and a couple of filthy hand towels hanging off the side. There are two rusty metal dining chairs and there's a grey plastic bucket underneath one of them.

I dump Footballer Dad onto the floor and he grunts. It's a relief to be able to let go of him; I would guess he weighs about fifteen stone or more. I take the car cover off and take a look at the car. While I'm here, I decide to charge the battery, so I open the bonnet and set up the CTEK charger.

In the boot, there's a small toolkit full of car stuff and, innocently circling a can of WD40, are a dozen plastic zip ties, which could look like something you might use to connect pipes and cables in the engine.

I drag Footballer Dad up to his feet, remove his jacket and shirt, and sit him down on one of the metal chairs, which I've placed right up against one of the brick walls so he can't rock the chair forward. I take his shoes and socks off and use the zip ties to connect his ankles to the front legs of the chair.

Using the same method, I tie his wrists to the mid rail across the back. I know that when he wakes up, the stretching sensation that this will produce will be extremely painful, but that's just tough.

I check his trouser pockets first, but there's nothing in them apart from a single spent match, a small amount of loose change and a crumpled mint wrapper. His jacket doesn't yield much; a mini spirit level key ring with two Yale keys, a Chubb mortice key and a Volkswagen car key.

In the inside pocket, there's a beer mat which has eighty pounds in ten pound notes carefully folded and attached to it with an elastic band. I take the money and put it in my pocket. I may buy Sara some flowers with it when all this is over. I'm a big fan of poetic justice.

No wallet, no ID of any kind. There's no way of telling whether this is an intentional thing or just the way he rolls.

He's still pretty out of it and his head hangs down against his chest. His nose has started bleeding again and blood drips down over his fat belly and his crotch. I take my jacket and my shirt off and put them on the roof of the car.

I go to the sink and fill up the grey plastic bucket with water. The bucket is slightly too big for the sink, which I've always found a little annoying, but it's a cross I have to bear. I place a hand under the tap. The water is so cold it numbs my skin almost immediately. This'll do fine.

I walk over to Footballer Dad and chuck the whole bucketful of freezing water straight at him. It soaks his head, his chest and a lot of the wall. Ideally, I'd get him full in the face, but that'll have to wait until he's a little more alert.

The effect is electrifying. He jerks his head up and performs a few high-pitched inhalations as the cold kicks in. I go back to the sink, fill up another bucket and throw that one over him as well. This time, I get his face and his full attention.

He screws up his eyes to clear the water and shakes his head from side to side like a wet dog. He's shivering and panting, his bloodshot eyes staring straight at me and he's probably wondering just what the fuck's going on. One minute he's strolling down old Piccadilly calling a pretty girl a stinking whore and the next he's in Hell. He coughs up some water he's inhaled and spits it onto the floor.

I have to try and see things from his point of view. This will be the first time he's actually got a good look at me. He got a glimmer when I assaulted him in the street, but after that it would have been all agony, delirium and pressure points. He's totally disorientated. He's in pain. He has no idea who I am, where he is or why he's here. This is good, and I'm going to keep him in the dark for a little while longer.

'What is it?' he says, his teeth chattering. 'Who are you? What d'you want? Is this some bleedin' queer thing?'

I don't say anything. I just look at him. He doesn't like this. His voice has an unpleasant rasping quality, which I realise is probably my doing. I'd almost forgotten that I'd whacked him hard in the throat back in Piccadilly. I heard the crunch of the cartilage. I know what that feels like and under other circumstances I might be a little sympathetic. His bafflement has now turned to aggression.

'I don't know who you are, mate, but you better let me

out of here right this *fuckin*' minute.' He allows himself a quick, frenzied, futile struggle against the zip ties. 'You are dead, my son, you are fuckin' dead.'

He's angry. He grinds his front teeth together so hard I'm afraid he might chip them. He expands his muscles in another useless attempt to damage the zip ties. I fill the kettle up with water and switch it on. There's some instant coffee left in a tin of Douwe Egberts Continental Coffee Rich Roast and it seems to be OK, so I put a spoonful in one of the mugs and wait, staring at him and saying nothing. Understandably, he still wants to chat: he's hoping to make sense of what's going on here and is looking for feedback.

'Who are you? Are you that slut's boyfriend or something? You piece of shit. You chickenshit fucker. You're fucking queer, aren't you. Why've you taken your shirt off? You fucking let me out of here or I'll fucking kill you. I'll rip your fucking guts out. I'll rip your guts out and shit in the hole. You are fucking going to wish you were dead when I've finished with you. You piece of fucking queer crap.'

He struggles once more. It's a waste of time. The kettle boils and clicks itself off. As I make my coffee, I take a long look at my Footballer Dad. I haven't decided precisely what I'm going to do with him yet. I know that he'll pick up on this and it'll make him even more uncertain about what's happening and how he should react. I can hear the thump of a bass guitar coming from the nearby rehearsal studio and I'm suddenly aware of a strong smell of chips.

I take a sip of coffee, pick up the kettle of boiling water and walk towards him. His eyes widen and for a second he looks frightened, then he looks contemptuous and scowls a little, like he's been threatened with boiling water a million times in the last fortnight and it's nothing to him. I hold the kettle up, glance at it and then look at him.

'You thought I was going to pour boiling water over you. It never occurred to me. That would be terrible. Can you imagine what that would feel like? A whole kettle of boiling water all over your face? Or actually poured down your *throat*? Or emptied all over your crotch? It doesn't bear thinking about, does it.'

He's looking at me like he wants to kill me, but his tone has changed.

'Listen, mate. I don't know what all this is about, but if you're smart – and I think you are – you'll let me out of here now. You have no idea what shit you're in if you keep me here. I'll just walk out the door of this place and you'll never see me again.'

'The problem with the boiling water is, of course, that you'd scream. This is quite a busy area. Somebody might hear. To be honest with you, I can't imagine what it would feel like to have boiling water poured all over your face. You'd probably be blinded at the very least. There is one way out of it, though. The screaming, that is.'

I take the kettle back over to the table and put it down. I get one of the filthy hand towels, soak it under the cold tap and walk towards my Footballer Dad. He knows what I'm going to do, closes his mouth tightly and turns his head to the side. He's struggling like crazy, but it's no good. He's helpless. I pinch his nose hard so he has to open his mouth to scream and then stuff a good wodge of the towel inside. He has to nose breathe now and it's not easy for him. His eyes are bulging and his face is going red.

I walk back to the metal table, take another sip of coffee and turn the kettle on again. I stare at him with expressionless eyes and I can feel his fear. His breathing is uneven and once more he starts to strain against the zip ties, trying to rock the chair from side to side. It doesn't work, not least because of the pain he'll be feeling in his shoulders, arms and wrists every time he moves. I don't know why he's bothering. Maybe he's hoping for a miracle. He's in the wrong place for miracles.

The kettle takes about fifty seconds to boil, though for Footballer Dad it must seem forever. When it finally clicks off and I pick it up and flash him a brief, sympathetic smile, it's too much for him. He makes a valiant but unsuccessful attempt to spit the towel out of his mouth then resignedly nods his head up and down, indicating that he's ready to talk.

We both know I'd have done it.

I drag the other chair across the floor and sit directly in front of him.

'OK. I'm going to ask you a few questions and I expect you to answer them quickly and accurately. If I sense for a second that you're not telling me the whole truth, or are holding something back, or are being smart, you'll be punished, and the punishment will be unpleasant and extreme.

'You asked me earlier why I'd taken my shirt off. The answer to that is that I don't want your blood spraying all over it. I'm sure you know how difficult it is to get blood stains out of cotton.'

I lean forward and pull the towel out of his mouth. He shakes his head from side to side and gasps. 'You really don't know what you're up against, mate. You are so fucked it's not true.'

He starts laughing, secure in the knowledge of his superior position in this encounter.

'OK. First question. This is the second time, to my knowledge, that you've harassed that young lady in the street. What's going on? What's happening?'

He laughs. I can smell cheap fags on his breath. 'I just don't like the bitch. She fucks me off, the little whore. She was lucky I didn't drag her off somewhere and…'

I flick my fist out in a punch that's so fast he doesn't even have time to blink before it crushes what's left of the cartilage in his nose. Luckily, the blood doesn't spray but just trickles. Footballer Dad looks somewhat displeased and grimaces in agony.

'Oh, Jesus. You bastard,' he says, not unreasonably.

'I'll ask you again. What's going on?'

'Look, mate. I'm seventy-one.'

'I don't give a toss how old you are. What's all this harassment about? Prevaricate once more and I boil the kettle. Then you know what will happen. Look at me. Look into my eyes. You know I'm not kidding.'

He purses his lips together. He's so furious he can barely speak. He hyperventilates to calm himself down and he's as white as a sheet. 'She's just a fucking slut who needed to be brought down a peg or two. He'll fucking get you for this, whoever you are.'

'Who will? The person who's organised all of this? Who is it? Look – you're just a foot soldier. I can tell. Whoever you're working for is just using you. They've got you into the mess you're in right now and you are in one *fuck* of a mess, believe you me. If they were worth looking up to they'd be doing this themselves, not getting some fuckin' pensioner to do it for them. I'm losing patience now. This is your last chance. Don't be their bitch.

What's going on?'

'Go fuck yourself, you fuckin' homo.'

'Well, girlfriend – don't say I didn't warn you.'

I pinch what's left of his nose until he opens his mouth again. I stuff the towel in his mouth. I walk over to the metal table and turn the kettle on again. I take another sip of my coffee, which is getting cold now. I chuck it down the sink and start to prepare another one.

Whoever this guy is, he's frightened of and is in awe of his boss. At least that tells me that there *is* a boss; someone who's organising all of this, which is what I'd suspected all along.

The fact that he told me that his boss will get me for this indicated that this is what usually happens when someone messes with one of his boss's foot soldiers. His boss is someone who doesn't fail. His boss is someone who wreaks vengeance.

You have no idea what shit you're in if you keep me here.
You really don't know what you're up against, mate.
He'll fuckin' get you for this, whoever you are.

Threats, threats and more threats; all based on my sad ignorance of the awesome, bone-chilling terror I'm dealing with and have inadvertently crossed. So we're certainly dealing with professional criminals, possibly even major players. This guy here has it written all over his face and his attitude confirms it.

Was he some sort of enforcer once? Is he still one, despite his age? What was his thing? Armed robbery? Breaking debtors' legs? He's in relatively good shape and still hits the gym regularly by the look of things, apart from his gut. Or conceivably he got that build pumping iron every day when he was inside; he's got that written all over his face, too.

Most people who were assaulted on the street and who came round tied to a chair in a cold garage with me boiling kettles would be absolutely terrified. Not this guy. He's too busy giving me all this macho bullshit, preserving what's left of his pride before it's all gone. Well, I'll find his breaking point soon and he'll be only too happy to tell me everything.

I'm actually pretty interested in all of this now, and I'm keen to discover why people like this would be interested enough in Sara Holt to take the sort of risks they've been taking. I can't imagine what their motivation would be. Money? Blackmail? Would they eventually tell Sara they'd stop if she paid them half a million?

I'm also interested that my friend here thought Sara needed to be taken down a peg or two. Do today's thugs look out for fashion designers who are getting too successful and exact retribution?

Aside from all of this, I get a mild feeling of satisfaction that I'm still only on Day One and have already caught one of the perpetrators and have him at my mercy. That's pretty good work, even if I say so myself, not to mention getting into Sara's place when no one thought it could be done.

I start thinking about Mrs Vasconselos. That was pretty good work, too. I wonder if she was walking around Piccadilly looking for a casual affair or was it just a chance meeting that went that way. The way she nudged the conversation was intelligent and direct, so perhaps she's done it before. From what I could see of her figure, I'm quite looking forward to her fitting at Rigby & Peller if I can make it.

And of course there's Klementina who likes Chinese food, though I can't think exactly when I'm going to fit her in. If it was a toss-up between Klementina and Mrs Vasconselos, I think I'd go for the latter, unless there was some way I could combine the two.

As I'm pouring hot water into another spoonful of instant I can tell he's dead. I'm not going to do a post mortem on him, but I would guess it's heart failure or lactic acidosis. Or maybe he couldn't breathe properly and simply suffocated; who knows. This is a real pain as I was just getting started, but as least I know I'm dealing with professionals, even if they're just professional criminals.

I untie him and let him slump to the floor. I'll stick him in the car and dump him somewhere the next chance I get. I put my shirt and jacket back on, switch off the battery charger, cover the car up and five minutes later I'm walking along Waterloo Road, looking for a cab. It's not even midnight.

15

BLOND HAIR

When I wake up the next morning, I notice a few aches and pains. The muscle strain of burglarising Sara's flat and dragging Footballer Dad around are taking their toll, and I mustn't forget my exertions with Aziza and Isolda. I must get down the gym more often. Thinking about it, I probably haven't been for about two months. In fact, I think I'll go this morning.

I swallow a couple of painkillers, decide to have a bath instead of a shower and load up the Siemens with Bourbon Espresso beans while the bath is running. I look in the fridge to see if there's anything to eat. I'm going to have to restock after Isolda's raid last night. There's a plum and coconut muffin I bought a few days ago and forgot about, so I take that out and put it on a plate. I fire the computer up and head towards the bathroom.

As I lie in the bath, I think about the events of last night. That harassment of Sara was a little more serious and aggressive than just being called a bitch, and I wonder if they're escalating things for some reason.

Would he have pulled her dress off in the street if he'd had time? Even on its own, that whole incident would have been enough to rattle most young women and it was starting to get pretty nasty before I intervened.

I did wonder about Footballer Dad's pejoratives while

I was chatting with him: 'bitch', 'whore', and all the rest of it, and began to wonder if it was personal in some way, but I think that was just his class, intelligence and generation speaking. He was just a dick, plain and simple, and this was just a job for him; a job that in his case went as badly as jobs like that can go. Tough break.

He would have been a great lead, though, but it was not to be. I try to put myself in the position of whoever his Scary Boss might be. He sends his man out for another spot of obnoxious, sexist harassment and his man disappears off the face of the planet. Now what on earth is he going to make of that?

If I was Scary Boss, I might try to give him a call, but he had no mobile on him. Perhaps he'll be calling him at home today. When are they going to realise he's missing? It might not be for some time. The bitch incident was about two weeks ago, if I remember Sara's comment correctly.

I think if I was doing the harassing and had maybe half a dozen people to help me, I'd rotate them to make the whole thing more confusing and difficult to describe. Footballer Dad may not have had another harassing gig for another two weeks.

The idea of there being a single individual pulling the strings behind all of this is still interesting. I've never come across anything quite like this and I still can't work out what the motivation might be, unless it's something completely random and crazy.

If, as I was led to believe, Scary Boss is such a Big Man, what is he doing wasting his time and energy on something like this? Answer: someone is paying him to do it, which brings me back to yesterday's speculations about the who and why of the whole thing.

Who would stand to gain if Sara screwed up these shows? I can't think my way out of the idea that is has to be a rival designer or someone similar. Perhaps it's someone she criticised in a magazine and they didn't take it too well.

Perhaps it's the editor of a fashion magazine who was promised some sort of exclusive and, for whatever reason, didn't get one. Perhaps it's a disgruntled ex-employee like Thai Hunter. It could have been something that happened ages ago that Sara has totally forgotten about.

Sara's success may well continue unimpeded if she fails to pull off doing New York and Milan at the same time, but she'd be forever known as someone who tried to bite off more than they could chew.

Is that important in the fashion industry, I wonder? Would that wipe her out or tarnish her reputation? I'm no expert, but I hardly think so, particularly if what had been happening to her got on the grapevine.

Bitchiness aside, I'm sure most of the people who know her would be extremely sympathetic if they knew what she'd had to put up with and they'd be looking for someone to blame and/or ostracise.

I decide to give Sara a call, firstly to see how she's doing as a professional courtesy, and secondly to make an appointment so I can run a couple of things past her.

'How d'you feel?'

'Hi. Fine. OK. Yes. I'm sorry – I've only just woken up.'

'What time are you going into work today?'

'Er, I want to be in by eleven.'

'I'll come and see you at eleven-thirty. I need to get you up to speed. I don't really want to tell you everything over the phone.'

'That'll be fine.'

'And listen – about what happened last night – put it out of your mind. At some point today it's going to catch up with you, but you mustn't dwell on it. Be tough. It's in the past now. And whatever you do, don't mention it to anybody.

'If anyone asks you about last night, tell them you had a great time. All your friends had dissipated by the time that guy appeared. No one saw what happened. Make your story convincing. Add an anecdote if you can think of one. OK?'

She laughs at this. 'An *anecdote*?'

'Sure. You bumped into one of your old lecturers from Saint Martin's who used to be a woman but who's now a man and you went to a burlesque club for drinks to catch up on old times. Anything.'

'Well, thank you for that suggestion.'

'My pleasure.'

'OK. I'll see you later. And thanks. Thanks for everything last night.'

'Don't mention it.'

I click my mobile off, get out of the bath and dry myself off.

Once I've made a coffee, I sit at the kitchen table and look at the list of Sara's engagements that Isolda printed off for me. She has a lunch date today, but that isn't highlighted. That means it's unlikely to be in the public domain and therefore technically hassle-free. But I have to remember that these things may have a tendency to leak out. The date is with a woman called Rachelle Beauchesne.

I drag the computer towards me and Google her

name. She's the director of a Paris-based PR company called Primeaux DD. I check to see whether she's got a Twitter account. She has. I look at her recent activity. Just a load of fashion-related retweets, then I see what I'm looking for: 'Lunch today with lovely @saraholt in ShahAb Persian restaurant. Diet out of window!!'

It was tweeted this morning at seven and has already been retweeted a hundred and forty-eight times. Even a private lunch date is news now. I check the location of the ShahAb and it's in Baker Street. Been open two years. Gets lots of five star reviews. She could walk there from Maccanti and probably wouldn't dream of taking a cab. I wonder if I can talk her out of it. Unlikely. I'll try, anyway.

Just as I'm going to get dressed, my mobile goes off. Isolda.

'So how did it go?'

I'm living in so many different realities that for a second I don't know what she's referring to. Then I remember.

'It was OK in the end. She'd taken some sort of exotic psychedelic fungus. I've no idea what it was. We just kept her awake, made her drink lots of orange juice and made sure that she was lying down on her side when she couldn't stand up anymore. She's OK now, but she's got quite a headache. I texted Ash this morning. I may have to pop around again to make sure everything's alright.'

That's obviously untrue, but it gives me an excuse the next time I have to slip away.

'What time did you get back?'

'I can't remember. I think it was around two.'

'You must be exhausted.'

'Not too bad. I'm going to the gym in half an hour, anyway.'

'Didn't you have enough of a workout yesterday? Where do you go? Gymbox?'

Gymbox is in St Martin's Lane. Lots of punch bags, a boxing ring, kickboxing lessons and a DJ. Went there once. Wasn't too keen. Too much testosterone flying around, some of it coming from the men.

'No. Soho Gyms in Macklin Street.'

'Are we going to see each other today?'

'I'm coming into the office at eleven-thirty to see Sara.'

'Should we – I mean…'

'Let her know about us? Not if you don't want to. It doesn't affect what I'm doing, so there's no reason why she should know.'

'I'd prefer it if she didn't. I'm not being funny. It just makes me look a bit slutty.'

'That's what attracted me to you in the first place.'

She laughs. 'Fuck off. What about tonight?'

'I'll give you a call when I know what's going on.'

'I miss being with you, you know.'

'Me too. See you later.'

I get my gym stuff together and head off to Macklin Street.

*

After an hour's workout and a forty-minute swim, which is all I can manage, I take a quick shower, leave my kit in my locker and walk up Drury Lane towards High Holborn. I've got plenty of time before I have to see Sara, so I can walk to Hinde Street and stop off at the Pret A Manger on New Oxford Street for a second breakfast.

It's as I'm turning left into High Holborn that I get another little warning tingle; the first I've had since yesterday. I keep walking and keep looking straight ahead. If this is the same person that I failed to spot in Manchester Square, St Martin's Lane and Wimpole Street, then I'm dealing with a fair level of professionalism and don't want to let them know that I'm switched on.

This is a major crossroads, and behind me I can hear a bunch of cars and lorries snarling angrily at a red traffic light. I can tell the lights have gone amber by the sound of the engines and run over to the other side of the road just as they turn green, glancing in the window of a Travelodge to see if anyone's following me.

It's clear, so I continue down the north side of the road and turn into Grape Street, a small thoroughfare that doesn't have much going on in it apart from a few office buildings, some vacant, some not, and the stage door for the Shaftesbury Theatre.

I have no idea who this might be, but I now have to assume it's connected to the case. Even if it isn't, I'll still have to neutralise it as it's getting on my nerves.

I risk a quick look over my shoulder. Still no one obvious. On a whim, I turn into one of the office buildings, pushing the double swing doors open and walk into the reception area like I know why I'm there and what I'm doing.

I have to take in my surroundings in a millisecond. Expensive décor. Air-conditioning. Clean smell. Pretty, well-dressed young girl behind a high reception desk. Lovely brown eyes, dyed blonde hair, gorgeous cleavage, late teens/early twenties. Bronze-tinted mirrors everywhere. There's a sign on the wall: Coggan Media Solutions. I catch the receptionist's eye and smile. She smiles back.

'Hi, there. I've come to pick up the proofs to be

delivered to Mr Allen.'

I think that sounded credible enough. I lean against the reception desk with an air of very slight impatience, then turn and give her a brief but hopefully engaging smile. She looks unsettled.

'Sorry, the – for who?'

'Mr Allen? Vector Studios?'

'I'm sorry; I don't know anything about this. Would you like to take a seat and I'll ask someone?'

'Sure.'

I sit down and position myself so that I can see the street outside reflected in one of the bronze wall mirrors. As she makes the call, I see my mark walking past at some speed. Late forties, running to fat, short blond hair, clean-shaven, expensive pale grey suit, black briefcase. I get up, wave at the baffled receptionist and go outside.

I can just see Blond Hair as he reaches the end of the street. He's assuming that I ran down this road as soon as I was out of sight. He stops and looks left and right. We're at the top end of Shaftesbury Avenue. Now he has to make a decision based on not much. There are about thirty places I could have gone before he caught up. I could even have got a cab or got on a bus.

After a few seconds of indecision, he opts to turn left. I wait for a while then follow, keeping on the right side of Grape Street. I don't want to turn around the corner at the end and get punched in the face.

When I think it's safe, I turn left and see him about ten yards away. He's crossed Shaftesbury Avenue as it gives him a better view of the road as it curves southwards. He's not rushing, he's not in a panic, he just moves along with a slow, purposeful walk, casually but thoroughly scanning the whole area without it being obvious what he's doing. Blond Hair is almost certainly police, or, more likely, ex-police.

I take my jacket off and sling it over my shoulder. It isn't a perfect disguise, but it might gain me a couple of seconds if he spots me. I allow him to get a little over a hundred yards ahead of me and keep on the other side of the road from him.

He strolls along at the same pace as a first-time tourist, then stops to look in the window of a shop selling expensive kitchen items, while using the reflection of the glass to look behind him, just in case. He gets his mobile out and makes a call, probably telling whoever it was who set him on me that I'd managed to escape his clutches and that he was very sorry and it wouldn't happen again. I wonder if he's talking to Scary Boss.

He takes off in the direction of New Oxford Street, stopping by a small coffee bar and going inside. After less than a minute, he comes out and sits on one of the metal chairs, still breezily scanning his surroundings, just in case.

When the waiter comes out with his coffee and distracts him for a second, I sit down at another table a couple of feet away. When he glances to the side and sees me, the reflex jerk it creates causes some of his coffee to spill into the saucer. He places his coffee on the table and nods his head resignedly at the predictability of being caught out like this. He turns and looks at me.

'You're looking a bit tired, my friend.'

God, he even sounds like a policeman; that offhand, blasé, mildly aggressive, condescending tone that I was frequently on the receiving end of as a teenager. I reply, but I don't turn to look at him or make eye contact.

'So what happened?' I say. 'Were you slung out of the

force for taking bribes? Beating a suspect to death? Falsifying evidence? Covering up child abuse by politicians? Go on – you can tell me. I'm very broad-minded.'

He ignores this, picks up his briefcase and takes out a brown Jiffy Bag. He tosses it so it lands on the table in front of me. The waiter comes out to see if I want anything. I say no thanks.

'As I was saying, you're looking a bit tired. I think you need a holiday.'

'Where would you suggest?'

'Somewhere hot, if it was me. Perhaps Malaysia. Somewhere like that. Far away.'

'How much is in the envelope?'

'Five thousand.'

'D'you think that'll be enough, officer?' I say the 'o' word to annoy him. He's absolutely not in the force anymore if he's doing stuff like this.

'More than enough, I would say. I think you've got a cracking deal there. Most private *dicks* would jump at the chance.'

'You were very good in Manchester Square, St Martin's Lane and Wimpole Street. I didn't see you at all.'

'What are you talking about?'

He looks truly baffled. Am I wrong about this? Interesting if I am.

'Forget it. So you want me to stop my current investigation with immediate effect, would that be correct?'

'That's about it, matey.'

'How do you even know I'm on a case? How do you even know I'm a private investigator? How did you even know where I'd be so you could trail me?'

I look at him for the first time. I want to see his face when he replies. He avoids my gaze by looking up at the sky.

'I'm sure I don't have to tell someone like you that there are ways of getting information like that. Technology is so vulnerable if you know what you're doing, don't you find that, matey?' He smiles smugly to himself and sips his coffee. A couple of drips fall from the bottom of the cup onto his trousers. I watch as the stain spreads.

His reply brings a whole number of new factors into play. Unless I'm mistaken, he's talking about phone hacking and listening devices. If that's what's been going on, then I'm going to have to take some major steps before I go any further with this case.

First of all, there's Sara's flat. Whoever got in there could well have planted a few bugs when they were busy moving coffee mugs around. Perhaps that was the main intention and all the rest was a smokescreen. That hadn't occurred to me. My focus and that of the police was on the breaking and entering aspect. It's equally possible that they may have tampered with her mobile while they were there or are intercepting the telephone signals in some other way.

Also, they know where she works. The scratching of her car right outside the building proves that. I didn't take any note of the security at the Maccanti building. If my bugging theory is correct, she may have the same problem in her office. Shit.

And if they're picking up intelligence from mobile phones, then it's a probability that they would target her MTA1 and MTA2. Maybe even other colleagues like Gaige. It's possible that someone was listening in on the conversation I had with Isolda this morning. I tell her where I was going to the gym and Blond Hair is on my back five minutes after I leave with a packet of bribe money. It can't be a coincidence. It occurs to me that he may have a car parked nearby.

If any of these guesses are true, then it's almost risible. What the hell is going on? What sort of ex-cop could manage this sort of stuff? I turn to Blond Hair once more.

'Were you in Special Branch, by any chance?'

'That's none of your business.'

So that's a 'yes', then. I look around to see if there's any conceivable way I could lift this guy, here, right now, in broad daylight, but it's impossible. Footballer Dad was a lot easier because of the time, location and crowds. Besides, he was busy, dim, and didn't see me coming. If I tried something like that here, it would be too conspicuous and I don't want the sort of trouble it would bring.

I really must have a think about all of this when I have a moment. As for now, I pick up the Jiffy Bag and throw it at Blond Hair's head. It bounces off and lands at his feet. He sighs, bends down, picks it up and puts it back in his briefcase.

He looks pissed, but like me, he can't really do anything here. He does, however, put on his best hard-man expression. You know the sort of thing: friendly tone, smiling mouth, threatening eyes. Never fails to give me a chill.

'I've tried to be nice and reasonable, my friend. If I see you again, I won't be so nice. You dump this right now. Right fucking now. My advice to you is fuck off and hide yourself somewhere. Now. This morning. You really don't want to get involved. You really don't.'

'Don't tell me – I don't know what I'm up against.'

A slight frown passes across his face when I say that. He gets up, gives me the mother of all hard looks and walks away in the direction of New Oxford Street.

I order a coffee and a croissant and sit and watch the world go by while I'm waiting. It's interesting that he didn't mention Footballer Dad. I'm assuming that he works for Scary Boss, so that was a little surprising. It could be that he's unaware of the activities of his colleagues. I think if he'd known about Footballer Dad's disappearance, he might have said something, maybe even questioned me about it, but it didn't come up at all.

But that's not necessarily unusual. If I was organising something like this, I'd run it all on a need-to-know basis, just in case one of my little helpers got caught. I doubt whether Footballer Dad could have told me anything about Blond Hair. He may not even have known of his existence.

Was it Blond Hair who broke into Sara's flat? Unlikely. He's almost three stone heavier than me and that extra weight would have brought down those cable coverings and believe me, it was a close thing when I was doing it.

'Sorry, sir. We haven't got any croissants left. Would you like anything else? We have carrot cake and lavender and coconut cake. Oh, and salted caramel and chocolate cookies.'

'It's OK. I'll just have the coffee.'

He places the coffee in front of me. I take a sip. It's almost cold and tastes of burnt milk. I leave the rest and decide to get a cab to Hinde Street.

It's just as I'm walking in the direction of Tottenham Court Road tube station, looking over my shoulder for a car, that I feel I'm being observed yet again. Well that's it. It can't be Blond Hair unless he's totally crazy. Would he have an assistant? Unlikely. I'm annoyed now; I haven't even started work and I'm working already. This time I'm going to catch this fucker, whoever it is.

16

RED HAIR

I walk down New Oxford Street using every reflective surface that I can, looking for suspicious activity to my rear. I use telephone kiosks, billboards on bus stops and shop windows. I try as hard as I can not to look too self-consciously switched on. I stop, bend down, and tie an imaginary shoelace while quickly looking behind me. Whoever it is that's tailing me is doing it, I suspect, from quite a distance.

This is a wide, three-lane road, with a lot of traffic, particularly buses, and a lot of pedestrian activity, not to mention the comings and goings from all the snack bars and cafés. It's also long and straight. If it was me doing this, I'd feel fairly confident that I could stay about two hundred yards behind my mark. I'd probably tail them from the opposite side of the road and keep one hundred per cent focus on them, so even if I lost visibility for a few seconds, I'd still know where they were from their probable trajectory and walking speed.

The advantage of tailing on the opposite side of the road is that it makes it more difficult for the person being followed to use reflective surfaces. I can see directly behind me and I can see directly across the road, but wider angles are virtually impossible, especially when the other person might be a few hundred yards to your rear.

Luckily, I'm getting help from the newer double decker buses. Every time they pull out, stop, start or change lanes, they're giving me a comprehensive view of the road behind me, the big curved glass on the front and back acting as constantly changing reflective surfaces. They're little distorted, shaky, unreliable and confusing from time to time, but they're all I've got at the moment.

Just as the wide windscreen of a Number 38 gives me a clear view of the other side of the road, I spot two contenders walking about a hundred and fifty yards back. Just a brief glimpse, but neither of them looks right.

One of them is a woman in her fifties in a red knee-length coat pushing a shopping trolley. She keeps stopping and looking in windows, but the windows she's looking in are those of sandwich shops and snack bars. She could be genuine, but I have to be suspicious. Maybe she's just hungry and fussy. New Oxford Street has a lot of stuff in it, but it's not the sort of place you'd go for your daily or weekly shop, so it's the shopping trolley that arouses my suspicion.

The other contender is a guy in his mid-thirties. Stocky, shortish red hair, over six foot and with a measured, ambling walk. He's wearing a grey waterproof more suited to a walk in the Peak District and a pair of pale khaki cargo pants. He, too, has an interest in the snack bars, but that casual, nothing-special-to-do walk is out of place here.

The shopping trolley woman looks at her watch and turns back the way she came. Red Hair loses interest in his snack bar window and keeps on ambling.

It's him. I just know it.

In thirty seconds I've got Centrepoint looming up on my left and Bainbridge Street on my right. I'm not familiar with Bainbridge Street; it looks like one of those nowhere roads, rather like Exeter Street, that is home to the back entrances of buildings on adjacent thoroughfares.

I take my wallet out, open it up like it's a book, look up at the street sign and turn into Nowhere Road, London WC1, hoping that Red Hair will follow.

After fifteen feet, there's a sharp right turn. This is a narrow road with double yellow lines on both sides and a lot of stuff going on. Two sets of minor road works and a couple of guys noisily removing a black metal bollard from the pavement.

I can see about two hundred yards ahead of me and there are roughly a dozen vans or cars parked all the way along. No shops, no big entrances, nowhere to hide. I walk along and don't look behind me. I don't know what I'm looking for, but I'll know it when I see it.

There is a fair amount of people about. This makes it a little difficult to sense Red Hair's presence, but not impossible. I cross over to the right-hand side of the road to get a better view of a doorway I spotted on the other side. It's actually two doorways.

One goes straight into the ground floor, but the other goes down into what I assume to be the basement. I can't tell what sort of building this is, but I can smell cooking, so it may be the back entrance to a restaurant or snack bar.

I walk for another few yards then cross the road again. I surreptitiously look over my shoulder, as if I don't want to be observed entering this building, but don't make any visual contact with Red Hair, who I can see down the far end of the road, sticking close to the buildings on the opposite side to me. If I was him, I'd dye my hair a different colour or wear a hat.

I quickly descend eleven steep steps. My guess was right; the food smell is stronger here and I can hear people shouting at each other in Austrian accents. This corridor is long. There are toilets to my left and a large kitchen to my right.

I walk into the kitchen, ready with my excuses, but there's nobody in here. I can't work out where the voices are coming from, but that hardly matters now.

I hear someone else coming down the steps. Almost certainly Red Hair. I count the steps off. Whoever it is stops when they get to the bottom. Like me, they're having a look around and listening. If I was Red Hair, my next move would be to check in this kitchen. It's unlikely that he's going to take a look at the toilets, but you never know.

I take a quick look around for weapons. I don't know what sort of person I'm dealing with here, but they're going to have to be on the receiving end of a bit of Shock and Awe, so I can get them out of here as fast as possible and find somewhere for the two of us to have an intimate tête-à-tête.

Hanging on the wall just behind me is a heavy-looking, thick-based copper frying pan with a twelve-inch diameter. That will have to do. I take it down and grip the silver handle in my right hand. There's a paper towel dispenser on a shelf near my shoulder. I pull out a handful and stuff them in my back pocket.

He's very quiet and is walking on soft-soled shoes. He's about four or five feet away from the kitchen door. As he gets closer, I can hear that he's a tiny bit out of breath and I assume he ran down the street to catch up when he saw me disappear into this place.

I stand on the right side of the door with my back pressed against the wall. This has to be done before he walks in and gets a visual on me, so I close my eyes and focus on the very slight sounds he's making; his breathing, the rustle of his clothing, his almost soundless footsteps.

The moment I sense he's about to turn and enter the kitchen, I swing the frying pan back and with a whiplash action of my wrist, slam it into his face as hard as I can.

He starts to cry out, but I clamp my hand across his mouth. His eyes bulge with surprise and fear. Using the hand that's still on his mouth, I quickly push him out of the kitchen and across the corridor until he makes contact with the wall on the other side with a dull thud.

From a distance of about a foot, I punch him, just the once, in the solar plexus. I take my hand off his mouth and place a finger to my lips. He gets the message.

I grab the four fingers of his left hand as tightly as I can, twist up the pain dial to ten and march him down the corridor and up the stairs to the street.

'Be discreet, please. We're going to have a quick chat.'

He nods his head. The expression on his face tells me he's wondering what the hell just happened and what the hell's going to happen next.

I hand him the paper tissues so he can mop the blood off his bleeding nose. We walk to the junction with Streatham Street. I'm sure it must look like we're holding hands, but there's nothing between us, honest.

There's a small café on the corner with a couple of rickety metal tables outside. I point to one of them. He sits down. I release his hand. He looks pained and massages each of his fingers in turn, his eyes darting from left to right, like he's looking for someone to come and rescue him. He's a big guy, but he looks so anguished and crestfallen that I almost feel sorry for him. Almost.

A smartly dressed waitress appears, hovering while she waits for our order. I ask for two black coffees. She smiles and disappears. I don't say anything while we wait for our coffees to arrive; I just look at him. He can't meet my gaze.

My hunch was right about him not being connected to Blond Hair. He just doesn't have the demeanour or bad vibes, for one thing, and he hasn't got any cocky talk, considering his circumstances. Also, he buckled too easily and doesn't look like he'll be attempting a getaway.

The coffees are placed in front of us. I don't touch mine. This guy still doesn't know where to look. I haven't got the time to waste with him, so I'm going to be direct and mildly sinister. I make him look me straight in the eye. There's something about his demeanour that reminds me of a scolded Cocker Spaniel.

'These are the rules. You're in deep trouble. Bullshit me and you'll regret it for the rest of your life. Got it?'

He nods and mops at his nose, which is still bleeding.

'Now. Who are you?'

'My name's Peter Dixon. I'm a private detective.'

Well, that's all I need.

'Show me your SIA licence.'

A Security Industry Authority licence is a recent thing, thought up by the government to regulate private investigators and others in the security business. Most straight-down-the-line investigators now have them. Some don't. I fall into the latter category.

Peter Dixon takes his wallet out of his jacket and hands me the licence. As he pulls it out, a key ring falls to the floor. The chain is attached to a real wine cork. Good idea. I notice it has four keys and a couple of slim burglar's tools on it. I take a look at the licence. It looks genuine. I hand it back.

'Business card.'

He hands me a light blue card. It reads 'London Surveillance Associates. Peter Dixon. Matrimonial Cases. Corporate Fraud. Technical Counter Measures'. There's a mobile number, a landline, two email addresses and an actual address in Chancery Lane. I put it in my wallet.

'I'm keeping this in case I have to find you. Who are the associates, or is that just drivel?'

'It's just drivel. There's only me.'

'Manchester Square, St Martin's Lane and Wimpole Street. That was you?'

He purses his lips and reluctantly confesses. 'Yeah.'

'I didn't see you.'

'You knew I was there, though. I could tell. Most people aren't that switched on.'

'Yeah, yeah. Who are you working for?'

'I don't know.'

'Remember what I said. Bullshit me and…'

'Really,' he says quickly. 'I really don't know who I'm working for. You've got to believe me.'

I believe him, but I'm not going to let him know that. I want him to be in a state of stress.

'Explain.'

He lifts his coffee cup up and takes a sip. He takes a deep breath and for the first time looks me straight in the eye. He has a slight Edinburgh accent, which I only notice after he's been speaking for a while.

'I do marital stuff. Divorce cases, infidelities, cheating, workplace affairs; you know the score. Sometimes I do child custody cases but not that often. It's all straightforward stuff, vehicle tracking, electronic eavesdropping, email tracing, Internet activity, asset searches; whatever it takes to do the job.'

'Go on.'

'This guy rang me up about a week ago. Said his name was Leo Hudson. Very well spoken, though it was hard to tell where he was from. I think he'd had elocution lessons. I've heard that type of voice before, y'know?

'He said he wanted a five-day surveillance on an individual calling himself Daniel Beckett. He wanted to know where Beckett lived, what he did, what places he went to, the whole lot. I have a PO box. He said he'd send me a stick with a photograph and some details. He also had a PO box number and that would be on the memory stick with the other stuff.'

'And when you'd finished your five days, you'd write your report, put it on the same memory stick and send it to his PO box. How was he paying you and how much?'

'Six thousand pounds. He asked for my bank account details. The whole job was for six thousand. Half the money was in my account an hour after the phone call. He said the other half would be put in after he'd received my report.'

'What was on the stick?'

'A photograph of you. It wasn't very good. It was a bit blurry, but good enough to ID you if I saw you. I would have said it was taken from some distance away, probably with a telephoto lens.

'It gave your name, eye colour, hair colour, height, build, age range thirty to thirty-five; all the relevant stuff. They suspected that you lived in WC2; Covent Garden or Leicester Square or thereabouts, but they didn't have a precise address.

'There was a warning about you. It said I was to be very careful as you were a dangerous individual. It said that you might be trained in counter-surveillance techniques, so I was to be extra cautious and give you a wide berth. Not to get caught. Words to that effect, anyway. I've been at this game for quite a few years now. I was pretty confident you wouldn't spot me.'

So far, so bad.

'You said you were asked to do five days. What day is this?'

'This is the fourth day.'

I'm trying to think whether this could be connected to the Sara Holt case. It doesn't seem like it is. It would be less of a headache if it was. The first time I noticed him was when Sara and I were heading towards the Wallace Collection for our initial meeting.

I felt I was being watched as we turned into Manchester Square. But I hadn't even taken the case at that point. And if today is Day Four, then he must have been on my tail the day before I met Sara and I somehow didn't notice him.

For him to have picked me up on my way to Sara's, I must assume that he had followed me from Exeter Street, which is moderately worrying.

'How did you track me to Manchester Square?'

'I followed you from Exeter Street.'

'How did you find that address?'

He shrugs his shoulders and sighs. 'I'd like to say it was a combination of my innate craftiness, skill and professionalism, but to be absolutely honest with you, it was dumb luck.' He sniffs and dabs at his nose, which has started to bleed again.

'Like I said, all they had as an area for you was WC2,

possibly Covent Garden and the surround. Maybe Leicester Square. Big area to cover. I had an image of you in my head based on your photograph and description. I spent five days wandering around Covent Garden. I went into shops, pubs, restaurants and bars. I was getting ready to report back and say I couldn't find you.'

'So how did you get lucky?'

'It was four days ago. I was feeling pretty low and exhausted, to be honest. I'd been doing a lot of walking around. I went in a bar for a drink. Place called Big Shots down by The Strand.'

I know what's coming. How could I be so stupid?

'There was a woman in there that everyone was looking at. Hard to tell her age. Mature, I would say, but with an amazing body. Long, blonde hair, but you could see the dark roots, but it looked good, you know? It was intentional. Expensively done, I would have said. Bright red lipstick. She was wearing this short sleeveless red dress that showed all the curves. She had a long rope of white pearls around her neck. A very big woman. Big in all the right places, I mean. Tiny waist.'

'OK. I get the idea.'

He's talking about Thea. I picked her up on the Jubilee Line during the rush hour about a month ago. She's forty-nine, divorced, demanding, a Virgo and she manages an upmarket shoe shop in Knightsbridge.

'Yeah. Well, anyway, you automatically looked to see who the lucky guy was. And it was you. I couldn't believe it. I couldn't believe my luck. As soon as I clocked you, I moved to the other end of the bar. Found a table. Started talking to some people. I didn't want you to see me. I remembered what they'd said about you.

'So I reckoned the best thing to do was to stay for as

long as possible. You didn't seem to be going anywhere and the both of you were knocking the booze back. I thought that if you'd been drinking, I might have a better chance of following you without you noticing me. That and the fact that the woman had been drinking, too. All your attention was on her.'

'So you followed us back to Exeter Street.'

'I couldn't see where it was you were going. Which building, I mean. I had to keep well back, but as soon as I could, I did a walk-through and worked out where you must have gone.

'I was pretty pleased with myself for that. I went home and got a couple of hours' shuteye, then drove up at five-thirty the next morning to make sure I caught you coming out.

'I parked about twenty yards away and kept an eye on your bit of the road through the rear view mirror. You came out with the woman at exactly eight-fifteen. I guess she had to go to work. After that it was relatively easy. You weren't expecting to be tailed; you were hung over and probably didn't get much sleep.

'Obviously I've lost you a few times, but managed to catch you enough for a decent report, but I couldn't work you out at all. I couldn't see any logic in your day. Sometimes you seemed to be taking evasive action just for the hell of it. How do you do it?'

'How do I do what?'

'All the women. The blonde one, the pretty Manchester Square one, and particularly that one with the long black hair all down her back. Jesus Christ. Are you sick?'

'What?'

'Well, I know you visited a psychiatrist yesterday.'

I almost have to laugh.

'Have you reported on me yet to whoever it is that hired you?'

'Of course not. I've got tomorrow to go before I do that. Day Five.'

'You do understand that you can't make that report.'

'I'm beginning to get the idea.'

'Is all of this anything to do with Sara Holt?'

'Who?'

'Sara Holt. The fashion designer.'

'I don't know what you're talking about.'

And I believe him. This is something else, but I don't know what. There's a link to his employer, whoever that may be, and it's through his report. There are a number of ways that report could be fixed so I can find out who's behind this and somehow apprehend them.

I could, if I had the time, even dust the memory stick with a few crushed crystals of strychnine, so whoever the recipient was would get a fatal dose as soon as they took it out of the Jiffy Bag or whatever.

It's a bit of a wake-up call for me. I've been careless, and I've ended up with this idiot on my back. Whoever is interested in me for whatever reason has narrowed the field down to a small area of London where I might be found. Not good; not good at all. I'll seriously have to look into this, but I can't do it now.

'What about my money?' he says, like I've just taken his favourite toy away.

'That's your problem. You shouldn't take cases like this. They're always bad news. If you can't meet someone face to face, forget it.'

'But...'

'I don't want to see you again. If I even *feel* you

hanging around, I'll be coming for you. This investigation of yours stops right now. Forget this contact with me ever happened. Tell your employers you couldn't find me. Return the money if you have to. Just put this down to experience.'

He nods his head and looks sheepish. He doesn't know what to do next. Maybe he expects me to buy him an almond croissant.

'What are you waiting for? Fuck off.'

He takes a final sip of his coffee, gets up and walks away. I take a deep breath, stretch and consider where the best place to get a cab to Hinde Street would be.

17

BAKER STREET EMBRACE

I pass Isolda as I'm on my way into Sara's office. She's wearing a maroon wrap-around cardigan and a black/grey below-the-knee skirt. Smart, professional and conservative, but it can't hope to conceal the curves and I can feel my insides turning to water and a contrasting dryness in my mouth.

'Good morning, Mr Beckett. How are you today?' she says, giving me an arch smile as we both pretend that we're not sleeping together.

'I'm fine, thanks. I'm sorry; I've forgotten your name.'

'Isolda.'

'Of course. Nice to see you again, Isolda.'

She passes by me, and I can hear the swish of her stockings as she walks down the corridor. She's wearing a different perfume today. Much darker than yesterday. Musk and patchouli, I think.

I pop my head around Sara's door. 'Can we go outside to a café or something?'

'Sounds very mysterious. Of course. If you want.'

We find a place on the corner of Thayer Street and Wigmore Street. A waitress takes our order and we sit outside. The traffic is busy here and it's a little too noisy, but that's OK.

Sara's looking a little bit pale. I can tell she has mixed feelings about what happened last night and is still a little shaken. She's probably also wondering what sort of person I am. She looks very lovely, though, and is wearing a pale brown short skirt and a matching blouse. She doesn't need makeup, but there's a dusting of cobalt blue eye shadow, which somehow highlights the unusual colour of her eyes.

'So what happened with him? Who was he? Did he tell you anything?'

I'd already rehearsed my story on the way here in the cab. 'It was the same guy who called you a bitch in Heddon Street that time. Your description of him enabled me to spot him straight away.

'He's a medium range crook. Retired now. Used to rob building societies and all the rest. Said that someone from the old days rang him up and asked him if he'd like to make a bit of easy money. He said yes.

'They sent him the cash, your photograph, where you could probably be found and at what time. Just told him to be aggressive and threatening towards you. It didn't matter how. He could improvise. He only did it on the two occasions we know about. There was another one that he was going to do, but you didn't appear so he abandoned it.'

So far, so good; I almost believe it myself.

'How much did they pay him?'

'Three hundred for each time.' I don't know where that figure came from. It just sounds good.

'Wow. I almost feel flattered.'

The waitress places our coffees on the wobbly table. I can tell by just looking at mine that it's going to taste awful. Contempt for the punter – found in coffee bars the world over.

'It couldn't have been him that broke into your flat, by the way. He was too old, too heavy and didn't strike me as agile enough. That would have been someone else. Presumably they were on a higher rate.'

'And he had no idea who it was that ordered this?'

'None at all, and I believed him.'

'Do you think he'll do it again?'

'Unlikely.'

'So what happens now?'

'I'd just like to ask you a couple more questions. I know we went over this before, but I keep wondering about the motivation for all of this. What would happen if these incidents caused you to completely screw up these two shows?'

She's sitting opposite me. I have to force myself not to look at her legs, but she suddenly crosses them and they demand my attention. She notices, smiles and flicks her hair back.

She's concentrating; thinking about what I've just asked. I don't imagine she considers screwing things up as an option and maybe has no way of articulating the concept.

'I'd be very disappointed.'

She plays with her hair for a few moments, trying to find the right words.

'I've always tried to improve on what I've done before. Once I've achieved one aim, the next one has to be an even greater challenge or you're just standing still. Doing just one show would seem an anti-climax once you've thought of doing two and I sort of get off on the challenge and the work that would be involved.'

'But what about your reputation as a designer? Would

that be damaged? Could you lose your position at Maccanti? Would you have trouble getting another job?'

'The next stage for me is to start my own label. I'm going to need suits for that.'

'Suits?'

'The money people. Investors. Backers. If I did these two shows at the same time and they were a success, it would be like – BANG! – it would make the suits sit up and take notice. I mean *really* take notice. It would be news. It would be news outside the fashion industry. It would mean a smooth transition to starting my own label. Now that's not to say that the suits aren't aware of me as a force right now, but what I'm hoping to do would certainly speed things up and get me better deals. Sometimes you have to whack the industry on the back of the head with a cricket bat.'

I clasp my fingers together behind my neck and stretch backwards in my chair, staring at the clouds. So this is not career damage, particularly. This is something that would inflict tremendous personal hurt on Sara. It would frustrate her. It would set her back a year or so. I remember what Footballer Dad said:

She's just a fucking slut who needed to be brought down a peg or two.

'I asked you before if you had any enemies. There's nothing at all that you can think of, no matter how trivial, that might have triggered something like this? Someone you criticised in a magazine or on a website. Someone you promised something to and didn't deliver on. An interview or an appointment you didn't turn up for.'

'I'm not like that. If there was someone I hurt, I'd have remembered and I'd remember because it would be so unusual for me to have done something like that.'

'Can I see your mobile?'

She looked baffled for a moment, but rummages in her bag and hands me a very smart Vertu Constellation in orange calf leather. I take it apart and check it for tampering. There's nothing in it that I can see, so I put it back together again and hand it back to her. I should really do the same with the phones belonging to both MTAs, but that can wait for the moment. If Sara's hasn't been physically bugged, it's unlikely theirs would have been, either. But you never know.

'Why did you do that?'

I may as well be honest with her on this. Keeping her in the dark about everything requires too much memory.

'I was approached by a guy this morning who offered me five thousand pounds to drop this case.'

Her eyes widen. 'What?'

'I said no. But whoever this guy was and whoever he worked for, he seemed to be a few steps ahead of me.'

'But how can that be possible?'

'I think that someone has access to the calls made on your mobile and I suspect the same may be true of Isolda and Melody. Maybe Gaige, too. I don't know who else because I don't know all of your staff. I'm also considering the fact that your flat and your office may be bugged. That's why we're out here and not inside.'

Her hand goes up to her mouth. 'I can't believe this is happening.'

'That makes two of us. Don't panic. I may be wrong about the bugging, but I want someone to check your offices and your flat, just to be on the safe side.

'There's a company called Marton Confidential, which is actually just one guy. He does a bug sweeping service. I'm going to give him a call and get him to check out your flat and your offices immediately.

'It won't take long and you don't have to explain to your staff what's going on. He's very discreet and will make it look like he's doing something else. You can tell Isolda: just let her know that he's coming when you get back to the office.

'Also, I'd like you to courier your two spare keys over to John Kimmons right now and ask if he can let a guy called Doug Teng into your flat. He can supervise him if he wishes. Doug is Chinese. He will have ID.'

I give Doug a call while Sara orders a motorcycle courier and rings Kimmons. Doug is working his bollocks off as per usual, so I have to sling him an extra five hundred to get him to do this ASAP. By the end of the conversation he's hailing a cab to get up to St John's Wood. He'll probably get there before the keys arrive. There are so many angles I have to check with Sara that they're beginning to drift out of my mind. Oh yes.

'Isolda mentioned that you had a previous MTA2 you had to let go. Thai something?'

'Thai Hunter. That's right. There was no bad feeling and she's doing well at Jigsaw now. It was just the stress of the work she couldn't cope with. You have to keep a lot of things in your head. Some people, like Isolda and Melody, have a talent for it, a knack for it, and some do not. I think she was relieved when it finally happened.'

'OK. This lunch you've got today…'

'I'm not cancelling.'

'But…'

'Listen. I feel much safer with you around, particularly after last night. But I'm not going to go and hide in my shell until all this shit is sorted out. What can happen? Rachelle is lovely and she's important to the shows I'll be doing. I really need to see her. Besides, the restaurant is only around the corner and it's the middle of the day. What could possibly happen?'

I press my fingers into my eyes and hope that my brain will suddenly allow all of this to fall into place. It doesn't.

'OK. Let's go back to your office and have a word with your MTAs, then I'll allow you to go to lunch.'

'You're so kind.'

'I'm famous for it.'

As soon as we get back, Sara removes her keys from the back of *The Makioka Sisters* book, pops them in an envelope with Kimmons' name on the front and hands them to the courier, who arrives three minutes later.

We get Isolda and Melody into Sara's office and I explain to them about Doug and what he'll be doing here when he arrives. I tell them that he'll probably come up with some cover story about who he is and what he's doing and they must stick to it. This ruse isn't totally necessary, but I don't want to create anxiety among the staff unnecessarily, and the fewer people who know what's going on, the better.

I take a look at Isolda's and Melody's mobiles, but once again, there's nothing physical inside either of them.

'I can't see how anyone could have put something in my mobile without me noticing,' says Melody. Melody Ribeiro is a devastatingly gorgeous black woman with a magenta streak through her hair; fantastic legs, an accent I can't place and a knowing look in her eyes, which I find faintly unsettling.

She's younger than Isolda, maybe twenty-two, and does a quick double take when she notices Isolda slowly lick her lips at me. She smirks to herself for the rest of the meeting.

'It's just something I wanted to rule out,' I say to Melody. 'There's a possibility that someone is listening in on telephone calls of people close to Sara. If *I* was doing this, her MTAs would be the people I'd be doing it to.'

'I think we should both get a pay rise, Sara,' says Melody, grinning. She looks directly at me and allows her eyes to slowly and slyly slide in Isolda's direction. She's enjoying this.

Isolda and Melody leave the office. Melody purses her lips and winks at me on her way out. She has a great mouth. I consider calling her when all of this is over.

Sara slumps back in her seat and sighs.

'Is it still only the morning?'

'What time is your lunch date, Sara?'

'I was going to walk over there now.'

'I'll come with you.'

'There's no need. Really.'

'I'm not going to come in the restaurant with you.'

'You'll want to if you catch sight of Rachelle.'

'Oh really? Tell me more.'

She laughs, grabs her jacket and bag and we head down the stairs and out to the street.

*

As we walk through Manchester Square towards Fitzhardinge Street I have both hands in my pockets and Sara snakes her arm through mine. We stroll along in the midday sunshine as if we're an item and it's not an unpleasant feeling.

I don't know whether she's doing this because she's friendly or whether it's because she feels safer. Whatever it is, the effect is the same for me; I feel rather light-headed as I always do when I have attractive females in close proximity.

She wears the same sweet, flowery perfume that she did when we first met and I slowly inhale it to add to the light intoxication that I'm feeling.

'What did you think of Melody?'

'Very, very attractive. Beautiful, stunning features, great mouth, fantastic legs. Liked the hair, too. Very sexy walk. Sensual, aggressive and passionate nature and very likely sexually dominant.'

She looks up at me and smiles. 'That's pretty detailed for such a short encounter. Is that a detective thing or is it just you?'

'I think it might be just me.'

'How would you describe me in those sorts of terms?'

'I wouldn't. You're one of my clients. It would be inappropriate and unprofessional.'

'But say I wasn't one of your clients.'

'But you are.'

'But say I wasn't. Come on, Daniel. I'm paying you. I insist.'

'Are you sure?'

'Yes.'

'And you won't be offended?'

'No.'

Oh well. Here goes.

'Strikingly beautiful, amazing eyes, sexy mouth, dazzling smile. A lissom, athletic, tantalising and sensual figure. A provocative and seductive walk. Passionate but more submissive than dominant.'

She looks up at me, her eyes widening. 'Wow. No one's ever sweet-talked me like that before.'

This makes me laugh. 'I'm a silver-tongued devil.'

We walk along in silence for a while, then turn into Baker Street.

'Is my walk really provocative and seductive?' she says, looking straight ahead.

'Yes. I noticed it straight away. I'm not saying it's an intentional thing on your part. It's just the way it is. Don't get big-headed.'

'Hm. And can you explain passionate but more submissive than dominant, sir?'

She said 'sir'. She's ribbing me.

'Just intuition on my part. I can pick things like that up off people. It's nothing personal. Just a comment. Just conjecture. An impression. Don't expect a collaring just yet.'

She tosses her head back and laughs. 'You're so funny. I like you.'

'Don't get too fond of me, baby. I'm a dangerous guy to be around.'

'I bet you say that to all the broads.'

'Only the ones with tantalising and sensual figures.'

We walk along Baker Street for a few hundred yards, heading north, until we're almost at Dorset Street.

'We have to cross over here,' she says. 'The restaurant's on the other side.'

Baker Street is one-way with three lanes of fast traffic aimed at unwary pedestrians who don't want to wait for any of the lights to change. We manage to dash across with only a couple of near misses to our credit.

When we reach the other side, I put a hand around her waist to help her up onto the pavement, but end up pulling her towards me. She places a hand on my shoulder. We have a brief moment of eye contact, then we're kissing, her mouth hard on mine, her body pressed tightly against me.

She places her arms around my neck and I hold her waist firmly, keeping her in place. I hear her bag drop to the floor. She pulls away, looks at me briefly and we start again with even more ferocity. I know this is unprofessional of me, but that's part of what's making it exciting.

She pulls away again, panting. She runs a hand through her hair. I grab her wrist, bending it to the right, and then hold the side of her neck, keeping her away from me, controlling her, as her open mouth greedily attempts to reach mine once more. I let the tension escalate for five excruciating seconds then release her, her kisses now urgent and impassioned.

She stops and looks downwards.

'I'm sorry,' she gasps. 'I shouldn't have done that. I've just – it's just all of this has – I don't know. I wanted you to stop me but I knew you wouldn't. Does that make sense?'

She puts her arms around me once more and holds on tightly. I stroke her hair. Her lipstick is a mess. It's busy here. Passers-by smile and stare. I'm aware of the traffic noise once more.

'It's OK,' I say. 'Don't worry about it.' She looks up at me and I run the back of my hand down her cheek. 'You're going to have to sort your makeup out before you meet your friend. It looks like you've been snogging.'

She picks her bag up, fishes out a small silver compact mirror and reapplies her lipstick. I hold the mirror up for her so she can brush her hair. About a hundred and fifty yards away I can see a tall blonde woman in a bright red coat who's ostentatiously waving at us. This must be Rachelle. I point her out to Sara who waves back.

'Go on. Have a nice lunch. I'll be in touch later today.'

She takes a few quick steps towards me and kisses me on the cheek, turning away quickly and making her way up the road, exaggerating her provocative and seductive walk for my benefit. She looks over her shoulder at me and sticks her tongue out.

I watch her wiggle up the road for about five seconds, then head down towards Wigmore Street. It's a little early, but I'll probably just pop in the Wagamama for a bite to eat. I'll have to have a think about what to do next, then I've got Mrs Doroteia Vasconselos at around three in Fortnum's.

It's terrible, but I've actually forgotten what she looks like, even though it was only about fifteen hours ago that we met. She had a lot of eye makeup on and a yummy mouth, but I can't quite bring her features into focus. I'm sure I'll recognise her when the time comes, though; at least I hope I do.

My mobile goes off. It's Doug Teng.

'Mr Beckett?'

'So what did you find?'

'Oh yeah. Very amusing. I've only just got inside. Any special instructions?'

'No, but make sure you check every room. When you get to Maccanti, ask for Isolda Jennison.'

'Okeydoke.'

'It's possible this woman is having her telephone calls listened to: possibly her colleagues as well. I couldn't find any physical evidence of this, but I need to rule out conventional bugging for my own peace of mind.'

'I'll do a scan for frequency interceptors at both sites.'

'OK. Good idea.'

'Speak later.'

I'm just clicking my mobile off and staring at a couple of girls on the other side of the road when I hear a screeching of tyres and a multiple car horn cacophony that makes me turn around to see where the accident is.

But it isn't an accident. A large, black SUV has pulled off the road and has mounted the pavement a couple of hundred yards away. Other cars are objecting and tooting their horns at this piece of insane driving. The doors open and two men in suits get out.

Even from this distance, I recognise one of them.

It's Blond Hair.

18

A DANGEROUS DRIVER

I start running, swerving past the shoppers, workers and tourists and trying to keep the SUV in my line of vision. Sara and Rachelle are six feet away from the two men and don't yet realise what's happening. I could shout, but I know they wouldn't hear.

They don't waste any time. Blond Hair strides over to Sara and punches her just once, in the face. She drops instantly and he and his colleague drag her towards the vehicle, open one of the back doors and chuck her inside like she's a sack of potatoes.

Rachelle starts screaming at them and Blond Hair's friend grabs her hair and smashes her head against a shop window. Luckily the glass doesn't break, but it looks like she's out for the count.

I'm about fifty yards away now and I can feel the strain of sprinting in my legs and lungs. It's a matter of seconds before I get to those bastards, but I can see both men have got in the vehicle and are now driving away. They're heading in my direction and are accelerating hard in first or second gear.

Where the assault happened, people are confused and shouting. They gawp but don't do anything, apart from an old woman who bends down to look at Rachelle.

I could do something insanely brave like jump onto the bonnet and hang on to the windscreen wipers, but I know that'll be a waste of time. There isn't much you can do with a vehicle this big and I'd be useless to Sara if I was wrapped under its wheels or unconscious or dead.

As it shoots past and changes lanes, Blond Hair gives me a quick, indifferent smirk, then gets back to the serious business of driving like a maniac.

There's a lot of traffic about, and the SUV is having to constantly change lanes and overtake to make progress. This is not a good road for quick escapes. It cuts up two taxis, almost hits an elderly pedestrian and causes a red BMW to brake hard, receiving a long horn blast from the driver.

It drifts into the bus lane then screeches out again. They're in a hurry to get away. I have no idea what they're doing or where they're going, but if I was them I'd want to get there before Sara regains consciousness.

Thanks to the vehicle's size and aggressive driving tactics, cars and cabs are quickly getting out of the way, allowing them to make good progress. I can hear the low-gear roar of the engine and the constant blasting of their horn. I have to act fast. I need a car. I need a fast car.

I look to my left and do a rapid scan of the traffic. Three black cabs, a bus, a Ford Ka, a four-ton flatback lorry, a VW Scirocco, a Mini and a Volvo S60. No good. Then I see a jet blue Audi R8 Coupé. That's it. Female driver and it's slowing down at a zebra crossing to let a bunch of tourists across.

I run as fast as I can to the crossing and knock on the window, fishing a business card out of my pocket. My card doesn't have anything on it apart from my name and mobile number, but it's made from a thin, silvery metal with miniature micro-grills on the top and bottom and looks pretty damn cool, classy, sassy and impressive. At least I hope it does.

The power window comes down. She's forty, blonde, red-framed glasses, grey business suit, dishy. The first thing I do is hand her my card so she doesn't think I'm robbing her or trying to clean her windscreen.

'Hi. This is going to sound insane. I'm a private investigator. My name's Daniel Beckett. My client is Sara Holt the fashion designer. She's just been assaulted and kidnapped. They've got a three-minute start in a fast, black SUV, which is heading south at some speed. Could you please give me a lift?'

She frowns and for a second I think she's going to drive off. She looks at my card and looks at me. Someone honks their horn at her. Vital seconds are ticking away.

'Sara Holt who designs for Maccanti?'

'Yes.'

'Get in.'

Well, *that* was easier than I thought it would be. I run around the car and get in the passenger side. The car smells of leather and perfume. Before I can get my seatbelt on, she puts her foot down and the acceleration is so great that it pins me back in the black leather bucket seat.

She's a good driver, maybe even a crazy one. We make sixty as we bomb down Baker Street and I'm amazed she doesn't hit anything.

She overtakes three cars on the inside using the bus lane and gets a chorus of complaining horns.

She cuts up an enormous coach and almost hits the back of a silver Mercedes, braking suddenly for a cyclist and rocking me forward in my seat.

My mouth is dry. She shakes my hand while steering with one finger on the steering wheel.

'I'm Eve Cook. Pleased to meet you, Mr Beckett. Which one is it we're following?'

For a second I can't see the SUV and my heart sinks as I think we've already lost them. Then it reappears, having been momentarily hidden in front of a huge lorry. I point straight ahead so there's no doubt.

'There. That one. The black one.'

Another snarl from the engine and we're about thirty feet behind the SUV. Under other circumstances, I'd make sure he didn't know I was tailing him, but this is different and unavoidable. I can tell he's spotted us as soon as he skips a red light and makes an illegal left turn into Wigmore Street. He wouldn't bother with the risk if he thought he was clear. I feel my stomach lurch as Ms Cook swerves around a purple Mini so we can keep the SUV in sight. She turns to me and smiles sweetly.

'Shall I go through the red light, too?'

'If you wouldn't mind.'

'No problem.'

She overtakes a slow-moving Bentley in the inside lane and I hear the tyres scream as she makes a wide illegal left into Wigmore. Two cars coming the other way blast their horns at her, people shout and point, and I hear the unmistakable sound of one vehicle rear-ending another. Oh well; just minor collateral damage.

Blond Hair is already about two hundred yards ahead, but there're no vehicles between him and us. Ms Cook puts her foot down again and we're soon catching up. Despite wearing a seatbelt, I find I have a white-knuckle grip on a black leather handle that's attached to the inside of the door.

He sails straight through another red light at the Wimpole Street crossroads and we follow, my driver narrowly avoiding being hit by a car transporter that hisses and rocks scarily on its suspension after a skilful emergency stop. People are looking at us now and this is getting too conspicuous. I suddenly feel nauseous.

I'm trying to work out where Blond Hair can be going. We can't keep on trailing him closely if he continues to drive this recklessly and his driving brings a new meaning to the word reckless. Eventually we're going to be in an accident and I can't inflict that on this car or its driver. Being ex-police and almost certainly Met, I have to assume he knows London like the back of his hand, so that'll make everything doubly problematic.

'So what is Sara doing next season, do you know?' says Eve Cook, noisily changing down from third into second for improved control. 'I've heard whispers.'

I lick my lips so I can speak, while being rocked from side to side. 'Well, she's working on some Basquiat-inspired designs at the moment. Very colourful. Could you watch that…'

She narrowly misses hitting another cyclist.

'Oh, marvellous. Have you seen the film about him? I've got one of her silk camisoles from last season.'

I can hear a police siren behind us. Probably nothing – we've only been at this for about thirty seconds. We continue along Wigmore Street at high speed, the engine screaming. Shocked pedestrians leap back onto the safety of the pavement.

The SUV takes a rubber-burning left turn into Harley Street, rocketing up the one-way system the wrong way. That's all I need. We follow at speed, but Ms Cook is looking a little perturbed.

'You know that we're going up a one-way street the wrong way?'

'Yes.'

'I'm not sure I'm skilled enough to do this. Do you want to swap places?'

The SUV is fifty yards ahead. I watch with horror as it narrowly misses hitting a huge, slow-moving Rolls Royce head-on. A big green jeep swerves to avoid the SUV and crashes into a stationary Renault Clio.

There are a lot of car horns being sounded now and it's hardly surprising. This insane manoeuvre tells me two things: he's getting desperate and the one-way system in Baker Street was taking him away from wherever it was he's trying to get to.

He's also hoping that driving up here will be an effective way of getting rid of me, but I'm afraid he's out of luck. A small florist's van does a hard turn to avoid the SUV, then jams on its brakes when it sees us coming. The woman driving looks insane with fear and rage.

'OK. Listen carefully,' I say, leaning toward her. 'Don't worry about hitting anything. He's clearing a path for us by doing this. Put your foot down and focus on getting right behind him.'

I look at the speedometer. We're only doing forty, but when all the other traffic is heading towards you and panicking, that's a fairly terrifying speed. A lorry loaded up with scaffolding narrowly misses scraping the side off us. I can see the driver swearing his head off.

I take my seat belt off and undo hers. 'I'm going to count to three, then I'm going to slide across into your seat. You must slide across me at exactly the same time. The car will lose power for a few seconds but that's not important. When you're in the passenger seat, get your safety belt on immediately, OK?'

She nods. Her eyes are bright with the excitement. A car pulls out from a parking place at the side of the road, then suddenly changes its mind as the SUV charges past, followed by us.

'Ready? One. Two. Three.'

Avoiding the gear stick, I grab the steering wheel with one hand and rapidly pull myself across into the driver's seat, grabbing her waist at the same time and helping chuck her across to the passenger side.

For a second she's on my lap and I can feel her suspender straps against my legs. Despite the situation, I can't help noting the gym-hard firmness of her body, the tiny waist and the scent of whatever it is she uses on her hair.

We're still in second gear, so the car slows down dramatically while there's no foot on the accelerator. I correct that and soon we're doing over fifty and avoiding the highly distressed lunchtime traffic once more. Two teenage girls point at us, but they're soon a blur.

This is a wide road, but parking is allowed on both sides, so we're basically dealing with two lanes. There's a cab parked on my left. I have to get past it while avoiding the bright yellow Peugeot on my right that's on its way to a head-on collision with us. I miss both with about two inches to spare on each side and take a deep breath to extinguish the big surge of adrenalin that my body just decided was an appropriate response.

I stay in second, playing the brakes against the accelerator from moment to moment in this breathtakingly mad obstacle course. My arms are straight, elbows locked, pushing against the steering wheel, my back pressed hard against the seat. If we avoid getting hit, it'll be an absolute fucking miracle.

I'm barely aware of the trees, houses, cars, window boxes and road works that are flashing by on each side. In a millisecond, I spot three Japanese girls taking photographs of us with their mobiles and a scaffolder dropping his Starbuck's coffee cup on the floor and swearing.

I keep my eyes burning into the back of the SUV, not giving him an inch of slack, speeding when he speeds, stopping when he stops, swerving when he swerves, avoiding when he avoids. I already feel exhausted.

'Her camisoles are marvellous, though,' Eve Cook continues, clicking her seatbelt on and readjusting her glasses. 'I find the touch of silk against my body such a sensual sensation.'

The SUV screeches to a halt, face to face with a people carrier whose driver swears and refuses to budge. It reverses a few feet, almost hits a motorcycle courier and a surprised pedestrian and continues on its way. I just catch sight of Blond Hair turning and looking straight at me. He doesn't seem concerned, but I bet he is. I'm catching up, but only because he's created a slipstream that I can follow. He's probably wondering where I got the car from. On my left, a woman in a fur coat has opened her handbag and is looking down into it. Bikes are tied against railings.

I still don't know where he's going, but it occurs to me that he must be heading towards Marylebone Road, where he can make a speedy escape to the west or east. He's got to be stopped before then; though as yet I have no idea how I'm going to do it. I can't really use offensive driving techniques with someone else's expensive car and driving in a built-up area on the wrong side of the road makes it a virtual impossibility anyway.

'Are you wearing any silk now?' I say. What am I talking about? I really must seek therapy. I can't help myself. An old black guy points angrily down the road, letting me know the proper direction I should be travelling in. Thanks for that.

'As a matter of fact, yes,' she says, crossing her legs. She's wearing red high heels, the same shade of red as her glasses. Black stockings. I wonder if her suspender belt is red with black straps.

The SUV takes a hard left into New Cavendish Street and I follow. It's a relief to be driving in the proper direction and I take another deep breath. Eve Cook runs a hand through her hair, looks at me and grins. She's having fun and genuinely can't give a shit about the car. Must be rich, I suppose. Or it's a company car.

The speed of both vehicles is attracting attention from pedestrians who stare in amazement. The SUV rips past a cyclist so closely that he falls off his bike onto the floor and I only just avoid driving over his bike and him. There're a couple of cars and a FedEx van up ahead of Blond Hair, but they're not slowing him down that much.

Then, in a flash of inspiration, I take a tyre burning right into Wimpole Mews. Hopefully, he'll check in his rear view mirror and wonder what the hell's happened to me. The mews road is wide and totally empty. I put my foot to the floorboard and I'm at the other end in a matter of seconds. This is a great car.

I take a stomach lurching left into Weymouth Street to be met with the usual loud objections and flashing headlamps you find when driving up a one-way street the wrong way at high speed, but fuck it; I'm starting to be an expert on this now.

'What is it you're wearing?' I ask Ms Cook. 'You don't have to answer if you feel it's too personal a question. I mean – we've only just met.'

I zigzag around a silver Toyota Yaris and a black Range Rover.

'Not at all. Remarkably, I'm wearing a pair of French knickers from Sara Holt's Oread line. Are you familiar with it? Two seasons ago now. The softness of the silk is like a caress.'

Weymouth Street also has car parking on each side of the road, but unlike Harley Street, it isn't quite wide enough for this kind of thing. I lurch to the right to avoid hitting a black cab, then swerve back to the left side to dodge a white Escort van. Eve Cook gasps, presses back into her seat and grabs my thigh. She has sharp fingernails, painted blood red.

As I pass Upper Wimpole Street on my left and jump a set of red lights that are facing the oncoming traffic, I'm gambling that I'm going much faster than the SUV, which had a couple of cars in front. I'm also gambling that he thinks he's given me the slip.

The two cars waiting at the lights rapidly move forward at awkward angles to give me the space to get past them. Perhaps they're used to this sort of thing around here.

'No. I'm not really familiar with Sara's lingerie lines, but obviously I'll have more of an interest now.' I keep forgetting that Sara is in the vehicle I'm in hot pursuit of.

I suddenly get the sensation that I'm in some insane, fast-moving computer game like Gran Turismo, except I'm facing the oncoming traffic rather than racing against it. I continue in second gear, my knuckles white on the wheel, turning it with small economic movements.

I'm focussing on the cars I'm trying to avoid so intensely it feels like I'm hallucinating. I can smell the clutch burning. There's a woman in a green top pushing a pram on my right. A man sprays the flowers in the window boxes on my left.

'Do you mean you'll have more of an interest because I'm wearing her lingerie?' She turns to look at me, waiting for my reaction.

I turn left into Westmoreland Street, which is thankfully two-way, and accelerate until I'm doing over seventy. A private ambulance starts to pull out from the parking bay of a small hospital until I give it a long blast of the horn.

'Well, that and the fact that I now know Sara.'

'Oh.' She gives a little moue. 'Could you introduce me to her? I'd love to meet her.'

Right turn only at the end of this road. I can see a zebra crossing. I open both windows so I can listen out for the SUV. I hear its engine about twenty feet to my left. A blue Ford S-MAX and the FedEx van pass by.

'Brace yourself.'

If this fails, Eve Cook will be the first casualty, not to mention her Audi R8. I'm depending on Blond Hair having good driving skills and speedy reactions. Let's hope he has both. I'll try and position the car so if he hits us, he'll hit the rear and not the passenger door.

Ignoring the right turn command, I drive straight ahead as if I'm aiming for the dining room of the house across the road then jam the brakes on hard. We both jerk forward and then backwards in our seats and I'm surprised the air bags didn't engage. I turn my head to the left and there's the SUV bearing down on us fast. For a second, I think he's going to hit us, but he screeches to a halt with a foot to spare.

There's a big John Lewis delivery lorry behind him, so he's blocked in. I pat Eve Cook on the leg, as if I'm just going to post a letter.

'Won't be a minute.'

I get out and walk around to the SUV. This has got to be quick and effective.

Blond Hair gets out and slams the door behind him. His face is red with anger and he looks like he means business. His suit jacket has gone and he rolls his shirtsleeves up in a way that's meant to be menacing. He slides a hand in his trouser pocket and slips a thick brass knuckle-duster over the fingers of his right hand. The old ways are always the best.

His associate, who I'll call Blue Suit, gets out the other side. He's a cocky-looking young guy wearing, as you may have surmised, a blue suit. He's a big fucker and I can tell he works out. He's got a low centre of gravity and big fists. He's grinning all over his face as if he knows what's going to happen next will be a foregone conclusion and is looking forward to it. Well, it won't be a foregone conclusion if I can help it. I remember what he did to Rachelle and I'll keep that in mind ten seconds from now. If there're just the two of them that means that Sara is probably unconscious or incapacitated in the back and they don't have to worry about her at the moment.

'I warned you, you piece of shit,' says Blond Hair, clenching his fat metal fist, his dead eyes threatening and sinister. He pulls his arm back ready for a fucker of a punch aimed at my face, but all that extra weight has made him too slow and he's telegraphing too much.

Just as he lets fly, I catch his wrist, turn my back to him and then use both hands to quickly and powerfully break his elbow over my shoulder.

His arm snaps ninety degrees the wrong way and I can hear the bone splinter and the cartilage crack. Blood sprays the side of my face and the scream he produces will be giving me tinnitus for the rest of the day.

While he's considering that, I elbow him in the side of the head and then grab his fucked arm by the wrist and bicep, twist it hard and use the excruciating pain to manipulate him to the floor. I kick him when he's down just because I can and for hitting Sara. Then I kick him again.

That all took five seconds and now I've got Blue Suit charging at me. His expression has changed and he's no longer grinning. Welcome to the party, shithead.

After what he's just seen, a normal person would think twice about continuing with this but I can tell this one is far too dim, despite the smart suit and confident swagger.

Stupid he may be, but he's got skills. His fists are up by his face and I can tell by what's he's doing with his feet that he's about to launch into some sort of spinning hook kick, probably aimed at my head.

This is never a good idea. Spin kicks looks great on film, but in reality that half second when you're standing on one leg and have your back to your opponent is fatal: bad balance, no visual. As Blue Suit gets to this point, I step forward and push him hard in the back. He falls flat on his face. I haven't got the time to allow him to get up, so I travel down with him, grab his hair and smash his head against the road surface three or four times until he's senseless. Forehead gashed, nose broken, front teeth out. That was for Rachelle, you piece of garbage.

Sara is just coming round when I open the back door of the SUV. She's mostly down in the footwell of the back seat, presumably as a result of the emergency stop. Despite that, she doesn't seem damaged. She puts her hands in front of her face in a defensive position and attempts to kick me. Well, at least she's conscious.

She's pale, groggy and has a swelling just starting to appear on the side of her face where Blond Hair punched her. I just hope she's not concussed, but I can check for that later. I can hear Eve Cook doing a screechy five-point turn so she's facing in the right direction. The John Lewis driver is tooting his horn impatiently. An old woman in a fur coat with a Chihuahua is pointing at me with her walking stick. No one has quite realised what's happened here yet, which is good. They probably think it's some sort of road traffic accident with added spectacular GBH.

I reach into the back of the car and start to help Sara out. She tries to kick me again. This time she clips me on the side of the arm and it hurts like a bastard.

'Sara, it's me. Come on. We've got to move.'

If she replied I didn't hear it as I'm slightly deaf on one side thanks to Blond Hair's scream. I take her hands and slowly help her out of the SUV until she's standing on the road. She throws up over my shoes.

There's a suit jacket hanging in the back of the car. Must be Blond Hair's. I grab it and put it over her shoulders. I take a last look at Blond Hair and Blue Suit. Blond Hair is as white as a sheet and has tears in his eyes. He's using his good arm to try and push himself up into a standing position, but he's too stunned and uncoordinated. It looks like he's pissed himself from the pain.

Blue Suit is on all fours and is throwing up over his hands. They'll both need to visit the hospital, and pretty fast in Blond Hair's case. That blood spray was from the brachial artery, which must have been ruptured by the elbow fracture. Bad break, in more ways than one. Still, I should care.

I propel Sara towards Ms Cook's car. She's trembling so much you could put a cocktail shaker in her hand and have a perfect vodka martini in less than five seconds. I get in the passenger seat and prop her up on my lap. She leans forward again and throws up.

'Are you alright, Mr Beckett? You've got blood all over the side of your face,' says Eve Cook, who seems remarkably unfazed by the last five terrifying minutes. Her skirt is rucked up and I can see her stocking tops and suspender straps.

'It's OK. It isn't mine.'

'I know this isn't quite the time or place, Miss Holt,' says Ms Cook to Sara as we drive away. 'But I am *such* a big fan of your work. I'm actually wearing a pair of your French knickers at the moment. The Oread line?'

Sara nods her head and throws up again, this time all over my shirt and trousers.

'If you wouldn't mind taking us to Covent Garden that would be fantastic.'

'It would be my pleasure.'

'And you've got my card. This car will need a full service and a good valeting after all of this. I insist on paying for all of that and for a rental car while you're inconvenienced. And thank you. You've probably saved her life.'

'Can I call you?'

'Yes. As soon as you know how much the car will cost, give me a call.'

'No. I mean can I *call* you?'

19

I NEVER SLEEP WITH CLIENTS

Eve Cook drops us off in Exeter Street amid the usual surprised comments that I actually live in Covent Garden. I make sure she still has my business card and she gives me hers. I tell her to call me as soon as the bill for her car needs to be paid. She asks me to call her as soon as I'm free. She says if I don't call her soon, she'll call me.

Sara is groggy and sick. She threw up again in the car just before we arrived here and both of us are now pretty thoroughly covered in her vomit. I feel bad about Eve Cook's car, and decide I'll take her out to dinner when I've finished with all of this. On top of everything else, she is an attractive woman and out of the whole dramatic episode, the most notable moment was when I felt her suspender straps as we swapped places in the car. I must be losing my mind.

It was incredibly lucky that she went along with the whole thing, because if she hadn't I'd certainly have lost Sara and God knows what would be happening to her by now. It was also a stroke of luck that she'd heard of Maccanti and was such a skilled driver, apart from the one-way insane scary bit.

I've got to get both of us inside and out of our clothes, and get her cleaned up and checked out. I've got to check if she's concussed and if she is I'll have no choice but to get her to a hospital. Immediate practicalities aside, I'm extremely concerned about this turn of events. Whatever this is, it's suddenly become a lot heavier.

She's small and light, so I lift her up in my arms and get her upstairs, laying her down on the hallway floor when I have to negotiate the locking system on my front door. I start to feel hungry, then remember that it's only a little past midday. I feel like it should be midnight.

Once we're inside, she moans a little as we walk over the nightingale floor, then quietens down as I take her into my bedroom and lay her on the bed.

I close the curtains to cut the light out and head into the bathroom, getting out of my vomit-soaked clothes, checking my blood-spattered face in the mirror and having a quick, hot shower.

When I've dried myself off, I put on a robe and go and check Sara. She's still lying on the bed, but at least she's conscious, if a little groggy. If you're not used to it, being hit hard in the face like that even once can be extremely traumatic, particularly if you're Sara's build and it's unexpected.

I still don't know if she totally lost consciousness in the SUV or not. Still, first things first. I put my arm around her shoulder and lift her to a sitting position. She's floppy and uncoordinated.

'Listen, Sara. You're covered in puke. I'm going to have to take these clothes off you and put them in the wash with mine. Then I want you to have a quick shower, then I'm going to take a look at you. You might be concussed and if you are, we're going to have to think about what to do next. We may have to go to a hospital. Understand?'

Her blouse is covered in dark patches from the vomit and her skirt is in an even worse mess. There are spots of blood on her clothing as well, but that's probably from me, or from Blond Hair, to be more accurate. The jacket I took from the SUV lies on the floor, also covered in vomit.

'Are you OK with me undressing you? I don't think you're up to it. We have to move on with all of this. We can't hang about.'

She looks up and gives me an arch glance. She sounds sleepy. 'I'm not wearing a bra under this. It might be too much for you. Men have taken their own lives.'

I suddenly remember our kiss on Baker Street and wonder where we stand now. That seems like it was a few days ago, but I can still remember the softness of her mouth.

'Listen, Sara. I've seen millions of naked women. Just in the last week there've been so many I've genuinely lost count. Think of me as a doctor or a priest.'

She laughs and holds her arms out to the side. I undo the buttons on her blouse and she moves each shoulder forward as I take the sleeves down. The fabric is soaking. I try to avoid looking at her breasts, but it's impossible. They're small and exquisitely well shaped. She catches my eye.

'I can see where you're looking, you know. I'm not silly.'

'You're imagining things. We're going to stand up now. Are you ready?'

'For what?'

I take her hands and get her to a standing position. I undo the clasp at the side of her skirt and let it fall to the floor. I'm obviously being punished for some appalling crime or crimes committed in a previous life, as she's wearing a tiny delicate black silk thong with lace around the edges.

I take her hand and lead her into the bathroom. She's a bit shaky, but nothing too serious. I resist putting an arm around her waist, patting her bottom, rubbing her back, biting her neck and a million other things that are occurring to me. I guess I'm something like a modern-day saint. I may have to contact the Church.

'Have a quick shower and wash your hair. There's some shampoo and conditioner in there and a Molton Brown shower gel. Don't be long or I'll be coming in to get you.'

'Promises, promises.'

'That's all I'm capable of at the moment.'

'That's what they all say at first.'

'You're asking to be disciplined, young lady.'

'They say that, too.'

She turns away from me and heads towards the shower. From behind, the thong can only be described as 'bottom-revealing'. She has a lovely, well-toned back. I wonder if she works out.

I pick up my clothes from the floor, get Sara's discarded items from the bedroom and stick them in the washing machine. She'll need something to wear, so I find her a worn-out blue sweatshirt that's a little too big for me, so it should cover her almost down to the knee. Just in case I've forgotten, I run a quick mantra through my head: *I never sleep with clients, I never sleep with clients.*

I'm going to have to have a serious think about all of this once I've checked that Sara's OK. I get an A4 pad of cartridge paper and a black uni-ball pen and stick them on the kitchen table. I need a blast of bean-to-cup, so fill up the Siemens with Café Français and stick it on. I can hear the shower running and stop myself visualising Sara in there, naked, working shampoo into her hair and rubbing shower gel over that sleek body.

Damn.

Just as the Siemens is completing its task, Sara appears in the kitchen doorway, wrapped in a dark red towel, her hair wet and slicked back. I point to the blue sweatshirt on the back of one of the chairs.

'Are you OK? You can wear this sweatshirt while your clothes are cooking.'

'Aw. I thought you'd have a big man's cotton shirt for me to wear so I looked like one of those sexy Sixties girls with tousled hair and a nonchalant pout.'

'A shirt would be too revealing. Would you like a coffee?'

'Hm.'

She picks up the sweatshirt and returns to the bathroom. I don't know what I'm going to do with her yet. She can't go back to work this afternoon, that's for sure. One of us is going to have to contact one of her MTAs and make up some story.

We also have to find out what happened to Rachelle Beauchesne, who may or may not have contacted the police, if she's not dead or in hospital after Blue Suit's assault. These are nasty guys, whoever they are. But I'm getting too far ahead of myself.

When she returns from the bathroom, her hair is starting to dry. It wasn't the effect I'd intended (I swear to you), but my old sweatshirt makes her look unbearably sexy and I can smell the Molton Brown Rhubarb and Rose Shower Gel on her. She sits across from me. I look at the small, blonde hairs on her legs. I hand her a coffee.

I attempt to be serious and concerned as opposed to desirous and sleazy. It's not easy. It's never easy.

'How do you feel?'

'Woozy.'

'After that guy hit you, do you think you were unconscious?'

She takes a sip of coffee, places her cup on the table and clasps her fingers together. 'I'm not sure. I don't quite remember everything. I remember the jeep or whatever it was stopping really suddenly and me being thrown forward onto the floor.'

'Before that; do you remember being thrown into the jeep after they hit you?'

'No.'

'OK. As you were sick a few times, I just want to do a few little checks on you.'

'I'm sorry about that. Being sick, I mean. And that woman's car…'

'Don't worry about her. She was delighted to meet you. She probably won't ever clean the car.' I drag my chair across the kitchen floor so I'm sitting opposite her. Her skin is warm and glowing from the shower.

'What's your name?'

'You've been working for me for two days and you don't know that? You're fired.'

'Seriously. Tell me.'

'Sara Holt.'

'What day is it?'

'Thursday.'

'Where are we, Sara?'

'I assume we're in your flat. It's amazing. Did you decorate it yourself?'

'No I didn't. This is going to sound silly, but would

you mind reciting the months of the year in reverse order?'

She looks puzzled, but she does it anyway. All OK.

'Can you remember what was happening before you were hit?'

'Hit? Rachelle. I was meeting Rachelle for lunch. She was waving at me from up Baker Street.'

'How do you feel? Do you feel ill? Do you have a headache? Do you feel dizzy or nauseous?'

'No. Just…' She places a hand against the side of her face. 'My face hurts all over here. Did you say I was hit? Was I punched?'

'Yes. I think you may have been knocked out cold, at least momentarily.'

'Hang on. I remember now; a big guy with blond hair.'

I get a torch from my man drawer, switch it on and shine it in her eyes. Her pupils constrict. All fine. I hold my finger up in front of me. 'As quickly as you can, touch my finger then touch your own nose.'

She smiles as if this is some eccentric game I've created, suddenly looking really young. She manages this small coordination task without any problems. All clear, I think.

'Let me know if you feel bad for any reason. I think you're OK under the circumstances. I was afraid you were concussed. I don't think you are but I had to check. But when all this is over you should go for a hospital check-up. Just to be on the safe side. Maybe get a dental appointment if you get any problems. Unusual aches and pains, bleeding from the mouth; that sort of thing.'

I touch the side of her face as gently as I can. There's swelling around her cheekbone and I think she's going to have a black eye. She flinches when my hand passes her jaw. Must have been one hell of a punch. I fetch a couple of paracetamol and a glass of water.

'Turn your mobile off. You need a break. If no one can get hold of you for a while, it's tough. I'm going out for a moment. I'm going to get some food. Have another coffee if you like. Under no circumstances answer the door to anyone.'

I'm very careful as I walk down Exeter Street and head towards The Strand, but there's no sign of anyone watching me, nor should there be.

I'm a bit concerned about Rachelle. Whatever happened to her, the police will certainly be involved by now, particularly if she was seriously hurt. If the police talk to her, she's going to tell them everything that happened and now they'll have to get involved with Sara's case, as this is no longer vague harassment but a kidnapping in broad daylight, albeit one that failed. I wanted Sara to turn her mobile off as I don't want anyone calling her and telling her about Rachelle. Not yet. She's had enough stress for one day.

I don't think I'm going to be able to meet up with Mrs Vasconselos at Fortnum's, which is a shame. Nevertheless, I know she's staying at the Hotel Café Royal, so all is not quite lost. I wonder if I should call her? I pop into Eat on The Strand and pick up a shitload of sandwiches, sushi and cookies, plus some fruit juice and mineral water in case Sara gets sick of coffee.

By the time I get back, she's got a bit more colour, but is starting to look tired. As we eat, she stretches her hand across the table and places it over mine.

'I'm afraid now, Daniel,' says Sara. She giggles, but it's fake and brittle. 'I feel as if someone's trying to do me serious harm. What would have happened if you hadn't caught up with those men?'

'I don't know. I don't know what they wanted. But know one thing: you're safe here, and I think you're going to have to stay here until I can get this mess sorted out. Unless you'd prefer me to hand the whole thing over to the police. Someone tried to kidnap you in broad daylight in front of witnesses. They have to take that seriously.'

She frowns and purses her lips. 'I told you. I want *you* to handle this. Do you mind if go and have a lie down on your bed? I feel a bit tired now. I think it's all catching up with me.'

'Sure. Lie on your side.'

She smiles at me as she heads for the bedroom. 'Don't think I've forgotten about what happened on Baker Street.'

'I'm sure I don't know what you're talking about, miss.'

'Oh yeah?' she says, without turning around.

I pour another coffee for myself and get my cartridge pad and pen in front of me on the table. I can see now why Blond Hair was so keen to buy me off. He obviously knew this kidnap attempt was happening – of course he did – and didn't want any interference from someone like me.

On the other hand, he obviously felt he had nothing to fear from my presence and he was almost right. I was just a minor problem that he wanted out of the way for his own peace of mind and so things ran smoothly.

He must have surmised that I wasn't guarding Sara day and night and that the chances of me being there when the snatch happened were remote, but he wanted to be on the safe side. As it turned out, I *was* there, but what the hell was I going to do against him and Blue Suit and their fuck-off SUV?

Also, they were prepared for someone trying to stop them or making a fuss; I suspect that's what Blue Suit was for and why Rachelle was dealt with so brutally. Blond Hair could easily have done the job on his own, so it must have been very important to him that nothing went wrong.

And now the next problem: what happened that changed all of this from harassment to kidnapping? Was it always going to be this way? Were the street hassles and breaking and entering just for starters, leading up to The Big One? And once they'd got Sara sequestered away somewhere, what were they going to do to her? A major premise of kidnapping is that at some point there's going to be a ransom demand. Who were they going to squeeze for the money?

But even the kidnapping idea doesn't really hold water. If I was going to grab Sara like that, I'd do it out of the blue, without any warning harassments or break-ins. So my first theory seems to be the most obvious solution: it was only meant to be harassment and hassle, but then something changed.

So what changed?

Kidnapping doesn't make sense on another level: if she was the daughter or wife of a well-known millionaire you could just about imagine it, but a single woman in her twenties making a success of herself in the fashion industry? I for one had never heard of her. If she hadn't contacted me, I wouldn't even have known of her existence.

So what other reason could they have for taking her away like that? Were they going to kill her? Rape her? Was it, as Isolda suggested, some disturbed guy who'd seen her photograph in a magazine and got a little too obsessed? Moreover, a disturbed guy with a mini-army of professional, motivated, moneyed, well-equipped criminals at his beck and call? I really can't get this straight in my head at all. I think of the words of wisdom of the late unlamented Footballer Dad:

She's just a fucking slut who needed to be brought down a peg or two.

And then:

He'll fucking get you for this, whoever you are.

No. The disturbed guy scenario doesn't really work, either. This is menacing, well-planned and professional, not crazy, random and unhinged. Was the fucking slut comment just a general insult he used all the time, or did he or whoever he worked for, actually know her personally, or at least know *of* her enough to hate her?

I'm going to write down the names of the players I know about so far on my cartridge pad. I'll add the first comments and thoughts that come to mind. If there's any justice in the world, which I know there isn't, something will gel and the answer will leap out and I'll know what to do. I'll start with:

1. Footballer Dad. Definitely a thug and definitely a foot soldier. Maybe brought out of retirement for this. Maybe still active. Responsible for at least two definite insulting, menacing harassments. Attempted to pull Sara's dress off in public. Despite his hard-man image, definitely fearful and/or respectful of Scary Boss. Which brings me to:

2. Scary Boss. Whoever the hell *he* is. The mastermind behind this whole thing? Reason unknown. The sort of criminal heavy that a hard man like Footballer Dad would fear or at least respect. Why is he bothering with this? So

high-risk, it must be worth it in some way. What's his motive and what's his reward? I'd like to meet him and ask WTF's going on. Then break his neck and dump his body in a skip.

3. Blond Hair. Ex-police. Possibly Special Branch. Bent former police working for criminals is not unknown, but the money has to be good. This would maybe make Scary Boss rich and influential. Blond Hair was a skilled pro; good tailing ability, fearless, risk-taking driving technique. Menacing, threatening, but too cocky and over-confident as it turned out. A senior player to Footballer Dad, that's for sure. His description didn't fit any of the men who Sara told me about, so he obviously didn't trouble himself with the minor stuff. Hits women. Is *he* Scary Boss? Unlikely.

4. Blue Suit. Another foot soldier, but younger and possibly more effective than Footballer Dad. One of those tossers with combat skills who use them to bully, overpower and feel good about themselves. Smartly dressed and well-groomed. That smirking expression expressed no doubt about the outcome of his altercation with me, but in the end he wasn't smart, skilled or fast enough. Second-class muscle. Hits women. Probably enjoys it.

5. Burglar Bill. Whoever broke into Sara's building was strong, not heavy or overweight, and skilled. We're most likely looking at a career burglar or a ninja. Most likely the former. So Scary Boss knows/employs people like this. Of the four gentlemen above, I would nominate Blue Suit as the most likely candidate, but I don't think he'd have the brains or chops for such a job.

Sara said that the two men who blocked her way one night were in their forties and that both had short dark hair. I have to assume that these two were one-offs. She never saw them again and they don't figure in my list of players. It could be that they were random wankers and nothing to do with all of this, but I somehow feel they were connected because of the technique and time frame. If Scary Boss is rotating the help, maybe the time hasn't come for these two to reappear quite yet.

Then there was the solitary guy in South Molton Street, the one who kept stepping in front of her. She said that his face was hard and serious and that she felt he would hit her if she tried to push past him. I didn't get a specific description of this guy, but he was using similar tactics to the other two. Once again, the 'hitting women' motif rears its ugly head and once again it may not yet be time for him to reappear. Maybe he never will.

Before the abduction attempt, I was wondering how long all of this would be kept up and when it would naturally end. When Sara announced she was no longer doing the two shows? When she had a nervous breakdown and was sent somewhere to 'rest'? Perhaps things weren't happening as fast as they planned, so the schedule had to be escalated, hence the SUV and its charming occupants. Maybe all of it was all just a game for them; a bit of fun.

Then we have Footballer Dad in Heddon Street, jostling her in the shoulder and calling her bitch. By the time he approached her in Piccadilly, he'd upped his game to 'fuckin' stinkin' whore' and tried to undo her dress. I must focus on the job of getting rid of his body when I have the time. It's pretty cold in the lock-up, so I reckon I've got three to five days before he starts to smell.

It's never been the same people twice, or if it has, I wasn't aware of it.

I take a look at the sheet of cartridge paper. I notice that my writing deteriorates as I get to the bottom of the page. So what do we have? At least eight of them, it would seem, unless Burglar Bill is doubling on harassment duties. A bunch of violent, misogynistic, ill-educated, macho bullies, all picking on the same girl.

I'm almost sorry that Footballer Dad died when he did. If I'd been able to get a solid hour with him, I'd have been able to make him tell me things he didn't even know he knew and then write me a polite thank-you note for listening, accompanied by a big bunch of in-season flowers. The frustration of not having any leads is beginning to annoy me intensely.

I rip a clean sheet of cartridge paper off the pad, grab the pen and absentmindedly wander into the bedroom, forgetting Sara is there. She's lying on her side and seems to be asleep. I realise that I've forgotten to do anything with Blond Hair's jacket, place the paper and pen on the bed and pick it up.

Without thinking, I start to rifle through the pockets. I find a number of pieces of pocket junk; some disposable tissues, chewing gum, lip balm, a silver fountain pen, a packet of Sudafed, a Leatherman Juice XE6 and a nine-inch Châtellerault stiletto flick knife. No wallet or keys. Was he being careful? Probably not. Keys still in the SUV and wallet probably in his trouser pocket. I take the Leatherman and the flick knife into the kitchen and hide them behind the food processor.

I'm just about to bin the jacket when I find a folded piece of red and white paper. It's the rental receipt for the SUV. Venture Car Hire, 36 Prideaux Road, Stockwell, London SW9 4AH. Black Ford Explorer. Rental period two days starting yesterday. There's an unreadable signature in three places on the sheet and a company name: T.R.J.E. Ltd.

Well, at bloody last. All I have to do is get down to Stockwell, find out who T.R.J.E. Ltd are and the whole thing'll be magically solved. Or not. It isn't much, but it's all I have to go on.

I get dressed, go in the bedroom, sit on the side of the bed and shake Sara awake. She rolls onto her back and looks up at me, smiling.

'Is it morning already?' she purrs. 'I'm exhausted after last night.'

'I have to go to work, darling. Remember to do the cleaning and particularly the inside of the oven. And the ironing. If this place isn't totally spotless by the time I return, you'll be getting a firm spanking.'

'I'm going to smear mud and offal over your carpets and furniture.'

Oh my God.

'Seriously – I'll let myself in when I get back. Don't answer the door and don't let anyone know where you are. Just go back to sleep.'

'Mm-hm. What was your name again?'

I grab my jacket, walk down to The Strand and get a cab to Stockwell. It's starting to rain.

20

VENTURE CAR HIRE

Prideaux Road is a small residential street filled mainly with terraced Edwardian houses. It's so deserted and quiet that I'm wondering if something terrible has happened here and the whole population has been evacuated.

Typically, number thirty-six is right down the other end from where the cab dropped me. There's a large, crappy-looking rusted gate with a wooden sign reading: Venture Cars. Tacky-looking purple writing on a green background. For a moment, I think I've somehow come to the wrong place or at least maybe to the wrong branch.

I push the gate open and walk into a wide, pothole-ridden yard. I can hear a bell go off somewhere, so presumably I've stepped on something without realising it. I look down, but I can't see anything. However run-down the whole operation looks from the outside, however, the rows of smart-looking vehicles tell a different story and maybe the rundown exterior is intentional.

There are several arc lights dotted around plus nine CCTV cameras, some discreet, some not so discreet. I assume the place is pretty well lit up at night to discourage casual theft or even casual inspection. It wouldn't surprise me if they hired a security firm to keep an eye on things when there was no one here, though I can't see any signs indicating a security presence, and they usually like to advertise.

The walls around the yard have broken glass embedded in them, which I thought was illegal, but I could be wrong. Not impossible to get past, but it would certainly discourage kids.

There's a wide, flat metal strip running across the base of the gate, probably some sort of security ramp, which is raised when the place is shut. There are about half a dozen SUVs like the one Blond Hair was driving, and the remaining vehicles are Daimlers, Jaguars, Nissans, Mercedes, BMWs and the like; all new, all clean and all in excellent condition. I can't imagine how much money it would take to set up an operation like this. Maybe they just started with a bank loan and two second hand Volkswagen Golfs or something.

There's a kid of about seventeen wearing a pink Ulan Bator t-shirt and he's cleaning the windscreen of a brand-new white Jaguar XK-R Coupé as if his life depended on it. He looks up when he sees me and nods towards a Portakabin to my left. Another bell goes off as I walk up the steps. There's a sign on the door: Reception.

The guy behind the reception counter is a heavily bearded, long-haired Asian dude in his mid-twenties, who is so big he seriously looks like he could be a Sumo wrestler.

He has a big pair of lime green Sennheiser headphones slung around his neck and one of his ears is pierced six times. He's wearing a red and white Kobayashi Porcelain Indonesia t-shirt. Left-handed. Copper bracelet on his right wrist. Rheumatism? I can't see how he would get through the door. He quickly walks around to greet me personally and even though he's smiling it's slightly intimidating. I'm expecting a bone-crusher handshake, but it's actually light and delicate, like he's barely touching me. He's been drinking Dr Pepper.

'Good morning, sir. I'm Nick Sarna. How can I help you?'

His voice is South London and educated. I wonder if he went to university but then decided to join the family business.

'Hi. My name's Daniel Beckett. I'm a private investigator. If you have the time, I'd like to talk to you about a vehicle that was rented here yesterday.'

He looks at me as if I've just told him I'm from outer space.

'You're shitting me.'

'About what?'

'That you're a private detective.'

'No.'

'You're actually a real private detective.'

'Yes.'

'Shit. It's like you're some fictional character and you've just walked in the fucking door in reality. This is really strange. You're even dressed like a cool fuck.'

'Thank you.'

'I don't mean that like it's a bad thing. Cool fuck, I mean. Yeah. Fucking great. Let's go in the office.'

He pokes his head out of the door and shouts at the kid. 'Szymon! Keep an eye out. I'm in a fucking meeting.'

Szymon waves and gets on with the windscreen.

'Szymon's got some sort of obsessive-compulsive disorder,' says Nick Sarna, grinning at me. 'It's great for keeping all the motors spotless, inside and out.'

We go through a back door into another, slightly larger

Portakabin. I watch him as he sidles through the door and still can't work out how he does it. This one is smartly decorated and has a huge tank of tropical fish in the corner. There are art prints all over the walls. There's a print of Nighthawks by Edward Hopper, which is the only one I recognise. I'm going to briefly soften him up. I point to the print.

'Hey. Nighthawks.'

'You like that? I fucking love his stuff. It's so creepy. Wait.'

He rummages around in a desk draw and produces a thick coffee table book full of Edward Hopper paintings. I take it and flick through it appreciatively.

'I did a BA in Fine Art at Northumbria University. He was one of the guys I tried to copy, but it's harder than it looks. It looks really simple, but it's not.'

'I'm sure.'

'You'd be amazed at how many people don't recognise stuff like this. I mean, he's one of the most famous artists in the fucking world. He's one of the greats. It's the same with others. People just don't – I mean, it's a big fucking thing. Art, I mean. And most people only recognise two or three artists, if that. Picasso, Van Gogh, stuff like that. Fucking Monet's water lilies on fucking tea towels.'

'Nothing wrong with them, though.'

'What – tea towels?'

'The artists.'

'No. Of course not. But there's so much more, y'know?'

I can see now that the bookshelf to my left is full of art books. Warhol, Kandinsky, Klein, Rothko, Chadwick. This is obviously his Big Thing. I don't want to get him started on why the hell he's working here. I don't have the time. I think I've broken the ice now, though, which is what I was aiming for.

'So let me just show you something…'

I fish the car rental receipt out of my pocket and put it on the desk in front of him. This is going OK so far. I'm not being too officious or pushing too hard. He's the type that would suddenly become unhelpful if you started sounding too much like authority.

'Yeah. I remember this. The black Explorer. Guy came in yesterday. I'm expecting him to bring it back today. Sneering, arrogant fucker. Impatient. Expected me to get down on my hands and knees in front of him. A face made for punching. Sighed irritably when he had to fill in the form. You know the type.'

'This guy. Did he have blond hair?'

'Yeah. Something of the copper about him, I thought.'

'You're right. I think he was in the police once.'

'Maybe I should be doing *your* job!'

'Maybe you should. What's the company on there? T.R.J.E. Ltd.'

'They've got a contract with us. They own a string of nightclubs.'

Nightclubs?

'What do they stand for? The initials, I mean.'

'I don't know. I think the E might stand for Enterprises. That's only a guess, though. It's just a name. I couldn't give a fuck as long as they pay, d'you know what I mean? We deal with loads of companies that have contracts. They do it because they get reductions and shit.'

'Sure. What does a company who own a string of nightclubs want with sleek high-end cars to the point where they have a contract?'

'No idea. They come in, they hire a car, they bring it back, y'know? I don't take much of an interest, to be honest. I block it all out.' He laughs. 'It's hell on earth. Hey, take a look at this guy.'

Another drawer opens and he hands me a thick art book. I can hardly believe it. It's Basquiat. Without giving her name, I tell him about Sara's interest and her designs inspired by his work. He seems genuinely surprised and impressed.

'That's so weird, though. Me handing you that book and you talking to someone about him just the other day.'

'Yeah.'

'Fuck.'

Now back to the story.

'You don't know any of your clients, then. Know their business or anything like that. Have a laugh and a joke with them. Meet up for a pint later.'

He laughs. 'Fuck *off!*'

'Well, you never know.'

'So – what – are you police? I mean are you ex-police? What's this all about? I love those Nordic Noir police shows. I'd like to live in Denmark. Do you belong to a company or are you on your own?'

'I'm on my own. And no, I'm not ex-police.'

'Have you ever been to Denmark?'

'Yes I have.'

'What's it like? Is it good?'

'Well, I was there on business. Just for half a day. Only saw a small part of it, really. Seemed very nice, though. I remember walking past a statue of Hans Christian Andersen.'

He nods. 'Let me get the file up on here.'

He taps away on a Toshiba Satellite Professional. He

screws his eyes up as if he needs glasses, but doesn't realise it yet. He looks up at me.

'What's this all about? What is it you're looking for?'

'I want a name and an address. I want to know the name of the guy that hired that vehicle and where he lives. If it's a company contract, as you say, I want the address of the head office and hopefully the director of the company. Anything you've got, really.' I laugh. I want to get him to collude with me. 'To be honest, I'm totally fucked with this so far. I've got nothing.'

'OK. Well, T.R.J.E. Ltd have a head office, but it's a nightclub. I told you they have a string of nightclubs. You'd think it might be an office or something, but it's just one of their biggest clubs. You might have heard of it. Dolly's? No?'

'No I haven't. Where is it?'

'249a Judd Street, WC1. Sort of Bloomsbury, I suppose. Near St Pancras railway. Well, not that near. That's just the nearest big thing.'

When I was pursuing the SUV it seemed to me that he was trying to get to Euston Road and travel either west or east. If he'd gone east, he could have been at St Pancras in about five minutes, awful lunchtime traffic allowing. Maybe that's what he had in mind. I remember Judd Street now. It's a long road that goes all the way down to Russell Square.

I'm interested that he used a hire car that could be traced back to a specific address. Presumably he wasn't expecting anyone to follow the abduction up, police or otherwise. And Sara would hardly have been in any position to chase it up if the whole thing had been successful. He was too cocky and arrogant by far.

If it had been me, I'd have used fake ID and a fake

address, so that if anyone came here asking questions they'd have hit a dead end. And if I was Blond Hair, I'd have dyed my hair and not been so obnoxious to the guy behind the counter. That way, he'd have had difficulty remembering me and wouldn't have been so keen to help.

'How come you've heard of it? Dolly's, I mean.'

'Oh, it's a big swanky place. Well, not that big. Sort of medium. Medium but smart. A wealthy friend of mine had his twenty-first there a few years ago. Five years ago, now I think of it. Really expensive, but OK for a one-off visit for a special occasion, I guess. We all had to dress in suits, which I hate.'

'Any name? A director or something?'

'Nothing like that. No need. The company pays us by direct debit.'

It still puzzles me. 'Why does a chain of nightclubs need hire cars?'

'No idea. Pick up people? Who knows?'

'What about the sneering, arrogant fucker who took the Explorer yesterday? Anything on him? Driving licence? Anything?'

'No. His name's Mr R. Hyland. There's an address in Harlesden. No telephone number. He's just one of the people who can sign for a car for T.R.J.E Ltd. It's a weird arrangement, but I'm not the one who made it. It was my brother when he was running this place. It looks like Mr R. Hyland had a driving licence and it was checked, but there's no details on it. Presumably it was valid and clean.

'The whole arrangement of this place is a bit chaotic, to be honest. Each company has a slightly different arrangement with us. My brother tended to do these businessy things by intuition.'

'Is there any way I can have a word with him?'

'My brother? Not really. He's dead. Died last year. August. Heart attack. He was thirty-three.'

'I'm sorry.'

'Doesn't bother me, mate. What's going on? What's happened?'

I may as well tell him. If nothing else, he may think twice about renting one of his flash cars to T.R.J.E Ltd in the future. If his brother died of a heart attack at thirty-three, it occurs to me that I should say something about his weight, just as a friendly gesture, but I don't want to spoil the atmosphere. He probably already knows, anyway.

'The Explorer was used in a kidnapping attempt.'

'What? You're fucking kidding, yeah?'

'No. It was involved in a high-speed car chase in the centre of London this morning. I was the one in pursuit. He was driving up one-way roads the wrong way. It was pretty crazy.'

'You're fucking kidding me. Was the Explorer damaged?'

I have to laugh at this. 'No. Not as far as I could tell. Clutch probably needs looking at.'

'Who did they kidnap?'

'My client. A woman. It was more of an abduction than a kidnapping, I suppose. But I managed to retrieve her. I had to get her away from the scene. Now I want to find the perpetrators.'

'Was it the Basquiat woman?'

'Yes.'

'And you rescued her?'

'Yes.'

'Shit. Fuck. Well fuck that. I'm not renting any cars to them anymore. Fuckers. If this business goes under because of it, then so be it. So what're you going to do now? You going to pistol-whip them? A bit of waterboarding? How did you find this place? Did you use clever detection techniques? Hey – why would someone go to Denmark just for a fucking half a day?' He laughs. 'Did you go over there to do a hit or something? Do you think he'll bring the SUV back?'

'The receipt fell out of the blond guy's jacket. It was all I had to go on. Anyway, I'm not going to waterboard anyone. I just want a chat. I don't know if he'll bring it back. If I find it I'll give you a call. Listen. Thanks for all your help. I know these things are kind of confidential.'

I hand him my business card and four fifties.

'What?! This is just a like in a film! Thanks, man. I'm not going to spend this. I'm gonna put this money and your card in a frame. This is so cool. This is real cinematic stuff. A fucking payoff. Money from a private dick. I'm going down IKEA tonight and get a frame.'

'Well, whatever you want to do with it, it's yours. You've done me a big favour. Is there anywhere I can get a cab around here?'

'You going up to Judd Street?'

'Yes.'

'You're fucked for cabs round here, mate. You could walk to the Lambeth Hospital, which is only around the corner, but that's just minicabs and they'll rip you off every time. There's a minicab company about half a mile away, but they'll rip you off as well. You'd have to walk towards Stockwell tube to find a black cab, but listen – I'll get Szymon to take you in one of the cars. It's the least I can do now you've made me feel like a real informant. Believe me, it'll save you a lot of time and you'll get a chance to travel in a flash motor.'

'Thanks. By the way. Those copper bracelets – they don't work.'

'No shit.'

Szymon, who only passed his test a week before and has serious ambitions to become a Formula One racing driver, gets me to Judd Street in precisely ten minutes in a Lotus Exige S2, which, he tells me, 'needed a good fuckin' blow out'. I won't cast aspersions on Szymon's driving, but compared to this journey, this morning's race up Harley Street on the wrong side of the road was like a restful half hour in a flotation tank.

Just as I'm getting out of the Lotus, Doug Teng calls me on my mobile. Sara's flat was clean and so are the offices at Maccanti. So at least there was no physical bugging or evidence of frequency interception, but it doesn't mean that someone wasn't listening in to the phone calls of Sara or her staff by other means. I'll have to put that information on ice until it becomes useful.

21

DOLLY'S NIGHTCLUB

Judd Street doesn't really look like the sort of place where you'd find an expensive nightclub, but as you walk further away from the St Pancras end, it gets rather more genteel and tree-lined and gradually more and more trendy restaurants and pubs start appearing, plus a small independent cinema.

I walk by Dolly's on the opposite side of the road. I wouldn't expect it to be open at this time of day, but I just want to get a quick look at its location and whether it's feasible for me to take a look inside if there's no one there.

There's a Japanese restaurant called Kanji, a pub and then Dolly's. If I didn't know the street number, I probably wouldn't have noticed it, and certainly wouldn't have identified it as a nightclub of any sort. There's a discreet white door right next to the pub. Single Yale lock, but despite the fact they've tried to disguise it, it's a steel security door, probably with an internal hinge chassis system. This would take less than ten minutes to get through, but I have no intention of attempting it, not in broad daylight and certainly not with thirteen people sitting outside the pub next door.

It looks as if Dolly's uses up the ground floor of the next three buildings along and possibly the basements, too. All of the ground floor windows are whited out and have dark brown wooden blinds outside.

The upper floors look like they're used as offices, and I can see two different company names in one of the windows on the first floor. There's a small gym on the third floor with people on exercise bikes wearing headphones. These other concerns are probably not connected with Dolly's and I suspect their opening hours would not coincide in any way.

A few doors away, there're two coffee bars and an estate agent's. On my side of the road there are three restaurants in a row (Turkish, Thai and Greek), a small supermarket and another pub. This is a busy area. I decide to see if I can take a look around the back, where there must be a service road of some sort.

Just as I'm crossing the road, my mobile goes off. It's Isolda.

'Are you OK?'

She sounds concerned.

'Sure. Why shouldn't I be OK?'

'Did you see the news? Oh my God, we've all been freaking out here. I can't get hold of Sara.'

'Hold on, hold on. What are you talking about?'

'It was on the television news. Rachelle Beauchesne. Some men attacked her in Baker Street and she's in a coma. Some building guy said he saw another woman attacked and pushed into some sort of jeep. A Range Rover or something, he thought. It must have been Sara, it *must* have been. She was going to have lunch with Rachelle today. The police are looking for the jeep. Is this more of the same? Is this the same people as all the other stuff? I've tried Sara's mobile, but she isn't answering.'

There are tears in her voice. I have to assimilate this

information quickly and decide what to do and say. Well, at least Rachelle's out of the loop for the moment and won't be talking to the police. Isolda didn't say anything about the car chase, which may well have been on the news if the police knew anything about it. I'm assuming they didn't. I think if I was a pedestrian and something like that passed me by, I'll be entertained, disturbed and amazed, but I don't think I'd call the cops. I'd leave that to someone else, like a typical don't-give-a-fuck Londoner.

Eventually, the police are going to get in touch with all of the staff at Maccanti, including the MTAs, and they're going to find out about me. I could play the game and give all of my information to them, but they'd have to fight their way through too much red tape to do anything quick and effective, and I think quick and effective is the way to go now.

I don't know Rachelle personally, but if I find Blue Suit again, he's going to get more than a battered face. I'm going to have to trust Isolda and tell her what's happened. If she thinks Sara has come to any harm, she'll be on the phone to the police. Maybe she's been in touch already.

'Isolda – when was all this on the news?'

'About five minutes ago.'

'Have you called the police?'

'No.'

'Good. Don't call them. Wait for them to call you, which'll be pretty soon, I would guess. Listen carefully. Sara is fine. She was abducted, but I managed to catch up with them and rescue her.'

'Oh, thank God. Where is she?'

'She's in my flat. She's safe. Please don't tell anyone

we've had this conversation.'

'I won't. Are you alright?'

'Yes.'

'I don't want you to get hurt.'

'I won't.'

'But if you did…'

'If the police ask, tell them you know that she hired a private investigator, but you don't know where I am or how to get in touch with me. There's no reason why you or anyone else should have my phone number, so they should believe you. I've got to go now; I'm following up a lead. I'll speak to you later. And remember – this conversation didn't happen.'

I'm sure Nick Sarna would have been delighted with that last comment.

'What can I do? There must be something I can do.' Her voice is trembling. Something in me wants to hold her. Something else wants me to tell her to pull herself together.

'I'll call you as soon as I know anything. Stay in the office. And don't worry. Just go with the flow. It'll be OK.'

'Are you sure?'

'Yes.'

I have to walk down half the length of the road before I spot the way around the back, in between a smart block of flats and a discreet new five-storey car park.

I made a point of counting how many buildings I passed so I could find the back entrance to Dolly's without any trouble, but there was no real need. Two hundred yards away, I can see the black SUV, parked on the right-hand side of the service road.

This means I have to be careful. One scenario could

be that Blue Suit and Blond Hair managed to get back here after their altercation with me and are now inside the nightclub, licking each other's wounds. That may not be the case, but I'm going have to act as if it is.

They may, of course, have just left the vehicle here temporarily and got themselves looked at. There's a big hospital complex about half a mile from here, but I'm not sure if it has an A&E department, which is certainly what my two friends will need, particularly Blonde Hair, after his inconvenient spot of brachial artery trouble.

I look behind me to see if anyone's hanging around, but it's clear like most service roads are. Keeping a careful eye on the buildings to my left, I walk past the SUV, quickly flicking the passenger door handle as I pass. It's locked and no alarm goes off. It's well placed in the road and hasn't been parked in a hurry.

Directly opposite is the back entrance to Dolly's. The pub next door has a small garden and there are maybe eight or nine people sitting outside, talking, drinking and smoking. No one is looking in my direction, and even if they were, they'd probably think nothing of it.

Dolly's can be reached by walking across a small yard with four big black portable bins and a sign on the wall with the club logo and underneath T.R.J.E Ltd in small black letters. I glance at the upper floors.

The only evidence of activity is on the second floor. There's a girl, probably an office worker of some type, holding a sheaf of papers and arguing with a fat guy with big circles of sweat under the armpits of his shirt. He has a supercilious expression on his face and is staring at her breasts as he talks.

Unbelievably, there's only a single large lock on the door into Dolly's and it takes an ordinary Yale key. I take my key chain out of my pocket. I started making Bump Keys years ago and always carry one just in case. It's just an ordinary Yale key with regularly spaced deep cuts filed into the business side. I guess the legal version of this would be called a Master Key or a Skeleton Key. I take it off the key chain and look for something I can hit it with. There's a rusted metal bar on the floor near one of the bins. Not perfect, but it'll have to do.

I push the Bump Key about two thirds of the way into the lock. It won't go in any further; they never do. I look over my shoulder and to my left and right to see if I'm clear, grab the metal bar in my right hand, press the bow of the key to the right with my thumb and hit it three times with the metal bar until it's in up to the hilt. It's not too noisy, but from the inside it may sound like someone's knocking on the door, so I wait for ten seconds and listen.

Nothing.

I turn the Bump Key to the right and the lock opens. Good. I remove the key, put it back on the key chain, open the door and go inside to be faced with total darkness and bone-chilling cold. I gently close the door behind me until I hear the click. It's so bright outside that it takes almost fifteen seconds for my eyes to get accustomed to the lack of light and even then I can only see vague outlines. I must eat more carrots.

I'm in a long, narrow corridor. I crouch down and pat my hands along the floor; some sort of ceramic tiling. There's a background noise of lightly running water, but I can't place where it's coming from; could be toilets somewhere in the building.

The walls either side of me feel like they're wallpapered. It's a remarkable thing; despite trying to convince myself that I'm just in some place that just happens to be without light at the moment, I always feel a worrying sensation of fear when I can't see where I'm going.

I stretch out a hand. I can see my fingers, so things can't be that bad. Keeping my hand in front of me, fingers stretched, I walk slowly along and wait for whichever tactile sensation I encounter first. After thirty seconds, I find it. It's a soft fabric, something like velvet, and it's covering another door. I run my hands over it until I find a handle. I grip it firmly and turn it down, then up. Thankfully, it opens, and I pull it towards me.

I can see what's going on now. This is a smartly decorated, well-lit little antechamber with male and female toilets to my right and three wood veneer doors to my left. One of these three doors says 'Kitchens. Private', another says 'Office' and the third one says nothing. The noise of running water is coming from the Ladies' toilet. I assume that the door with nothing on it leads directly into the nightclub, so decide to go and have a look.

It's much bigger than I imagined, and my guess about the club running into the buildings next door, at least on the ground floor, was correct.

Any type of club has a unique atmosphere and smell during the day when it isn't open to the public. It has a brittle, unsettling ambience, not helped by the total silence, as if it's waiting to be filled with people before it can properly be said to exist.

The predominant smell is of stale alcohol, but with notes of sweat, perfume, plastic and leather. In the past, you'd have smelt stale tobacco, but not anymore. All of the bars are closed up, with metal shutters preventing out-of-hours access to all the booze. It looks neat and tidy, so either it wasn't open last night or the cleaners come in for a few hours immediately after closing time.

There are no windows, and what illumination there is comes from bright sub-floor lighting, which I assume is left on twenty-four hours a day. There are lights on the walls, coloured LED spotlights and hanging from the ceiling are a dozen or so electric chandeliers and banks of hi-tech mobile disco lights, particularly over the dance floor area down the far end.

Most of the interior consists of long leather seating units, each with its own wide glass table. Each table has a couple of glass lamps, designed to look like chunky church candles.

Walking past the dance floor takes you to another seating area and then into a kind of restaurant zone, with smoked glass tables and chairs. To my untrained eye, it all looks pretty upscale. As Nick Sarna said, really expensive, but OK for a one-off visit for a special occasion.

A couple of double doors lead into the large reception area at the front of the building. There's a large cloakroom and more toilets. If there is a basement, there's no obvious way down to it that I can see. I go back to the antechamber and give the door of the office a try. It's locked. I can't be bothered with that at the moment, so try the kitchen. This is open.

It looks like any professional kitchen; the type you might find in a restaurant or club. It smells of lemon-scented cleaner and my footsteps echo as I walk around. Everything is stainless steel and meticulously tidy. Spotless preparation areas have shelves above them with piles of brand-new looking crockery and shiny steel and copper utensils.

I feel that I'm wasting my time and decide to take a

look at the office, but just as I'm about to leave I get a strong feeling that something's not right in here. I actually feel slightly dizzy and reach out to steady myself on one of the steel surfaces. Perhaps I'm suffering delayed shock from this morning's activities or, more likely, I'm just knackered.

On a whim, I walk down to the far end of the kitchen. There's a metal table on castors with what looks like a giant food mixer on top. There's a left turn into an area with more giant versions of stuff you'd see in a normal kitchen. Some of it is professional catering machinery, which I can't identify or see any use for.

There are three big steel bins with black bin bags hanging out of them. There's a loud air-conditioning noise down this end; it rattles like it needs to be fixed. There's a long steel table with a body on it. This is covered in a light brown sheet of some sort; cotton, by the look of it.

Even though I can't hear anything, I look over my shoulder and then walk back to check that the kitchen's still empty before I take a look at whoever this is. When I pull the sheet back, I'm not totally surprised to discover that it's Blond Hair.

No one's bothered to close his eyes. They've undone the top couple of buttons of his shirt, but that was never going to do much good. Just to be absolutely sure, I place two fingers against the pulse point on the side of his neck. Now I'm absolutely sure. On the side where I broke his elbow, the shirt is soaked with his blood and it's all down his trousers on that side. There's a big pool of blood on the floor underneath him.

His elbow is severely bruised with a big tear in the flesh and a large reddish patch on the reverse side of the bicep. Whoever brought him here, and I'm guessing it was Blue Suit, decided that there was no need to visit a hospital and Blond Hair simply bled to death or died of shock or a combination of both.

Well, that's too bad and it still doesn't tell me what I need to know, other than the pair of them were idiots.

Remembering the useful clue that I found in Blond Hair's jacket, I search his trouser pockets, but there's nothing in them at all. I'm going to have to break into the office.

As I turn around to leave the kitchen, I'm amazed to see a guy pointing a gun at me. I say amazed, because I really didn't hear anything at all, focused as I was on Blond Hair's cadaver. And the air-conditioning noise, of course. I've got a shitload of excuses and they all make me feel really efficient and professional. I'm annoyed with myself as I don't like to feel I'm slipping in any way. As I'm taking him in, I notice that he's not wearing any shoes. Smart.

He's in his twenties, pretty tall, beefy, bald, bearded and looks cut from the same mould as Blue Suit, except he's wearing a black suit. He's calm, curious, slightly annoyed and holding a Taurus PT 100. It's a nice-looking pistol, made in Brazil and popular with civilians in the US. Ten to fifteen rounds, depending on whether it's manufactured for the police or ordinary mortals.

I don't raise my hands or anything like that. That would indicate that I thought I was doing something wrong. It's a new theory and one I'm testing out for the first time.

'Who the *fuck* are you?'

'Health and Safety. I'm afraid we have some issues with corpses in food preparation areas. It's to do with bacterial cross-contamination.'

There's a millisecond, *a millisecond* where a flicker of doubt crosses his features, like he thinks that this preposterous story might be true, that someone who's obviously broken in to a locked premises to check kitchen hygiene and casually comments on a fresh corpse breaking H&S rules might be in any way sane and/or slightly honest. This tells me he isn't too bright.

He's holding the gun steadily and professionally and it's aimed at my head, grip in his right hand and his left hand supporting his right wrist. The safety is on, but his left hand is two inches away from it and he could flick it off in a second. I'm assuming it's loaded.

'Take your jacket off. Throw it towards me. Don't try anything stupid. I've got a gun.'

No shit.

I slowly remove my jacket, making a quick mental inventory of what's in the pockets: mobile, wallet, small pack of my business cards, tactical pen. If he's bright, which I don't think he is, it'll take him a couple of minutes to work out what I am and possibly even what I'm doing here.

My wallet contains the usual wallet stuff, plus six hundred bribery money. My business cards only have my name and my mobile number. My mobile will be virtually useless as I use initials and numbers for all contacts, and besides, it's got a difficult lock screen pattern, which I'm not going to help him with.

The tactical pen is actually (in my hands) a dangerous weapon, made from aircraft grade aluminium and used in the same way you'd use a Kubotan, a small martial arts weapon. Whether he'll recognise it as such is another thing altogether; most people don't, often to their cost.

I chuck the jacket so it lands at his feet.

'Right. Now put your hands behind your head. Remember. No clever stuff.'

I do what he says. No point arguing. Not yet, at least. Keeping the gun on me, he picks my jacket up and takes a cursory look at the contents. He takes the money out of the wallet and puts it in his pocket, smirking at me as he throws the wallet onto the floor. Good. It's not occurring to him to take a detailed look at everything as he has no idea who I might be or why I'm here.

'OK, my friend. Who are you and what are you doing here? Believe me; I'm not going to ask you twice.'

He's standing eight feet away from me, close enough for me to be able to smell the Hoppe's Precision Lubricating Oil that he's used on the Taurus. I can also smell some unpleasantly sharp aftershave or cologne.

Naturally, he's banking on me being a little in awe of the gun, but I don't think he'd really shoot. There's no silencer and that gun takes a .40 S&W; you'd hear a shot being fired in the pub next door and in the street. I just hope he knows this. I've got to think of something to delay him.

'I work for Keegan's. Keegan's Nightclub in King's Cross.'

'Never heard of them.'

Neither have I. I don't know what I'm talking about. He takes his mobile out of his pocket and presses something on it. As he's waiting for whoever it is to answer, I take a look at him. This is not one of Sara's assailants, at least not from her descriptions, anyway. How many of these people are there? What *is* this?

'They sent me here to check out the club and see if I could find out the money situation. I thought I'd be able to break into the office. They think you're not doing too well and were going to make you a rather aggressive offer. I just work for them. This is nothing to do with me. I don't know anything about their business matters.'

'Oh, really? This sounds like bullshit to me, my friend.'

That's a pretty fair comment, to be honest. 'Why don't you just let me go. Come on, mate. I haven't been able to get what I wanted.' I try to sound plaintive and pathetic; anything to make him think I'm no real threat to him. Anything to slightly alter the atmosphere; to get him off high alert.

Whoever he's calling responds. They say something. He laughs.

'Yeah, listen. I just popped into the club to pick some stuff up and there's this guy here. I don't know who the fuck he is and he's got some bullshit story about being from a club called Keegan's. Do you know anything about this?'

All the while, I'm watching and waiting. Waiting for a miniscule moment of relaxation, waiting for him to be distracted by something, waiting for something, anything, to happen; something that will kill his composure or impair his concentration; a noise, a gust of wind; anything.

The distance between us is too great for me to jump him; he'd easily have time to get the safety off and shoot me. But that option may be the only one I have. Maybe there isn't a bullet in the chamber. Maybe he's not a good shot, even at a distance like this. Maybe the gun will jam. I can feel the adrenalin starting to rev up inside me, my heart rate rising and my saliva starting to dry up.

He looks me over. His eyes have no humour in them whatsoever, just a vacant malevolence. He's got to be disposed of. He starts describing me to whoever's on the phone. It's almost flattering. Maybe we should get married and start a family. One day we'd talk about how we met and have a laugh.

'He's over six foot, early thirties, athletic build, dark brown hair and eyes, good-looking in a poncy actor way. Yeah – he's seen Robbie. He was looking at him when I came in. There's no way he's going anywhere after seeing that. Fuck, no. I didn't think of that. Hang on. Just *wait*!'

So that's Blond Hair's name: Robbie. Robbie Hyland. I'll try and remember that, for all the good it'll probably do me.

He reaches down and picks my wallet up. Unfortunately his concentration is good and he doesn't take his focus or the gun off me for a second. He takes one of my business cards out of the wallet, stares at it, and resumes his conversation. I notice that sweat is gathering on his upper lip and he's starting to smell.

'Daniel Beckett. It's on a poncy metal business card. No, me neither. There's a phone number. Look, can Jackie get a cab over and sort this out? I really haven't got the time and he likes this sort of thing. What do you mean? What?'

He has a hurried series of exchanges about Jackie and how they haven't seen him for over twenty-four hours. I soon pick up that they're talking about Footballer Dad.

'OK. OK. Well, send Derek over. I'll wait with this prick until he gets here. Someone better go round Jackie's flat and have a look. No, of course he hasn't got a fuckin' mobile. Are you kidding? You know what he's like about that sort of shit. What? Well, that's no good. Where's Derek now?'

I'm still watching, still waiting. He's having staff

problems. Perhaps it's an occupational scumbag hazard. There are a few physical signs that he's getting a little impatient and rattled; he's shaking his head, pouting and taking deep breaths.

'What? He's in Exeter Street? Where the fuck is Exeter Street?'

My stomach turns to water as I realise the missing piece of the jigsaw has just fallen into place.

Isolda.

22

BLACK SUIT

Isolda.

It was staring me in the face the whole time and I just didn't see it. I was too overwhelmed by her physicality, wanton beauty and the thrill of a fresh, voracious sexual encounter.

'OK,' says Black Suit. 'Well you've got to get someone else who can get over here and take over from me. I can't deal with this right now. I have to be up in Tottenham.'

Her concern for Sara, her sympathy for Sara, her admiration for Sara, her appreciation of Sara's talent, even her job title: *Most Trusted Assistant*.

'What about Oliver. Where is he at the moment?'

Using sex to distract me; to keep an eye on me. Her warped passion and taste for deviance keeping her on my mind when I should have been more focussed on the case and observing her more objectively.

Continually checking up on how I was doing; the phone calls, the trysts, the convincingly reluctant hints that Sara might be imagining the whole thing.

'Good. That's good. That's ten minutes away. Give him a call and tell him to get over here ASAP. He can park around the back. I'll disable this guy and then we can have a good chat with him later tonight.' He laughs coldly. 'Yeah. Yeah. With extreme prejudice. See you, mate.'

It explains how Blond Hair knew how to catch me as I was leaving the gym. No one knew where I was going apart from Isolda. All those suggestions about phones being tapped and premises being bugged were bullshit. Blond Hair was simply protecting his source. Ridiculously, I'm annoyed that I wasted Doug Teng's time and Sara's money.

'And give the boss a bell anyway. Ask about this Keegan's club thing. There might be something in it. This guy ain't going nowhere.'

And the most obvious factor; Isolda knew where Sara would be at all times, whether it cropped up on social media or not, whether it was professional or personal or somewhere in between. She knew where she lived and she knew her background; the nervous breakdown, what sort of person she was, how she could be intimidated, how to put her off her stroke.

And short of Sara announcing the fact on social media and in the press, there is no way on earth that anyone could know she was in my flat; only Isolda knew and she knew because I told her and I told her to make her feel better about Sara and I wanted her to feel better because I like her, perhaps a little too much if I'm being honest with myself, which I never am.

Hell.

'OK. Tell Oliver I'm waiting. Do it now. See you later.'

Black Suit flicks his mobile off and drops it in his jacket pocket. His attention is back on me. I have to get him out of the way so I can get over to Covent Garden. I may be too late, but I have to try, if only to see what's happened. Then I have to find Isolda.

'So here we are, Mr Daniel Beckett. We're going to wait for my associate to arrive, then we're going to restrain you and have a more detailed word this evening. Whether your story is true or not – and I don't think it is – you're in the deepest shit you've ever been in.'

He's a little more relaxed with me now. His focus has decreased slightly now he's sorted his personnel problem. I still have my hands behind my head.

'Can I sit down? All this standing up is getting a bit much.'

'Oh yeah. Sure. I'll get you a fuckin' comfy armchair. I'll tell you what, though. You can get down on your knees. That'll be nice and comfortable for you. Right down on your knees where you belong.'

I comply with his request and sit in the *seiza* position. He'll naturally think that I'm at a considerable physical disadvantage. Now I have to needle him, probably at tremendous risk to my life. Ah well. All part of the job.

'I'm afraid I don't have anything to tie you up with while we wait for my colleague,' he sneers. 'So I'm going to have to find something to knock you out cold with. Sorry about that, old chum. Can't spend all day aiming a gun at you. My arm's starting to ache.'

'That guy you were talking about on the phone. Jackie, was it?'

He looks baffled – firstly, that I should engage him in casual conversation and secondly that it should be about his phone call and someone he knows.

'What the hell's that got to do with you?'

'Is he like – you know – in his seventies? Quite rugged looking? White hair? Lined face? Bit of a gut. Swears a lot?'

Still holding the gun at my head, Black Suit takes a few

steps towards me. He looks suspicious, but he's curious at the same time.

'What do *you* know about him?'

'Well, he's dead. Sorry.'

I stop it there. I don't want to give him too much in one go. It may give him a headache and I wouldn't want that.

'What are you talking about?'

'Well, I had him in a lock-up last night and I was torturing him and he died.'

He chuckles. 'What a fuckin' load of shit. You? How were *you* torturing Jackie? He could beat the crap out of someone like you.'

I keep my voice calm and soft, as if I'm talking about a visit to the theatre. 'I'm not saying he's not a strong guy, but that's what happened. I think he may have died of heart failure or suffocated or something. I'm not a doctor; it can be hard to tell sometimes. He was tied up and I'd stuffed a wet towel halfway down his throat.'

He's getting angry now. He doesn't really believe me, but he can't deny that I gave him a good description of Footballer Dad. The tops of my arms are aching from clasping them behind my neck.

'You don't say things like that. You don't talk about people like that. Jackie's my uncle. That's family. You don't talk about family like that.'

He's waving the pistol at me, but still hasn't taken the safety off. I'm trying to get his attention away from the gun and onto me. I think I'm succeeding.

'OK. He's not dead. Everything's alright. I'm just lying to amuse myself.' I tilt my head to the side and look him straight in the eye. 'And I'm a little reluctant to tell you this under the circumstances, but your mate Robbie on the table over there? I'm afraid that was me, too.'

'Yeah. Sure it was.'

He looks at me as if I'm some nutbag who goes around confessing to crimes he didn't commit. I have no idea which road this is taking me down, but anything's better than a stalemate.

'He used to be in the police, didn't he? Robbie. Carries a knuckleduster. He was on the point of using it on me this morning, but I didn't really want that, so I broke his elbow over my shoulder. This caused the bone to splinter and rupture a major artery. I think he probably bled to death. To be honest, he should have been taken to a hospital immediately. You can go and check the injury if you don't believe me.'

He doesn't respond. He's trying to take all of this in and make his mind up whether any of it could be true. His eyes harden and a petulant little pout appears on his mouth. He flips the gun around in his hand so he's holding the barrel. Excellent. He's considering pistol-whipping me while I'm on my knees in front of him. I'm controlling him now, but he doesn't realise it yet.

'I'll tell you – Robbie there screamed so loudly when I did that to him that I've still got ringing in my ears from it. But Jackie…'

'You better shut your mouth right now, friend.'

'Jackie was pathetic. Or should I call him Uncle Jackie. Jackie is normally a girl's name, isn't it? Anyway, Uncle Jackie was very tough at first, kept telling me that I didn't know who I was dealing with and all that sort of threatening crap that idiots like him come up with when they know they're in deep shit. When they're pissing themselves with fear, which is what good old Uncle Jackie did.'

He's glowering. His face is darkening. I wonder how close he and Uncle Jackie were? Maybe they used to go fishing together. Maybe Uncle Jackie was like a father to him. He's willing me not to go on. His grip on the gun barrel is making his knuckles white. His body odour is getting worse.

'Then he started crying and begging for mercy.'

'Right, you fuck.'

With the gun in his right hand he swings it over his left shoulder to get momentum and slashes it down towards my face. If you telegraph your moves like this, you have to expect the worst and that's what he's going to get.

Still on my knees I block his arm with my left hand, grab his elbow, turn sharply to my right and slam him down on the floor, face first, pinning his arm at the shoulder and the wrist. It all happened so fast I didn't see what happened to his gun, but heard it slide across the floor somewhere. I'll worry about that later.

I move in close to him, bring his arm up high behind his back, close my eyes tightly and wrench it towards his head as hard as I can, dislocating his shoulder. I do it so well I can feel the dull thump as the bone pops out of the socket. He shrieks, as well he might.

I get up and pat him down. No other weapons. I take his wallet and retrieve my money, plus all of his, which comes to a tidy five hundred. He's panting, sobbing and in considerable pain and distress. He remains face down as he can't do much else. It takes me thirty seconds to find his gun, which had skittered along the floor and hidden itself under some drawers near one of the ovens.

I get my jacket back on, stick the gun in an inside pocket and head for the office. I've got no time for subtlety, so I take a step back and kick the door hard, about a foot below the lock. It splinters and opens straight away. I turn the lights on and look around.

I'm looking for two things; the keys to the SUV and something to tie Black Suit up with. He's coming with me. I'm not going to leave him here to report to whichever gorilla turns up. He's a loose end and I can't afford any at the moment. I've probably got a little over five minutes to sort this.

There's a filing cabinet, but it's locked. No time for that. I frantically search the desk for the keys but can't find anything. Did Blue Suit take them with him when he left here? I'm about to give up, then I see what looks like a psychedelic penholder on the windowsill. Two pens poking out and there are the keys, attached to a big purple and green Venture Cars key ring, which is hanging over the side. I grab the keys and drop them into my pocket. Let's hope they're the right ones. I think they are.

I take a quick look around but can't see anything I can use to tie Black Suit up with. I go back into the kitchen and rapidly open drawer after drawer. Finally I find a ball of white cooking string. Not really what I'm after, but it'll have to do. In another drawer there's a small amount of silver duct tape left on a small roll, so I take that as well.

I manhandle Black Suit to a sitting up position. He moans as my hand grips him under the armpit where the dislocation happened. I squat in front of him and slap his face to get his attention. He's sweating and shivering.

'This is what's going to happen. I'm going to use this string to tie your hands behind your back. It's going to be very painful because your shoulder's dislocated. But once I've finished it'll settle as long as you don't move a muscle.

'I'm going to tape your mouth up because you're

probably going to want to scream a few times over the next few minutes. Then we're going out to the SUV. You're going in the boot. Getting you in will hurt. Once you're in there, I'm tying your ankles together. Keep still and the pain will be minimal. Move around and you won't believe what happens. Got it?'

He nods his head. He's defeated. He's perspiring. He's as white as a sheet. I wind a couple of feet of duct tape around his head, covering his mouth. I can hear a low, guttural scream trying to escape from his throat as I whip both arms behind his back and tie his wrists together. This sort of string would be totally useless under normal circumstances, but not when one of your shoulders is as wrecked as his is. I wind it round and round; it looks OK.

I grab his arms on the bicep. 'Now you're going to stand up. It will hurt as I help you up. You will scream. You will not faint. Then we're going outside. One, two…'

Another muffled, agonised scream and he's on his feet. His eyes roll up into his head. We get out of the kitchen and into the antechamber. I hold the back of his neck to guide him as he staggers along. I just hope he doesn't faint; that would be a real pain. Then we're outside. I press the control on the keys and the SUV's lights flash. Thank God for that.

I check the service road to make sure it's clear and walk Black Suit over to the SUV. I open the boot and indicate he should get in. He sits down and swings his legs to the left, propping himself up against the side. I tie his ankles together with the string. Again, bloody useless, but I don't think he'll get a chance to untie himself.

I slam the boot shut, get in the driver's seat and turn the engine over, wondering how long it'll take me to get to Covent Garden in weekday traffic. That's the problem with Szymon; he's never around when you need him.

23

LOVERS' TIFF

When I get to Exeter Street, I stop at the end of the road and wait. I can feel my heart thumping in my chest. I can hear Black Suit groaning in the back. I hope the string holds. Nothing's parked here as there are double yellow lines on each side of the road.

The only visible vehicle is a small van parked up on the pavement delivering stuff to a nearby restaurant. It says Orel Fruit Supplies on the side of the van. A tall girl appears wearing a polo shirt with the same logo on the front. On the right, there's a woman picking up a load of shopping from the floor, the result of a split carrier bag. On the left, two Chinese teenagers walk along arguing, passing a spliff to and fro and laughing.

All quiet.

I get out of the SUV, lock it and pat the side of my jacket to make sure I'm still carrying Black Suit's Taurus PT 100. I try to avoid carrying guns, but these people seem to find them useful and I don't want to walk in on one of them without some sort of ballistic assistance.

The ground floor entrance to my flat is closed, so at least they didn't smash the door down, if, indeed, they've got here yet. On the way up the stairs, I take the safety off the Taurus and slide a bullet into the chamber. I realise now that I could have taken Black Suit when he had this aimed at my head, but I couldn't have known that at the time, so tough luck me.

I'm as quiet as I can be under the circumstances. I concentrate on each step I take, putting firm pressure on each wooden tread to avoid any creaking. I can feel my hand sweating on the grip of the gun and I'm aware of each small noise, each alteration in atmosphere. I'm conscious of vague and unfamiliar scents; sour male sweat, cheap deodorant, Sara's perfume.

After what seems like hours, I'm standing outside the door to my flat. I place the palm of my hand against it and apply the tiniest amount of pressure, all the while listening for sounds from within. The door is closed. The locks don't seem to be damaged. Whoever broke in would have to be a pretty skilled burglar; perhaps the same person who got into Sara's flat.

I think of Isolda saying how all that burglarising business at Sara's gave her the creeps.

Slowly and as quietly as possible, I turn both locks over at the same time and tap the door open with my foot. I stand at the entrance for a moment. The scents I noticed on the stairs are marginally stronger in here. I close my eyes for a couple of seconds, trying to sense a presence inside. There's nothing, so I walk in, checking each room, negotiating the nightingale floor and looking around for signs of disturbance. I hold the gun straight ahead at eye level, my finger lightly resting on the trigger.

I tap the bedroom door open with my foot and look inside. When I left here, Sara was lying on the bed. I can still see her shape on the top sheet. Everything looks OK and there seems to have been no sign of a struggle. How did they get in without her noticing? Did the squeaks from the nightingale floor not wake her? How did they get her out of here without it being conspicuous? None of that matters. Bottom line is she's gone and it's partly my fault.

*

When I get to Maccanti, I get buzzed in and take the stairs three at a time, not bothering to wait for the lift. When I get to reception, I run straight into Melody Ribeiro, almost knocking her down.

'Where's Isolda?'

'God Almighty. What *has* that girl got?'

I'd almost forgotten how attractive Melody was and it was what – a few hours ago that I last saw her? How time flies.

'It's nothing to do with that. Where is she?'

'She's in Sara's office. Look, if you ever…I mean, if you and her…'

But I don't stay to listen to whatever it is. I stride down the corridor towards Sara's office. Her door is closed. I've got to control myself and not raise my voice. I mustn't do anything to distract Isolda while I get the truth out of her.

I push the door wide open with the ball of my hand. She's leaning over Sara's book table. She's still wearing the maroon wrap-around cardigan and my eyes go straight to her inflammatory cleavage and the wide swell of her breasts. I have to stop this right now.

When she sees me, she stops what she's doing, runs towards me and puts both of her arms around my neck, pressing herself against me. I don't reciprocate, and hold my arms out to the side like it's a stick-up.

When she speaks, there a hint of a sob in her voice,

but I don't think it's connected to what she's about to say. I think it's connected to the fact that she knows she's been found out.

'Oh, thank God you're here. What's going on, Daniel? I've been so worried. How's Sara? How's she coping with all of this? I'm going to have to find out which hospital Rachelle's been taken to. Do you think they'll let me see her? What sort of people would do something like that?'

She gasps with pleasure as I grab both of her shoulders, then looks dismayed as I push her down onto a chair. I lean against the edge of the table. I fold my arms. I make my face expressionless. I look directly into her eyes and I can tell it's giving her the wrong type of chill.

'Sara's gone, Isolda. Whoever the hell they are, they've taken her. They've been in my flat and they've taken her.'

She covers her mouth with her hand. 'Oh my God.'

'What's going on, Isolda? I tell you I've got Sara at my flat. Ten minutes later I hear my address mentioned by a gun-wielding thug whom I know to have direct links to Sara's harassment and abduction.

'No one else knew where Sara was. Only you. I rush back to my flat and there's no sign of her. I don't think she popped out to watch *The Lion King* or do a bit of souvenir shopping, do you? Not after some piece of shit had tried to kidnap her.'

'I don't know what you mean, I…'

'Listen.' I spit the word out with enough *ki* to make her jerk back in her seat. 'I don't know why, but I know you're somehow involved in this if not actually behind all of it. I tell you which gym I'm going to and when I leave I've got some bent ex-cop on my tail wielding a pack of bribery money and telling me to get lost.

'I tell you where I'm keeping Sara and people break into my flat and take her away. You're the only possible culprit. You know where Sara's going to be the whole time. You know where she lives, you know what she's like, you know what work she's doing and you know what it would take to put her off her stride.

'You've got to tell me right now. I don't know what they're going to do with Sara but I can't imagine it's good. Her life is probably in danger. Maybe they want her for something else; something I can't imagine. I don't know. But every second that goes by makes it worse for her. Now you can tell me of your own volition or I can make you tell me. It doesn't make any difference to me.'

She starts sobbing, her hand up against her face, her body convulsing. She hyperventilates, trying to catch my eye the whole time, trying desperately to work that magic on me once again, but I've already cut her out of my emotions.

'Please. I swear. I haven't got anything to do with this. I'm just so worried about Sara and Rachelle…'

'Bullshit. You don't give a toss about Sara or Rachelle. If you did, you wouldn't be involved in this and you are most certainly involved in it. Do I look that stupid, Isolda?'

'How can you say things like that to me?' She looks up, her eyes moist, her lips trembling. 'Even if the last couple of days have meant nothing to you, they certainly have to me. I've never felt like this about anyone.'

Here we go.

'Shut up. Tell me what's going on. Last chance.'

Melody pops her head around the door to see what all the fuss is about. She takes a look at the red-eyed Isolda, then observes my dark expression. I turn to look at her.

'Lovers' tiff.'

'Ah. OK. Sorry.'

She backs out of the room just as one of the phones goes off. This is too busy here: too many distractions. I grab Isolda's arm and pull her up to her feet. She looks sullen; she's given up the faking. We go down the stairs that I went down with Sara on my first day here.

I remember the moment that Sara tripped and almost fell and I grabbed her. That was when I realised she was on medication. And now she's gone. I'm still not close to finding out the cause for all of this this, but I'm getting closer.

I parked the SUV in Manchester Square, with Black Suit presumably still in agony in the boot, if he hasn't gone the way of Footballer Dad. I march Isolda towards it and we get in. I must remember to let Venture Car Hire know where their vehicle is when I've finished with it, whenever that will be.

I spot a traffic warden watching me. I get Isolda into the passenger seat, walk around and get in the driver's side. I take off my jacket and shove it in the back, noticing for the first time that the seat and the floor beneath it are covered in blood. I think of taking the gun out of the jacket and sticking it somewhere else, but I don't want Isolda to see it, so I leave it where it is. Producing a gun right now would freak her out completely.

'Right. Let's have it. You're not leaving here until you've told me everything.'

I rest my hands on the steering wheel and look straight ahead. Sometimes not making eye contact helps people spill their guts more readily.

I keep an eye on her with my peripheral vision. She's

looking at a couple of colourful hanging baskets attached to a lamppost. Mainly pink and purple. Mainly petunias. She watches a couple of elderly tourists walk towards us, then watches them as they walk past.

She starts to bite one of her fingernails, then thinks better of it and wipes the saliva off onto her skirt. She clenches and unclenches her fists. She looks at me; I don't react. She looks out of the window again. Then she starts talking.

'It's my father.'

'*What*? What is? What's your father?'

'I don't know where to start. My father's Tommy Jennison.'

She turns to look at me as if this name may mean something to me. It doesn't.

'I don't know who that is.'

'I was afraid when Sara hired you that you might be ex-police. Lots of private investigators are, apparently. I was so relieved when Sara happened to mention that you weren't.'

'What difference would that have made to you?'

'This is a difficult thing for me to talk about and I've never really spoken about it to anyone before. It really, really isn't the sort of thing you tell people.'

I've started her off. I won't respond now. I'll just let it flow. She's crying, but this time the tears seem genuine.

'When I was two, my dad went to prison. It was in all the papers, but I don't really remember it, you know? It was a twenty-three-year sentence, but he got out after about sixteen years.'

She runs a hand through her hair and shakes her head. This releases a cloud of her perfume into the air. I have to concentrate.

'He'd been like, I suppose, a career criminal; mainly protection and extortion at first, but he'd also taken part in some big robberies. You have to understand that even now I don't know the whole extent of what he did. It wasn't something he was going to tell me about. I think the robberies were mainly to do with security vans, things like that. Some of them were quite violent.

'It was all very well organised. He had like a 'family' of people who worked for him. He was opportunistic; he'd sometimes rob things like fur warehouses; anything where a lot of big money could be made. My grandmother told me she remembered the house being full of mink and silver fox furs and the awful smell they made. She was afraid of catching anthrax. Whatever, he was a big name in the criminal underworld and was very successful.'

The atmosphere is a little calmer, and even though there are tears streaming down her face, she's stopped sobbing. I'm going to push her along now. This is going too slowly for my liking and I can't see any relevancy yet. I'll start gently.

'OK. What happened that caused him to go to prison?'

'I still don't know the precise details, but it was to do with someone from a rival operation. Something to do with rival criminal operations after the same thing, you know? It was always happening, apparently. Anyway, he…'

She suddenly brings a hand up to her mouth and the sobs wrack her body once more. Whatever this is, it's a painful memory. I decide to shut up and let it come out naturally. If the flow stops, it may be to Sara's disadvantage. I have to keep thinking of Sara.

'There was a man called Jason Marshall. He'd been running an operation much like Dad's. As I said, I don't know precisely what led to all of this. Dad and one of his friends lifted him and tortured him pretty horribly. Dad's friend was a man called Jack Heath. Dad and him had been in school together. They'd know each other for years.

'Jack Heath was a pretty inventive enforcer and torturer. He liked doing it and was full of ideas. People were afraid of him. He and Dad hammered six-inch nails into Jason Marshall. I think this went on for a long time. He almost died. He was certainly finished physically and mentally.'

Jack Heath? This must be Uncle Jackie aka Footballer Dad. It always does the heart good to know you've offed a major lowlife, even if accidentally.

'Dad didn't know that the police were observing him for something else altogether; one of his jobs, I mean. There was one particular police officer, a detective, who'd been on Dad's case for three years or more. The police were always after him, but they could never get a conviction. He was too smart for them.

'This detective was hoping to catch Dad with a load of stolen goods from a warehouse robbery at some electrical goods place in Lewisham or somewhere. Maybe it was Ladywell, not Lewisham. Instead, he and his men came upon this torture scene.

'It was a big thing. Finally, after all those years, someone had got something on Tommy Jennison. He seemed to be invulnerable and it really pissed the police off. The upshot was that both he and Jack Heath were arrested, charged and put away. Can you…'

She opens the door. I reach out to stop her, but she's only going to be sick in the road. She spits a few times and gets back in, shutting the door again.

'I don't understand, Isolda. I don't understand what this has got to do with all that's been going on with Sara.'

'I have to tell you all of this, so you'll see how it's happened. When my father went to prison, my mum coped for a while, but she committed suicide when I was six. She took an overdose of paracetamol. I don't really know why. She just…I don't know.' She stops to wipe the tears out of her eyes. 'After that, I was brought up by my grandmother; my dad's mum.

'It wasn't too bad, except she was ill a lot of the time and couldn't do parent stuff with me; take me to places. It was a bit grim. I never had birthday parties and could never have friends around. I had friends in school, but my grandmother wouldn't have them in the house and their parents didn't want them hanging around with me anyway. I never visited Dad in prison. It was just never on the cards.

'We lived in this huge house because of Dad's money from his jobs. The police or the courts took a lot, but they couldn't take everything. They couldn't take the house, and a lot of the money was invested in various things that no one knew about, so it was out of their reach.

'When Dad got out, I was eighteen. I was like this person he didn't know. He felt really upset, guilty and angry that he'd missed me growing up. He was really, really guilty about Mum killing herself. He felt that was his fault, too, and I suppose it was. Before she killed herself, she had lots of affairs and he found out about some of them and had the perpetrators taken care of whenever he thought he could get away with it.

'As a result of all of that, there was nothing he wouldn't do for me. When I wanted to be a fashion designer, he backed me all the way. When I was in St Martin's, he set me up in a fabulous flat in Notting Hill so I wouldn't have to live like a student. He hated that. He hated students. I had a ball. Everything I wanted I could have, whether it was books, clothes, holidays – you name it.

'Dad soon got back into his old ways again once he was out, but on a more subtle level. I don't really know what he gets up to now and I don't want to. He's often said that he won't tell me for my own protection. He owns a couple of nightclubs, but I haven't been to any of them. I think they're just fronts for the taxman and the law.

'Whatever he does, I always feel he's a little ashamed because of what happened when I was small, but it's like it's all he can do, you know? I'm surprised he's still at it, to be honest. I thought he might have retired by now. Maybe he can't.'

She turns to me and puts a hand on my thigh. 'You liked it with me, didn't you? I'm good at it, aren't I? I thought some of it might freak you out, but it didn't, did it. Some men I've been with, they won't go along with…'

'Can we get on with it, Isolda? We really can't waste any time now.'

She looks away sharply. Despite herself, she's still trying it on. She smiles at me, then opens the car door and throws up again. At least the vomit looks genuine.

24

THE CAMPAIGN

We both stare out of the windows of the SUV, watching tourists, watching people embarking from taxis, watching the wind blow the leaves on the trees. I start wondering about how they managed to take Sara from my flat without a struggle. Was it one monumental punch in the face again, like in Baker Street? I get a chill in my stomach when I remember she was only wearing my sweatshirt.

It concerns me that she's so attractive and what thugs like these guys might decide to do to her. Perhaps they just aimed a gun at her head and simply told her to come quietly or else. What were the chances of someone being escorted out of my flat at gunpoint and nobody noticing? Moderate, I would say. Apart from the evenings, Exeter Street is pretty deserted, three or four people walking around at the most, many of them lost or going somewhere else.

'I was good at St Martin's,' continues Isolda after a few minutes, 'but I wasn't good *enough* and I knew it. Some people have a natural talent for design. Ideas just pop into their heads. They can't get them down on paper fast enough. One girl I knew said she could actually close her eyes and see models walking by wearing all these clothes she'd been thinking about. All she had to do was to sketch them as quickly as she could before they vanished from her thoughts. I was so jealous of that. That was the exact opposite of what it was like for me.

'For me it was a slog. I used to read book after book about top designers from the past. My flat was like Sara's office. I just hoped that if I read enough and practised enough and looked at enough pictures and went to enough fashion shows that some of it would rub off on me and one day I'd just be magically able to do it like the big names.

'I'd always been good at drawing and had a good sense of what colours to use. I knew what was good and bad and understood the history of the whole thing. But when it came to coming up with the goods I knew deep down that I couldn't cut it.

'When I graduated, I could probably have got a job with some Z-grade manufacturer, designing clothes for some bloody supermarket chain's own brand or something, but I wanted to be up there at the top, I wanted to be involved with haute couture, I wanted to *be* somebody.'

'So the closest you could get to the top echelons was being an MTA to someone who already *was* somebody,' I say, the whole mess starting to coalesce in my mind, at long bloody last.

'Exactly that. Top designers will always want assistants who know the score as far as design goes. They want someone smart, someone who knows all the history, someone who they can bounce ideas off, someone who can tell them when they're repeating themselves or are being unconsciously derivative. If you've got a BA in fashion from St Martin's they'll know you've got the stuff to be a good MTA.

'As long as you present yourself well at the interview;

as long as you look the part and sound enthusiastic. And I was good at that – sounding enthusiastic, I mean. And thanks to Dad I had all the latest clothes. I knew I looked spectacular.

'Fashion designers are confident, bright, fun, outgoing people. They like having people like me around them. I was a real fashionista. Maccanti was big, Sara was becoming big – it was exactly where I wanted to be, even if I wasn't actually doing the designing.'

'So you started working for Sara.'

'Yes. I have to say that it irritated me straight away that she had so much going for her so soon. She had – well, I wouldn't call it a stroke of luck – she had *life circumstances* that favoured her getting on in the fashion world. She had the gift, of course, just like I was telling you before. Ideas simply pour out of her. But her family background, even though it was unfortunate, certainly gave her an advantage.'

'Tell me.'

'Her father died when she was fairly young. He had a heart condition. Her mother remarried. Her stepfather was American and they relocated to New York when Sara was in her teens.'

'So did her stepfather have some influence in the fashion industry? Did he give her a leg up?'

'Oh no. Nothing like that. But he was pretty well off and easily able to foot the bill for a suitable university education for her. Sara was very good at art while she was in school. One of her teachers suggested that she think about going to Brown's. I mean, that is *the* way to do it if you're going into fashion design. A liberal arts degree from Brown's, then an MA from St Martin's. So she left Brown's with her BA and then came to London. She was certainly a high flyer when she was at St Martin's. We weren't contemporaries, we just missed each other, but everyone was still talking about her and you were shown her work as an example of *what to do*.

'I'd heard that she had some sort of breakdown and took some time off while she was at St Martin's, but she picked herself up again and just finished the course with honours.

'After London, it just took her five years to get to where she is today, which is absolutely amazing. And she's amazingly popular. Everyone loves her. It helps that she's so cute and pretty, I guess, but so, *so* bloody talented. God knows where she'll be in five years.'

'OK, Isolda. So what happened? What started to go wrong for you?'

She looks down at her lap, brushing imaginary lint off her skirt. 'You keep a lid on it, you know? I knew that I could never be like Sara. I'd always known that. And I really admired her. I loved her work. But her progression and acclaim was *so* fast, *so* meteoric that it started to grate.

'It was as if she had a charmed life. I'd sit in at meetings with her and she'd be coming out with all these great ideas and I'd wish she'd shut up, you know? It was like being bludgeoned with greatness. It really started to get annoying.

'I didn't have anything to complain about, not really, and it's been a great ride working for her for the last two years, but it must have been the gap between us that began to irk me. It was so big. Her success as a designer and my lack of it; it was like a worm, burrowing away day and night. She never said anything, but I knew that she must have regarded me as an inferior in some way. That might not be true, of course, but it was the way I looked at it. I couldn't help myself.

'She knew, obviously, that I'd done my BA at St Martin's and all that, so it was clear that I'd originally wanted to do what she did. We never talked about it, of course, not even at my interview. She was so nice. It might have been preferable if she'd had been a bitch, do you know what I mean? But generally it was all OK. I managed to suppress it all. I wasn't unhappy or anything like that, you know?

'I've always had a great time at Maccanti and I've always had a great time working for Sara. In fact, I sometimes resented how I was feeling. I resented *myself*, if you like. I actually thought of going to see a psychiatrist or psychologist about it. Someone who could talk me through it and help me eradicate it all. But in the end I didn't bother. I just let it happen. I just let it eat away at me.'

I'm getting bored with this now and I start to wonder whether she's just buying time, for herself or for someone else. It's all very interesting, though, if you're intrigued by self-pitying psychobabble.

Anyway, we're a little further on than we were five minutes ago and I still get a strong feeling that she'll just shut down if I push her too hard and I can't have that happening, not when I'm so close.

While I'm waiting, I try to remember how long I've been on this case and it's difficult. Then I realise that this only Day Two. This wouldn't be bad progress at all, were it not for the fact that my client has been abducted from right under my nose.

'So what happened next, Isolda? Can we move forward a little?'

'It was about a month and a half ago. Sara had a

meeting with me, Melody, Gaige and Maria Auclair, the business head. She said she intended to try something that was either going to make us all groan with all the work it would involve or it would be the most exciting thing we'd ever heard of.

'She was going to attempt to do the autumn Milan and New York Fashion Weeks simultaneously. Well, almost simultaneously, maybe three days break in between the two. No one had done it. Everyone went *WOW* and we all leapt around, but – and I couldn't understand it and tried to suppress it – I felt really tearful.'

'I understand.'

'Do you?'

'The meteoric rise, the talent, the energy, the industry and public reception to her work and to her as a person – *and now this.*'

She half laughs and wipes away a tear that's slowly falling down her cheek. 'So a couple of nights later I was round my dad's place for dinner. My grandmother was there, too. We were just talking about this and that and Dad started asking me about work and what the famous Sara was doing and I told him about the shows. My dad must have seen there was something wrong and pressed and pressed and pressed until I came out with it.

'I started crying. I couldn't help myself. All of it came out in one tearful torrent; the fact that I was only a few years younger than her, the fact that we'd both been to fashion school but she was doing it and I was only a helper, the fact that nothing could stop her and she'd been going from one success to another since she'd started and now this amazing thing she was going to do with New York and Milan. It was as if I'd chosen the worst possible person to be associated with. I was hand in glove with someone who was everything that I wasn't.

'After a while I stopped. I was shocked. Shocked with what I'd come out with and shocked by myself. I was jealous of her. I was jealous of Sara Holt. I'd never thought it before and I'd certainly never said it out loud. I couldn't believe it. It was like a weight had been lifted. This is going to sound ridiculous, but I felt cleansed by thinking it. I actually felt physically lighter.

'My dad was clearly upset. He'd helped me so much – as much as he could, anyway. And here I was in my mid-twenties and seriously unhappy. I could see his mind ticking over. I could see he was trying to think of something he could do to alleviate my pain. Then he came up with it. Nothing too nasty. Nothing physical. Just a few scary encounters to spook her. Not regular; just now and again. Just enough to put her off her stroke.

'I'd told him that she seemed highly-strung and had had some sort of nervous breakdown in the past. I think that's why he thought of The Campaign, as he called it.'

Jesus Christ. 'And you didn't try and stop him? Discourage him? You saw the effect it was having on Sara. You could have gone to the police straight away. If you'd have done that, we wouldn't be in the mess we're in now.'

'How…' She sighs, pulls down the sun visor and examines her face in the vanity mirror, wiping the smudged makeup from around her eyes with the tip of a finger. Her movements are so delicate, vulnerable and feminine that it's difficult to not want to reach out and touch her and comfort her.

'How could I possibly have reported him to the police? He's my father. I owed him so much. He thought he was doing the best for me. And he's still involved in some heavy stuff, you know? Not as bad as in his heyday, but the last thing he'd want would be the police sniffing around for something like this. And with his past record, they'd take what he was doing very seriously indeed.'

She turns to face me for the first time since we've been sitting here. I try to keep my expression blank.

'You don't know what he's like. Once he's got something in his head he's unstoppable. All the ideas pile into his head one after another and he has to carry them out. Besides, I thought it would be untraceable, do you understand? It would just seem like a random load of events. Never the same people twice. It would just seem like typical London stuff. He didn't mention breaking into her flat, but he said there were things he could do that would make Sara think she was going a bit batty. Those were his words: *a bit batty*.

'It seemed harmless enough. I was the only one she confided in at first. It was hard not to laugh because I knew who was doing it and why. It was me who suggested she get a bodyguard and that translated into you.

'I never thought she'd take it all so seriously that she'd hire someone to investigate it. I thought when the police couldn't find anything that would be the end of it. I didn't even think she'd get the police involved. It was all deniable stuff. All of it could be explained away.'

She starts crying again. I fold my arms. Well, at least my guess about all this having all the hallmarks of professionals was correct. Her father must have got all his bent mates to chip in on this. He'd sling them a wad of cash, tell them what to do and let them get on with it.

They probably all thought it was a big laugh. Freaking out some fashion designer bird who'd got too big for her boots. Instead, he'd got a perfectly charming, hard-working, talented woman on diazepam, worried out of her mind, frightened for her safety and wondering if she was going insane.

He'd also pushed two of his foot soldiers directly into my path where they met a sticky end. He could never have banked on that happening in a million years and I'm wondering what he'll do when he finds out. As if on cue, Black Suit does a little bit of pained murmuring from the boot, which makes Isolda jump.

'What was that?'

'Just some guy. I'll tell you about it later. Listen, Isolda. This has become really serious now. You're in a lot of shit. And I suspect Sara's in real danger. But there's one thing I still don't understand. When did this suddenly change from harassment to abduction? What happened?'

She looks down again and shakes her head from side to side. 'It was my fault, but I didn't realise what I'd done until it was too late. It was yesterday. I had lunch with Dad.'

'I remember. Romanian restaurant. You looked slightly perturbed when the subject was brought up.'

'He was a bit concerned that Sara had hired you. He asked about you; what sort of person you were, whether you looked like you might have been police, whether you might have heard of him or any of his friends. I told him no.

'He wanted to know whether or not you could handle yourself in a fight. That seemed important to him. I told him that I had no idea, that I didn't know anything about you.

'I told him that you'd been recommended to Sara by a woman called Gracie Short who did a fashion blog. I thought you'd handled some sort of marital problem for her. Apart from that, we didn't really know anything about you. I think he tried to check you out on the Internet, but found nothing.'

Her face is soaked with tears now. There's still something in me that wants to touch that face, to wipe those tears away, but that isn't going to happen.

'Daniel – I hope you don't think that you and me…that I came on to you because of all of this…'

'That's exactly what I think.'

That was a cruel shot, but it's just tough luck and she has to take it on the chin. I don't really know if that's true; whether I really *do* think that her interest in me was one hundred per cent to do with the case.

Part of me would like to think it wasn't. Part of me would like to think it was genuine. Part of me would like to take her; here, now, in broad daylight in Manchester Square.

I can recall the immediate, provocative body language, the continuous, casual touching, the teasing eye contact. Sensing that I was attracted to her and getting me to take her to dinner when we barely knew each other. The whole thing was probably just an added, enjoyable bonus for her; a bit of fun, just like Sara's harassment.

I try to remember every single word we've spoken over the last few days; her reluctant but steady questioning about the case, her touching concern for Sara. Could all of it have been fake? I really have no idea, but I have to assume it was. I have to be extremely careful dealing with her now. I have to treat her as the enemy. When I think of all the progress reports I'd given her I could kick myself into the middle of next week.

'I wanted to get close to you, it's true.' She continues.

'That was the reason I suggested going to The Perfume River. I thought I could get an idea of how likely it was that Dad's activities could be detected, how likely it was that you'd see that it wasn't all in Sara's mind.

'That date was ostensibly meant to be a professional evening; concerned colleague seeing if she could help in any way. I thought I may get enough info from that evening to tell Dad to back off, if I thought that's what was needed. That's what was in my mind at first, anyway.

'But as soon as I walked in that bar – perhaps even before that – I could tell by the way you looked at me that you wanted to sleep with me. And that's a turn on for me, it always is. I never get used to it.

'And as I listened to you talk, as I watched you, I started imagining us together and it became overwhelming for me. I knew it was going to be difficult for me to keep my focus. I wanted you so badly it was like a pain. I just decided to go with it and see what happened.'

Yeah, yeah, yeah.

'What happened when you had lunch with your father?'

'I don't remember when it came up. I was telling him about you. The questions you asked. How thorough you were. He said not to worry about it. How there was no way you could outfox his mates. Then I started bitching about Sara again. I had a rant about how phoney she was, how much her nice-girl image was put on to get people to like her professionally. There were so many phonies in the fashion world that she made a point of not being seen like that, but even *she* was phoney underneath.'

'Then what?'

'Then I went further and said that even her *name*

wasn't her real one. I'd never mentioned this to dad before. I had no reason to. It sounds so cool, doesn't it? *Sara Holt*. It's just one of *those names*. Memorable and snappy; easy to spell, a fashionista name, a brand name. But it's not her original name; it's her American stepdad's name. She took his surname when her mum remarried, when she was fifteen.

'Her real name, her *birth* name was Sara MacQuoid. Not quite so cool, too much of a mouthful, difficult to spell, very unusual. When I told Dad this, he looked like someone had just slapped him in the face. He went as white as a sheet. For a second, I thought he was having a stroke or something. Then he asked me to spell MacQuoid, so I did.'

'And?'

'You must believe me when I tell that you that I had no idea about this. It was the first time that Dad had ever mentioned it. He didn't like talking to me about his past.'

'What was it? What did he tell you?'

'MacQuoid was the surname of the detective who put Dad in prison. DS Alistair MacQuoid, Sara's father.'

25

HYPODERMIC

I keep under the speed limit as much as possible as I'm still not sure whether the police will be looking for the SUV after this morning's antics. I'm slightly worried that Nick Sarna may report it as stolen or AWOL at some point and I don't know how long I might require it. I decide to give him a call.

'Hi. Daniel Beckett. I'm just letting you know that I'm in the Explorer. I'm going to need it for a while. I'll let you know where it is when I've finished with it.'

'Will it be in one piece?'

'It'll have a huge scrapes down the sides, wing mirrors hanging off, bullet holes in all the windows and I'll have kicked the windscreen out.'

'Fuckin' A. How's it going with the Basquiat woman?'

'Disastrous. I'll speak to you later.'

'Hey. Make sure you bring it back with a full tank.'

I hope he's kidding.

We're heading up through Camden on our way to Kenwood, a leafy area of Hampstead Heath where Isolda's father is ensconced in some gigantic mansion, bought years ago with his ill-gotten gains.

I get Isolda to give him a call on some fake pretext or other, just to let me know for sure that he's home. Even if they don't have Sara there, I'll be taking him in exchange for her. I'll need to know what to expect, but before I start questioning Isolda again I attempt to run this insane situation through my mind. Isolda has a quick chat to him and turns to me.

'Dad's at home. He'll be there for the rest of the day. He sounded pretty relaxed and cheerful.'

'Well, that's put my mind at rest.'

Relaxed and cheerful? She folds her mobile away and stares out of the window just as we pass the Roundhouse. I think she's a little stunned. I'm trying to put the timeline together. She has lunch with her dad who finds out that the girl whose life he's been making a misery is the daughter of the detective who put him away. But despite that, Footballer Dad/Uncle Jackie/Jack Heath is still at it with the harassment that very evening.

That doesn't quite make sense, unless Uncle Jackie couldn't be contacted and couldn't be called off. Or perhaps Tommy Jennison had to have a really profound, deep think about the whole situation, which took him the rest of that day and the early hours of the next one.

Maybe he simply forgot or it slipped his mind in all the excitement. Maybe someone else was handling that side of things and didn't get the info in time. Black Suit said something about Uncle Jackie not using a mobile phone and was annoyed that they could never get hold of him.

No, of course he hasn't got a fuckin' mobile. Are you kidding?

Whatever, Tommy Jennison acted fast. He must have spoken to Isolda who told him about the lunch date with Rachelle Beauchesne. Let's face it; it's pretty unlikely he found out about it through Twitter.

He was concerned about me interfering with the whole process, found out from Isolda where I'd be that morning and sent Blond Hair/Robbie Hyland to try and get me out of the picture, with a potent but ultimately useless cocktail of money and menaces.

Maybe, under normal circumstances, he'd have set Uncle Jackie on me. I can hear Black Suit groaning in the boot once more. I wish he'd shut up; he's spoiling my concentration.

They must have just hoped/assumed that I wouldn't be babysitting Sara the whole time and wouldn't be there when they attempted to snatch her, and even if I was, so what? They'd have been confident that Blond Hair and Blue Suit could easily have taken care of some lowlife private investigator, particularly one who didn't seem to use a vehicle of any sort. Big mistake; and not the first one they'd made.

Isolda puts her hand on my knee and give it a squeeze, as if we're partners in crime or are on our first date in school. I ignore the squeeze and don't look at her. It still feels like an electric shock, though.

I can't imagine what's going to happen to her if and when this whole thing is sorted out. Has she even thought it through, I wonder? It's the sort of thing I'd have to ask DI Bream about. I'm not even sure what you'd call Isolda's type of crime. Conspiracy to abduct, psychologically harass, trespass, burglarise and assault? Something like that? Who knows?

One thing's for sure, she and her dad and his surviving cohorts will have to have a damn good squadron of high-flying hyper-expensive lawyers to prevent them doing jail time, particularly Tommy Jennison with his unsavoury record. What an idiot. He obviously can't help himself.

At the very least, Isolda will lose her job at Maccanti and will never work in the fashion industry again. Well, that's tough. She's been an idiot, too, just like her dad. It obviously runs in the family. The awful thing is that I still really fancy her, can't stop looking at her breasts out of the corner of my eye and under other circumstances would stop the car right here and ravish her. I must book a formal appointment with Aziza.

As we head up Haverstock Hill, I suddenly remember that Sara told me her dad had been a detective with the Met, but it didn't register as being important or relevant at the time.

Of course with hindsight I can see that it was the key to the whole thing, but my initial focus had to be on who was breaking into her home and hassling her on the street and how to identify them and stop them. I must remember that I've still got Footballer Dad in my lock-up. Wouldn't do to forget that.

'Where am I going now, Isolda?'

We're in Hampstead High Street. It's not a place I'm too familiar with. Everything's getting very leafy and affluent. Despite that, I don't like the look of it very much, which I'm sure will cause the residents a few sleepless nights if not uncontrollable panic.

'Straight on,' she says, her voice flat and lethargic. 'We pass through Hampstead. In five or so minutes, you'll see a big park on your right, then there's a roundabout. Take the second exit. You'll be in Spaniard's Road, then you go straight on again for a while.'

I'm not going to question Isolda about her father's motives; it'll be much better to get it from the horse's mouth. What's puzzling me and worrying me is what Tommy Jennison is going to do with Sara now he's got her. Isolda has suggested nothing and it's likely she's as much in the dark regarding Sara's fate as I am.

All those years ago, DS Alistair MacQuoid gives him a

well-deserved prison sentence. In a sense, it was a bit of bad luck. He'd have got a smaller sentence if it had just been harbouring stolen goods or whatever the hell it was. As it was, he was discovered hammering nails into a fellow crook, which probably didn't go down too well with the jury.

At the time, Jennison was married, had a two-year-old daughter, a wife, an ailing mother and a well-oiled little organisation. By the time he got out, his daughter was a grown woman, his wife had committed suicide after various affairs and his crime business was undoubtedly down the pan to one degree or another. On the plus side, he still had an ailing mother.

I'm sure his associates on the outside would have maintained his crooked empire for him, but things would never be the same again. I'm guessing that sixteen years is a long time to be gone in the crime biz.

He would have been resentful, furious, bitter and remorseful. He would have had years to think about what he was going to do when he finally got out. He'd have been looking for someone to blame for his misfortune. They always do.

He would not have considered for a moment that he'd done anything wrong. I'm guessing that he wouldn't be too bright, so he'd probably be thinking of revenge, despite the time that had elapsed and consequences that it might bring. Maybe you have to have something like that in your head when you're in prison, just to get you from one day to the next.

So he gets out and asks around about DS MacQuoid. But DS MacQuoid is no longer with us and hasn't been for some time. The wife of DS MacQuoid has lived in New York for years, has a new surname, would be difficult to trace, and, besides, lives too far away for practical revenge purposes.

There's no way he could locate her, travel to the States, kill her and get back to the UK in time for tea. He just wouldn't have the skills, the contacts or the brains, so he was undoubtedly resigned to giving up the revenge idea as a bad job. But I can't imagine he'd ever forget about the whole affair.

Then out of the blue, years later, his daughter drops a bombshell. Her boss, the woman that he and his boys have been giving a hard time to, having a bit of a laugh with, turns out to be the daughter of his nemesis, DS MacQuoid.

Like his daughter, Sara Holt is now a grown woman, too. But she's a very successful, well-known, rich, beautiful, grown woman. And Tommy Jennison knows everything about her and her movements.

He knows what she does, where she works and where she lives. He's got a one-woman intelligence unit in his own daughter, supplying all the information he needs to intimidate and persecute.

He's had a load of his guys making her life hell for almost a month. She's hired a private investigator, but what the fuck; he knows their sort and has dealt with them before.

I try to put myself in his place. I try to imagine what action I'd take. I couldn't get MacQuoid, I couldn't get his wife, but I *can* get to his daughter. She's been handed to me on a plate. I have to do *something*. I can't just let this go. It's just too good an opportunity to miss. That bastard MacQuoid's daughter; *she'll* be the payment for all I've had to go through.

Would he be thinking of siphoning money out of her

company? Resuscitating the protection business that Isolda said he once had? Some form of extortion? I can't see how that would work. You don't start off an enterprise like that by abducting your mark.

The obvious thing is that he'll just kill her or torture her to death, just so he can feel good and self-righteous about himself. Is he that mad? Is it worth the risk? Maybe it's not. First of all, if Sara was found dead somewhere or just vanished into thin air, Isolda would know who was behind it.

Hasn't he done enough damage to Isolda already without something like that happening? Would Isolda have such a lack of moral fibre that she'd keep quiet about it? Just let her dad get away with anything because he was her dad and she owed him?

Secondly, if he disposed of Sara in some way, the police would be involved. I'd make sure of it even if Isolda didn't. This whole thing is a mess now. Tommy and his boys have fucked up too many times. The link between Tommy Jennison and Sara is too strong and it supplies a great motive; it would be easy to convict him. There are a fair few people outside the Jennison magic circle who know some of what's going on. There's me, for a start, then there's DI Bream, for another.

But what if he doesn't care who knows? Isolda told me that her dad and Uncle Jackie had been in school together. Uncle Jackie was seventy-one, so her dad must be around the same age. Maybe Tommy thinks that whatever he does would be worth it. He isn't a young man. He may be resigned to being caught whatever it is he decides to do. He just wants to have his pound of flesh.

He may accept that going to prison again would be a

fair price to pay for avenging himself on one of MacQuoid's family, for rubbing MacQuoid's line out of existence. Isolda can look after herself now. Except she'll probably be in prison. Perhaps he didn't think that bit of it through or perhaps it's relatively unimportant in the scheme of things.

I'm getting a headache from speculating, and it's all bullshit, really. I'll just have to see what happens and play it by ear. My main aim at the moment is simply to rescue Sara and come down hard on these scumbags, if need be.

I get to the roundabout and take the second exit into Spaniard's Road. This is a long, straight dual carriageway with parks and woodland on either side. This goes on for quite a while until we enter a built-up area with big houses and even bigger trees. Once we're through that bit, we drive along for three or four miles until Isolda points to a turning on our right that I almost miss.

It's the entrance to a private road. There's a red and white traffic barrier with a drop skirt blocking our way. To the right of the barrier, there's a modern, metal gatehouse with two uniformed staff inside. There are four obvious security cameras on top of the gatehouse, two attached to a wall on the other side and a couple of dummy cameras attached to a tree. I drive up to the barrier and stop.

When they see us, both security guards get out to have a closer look. I open my window and lean backward in my seat so they can see my passenger.

'Miss Jennison! How are you?' says the older of the two, an elderly ex something-or-other with a grey moustache and tea on his breath.

'I'm fine, George. Just popping in on my dad for a surprise visit.'

'Ah. I won't bother to ring him and tell him you're on your way, then!'

She laughs. He melts. 'No. There'll be no need for that, George. Thank you anyway. See you later. Oh, and George – don't work too hard, will you.'

'See you later, Miss Jennison.'

He gives me a brief, frosty grin. For a moment there I thought I'd become invisible. The traffic barrier ascends and we continue on our way.

We drive along fairly slowly. There are speed bumps every ten feet or so. I don't slow down for them to give Black Suit a little jolt of well-deserved pain in his dislocated shoulder. He groans the first and second times, and then he's quiet. After a while, I start seeing big houses on both sides of the road, usually pretty well hidden by large trees.

We pass maybe eight or nine of these before Isolda points to a gated entrance on our left. I turn in and stop. She gets out and presses a discreet black entry phone, says something, then gets back in the SUV. The gate opens and we drive on.

The house is enormous. If someone told me that it belonged to some wealthy stockbroker I wouldn't hesitate to believe them. In fact, it looks like there are three houses in the same plot of land, unless the two smaller ones are extremely elaborate and ornate garages or dog kennels.

I'm no estate agent, but I would guess we're looking at a seven or eight bedroom place here. There's a central front door flanked by Doric columns, ten big windows on the ground floor, eight on the first floor. Built, I would imagine, in the 1940s or 1950s. Price? In this area, somewhere in the region of five or six million at the very least. So it's official; crime does pay.

The SUV crunches its way around a semi-circular gravel drive. Black Suit has another moan as I brake suddenly. I get out and Isolda follows after a couple of seconds. The front door opens. Three men appear.

The first one I take to be Tommy Jennison. This is purely from my assessment of his age. Other than that, he's quite unlike how I imagined. I was thinking of someone cut from the same cloth as Footballer Dad, but Tommy is different. Tall, good posture, handsome in an ageing chat show host way, perma-tanned and greying but not completely grey; definite pension advert material. One hand in his trouser pocket the other by his side. His eyes are on Isolda and he's grinning.

The second guy is about five ten and wide and I mean *wide*. Fifty-inch chest at least and certainly XXXL in t-shirts, which I'm sure he never wears. Prime bodyguard/bouncer material with piggy eyes like two piss-holes in the snow. Probably early fifties, could be younger. Humourless, grim mouth, badly broken nose that wasn't set properly and big hands covered in thick black hair. He's carrying a small yellow plastic box. Maybe it's his sandwiches.

But it's the third guy that disorientates me the most. For a fraction of a second, I think it's someone that I know, someone I encountered in the past or someone I once worked with. I process his appearance: thirty, noticeably short, big fists, bad teeth, neck tattoo, angry demeanour. Then it hits me like an avalanche.

This is the guy I encountered in Marylebone High Street on my way to the initial meeting with Sara. The little shit who was jostling people left right and centre. The one I decided to deal with. The one I called shortass.

The one I called girlfriend. The one who tried to punch me and got smacked into the pavement for his trouble. The one who ended up having the shit kicked out of him by a bunch of office girls.

And I suddenly know for certain that this is Isolda's boyfriend. Gaige joked about them having a lunchtime row when I was in Sara's office. When I first met her, Isolda's eyes were a little red-rimmed, as if she'd been crying.

I remember this guy storming down the street with a black cloud over his head and wondering what the problem was. Did he know what she had in mind with me? No. That would be virtually impossible. I knew there must have been a problem with her personal life, but couldn't guess and/or didn't care what it was. Once again, she'd overwhelmed me and made me take my eye off the ball.

It's an inappropriate time for clichéd observations, but *I can't imagine what she can possibly see in him.* He must be only five foot tall and has a face like a petulant little monkey. Isolda is tall, strikingly beautiful and extremely voluptuous. I try not to think about them together; I may throw up. Is it because he works for her father in some capacity? Is she being coerced? My God – was he Burglar Bill?

I see him staring at Isolda and smirking. I turn to look at her and find I'm peering down the barrel of Black Suit's Taurus PT 100. She's holding it like a pro and it's aimed straight at my head. The safety's off and my stomach goes cold as I hear her racking the slide and a round going into the chamber. Who taught her how to do that? Her dad? Shortass?

It was in my jacket in the back seat of the SUV. All the

speed bumps must have gradually made it visible and she chose her moment and grabbed it when I got out. I'm bloody useless. I'll have to give Sara a full refund if she's still alive.

'I'm sorry, Daniel.'

Tears are flowing down her face. Her lower lip is quivering. I can't stand it, I really can't.

'I wouldn't expect anything less from you, Isolda.'

'You don't understand.'

'I never do.'

It happens really fast. Wide Chest throws the plastic yellow box to Shortass who catches it and opens it up. Wide Chest then strides over and pulls both of my arms behind my back. Under normal circumstances I could have him on the floor in half a second, but not with a gun aimed at my head. That would be asking for trouble and I think I've got enough as it is.

His grip on my biceps is powerful and extremely painful, making me feel light-headed and nauseous. Tommy Jennison watches and smiles pleasantly. I think of his pleasant smile then of the six-inch nails torture. I mustn't forget that if I survive whatever's going to happen next.

Shortass takes a small syringe out the yellow plastic box, holds it up and pushes the plunger. Fluid sprays into the air. I'm guessing it's not vitamin B. He holds it in his fist and jabs it into my shoulder. There's a dull ache as he injects whatever it is into my bloodstream. I look down at him.

'Are you sure you don't need to stand on a box, sonny?'

I get a swift punch in the stomach for that, though I think if those turn out to be my last words, that punch would be an OK price to pay; it was moderately witty, cruel and demonstrated a certain insouciance in the face of possible death/danger/whatever.

Shortass's grinning monkey face is the last thing I see as the darkness starts to arrive. The sensation isn't that unpleasant. I wonder if he recognises me from the other day. I rather hope he doesn't.

26

THE DARK PLACE

I decide that I've been lying on my side long enough when my hip really starts to ache. The side of my neck doesn't feel too good, either, and my right hand seems to have gone to sleep.

I roll over so I'm lying on my back and that helps a little. I massage my hand and gradually the tingling goes away and I can feel it again. I rest both hands on my stomach and lie there.

I'm just on the edge of nausea. I think if I moved too rapidly or tried to get up or had to speak to someone, then I'd probably throw up, so I lie still, breathe steadily but not too deeply, and try to focus on something.

But I can't.

I'm not really sure whether I'm awake or asleep. Do I wake or sleep? Where's that from? I open my eyes; at least I *think* I'm opening my eyes, because it's as pitch black as when I think I've got them shut. There is a slight difference, though. When I think I've got them shut, I experience an unpleasant rushing sensation, as if I'm speeding along in some out-of-control fairground ride. This brings nausea with it. When I think I've got them open, that sensation goes away and so does the nausea.

I lie still for a little while more. I'm not sure how long for. I'm not sure if I fell asleep. It could have been minutes or it could have been hours. I'm not sure if my eyes are open. Perhaps my eyes are open and I'm blind. That thought creates slight panic and with it comes the nausea, so I crumple that consideration up and throw it away.

It's very quiet here and I'm not quite sure where I am. I wonder which country I'm in. Am I on a job? An assignment? Somewhere abroad? Have I been caught? I'm definitely not at home. The hardness and coldness of this floor doesn't feel like anywhere that I can remember lying before.

I can feel my heart beating, so I'm definitely alive, which is something. Unless I'm imagining my heart beating. I can feel my tongue tingling in my mouth. Odd sensation. Not sure why that is happening.

During the action of closing and opening my eyes, I'm seeing or perceiving bright flashes of colour: purples, greens and oranges. They are still there when I assume my eyes are completely shut.

Just now, on the very edge of my perception, I could see a big fluorescent green ball with a corona of orange. I can follow these things around as they move and I can feel my eyeballs moving from left to right, trying to keep up with them, trying to keep them in one place long enough for me to have a good look. But they're always just on the edge of my direct vision.

Unlike something ordinary, like floaters, it isn't the movement of my eyeballs that is giving these coloured shapes motion. They're doing it on their own, quite independently, even though that's not strictly true as they're almost certainly a product of my mind. *Ode to a Nightingale*; that was it. Written in Hampstead. What a coincidence.

It does occur to me, however, that these things actually really exist; they're always there and something you don't usually notice, for various reasons.

Sometimes the blackness I perceive with my eyes shut or open becomes a bright white. But it's so white that it's actually black. It's like someone or something is demonstrating to me that black and white are the same thing. Why would they want to do that?

As I lie here, I get the idea that there's nothing beneath me; that I'm floating a few inches above the floor; or that the floor is absent altogether and there's nothing there at all. I know that can't be true, but I touch the floor with one of my fingers, just to check.

The floor is where it should be, but just that small finger movement has replaced the floating sensation with the high-speed rush, which is both unsettling and nauseating, though I know if I do nothing and don't think of anything it'll eventually stop.

I start thinking of that girl, the waitress, Klementina. She was Swedish. Mobile number was 07002690444. Liked Chinese food. How do I know that? Did I arrange to take her out? Have I already taken her out? How did it go? Blonde hair and a remarkable bust. Strong accent. She was called Klementina. Her hair was blonde and there was loads of it. Was she a student?

I decide that I'm going to sit up. That should answer a lot of questions about my physical and mental state, so I steel myself and focus on raising my upper body a few inches off the ground. This is more difficult than I thought and I immediately feel rapidly and spectacularly dizzy.

I stay still. I don't return to my prostrate position, even though my body is demanding that I do. My stomach muscles hurt, but they hurt a little too much, and I wonder if I've been in an accident of some kind.

I attempt to push myself up a little further. This time, I place the palms of both hands against the floor to give myself a little support. The floor is concrete, or something similar. It's gritty and dirty. Is this a garage, perhaps?

I push myself up as slowly as possible to prevent the dizziness and nausea until I'm actually sitting up. The pain from doing this was remarkable, but not too debilitating. Eventually, I use my right hand to grip my right thigh and pull, and place my left hand flat on the floor to keep my balance.

The first thing I do is to manually open my eyelids with my fingers. It's still pitch black. Maybe I *am* blind. I hold my hand six inches away from my eyes, but still can't see anything. I wiggle my fingers and wave my hand from left to right, but still there's nothing.

I can feel my heart beating faster from the effort of getting this far, then it slowly starts coming back to me, courtesy of the pain in my stomach. Someone punched me. Some guy I don't know. I can't remember why he did it. Maybe he didn't like me. Was I in a fight in a pub?

My hand moves up to rub my shoulder. Something is making it itch and there's a dull pain there, too. A hypodermic syringe. Some liquid spraying up into the air. I can remember the jab as the needle went in.

Am I sick? Was I in a hospital? The punch makes that unlikely. The punch was close in time to the jab in my arm, I'm sure of it. They don't punch you in hospitals, not regularly, anyway. I've got a slight ringing in one of my ears. I don't understand where that came from. A loud noise?

There's a woman holding a gun. She's beautiful, but she's crying about something. She seems to be unhappy. She's pointing the gun at me. Was it me that made her cry? Have I been caught? Is she going to kill me? I'm on my own if I've been caught. That's what they always tell you.

It's a good-looking gun. Silver. I can see her face in my mind. I try to focus on it. It's like an anchor for me. If I can look at her face then I may be able to think more coherently. Maybe I can discover who this woman is. Maybe it's someone I'm seeing socially. Maybe it's someone I work with. Do I work with people who look like that? It must be a good job if that's the case.

Her lips are full. Kissable lips. Dark red lipstick. It's called Dark Plum. The lipstick, I mean. How do I know that? White, even teeth. Her skin is pale. Her mouth is turned up at the edges, but she's not smiling. Her mouth is always like that. Beautiful brown eyes. Quite a dark brown, really. Her eyes might even look totally black from a distance.

She has long, black eyelashes. Long black hair. Delicate features. Good cheekbones. There's personality in the eyes. Humour. Passion. Is this someone I work for? She's talking to someone called George. Who's George? Do I work for George?

George is letting us in somewhere. He knows this woman. I'm driving. It's like a big jeep. I get the feeling that we're going to a hotel. Are we having an affair? Is she married and I'm taking her to a hotel? Have we just met? Are we married to each other and we're on holiday? Is it a business conference? What sort of business?

There are no cars on this road; only us. I turn to look at her. She has really long, black hair. It looks fabulous. It reaches all the way down her back to her coccyx. I'm wondering what she'd look like naked with hair like that cascading down her back. Her figure is full and voluptuous. But somehow, I already know what she looks like naked; obscenely curvaceous, wide hips, big, plump, firm breasts. This is not the first time we've been together.

So why is she trying to shoot me?

I get a vision of her laughing, then one of her face frowning with fierce concentration in the throes of an intense and protracted climax.

Isolda.

And my name's Daniel Beckett.

*

I must have drifted away again. Did I fall asleep or was I knocked out by the chemicals in my bloodstream? Well, at least my thinking capacity seems to have returned, even if it's a little shaky. I have to try and concentrate.

Well, first things first. I've been pretty well incapacitated by an intramuscular dose of some drug or other. Probably a cocktail of drugs. It seems a shame to soil the word cocktail when you're using it in this context. What a strange thing to think. Let's hope it's something they got from a professional rather than something Tommy Jennison cobbled together with his school chemistry set in the garage. Tommy Jennison: now I remember.

At the moment, it feels like it could easily be a mixture of horse tranquiliser, mescaline and some benzodiazepine or other. Perhaps it's just a single drug that has all of those qualities. My muscle movements are sluggish, my thoughts are wandering, I'm losing track of time and I'm hallucinating. It's just a normal day at the office, then.

Sometimes I can think quickly and lucidly, other times I can't remember what I was thinking about a few seconds after I was thinking about it. This isn't the case with the physical effects; they're pretty well consistently awful, especially the nausea.

With any drug (or drugs), every second that passes allows your body to break it down and get rid of it, though some are more difficult to get rid of than others.

Some drugs can be flushed out with water or fruit drinks and others can't. Some drugs stay in your system for a few hours, others stay there for a few days. In some cases, there may be an antidote available; something that you can take orally or intravenously which will neutralise the effects of whatever it is in a matter of seconds or minutes.

Well, no one's going to be popping in here with a glass of orange juice or some useful pills, so I'm going to have to attempt to do it myself.

I've known how to do this for so long now that it's difficult for me to put into words. It's a little like the mental techniques for controlling pain. Everyone knows that when you accidentally put your finger on a hot surface, there are a couple of seconds before you feel the pain. You know it's coming and you can brace yourself. It's possible to increase that gap; to stretch it from a couple of seconds to five seconds to ten seconds to twenty seconds, until the sensation gets lost in there somewhere or you're better prepared for it. I had it explained to me once and I still don't understand it.

Another technique is to temporarily place your mind elsewhere. Into a nearby inanimate object, for example.

This takes more concentration and is tremendously difficult to master. Any distraction, small or large, can put you off your stroke and the whole endeavour can rapidly collapse.

How can I possibly know how to do something like that?

But I know that both of these techniques can work, albeit temporarily, against unwanted drugs in your system. They don't flush the drugs out of your system, but they may allow you to perform small tasks that would be impossible otherwise.

In my case, I want to be able to stand up and find out where the hell I am and how I can get out. I'm hoping that just the act of getting up and walking may reduce the effect of the drugs even further. It may not work, but it's worth a try, and I've got nothing else to do.

Still sitting up, I try to visualise the drug or drugs as a single molecule. This molecule is in my bloodstream. It passes into my nervous system and is travelling along my nerve fibres, jumping the synapses, trying to get to the relevant bits of my brain.

Its journey is so rapid as to be virtually unmeasurable. I'm trying to imagine the molecules slowing down slightly, not so much that I annoy them, but enough to actually perceive their journey and attempt to decrease its speed. I'm aware that this must sound like codswallop.

While I'm doing this, I slowly raise my knees and get my feet flat on the floor. This takes a tremendous effort of will, but at least it's something. It's almost as if I'm doing something forbidden while the drug molecules are looking the other way.

I keep my focus on the molecules. That's all that matters. I can see them passing by at an incredible speed and concentrate on attempting to slow them down, just a tiny bit, so they're not getting into my brain so swiftly.

I raise my head up and make sure that I think my eyes are open. I feel my eyelids with my fingers, but am unsure I can trust what my fingers are feeling. It's a worrying sensation. I don't want the nausea to return while I'm doing this. I breathe deeply. Doing this isn't making me feel sick, which is a good sign.

After a possible five minutes, I finally get the nerve to attempt standing up. I know this isn't going to be easy, but I have to have a go, for my own curiosity if nothing else.

I press down onto the floor with both hands and somehow get into a crouching position. The floor feels colder. Then I straighten my legs, take my hands off the floor, and after a few wobbles I'm almost standing up straight.

I feel dizzy once more, but at least there's no nausea. I blink once, and this brings with it a dazzling display of orange circles, which fly away to the edge of my visual range and then disappear. Wow.

Despite the fact I feel like I'm wearing lead shoes, I stretch my hands in front of me and attempt a few steps. I must look crazy. I hope no one's watching this on infrared. I hope this isn't being recorded for training purposes. It's easier than I thought. I'm taking it slowly, waiting for some obstruction.

After eleven slow steps I notice a very slight change in temperature. I stretch my hands out a little further and come into contact with what I assume to be a brick wall. I run my fingers across the grouting; definitely bricks. I start to feel a little sick again, so use the wall to support myself while I attempt a little deep breathing.

I've been concentrating so much on getting to this stage, that only now do some of the other factors involved in my current circumstances start flooding back into my head. But it's hard to focus on them and arrange them in any way that makes sense.

I've got a definite image of Isolda aiming that gun at my head. OK, so that was my fault, my carelessness and my naivety. As soon as we started heading over to her dad's place, she must have known that she was leading me straight into a trap. But the gun falling out of my jacket was pure chance. For Isolda, it was a bit of opportunistic luck.

I remember being surprised she could handle that gun so well, but then she might have been familiar with that exact model. It belonged to Black Suit, after all. Perhaps her dad and his boys all used the same type of shooter, as I'm sure they call it. Well, she may not have been able to handle it very well, but at least she knew how to hold it and aim it, which is always useful with a gun.

I try to think about what would have happened if she hadn't discovered the gun, but she did, so it isn't really worth any conjecture. Despite that, it still gives me pleasure to think of her not discovering the gun. It's so enjoyable that I may have been thinking about it for five minutes or more. I really must get my brain to work properly.

Is Sara inside that house somewhere? Almost certainly. That's what I'm here for, of course. I'm here to rescue Sara, except I'm in a dark place with stone floors and so debilitated with drugs I can hardly walk, let alone think straight.

So the baddies have at least one gun. Are there more in the house? Possibly; unless Isolda's dad is being careful. Maybe he has to keep his nose clean. One is enough, though.

And now I start thinking about Tommy Jennison's staff. The guy with the broken nose. Wide Chest, as I designated him. Certainly a tough character who could easily beat the crap out of you and enjoy doing it.

Not infallible, though, I suspect. Creeps like that never are. The fact that they usually think they are means they aren't.

And then there's Shortass, of course. Quick temper, smirking and violent. It's still shocking that he must be Isolda's boyfriend. Is she insane? I mean, *really* insane? Maybe that would explain everything that's been going on. Nobody apart from me knows that I took him down on Marylebone High Street a few days ago and it has to stay that way for as long as possible.

And God knows what he'd do if he found out about Isolda and me. Maybe he already knows. Maybe she's told him. There's nothing I wouldn't put past her now.

Maybe Shortass recognised me straight away, but didn't say anything because it was so embarrassing. Whatever; for a number of reasons it's not good that he has me at quite a big disadvantage here.

I start to feel a little better and slowly work my way along the wall, one languid step at a time. I've never used them, but I imagine this is what it's like when you have a really heavy pair of those ankle weights on. I feel cold, then suddenly realise that I'm covered in sweat. I'm soaked in it. I can feel it dripping down the sides of my body from my armpits.

I start to think that it's getting lighter in here, but I suspect it's just a side-effect of whatever's coursing through my bloodstream at present. Was it Fortnum's she said? I can't remember the hotel she was staying at. Is there a Fortnum's hotel?

And Tommy Jennison didn't look like the psychopath I was expecting. Looked like he was a retired businessman of some sort. In fact, that's probably the way he sees himself. A businessman. Career criminals are often inclined to anoint themselves with respectable-sounding appellations. Did I really just say that?

Of course, in the real world, it's unlikely that someone like Tommy Jennison would have had the brains to be a businessman in any normal sense of the word. Does he know about Isolda and me? Would it make any difference to him? Will he force me to get married to her?

I suddenly feel a little surge of panic. There's something I have to do; something I've forgotten about. Then I laugh as I realise that it's Mrs Vasconselos. She's probably at Fortnum's right now, wondering where I am and why I haven't bothered to turn up. I know I shouldn't be thinking about this, but it suddenly seems the only important thing there is.

The bricks have stopped and I can feel my hands on a smoother surface. Is this a door? I try to remember what doors are usually made of. Wood? Metal? This is like ridged metal. I run my hands around it and eventually work out that it's door-shaped. It seems the right size, too. But there's something missing. It's the handle. There's no handle in here. I feel nauseous and excessively sweaty again. I keep my hands flat against this door without a handle and let my head droop down. I close my eyes tightly and see big fuzzy orbs of emerald and tangerine.

I remember that Black Suit was in the boot of the SUV. I'd damaged him in some way, but I can't remember how. I try to concentrate on what I did to him, but it just won't come. I'm breathing slowly. I can feel the air go down into my lungs and then come up again. I push myself back into a proper standing position, but I'm not confident about walking.

The pleasing image of Sara drifts into my brain again. This is good. This is why I'm here, but I keep forgetting about it. They're going to be angry about what I did to Black Suit, whatever it was. He's an asset. They must know about Blond Hair because Black Suit was there when I found him and he didn't seem surprised. He had phone conversations with people, but I can't recall them now.

And Footballer Dad. They don't know what happened to him, but if they've got Sara she'll know that I grabbed him. That's if she knows who they're talking about, of course. They may not bother to ask her. They have no idea where he is. It's only me that knows where he is, or at least I think it is.

I just realised that I don't know who it is I'm talking about. I can't keep a thought going. It'd be handy to know what this stuff is. Oh, hang on: I told Black Suit about Footballer Dad. That's a bit of a pain, but, um…

I take a few steps back from the door. I can hear someone outside it, or at least I *think* I can. There's a metallic sliding noise. It opens with a bang and the bright light that floods in is burning the back of my eyeballs. It's just unbearable.

I can see a big shape stride into this room or whatever it is. I think the big shape is Wide Chest. It is. For the first time I get a miniscule glimpse of this place. It's big; totally windowless, square and featureless, apart from a loft hatch door dead in the centre of the ceiling.

He grabs my hair and marches me out into the sunlight. He'd never have managed that normally. I'd have stopped him before his hand had got anywhere near me. He'd be lying on the floor by now with a broken arm at the very least. That makes me feel a little better as I'm dragged through a courtyard towards a big house, throwing up twice on the way.

27

WITHERED ARM

I'm feeling so feeble and useless that it's easy for Wide Chest to manhandle me in this way. I keep tripping up and falling over, and each time it happens, he grins and impatiently drags me up to my feet. I wish I could kill him. He smells of peaches. Perhaps it's the shampoo he uses.

We're making slow and erratic progress down a long corridor. Very tasteful carpet, I notice; one of those complex Turkish designs that you see in hotels or country houses. I become fixated on the complex interlocking patterns and the way they've used three different shades of red. I start breathing slowly through my nostrils so I don't feel the urge to be sick over it. That would be such a shame. It's such a nice carpet.

I suddenly wonder where my jacket is. Is it still in the car? I wonder if they've discovered Black Suit yet. I dislocated his shoulder. I remember now. That'll need a hospital visit. Then physiotherapy. Three or four months for a full recovery.

Wide Chest opens a couple of cream Regency doors and we're in a rather lovely, well-decorated living room. This is definitely the work of an expensive and stylish interior decorator.

Like the rest of the house, it's enormous, but despite

that, they've still taken the trouble to attach a conservatory to it. This catastrophically destroys the well-thought-out, tasteful Italianate theme of the interior.

Beyond the conservatory, which contains half a dozen basket chairs and a couple of matching tables, there's a big lake. It's still and peaceful. You could easily imagine rowing a small boat out to the centre and just chilling with a good book.

There are a couple of small wooden jetties a few feet away from the conservatory, but no visible watercraft. There are several weeping willows on the far side and some ducks swimming around. It's a charming, peaceful scene.

There's an enormous painting above the fireplace. Looks like a Raphael or something. There are naked angel/baby things floating in the air firing arrows at a half-nude woman, while satyrs grab other passing scantily clad females. I'm sure it has a theme, but I can't focus on what that theme might be at the moment. I start to get obsessed with it, so Wide Chest gives me a slight nudge forward.

The floor is made up of what looks like reclaimed terracotta tiles in brown, cream, red and pink, giving the place a cool hint of the Mediterranean. I can imagine it must feel great walking barefoot on these in the summer. For a second, I start to have double vision, then it clears up as quickly as it appeared. I have quite a bad headache.

There are three big sofas in here. Each one of them could easily seat four or five people. In the centre of the room is a big green marble coffee table. There are a couple of large books on it, but I can't read the titles upside down.

One of the walls is almost entirely covered in a bank

of huge mirrors. I look longingly at the sofas again. I want to lie down on one of them and go to sleep.

It says something about my state that I notice the furnishing, decorations and exterior view before I notice the people.

Wide Chest drags me over towards the sofa nearest the fireplace. Sitting down is Tommy Jennison. He's wearing a short-sleeved shirt with awful pink, white and blue checks all over it. Grey casual trousers, white socks, and light brown leather moccasins. Now I can see him up close, it's plain that his greying hair is actually a wig.

One of his arms is short and withered. Can't imagine what the trouble must be. Whatever it is, he has that arm around the shoulder of a very pretty girl who's sitting right next to him on the sofa. I really wish Wide Chest wouldn't grab my bicep that hard. It's really starting to hurt.

The girl who's next to Tommy Jennison is wearing a purple see-though baby doll with a matching thong underneath, the sort of thing you'd get from one of the tackier sex shops. It's open all the way down the front, except where it's tied with a bow at the breasts. She has fabulous breasts; small, round, a sexy shape.

I wonder if I should be staring at her this much. I don't want to appear impolite. Her shoulders are bare, with little bows on the upper arm. She also has great legs.

It's because this girl seems to be pissed or stoned or whatever, her head resting listlessly on Jennison's arm, her hair partially covering her face, that I don't recognise her at first.

It's Sara, of course. It looks like she's had a big dose of whatever they gave to me and is pretty well out of it. I feel very slight alarm. I'm sure I should be feeling more.

She slowly tucks her legs underneath herself and leans into Jennison. Does she have any idea what's going on or where she is? How long has she been here? I was in that club. When was that? Two, three hours ago?

Jennison puts his withered arm around her and holds her close. He starts kissing her; clumsy, slobbering kisses, like an inexperienced teenager. I want him to stop it. She moans, and I can see her body starting to react as he runs his hand up her thigh.

I start to feel nauseous again. Wide Chest is still gripping my arm. I'm totally defenceless against him. His body odour reminds me of wet canvas.

He drags me over to another sofa and pushes me into it. It's incredibly soft. I can feel myself sink into it. I could just fall asleep here, but I know that's not a good idea. I take a deep breath in an attempt to clear my head. It doesn't work.

I'm sitting opposite Jennison and Sara. The big marble coffee table is in between us. There are a couple of hefty coffee table books on it. I couldn't read the titles when I came in here, but I can now.

One is a National Geographic book called *Simply Beautiful Photographs*, and the other is called *The Cambridge World History of Food Volume Two*. That reminds me of Imperial China in Lisle Street for some reason. Great Chinese restaurant. Why am I thinking about that? Oh yes. That girl. Swedish with a name beginning with a K.

The food book looks interesting, so I lean forward to have a look, but my balance goes and I have to rest my hand against the edge of the table to avoid falling over. My sinuses feel inflamed. I have to shake this stuff off, whatever it is. Klementina. Very pretty. I can see Jennison grinning at me. I think he's got false teeth.

Sara looks over at me and there's a spark of recognition in her eyes, followed by panic. For a second, she attempts to get up, but she can't get the momentum going to get off that soft sofa. Besides, Jennison still has his withered arm around her and is holding one of her shoulders pretty firmly. She isn't going anywhere.

I thought Wide Chest had disappeared, but he's still in the room, standing next to a colossal salt-water aquarium which I'd somehow failed to notice. I get hypnotised by it for a short while; black and white Clownfish, big yellow Angelfish, tiny, delicate red and white shrimps, a couple of Dragonets and even a blue starfish.

'Beautiful but captive, eh, Mr Beckett?'

'Sorry. What?'

Is he talking to me or just pontificating? Somewhere in my head, I realise that I should or could be responding to this statement, but nothing comes. I just hope this condition isn't permanent.

Jennison takes an adoring look at Sara and gently pushes her hair out of her face. He gives her a couple of light kisses on the lips. She barely responds. It's like an excruciatingly unsuccessful teenage date. He looks at me as if he's seeking my approval for his necking skills.

'She's what we used to call a little darlin'. Got all the gear; everything in the right place, everything the right size. She's a lovely little thing. What's more, I bet she likes to get down and dirty, you know what I'm sayin'? I can always tell the sort. All that girl next door stuff, but underneath…'

She's my client.

Jennison babbles on with this adolescent tripe. How long have I been here? I look out of the window. It's still light. I just hope it's the same day as when I arrived. I notice I've got the cold sweats again. My mouth is dry. I'm aware of my heart beating fast. When I move my head I get triple vision.

'She was wearing fuck all when she got here. Just some crappy old sweatshirt. I wanted her in something more feminine. It was a bit sweaty, too, to be honest with you. The sweatshirt, I mean. I binned it. We just left her on the floor in the toilet until we could get something sorted out. She pissed herself, which I can't stand in a woman. It isn't ladylike. It makes me sick. She looks nice and decent now, though, don't you think?'

Was that a rhetorical question or is he waiting for a reply? All I can manage is a half-hearted shrug. Jennison starts necking with her again. Wide Chest looks on with a smirk on his stupid face, impressed with his boss's way with the ladies, no doubt. I start laughing for no apparent reason. Jennison's head snaps away from Sara and he looks straight at me. His expression is meant to be scary, but I just find it hilarious and laugh some more.

He nods just once at Wide Chest, who walks over to me, lifts me off the sofa by my hair and punches me just once in the solar plexus. He lets me go and I plop down onto the sofa again, feeling stunned and disorientated.

The strange thing is that I don't feel the sort of pain I'd expect to after a punch like that. The hair pull was worse. Maybe whatever I've been given has an anaesthetic effect. I think I'm going to be sick, but nothing happens. I have tinnitus in one of my ears.

It may have been the surge of adrenalin I just experienced, but I suddenly feel a little more 'in the room' than I did a few minutes ago. I have to keep focussing on recovering. Every second that goes by, my body will be getting rid of this shit, molecule by molecule.

It feels like I've been in this room with Jennison for an hour, though it must be less than five minutes. I think my guess about there being benzodiazepines in the mix must have been correct. Where did they get this shit from?

I try to curtail all of this speculation. I'm suddenly and inexplicably worried that everyone in the room can hear my thoughts. I need to get a drink of water. Someone starts talking to me. It sounds like they're miles away and speaking from the far end of a long metal tunnel.

'So we meet at last, Mr Beckett,' says Jennison, like he's some bloody cut-price Bond villain. 'You've caused me a lot of trouble. We've got a lot to talk about.'

'Have we?'

Well, at least I can speak. It wasn't as hard as I imagined it would be.

'All that's been going on. It was meant to be a secret, you see. *Deniable* they call it in the spy films. Now *you're* here, poking your nose in where it isn't wanted.

'I want to know who else knows about this. I want to know how you found out about Dolly's, for example. How did you know to go there? You've been working on this for two days from what I can gather. You can't have just turned up there as if by magic. You must have spoken to people. I want to know who they were. I want to know where I can find them.'

He smiles at me like a friendly pervert uncle. I can't have this guy visiting innocents like Nick Sarna.

'I realise that you're in no position to have a coherent conversation at the moment, but you will be soon. Maybe in a few hours or so, maybe less. It's different for each individual, I'm told. Some things you can tell me now, other things I'll make you tell me later.'

I nod towards Sara. 'Let her go.'

My words seem isolated and meaningless. They don't resonate in any way. They're dry and flat. I wonder if I even said anything. Maybe I just thought it. Jennison laughs and holds Sara tightly against him.

'I don't think that would be a good idea at all, Mr Beckett. If I let her out of here, anything might happen to her. She's so smashed she could walk under a fucking car and not even notice!'

He laughs at this amusing idea. After a moment, Wide Chest decides it's safe to laugh along with his boss and allows himself a mild, throaty chuckle. I am reminded of Muttley.

'And I can't have that happen, you see, Mr Beckett. And the reason I can't have that happen is that I don't like my property being damaged.

'And have no doubt about it, Mr Beckett; Miss Holt slash MacQuoid here is definitely my property now. I own her like I own that fish tank over there that you were so admiring of. She is now one of my *things*. She belongs to me. She's mine.'

I clasp my hands behind my neck and stretch. I can feel things click in my back. I sink a little further into this amazing sofa. 'You're pathetic.'

Did I actually *say* that? That was a comment that I would usually just *think*, not say out loud, particularly in my current circumstances. Wide Chest frowns and looks to Jennison for instruction. That confirms it; I *did* say that out loud. Have to be more careful. Have to be aware of that. Don't want them knowing what I'm thinking. Not good.

Jennison shakes his head, whether at Wide Chest or at me I can't tell. I try to think of something neutral so they can't read my thoughts. I think of a wooden gate in the country. I lean against it and look at some crops in a field. It's the summer. Birds tweet, insects buzz.

He fiddles with a strand of Sara's hair. 'I'm doing her a favour. Women can't handle success. It goes to their heads. They think they're God Almighty. Some women you have to put on a pedestal. The rest are whores, plain and simple. This is the sort of woman you put on a pedestal.'

'What a load of bollocks.'

Wide Chest looks at Jennison. Jennison nods his head. Wide Chest lifts me off the sofa by my hair again, but this time he punches me in the balls, before pushing me back down onto the sofa.

I bend double with the pain and can feel the dull ache spread up my back, as if someone's frying my kidneys. My eyes are watering. The dizziness and nausea return with a vengeance. I'm going to kill this guy.

'Have you ever been in prison, Mr Beckett? I doubt that you have. It wasn't so bad for me, all things considered. People knew me. They knew that I wasn't a man to cross. I got respect.

'But it wasn't what went on inside prison that bothered me. It was what was going on outside prison. That's what was the killer. Do you know how old Isolda was when I was put away?'

'Yes.'

'She was only two years old. It's a lovely name, don't you think? Isolda. It's from an Arthurian legend. Can't remember the whole story. My wife knew. It's a Welsh name. It means 'beautiful' or 'fair', and she's certainly that.

'Do you know what we used to call her when she was a little baby? We used to call her Dolly. My wife found it out. It's one of the nicknames for Isolda. Dolly seemed nice. It suited her.'

'Fuck.'

'The nightclub's named after her, of course. I'm sure you worked that one out.'

'It was a classy joint.'

He laughs. Well, at least my sarcasm is still functioning. The door opens and in strides Shortass. I feel slight anxiety when I see him. He gestures to Wide Chest who leaves the room. Shortass is about to sit down on a straight-backed wooden chair when Sara slides to the floor, her eyes rolling up into her head. She looks sick, frail and pale.

Shortass runs over, grabs Sara under both arms and hoists her upright, placing her carefully next to Jennison, who puts his withered arm around her shoulders again. Shortass returns to his chair, sits down and crosses his hands across his lap. He stares at me indifferently. This is good. This means he doesn't recognise me from the other day.

I notice he has a big, yellowing bruise on the side of his head, near one of his cheekbones. There's also a nasty graze down one side of his nose. Presumably this is from the kicking he got at the hands of those girls in Marylebone High Street. He also has a slowly healing split lip. I think I may be responsible for that, but I can't remember what I did to cause it. Serves him right, whatever it was.

Sara's head lolls back, as if she's passed out. Jennison casually fondles her breasts through the baby doll. Her nipples harden. He winks at Shortass. Shortass gives him a lecherous grin. Jennison picks his false teeth. Shortass smiles idiotically. I feel like I'm a participant in someone's deranged strung-out nightmare.

'I was just telling Mr Beckett here about Isolda's name, Timmy.'

Timmy! I much prefer Shortass. I want to laugh again. I bite the inside of my lip to stifle it. Shortass seems to have a pale purple aura around him. I know it's not really there, but I stare at it intently as it looks quite nice.

Shortass catches my stare, assumes it to be contemptuous and gives me a menacing scowl. 'Oh yeah. Means 'beautiful', don't it?' he says.

I can see Shortass's neck tattoo more clearly now. Quite detailed and delicate, like a Hokusai snake. Did Hokusai draw snakes? I wonder how far down it goes. I wonder if he's got any others. Perhaps he's covered in them.

Snake tattoo, short, scowling, says 'don't it', bad teeth, face like a petulant little monkey; Christ, Isolda – where were you when they were handing out the good taste?

'That's right,' says Jennison, after what seems like an age. 'She was a beautiful Irish princess in the legend. 'Fair lady', 'beautiful' – it means all of those things. What about you, Mr Beckett? Do you think my Isolda is beautiful?'

He looks at me then glances slyly at Shortass. Is this a trick question? This is unreal and unhealthy. This is a demented, diseased scenario.

I take a deep breath and it morphs into a big yawn. I wipe the tears from my eyes with both hands. Irish princess? Didn't he just say that Isolda was a Welsh name?

I can see Shortass staring daggers at me, willing me to give some sort of inappropriate answer. I must concentrate. I mustn't give them what they want. I mustn't say what I'm thinking, but it oozes out anyway.

'Yeah, she's beautiful. She's probably one of the best-looking women I've slept with. When she's naked, she…'

I don't get a chance to finish whatever half thought out drivel I was going to slur. Shortass dives across the room, his eyes wild and his fists flailing.

I put my hands up to protect my face against the rain of punches and try to go into a foetal position to protect the rest of me. Apart from the punches, he repeatedly kicks me in the shins, which even in my current state I think is a bit pathetic. He's like an angry little boy.

Jennison barks his name once and the onslaught stops instantly. Shortass stands up straight, nostril breathing heavily, and walks backwards towards his seat, rubbing his knuckles.

Jennison smirks at me, pleased that I fell into his trap. Wide Chest pops his head around the door, then disappears again.

'Now where was I?' continues Jennison. 'Oh yes, Isolda. She was a beautiful baby and she's a beautiful woman. But I missed all the bits in between, d'you know what I'm saying? Because I was in fucking prison for sixteen years. I missed her growing up.

'I missed her being a little girl. I missed her being a teenager. I missed buying her presents. I missed all those birthdays. I missed all those successes and I missed all those failures; times when I could have been giving her a cuddle.'

I want to puke.

'I told my wife never to bring her to see me. I didn't think it was right that she should see her daddy in prison. When *her* mummy died, *my* mummy looked after her. And I told *my* mummy never to bring little Isolda to see me in prison.'

I have to laugh at this sentimental claptrap. All this mummy and daddy stuff. He just sounds like a feeble-minded, self-pitying, self-justifying numbskull. I don't want to hear this shit. I want him to shut up.

I want to get away from here. I want to get Sara away from this toxic situation. Jennison is fondling her again. She looks half asleep. This seems to be going on forever.

'You might find it all funny, Mr Beckett, but it wasn't funny at all. Not to me. To have a daughter and to miss that hugely important part of her life. It almost killed me. There were times, when I was in prison when I felt like ending it all.'

I give him a friendly smile. 'You should have done it.'

Jennison's face darkens and I get another tough look. My body continues to feel heavy. I'm intrigued by this stuff, whatever it is. If I get out of this, I must have my blood analysed. Jennison leans over Sara and loudly sniffs her neck.

'And then came the news that every prisoner dreads. It was about my wife, Yazmine. My business was still ticking along nicely while I was inside. Of course, it had to be more low-key and all the big jobs had to be shut down. They required brains, and good as my boys were, none of them had the nous to carry on my work in the same style, if you get my drift.'

'Yeah. Could I have a drink of water?'

I'm not sure whether I said that out loud. No one gets me a drink, so I suppose I just thought it. As Jennison reminisces, he casually strokes Sara's hair. Shortass gazes at him adoringly. He's heard all this miserably sentimental bullshit prisoner wank before, but I'm sure he never gets tired of it.

'But I was hearing nasty rumours about Yazmine,' he

continues. 'There was a club she used to go to. It was a good, classy place in Peckham. We'd been there plenty of times. I was known there.'

Shortass suddenly looks sad and hangs his head.

'Yazmine was picking up men there and bringing them back here. Now don't get me wrong; you can't expect a woman in her late thirties to go without being banged for sixteen years. She had needs. I understood that completely. But she didn't get it; all that has to stop once you're a mum.

'I was worried about how little Dolly would be taking it, having so many uncles around the place at all hours of the day and night. All the stuff she's be hearing coming out of Yazmine's bedroom. Yazmine wasn't one to be quiet, if you get my drift, and always used quite a lot of putrid language, which I couldn't stand.'

'Nice.'

'So all of that was going on. Years and years it went on. So I moved my mummy in with her. Mummy's health wasn't good; it still isn't good even today, but I needed to make sure that little Dolly was well looked after. I needed someone to keep my Yazmine in check.

'Then a year later, the stupid cow killed herself. Took a load of paracetamol. They tried to pump her stomach, but it was no good. Some of my boys took care of the funeral arrangements. They wouldn't let me go to her funeral. The prison authorities, I mean. I was too high risk.' He nods his head proudly. 'They reckoned that some of my boys would try something and they were probably right.'

God, this is so tedious. I've already had the back-story from Isolda. It seems like he's been telling me this tedious crap for about three days. Still, each second he talks, it's another second I'm still here and another second for my liver to sort out the toxins, so I'm letting him get on with it.

'You see, it could be said that being sent to prison wrecked my life, and when someone wrecks your life, you have to wreck theirs back. That's only fair, isn't it, Mr Beckett. And if they're not around, you have to wreck the lives of their nearest and dearest.'

I listen to his bullshit and watch helplessly as he gropes Sara once more. He kisses her mouth and licks her face. Her skin glistens with his saliva. He pulls at the bow on Sara's baby doll and it comes undone. Shortass smiles. It's not a nice smile.

Inexplicably, I start to feel profoundly sorry for Isolda.

28

THE WENDY HOUSE

For a second, I think there's a dog scratching at the door, trying to get in. I can also hear a sound like a small electrical motor. Jennison notices the noise, quickly re-ties the bow on Sara's baby doll and props her up against the back of the sofa. I think she's asleep. I hope she's not dead. He nods to Shortass who walks over to the Regency doors and opens both of them wide.

What comes in through the door is, under the circumstances, such a surreal sight, that I wonder if it's a side effect of whatever's whizzing though my blood. Then I realise that it's so surreal that it can't be.

It's an old woman. If I had to guess her age, I'd have to say somewhere between ninety and one hundred and ten. She's in a hi-tech electric wheelchair. It looks expensive. It's sleek, matt black and well designed with four grey castor wheels and two bigger wheels with white tyres that are powered by an electrical engine of some sort.

As she proceeds into the room, you can hear lots of small hydraulic engine noises. On the left side of the chair there's a small platform supporting two blue gas cylinders, presumably containing oxygen.

There's a green plastic tube coming out of one of the cylinders, which terminates in a transparent plastic mask, held to her face with a length of green elastic. I wonder why the chair doesn't tip over due to the weight of the cylinders.

I can hear her strained breathing and there's a strong smell of antiseptics. On the right-hand side of the chair is a small, see-through compartment full of drug bottles and dressings.

Her skin is sallow and waxy, her hair white and brittle. She's operating the chair using a joystick in her right hand. She's wearing a huge, and under the circumstances, ridiculous flowery hat that you might have seen at a wedding in the 1950s.

As she passes Sara, she does a rapid ninety-degree turns so that she can get a good view. She stares at Sara for four or five seconds, but doesn't say anything. I spot an intravenous drip going into the rear of her neck, but can't see where it's coming from.

After she's inspected Sara, she trundles past Jennison then positions herself to the left of the sofa he and Sara are sitting on. She's now looking directly at me.

No one is saying anything, but everyone's looking very respectful and happy. It's as if the Pope has trundled into the room wearing a flowery hat. I decide to break the silence, just for the hell of it. I look straight at Jennison.

'Aren't you going to introduce me to your fiancée?'

He grins but his eyes are dead. 'What a funny man.' He gives a little nod to Shortass, who walks pasts the old woman, turns towards me and gives me an almighty punch to the face with one of his big fists.

It lands right on my cheekbone and knocks me on my side. I hate being hit there. I'm almost certainly going to have a black eye from that. I notice that it hurt quite a bit and wonder if the sedative effects of the drugs are very slowly wearing off. Jennison turns to the old lady.

'Mummy. I'm just going to show Mr Beckett the Wendy House. Can you look after Sara and make sure she doesn't hurt herself?'

How Mummy is going to do that, I can't imagine. She takes her oxygen mask off. She's going to speak!

'I'll make sure the little whore doesn't do anything.'

It's quite a shock when she speaks. I'd expected a frail little-old-lady voice, but she has a nasty, deep, cawing, grating East London accent that drips with venom. She seems to get short of breath immediately and puts the mask back over her mouth.

The electronic sounds coming from her wheelchair are filling my head. Are they really that loud or is it me? My face is throbbing from Shortass's punch. I don't like leaving Sara here with her, but I have no choice. This is not looking good. She leans over precariously and slaps Sara across the face.

'Little bitch and whore!'

What the hell? Jennison watches as Shortass grabs my arm and pulls me to my feet. I feel instantly dizzy and close to passing out. Little white lights dance in front of my eyes. I take a few deep breaths. Jennison stands, leans over his mother and gives her a kiss on the top of her flowery hat.

'Won't be long, Mummy. Dolly's back. She's taken the day off work to come and see you. She's just having a bath and getting changed.'

'A bath? Was she sweaty? That girl needs to lose some weight,' says Mrs Jennison, whom I'm beginning to dislike.

I had wondered where Isolda was. I thought she might be a tad more proactive in all of this. Perhaps she's trying to avoid seeing Sara. Perhaps she's trying to avoid seeing me.

I thought I was recovering slightly, but as we all go out of the front door and walk across the courtyard, I feel groggy and disorientated again. It's not very sunny now, but it's still too bright for me and I have to squint to see where we're going.

I try to work out what time it must be. From the position of the sun in the sky I'm guessing that it's somewhere between six and seven in the evening. There's a strong scent of some sort of flower in the air. Don't know what it is. Nice, though.

We walk down the side of the house. For a moment, I think we're going to the lake and they're going to drown me, but we stop before that and I have to smile when I see where we're going.

It's like a fairy-tale cottage. It has a tiny wooden front door, a window either side with wooden shutters, a genuine thatched roof and a small brick chimney. The whole thing is maybe ten feet tall and there's certainly no first floor. I'm assuming it must have been built as a folly of some sort or maybe as a plaything for spoilt kids. I expect a witch to come out and greet us.

Shortass holds my arm as Jennison open the front door. It takes him a while, as there's a Yale and three mortice locks; obviously a security conscious witch.

As soon as we're inside, you can tell that no one lives here. The air is dead. It's not a dirty place and it's been kept tidy, but it has no atmosphere. I suddenly feel groggy and lean against a wall. Shortass doesn't like this and pulls me away.

There's a small kitchen ahead of us, but we're not going that way. We turn right, into a sitting room. There's a chintzy three-piece suite, a small desk and a glass-topped coffee table. Shortass shoves me down onto one of the chairs. I'm starting to get used to this happening. I feel vomit start to rise up into the lower part of my throat, but luckily it doesn't get any further. That point on my shoulder where the needle went in is hurting again.

I look around the place and wonder why I'm in here. It's all very well coordinated. There's a design on the sofa covers and cushions – a sort of plum, yellow and cream spider web thing – that's also featured on the curtains. The curtains are open slightly. I can't see the shutters on the windows. Instead of glass, there are sheets of metal. There's a fireplace, but the chimney is sealed off. This is a prison.

I'm still finding it difficult to keep thoughts going. I start thinking about Klementina. She had amazing hair. I try to think of things I can talk about to her. I've been to Sweden on several occasions, but can't remember where.

Jennison asks Shortass to go and make some coffee. Shortass disappears. Jennison sits opposite me. It's the first time we've been alone. I'm obviously no threat whatsoever to him in this state and he knows it.

He stares at me in a way I don't like. It's almost sympathetic, as if he knows what's going to happen to me and feels sorry for me.

'What is this place?' I say, surprised at how my voice sounds.

'Be patient, Mr Beckett,' says Jennison, getting himself comfortable on the sofa. 'We'll be getting to that soon enough.'

I can hear Shortass clanking around in the kitchen. I can hear a kettle start to boil.

'I was telling you about my prison days, wasn't I. Do

you know, I still dream that I'm inside? The relief when I wake up is incredible.'

'Well, you'll soon be back there for real.'

Either I just thought that or he's ignoring me. I'm feeling a little panicky. I want to know what's going to happen and where all this is going. All this maudlin chat and prevarication is beginning to irritate me. Maybe that's the intention.

'There was one thing that kept me going in prison. Do you know what it was, Mr Beckett?'

I look at a print that's hanging above the fireplace. It's Victorian, I think. It's of two sickeningly cute fairies leaning across a toadstool, kissing each other. Eskilstuna: that was one of the places I went in Sweden.

'It was the fact that when I got out, I was going to make the bastard that put me inside suffer. DS MacQuoid. And then I get out and the bastard's dead! His wife's fucked off to the States; the whole revenge thing became too much trouble, too complicated. If his wife had still been in the country, she'd have been dead meat; after I'd had my fun with her, of course. I didn't even know about his fucking daughter. Didn't even know she existed. Can you believe that?'

'I know all of this. Isolda told me. Could you shut up for a minute? I don't feel well. Did I ask you for water?'

I'm sounding more lucid. I must be recovering. A sudden millisecond of double vision tells me I'm not there yet.

'Well, you know that Isolda wanted these fashion shows MacQuoid's daughter was doing well and truly fucked up. Well, that was the least I could do for her.

'Everything Holt did was starting to cause her pain. Anything to make her happy, you know how it is. I just slung my lads a couple of hundred each. It was nothing to them. Just a bit of fun, considering what they were used to doing, d'you get me?

'Timmy out there; he broke into her flat. He was a bit out of practice, but he still managed it without a single person noticing, least of all Miss Holt. He's a good boy. Skilled. That put the shits up her; someone breaking into her flat but taking nothing. I thought that one up. Isolda told me Holt had a nervous breakdown or something. In the past, I mean. I know the type. Jittery. Easily spooked.

'I know the police. I know what your average plod would think if some bint told them that someone had been breaking in but took nothing and she had no evidence. They'd think she was a bit mad and then *she'd* think she was a bit mad, too.'

Shortass reappears with a tray with coffee things on and places them on the glass-topped coffee table. Three powder blue cups and saucers and a large lime green cafetière. No biscuits, which is a bit of a disappointment, but otherwise very genteel.

He pours the coffee out and carefully pushes a cup and saucer towards me, a surprisingly polite gesture coming from someone who's already savagely attacked me once and then punched me in the face at his boss's request.

'All the other stuff. It was choreographed, that's the only word for it,' continues Jennison, proudly. 'Little incidents that could happen to anybody. Women get called bitch, slut and whore all the time. It's just part of normal life for women all over the world. Who's going to know if one of those incidents was planned or not?'

I take a sip of coffee. It's not bad. I start to feel a little better. I'm still not up to anything, though. If I was functioning properly, these two would already be dead. I keep having to wipe tears from my eyes. Jennison continues his monologue. He's proud of his achievements and just has to tell someone about them.

'And then Isolda just happens to mention it. *Just happens to mention it*! That Miss la-di-dah Holt's original name was MacQuoid. I felt sick; I'll tell you that for nothing. I thought that it couldn't be, d'you know what I mean? But that surname. Rare, that is. I'd never heard that surname anywhere else. Have you ever heard of that surname? That bastard's daughter, and my girl was her bloody assistant. I check her on the Internet and it all fell into place.'

'So you decided you were going to abduct her.' That was weird. I can hear my voice in my ears.

'I detect a sneer in your voice, Mr Beckett. You clearly don't understand me. It's to do with morals. It's to do with right and wrong. MacQuoid send me to prison. That was wrong. I missed my daughter growing up. That was wrong. My wife fucks around and then kills herself. That was wrong, too. So many wrongs.

'So when I come out, MacQuoid has to die. That is morally correct. But he's already dead. His wife is out of the loop. But now I've got his daughter. It's like a natural law. It's the law of the jungle. I was *owed* his daughter for what he did to me. Is that too difficult to understand?'

'She's got nothing to do with your sad criminal career, you inadequate shit. Let her go.'

Shortass starts to get up, but Jennison raises a hand to stop him.

'I can't do that, Mr Beckett. Let her go, I mean. She's going to be my new mistress. My girlfriend. My wife.'

All my smart comments die on my lips. Jennison looks

pleased that I'm shocked and speechless.

'That's why I brought you in here; to show you where she's going to live. To show you how much you've messed up. I may be getting on a bit, but I've still got what it takes to please the ladies. Can you imagine what DS MacQuoid would think? He'd be rolling in his grave. Me, Tommy Jennison, banging his daughter. And it won't be just me, either. I like to treat my men. I like to keep them sweet. Give 'em a nice little gift every now and then. Of course, we'll have to keep her medicated. But that stuff she's on now, we can't keep her on that forever. She's no good to me on that. We'll just put something else in her food every day. Not too little, not too much.'

He laughs and rubs his hands up and down his thighs. Shortass has a laugh as well. I feel sick.

'It'll just be like having a little toy. Like one of them sex dolls, but real, you get the picture? I'm going to have me a really bloody good time, Sonny Jim, a really bloody good time. So's Timmy here. And Derek. It's sweet. I couldn't have asked for anything more sweet than this. She looks like one of them models in a magazine. Certainly out of Derek's league; and Timmy's too, truth be told. Old MacQuoid'll be rolling in his grave. He'll be rolling in it every time I have her. Bringing my boys in on it just makes it better, understand? More satisfying. More revengeful.'

He cackles to himself, his false teeth whistling.

I close my eyes and exhale slowly. I feel suddenly and inexorably depressed. I have completely failed this client. I have completely fucked up. It couldn't get any worse than this. A young, intelligent, successful woman asks me to investigate some incidents of harassment and a couple of days later she's the drugged-out concubine/prisoner of a wig-wearing, seventy-year-old animal with false teeth and a withered arm. Good work, Beckett.

'With all no respect, you're a complete simpleton,' I say, probably risking another punch from Shortass. 'You're never going to get away with this.'

That was awful. I never usually drift into speaking in clichés.

'Oh yes I am, Sonny Jim. Think about it. Who knows she's here? Who will ever know?'

This is a difficult one to think about in my state. Who knows Sara's here apart from this lot? Well, me, for a start, but I don't count; not at the moment. At some point she'll be reported missing, probably by Isolda if she's devious enough and I think she is. But I'm forgetting Rachelle Beauchesne. That incident will point the police in Sara's direction. They'll look at her Twitter account. If Rachelle dies, it'll be a murder inquiry. They'll be looking for Blue Suit and won't stop until they find him.

Isolda, of course, will have to hold it together should she be interviewed by the police. Would she buckle under that type of pressure? She'll be upset and falling to pieces, but then the police would expect her to be like that. She did a damn good job of pretending to be Sara Holt's biggest fan. It certainly fooled me, but then my judgment was clouded by lust.

So it's certain the police would investigate. Someone will doubtless launch an appeal. It'll make the news. Sara's mother and stepfather will come over from the States. They'll put pressure on the police. The police will ask for witnesses. They'll want to speak to anyone who might have seen Sara in the previous forty-eight hours or whatever. Who would come forward? If Eve Cook saw an appeal like that she'd go straight to the authorities.

She'll tell them how I commandeered her car after Sara was grabbed. She'll tell them how I rescued Sara, how she dropped us off at Exeter Street. She'll show them my business card. They'll check my flat. They may not find signs of a struggle, but forensics might find something, some proof she was there.

But it's unlikely they'd find any evidence of Jennison's goons. They'd have been too careful. They'd have worn gloves. All of the evidence and testimonials might even point to *me*, and if I turn out to have vanished into thin air, they might think it's case closed.

As soon as I discovered Sara had been grabbed, I went straight over to Maccanti. Melody, Sara's MTA2 would tell the police, if they thought to ask, that I'd barged into the offices and was having some sort of altercation with Isolda.

But Melody suspected that there was something going on between me and Isolda and it could be interpreted that we were having a row. I'd said as much. I said we were having a lovers' tiff. I don't know whether she believed that or not. Did she know about Rachelle? Isolda and I left, but where we were going would be anybody's guess.

Any reporting of Sara's going missing would hopefully attract the attention of DI Bream. She'd try to get in touch with me. When that failed she may or may not look into it.

But she'd have to make the connection between Sara and Isolda. She'd have to discover that Sara's original surname was MacQuoid. Then she'd have to make the MacQuoid/Jennison connection. Only then could the blame be laid at Jennison's door.

But Olivia Bream is the wrong generation. The sort of

police officer who would be familiar with The Legend of Tommy Jennison would be retired by now. The trail, in effect, would end at the point that Eve Cook dropped us off at Exeter Street. Is that right? My thought processes are still foggy.

I try to remember how I got here in the first place. How I made the link with Isolda. It was pure chance. I just happened to get a lead that took me to Dolly's. While I was there, Black Suit mentioned Exeter Street when he was on the phone. That was it. That was the lead. Isolda was the only person who knew that Sara was at my place.

If Black Suit hadn't rung whoever it was to check up on me, I would never have known about Isolda's involvement. It was an unrepeatable and fortuitous set of circumstances that the police would never be lucky enough to encounter.

That makes me the only outsider who knows or could even *suspect* where Sara is and indubitably puts me in the deepest shit. It also puts Sara in deep shit, of course. I have to get Sara out of this. But how? This is the deepest of deep shit.

'Now I know what you're thinking,' smiles Jennison. 'Age difference of over forty years; it won't work!'

He and Shortass have a good old snigger at this.

My head is spinning. I'm trying to decide whether Jennison is altogether sane. I think he probably is. Sane but twisted; sane but with the morals of a rattlesnake and that's an insult to rattlesnakes.

All this makes total sense to him. It's the way of things. It's what you do. It's the rules. He's conservative and inflexible.

'I don't know why they built this place,' says Jennison, looking around as if he'd never been in here before. 'Just a bit of fun for someone, I think. Isolda used to play here when she was little. As I said, this is where Miss Sara Holt will live. I won't be having her in the main house. Don't want Mummy to hear what'll be going on. It'd be embarrassing.

'It's totally escape-proof. Had it altered in the Nineties. Just some justice being served, that's all you need to know. She'll get used to it. It's got a bedroom, bathroom, toilet and kitchen. Her dad put me in prison and now she's going to be in prison. But it's a nice prison, I think you'll agree. No slopping out in the morning and conjugal visits whenever me or the boys feel like it. It's a sweet arrangement.'

Jennison glances at Shortass, who gives him a matey, obsequious grin. He leans forwards so our faces are six inches apart. I can smell his breath. 'And now, Mr Beckett, we come to the interesting subject of *you*.'

29

A HOT KNIFE THROUGH BUTTER

In the last five minutes I've noticed that I'm feeling a little better. I'm getting intermittent cold sweats, but the hallucinations seem to have died down, apart from a vague orange glow around Jennison's face, which may well be the result of too many tanning bed sessions.

My body still feels like it's made of lead, but it's not quite as bad as when I woke up in that room. I'm still feeling symptoms of disassociation, as if my consciousness is trying to leave my body. It's a bit panic inducing, but deep breathing helps a little.

I have to assume that Jennison has used this drug on others, so he'll know the symptoms and he'll know the signs of recovery. But recovery must be different for each individual; it always is when you're dealing with downers. I just wish I knew exactly what I'd been given. If I knew that, I could fake it more convincingly. I'll just have to improvise and hope for the best.

I can't allow Jennison to glimpse even the tiniest improvement. I let my eyes go out of focus. I let my head droop onto my chest. I scratch at my arms. I lick my lips. I make my breathing shallow. I make my breathing deep. I allow expressions of bafflement and/or confusion to pass across my features. It may work, it may not.

'I realise that this was just a job for you, Mr Beckett. I imagine you were pretty suspicious when you first took it on. It must have seemed like Holt was making it all up and that was part of the point, yeah?

'I know that it was Isolda who suggested to her that she get a bodyguard and that led to her hiring you. Bit of a pain, but what could we do?

'When you got here Isolda asked me not to hurt you and she asked me not to kill you. I'm sorry she's not around at the moment, by the way. I think she was a little surprised it all went this way, but she's only got herself to blame. I don't think she really felt comfortable seeing you or Miss Holt. I'm sure you understand.'

'Of course. I wouldn't want to embarrass her by letting her see me like this.'

'I'll do anything for her; she knows that she can twist me around her little finger. But even though I love her, I can't have her telling me who to kill and who not to kill and who to hurt and who not to hurt. This is business and she's just a woman.

'I told her we'd just give you an injection of that stuff. Give you a bit of a scare, pay you off and then send you packing. Of course you and I know that isn't what's going to happen, don't we, Mr Beckett. We're men of the world. We both understand the reality of situations like this where a mere girl like Isolda certainly doesn't.'

His eyes narrow menacingly. 'I've also got a pretty good idea *why* she's so concerned about you. But that's her business. She's a grown woman. She can do what she likes.

'But I'm not going to kill you yet. I want to know what the hell's been going on with you and my boys and I want to know who knows about all of this apart from you. Like

I said earlier, you somehow found Dolly's and I want to know how that happened.

'This has got out of control. I have to keep my nose clean, you get me? I can't have stuff like this happening. I can't be investigated. I can't have loose ends like you hanging about. It's like in a film: you know too much.'

I nod my head like this is some sort of business meeting, which he probably thinks it is.

I'd like to have met his wife. I'd like to see a photograph of her, at least. It must be Yazmine that Isolda takes after. I can't see any of her in old Tommy at all. I wonder where Isolda is? I wonder if Yazmine had a knockout figure like Isolda? If she did, she was too good for Tommy. Yazmine. Such a lovely name. Must be a variant of Jasmine.

'You see, Mr Beckett, if it was just you turning up as a meddlesome private investigator and sticking your nose where it wasn't wanted, I could probably have made a deal with you.

'We tried that already, as you know. We tried to give you five grand to disappear before we snatched Miss Holt. You turned it down, I don't know why; maybe you don't need the money. Can I ask you how much you charge? Just out of interest?'

'A thousand a day plus non-negotiable expenses.' I'm amazed I can remember. Jennison and Shortass have a little schoolboy snigger together. I've no doubt that money like that is peanuts to them both, big time bastards that they are.

'Maybe you turned it down because of some sense of duty you have to your client. I can understand that. I like integrity. Maybe you fancied her. Maybe you thought you might get to sleep with her, but it's *me* that's going to be doing that! It's *me* that's going to be having the time of my fucking life with her!'

He and Shortass have another snigger session. It takes them a minute or so to recover.

'But anyway, what I'm saying is if it was just a matter of making you go away and forgetting all of this I think we could have been talking business. I would have been prepared to offer you something in the region of twenty grand to just lose yourself. Would that have been enough for a man like you? Or would it have to have been more? I'll be honest with you; I can't tell. I can't work you out.'

'I'm too enigmatic for you.'

'But this is all irrelevant. It's too late now. You're going to have to go,' he continues. 'Because apart from the fact you know too much, you also ripped through some of my best boys like a hot knife through butter. I've never seen anything like it. It's almost admirable.'

'Thank you.'

'In my book, that gets the death penalty. If I could kill you twice, I would, and I'd take great pleasure in doing it.

'Those two boys who took Miss Holt from Baker Street in the Explorer out there. Jake Merriman was one of my up-and-coming lads. He's a fucking kickboxing champion. Has been for seven years. He said that you took on him and Robbie Hyland like it was nothing. He said you almost snapped Robbie's arm off at the elbow.'

For a moment, I don't know who he's talking about, then I remember. This is Blue Suit and Blond Hair.

'And Robbie's dead. Well, you know that. You saw him.'

I shrug. 'You should have got him faster medical treatment.'

'And Jake is in intensive care. He's severely concussed.

They think he might have brain damage. His jaw is broken. His nose and forehead is smashed so bad that he's going to have to have plastic bloody surgery when he comes round, *if* he comes round. Five of his teeth snapped off, as well.'

'So much for kickboxing, then.'

'And then there's Colin who had the misfortune to run into you at Dolly's. The one you shoved in the car boot. He's in the Royal Free Hospital. Timmy here spoke to one of the doctors. One of the worst shoulder dislocations she'd ever seen. Ripped ligaments, ruptured tendons, torn muscles, nerve damage, severed blood vessels; the fucking works. Probably never be able to use that arm properly again. They said he was delirious with it.'

He glares at me like this is all my fault or something. People are always looking to put the blame onto someone else. I can see Shortass looking at me in a strange way. I'm afraid it may all be coming back to him.

'And then,' continues Jennison, 'we have the mystery of what happened to Jackie Heath. That was Colin's uncle, did you know that? What's more, he was one of my oldest friends.'

'You have friends?'

I don't think that Black Suit/Colin was well enough to repeat what I'd told him about Footballer Dad. If he had, Jennison would be a lot angrier than he is.

'Jackie Heath goes out to lay a bit of hassle on Miss Holt – some poncy fashion thing off Piccadilly – and no one's heard from him since. Now I don't care if that name means nothing to you, but I reckon you were behind that as well. Where is he? What happened to him?'

I can't be bothered to lie and I want to see what

happens when I tell him. I want him to know. I want to hurt him.

'He's dead. You put him in a situation that he simply wasn't up to handling. I didn't kill him. He just died. Heart attack probably. I was questioning him at the time.'

'*Questioning* him? You mean *torturing* him?'

'Yeah, I guess you could say that, but I hadn't really started. Not properly.'

I wish I could shut up. It takes five or six seconds of goggle-eyed incredulity for this bombshell to sink in, then Jennison gets up and slaps me around for a bit. He goes a bit berserk, really. He grabs my hair. He punches me again and again. I can't do much against this, but I keep turning my head to the side so he doesn't break my nose. Vanity will be the death of me.

He shoves me back into the chair. He's getting pissed that I'm being so unresponsive. I'm sure I'll have many marks and bruises on my face and neck from this, but it doesn't really hurt that much. I'm lucky that there's little real strength in his withered arm. He has a good left hook, though. I spit into my hand. There's quite a bit of blood in my saliva.

He sits back down on the sofa, drops his head into his hands and sobs. I feel so guilty now.

'Oh no. Oh God. Not Jackie. Oh fuck. Oh, Jackie, mate. Oh, Jackie. I'll tell Nancy for you, mate. I'll tell her, I'll tell her. I'll look after her.' He looks up at me. His eyes are dead. 'You are not going to believe what's going to happen to you, Beckett. I'm going to make it last a long, long time.'

'Just make sure you sterilise the six-inch nails. I wouldn't want to get an infection.'

Suddenly, Shortass's eyes widen. He's so angry he can

barely speak. He points a finger at me.

'You! It was you!'

He launches himself at me and once again I try to protect myself against another volley of punches and kicks. This is awful and painful, but the adrenalin it's producing is helping to wake me up. Jennison looks amazed; he doesn't understand what the problem is.

'Timmy! What the hell's the matter with you?'

After another dozen or so blows to my head, Shortass pulls away and stands up straight, angrily nose breathing and vibrating with rage. He points at me once more.

'This guy. This is the guy that did this to my face. He took me by surprise. Right out of the blue it was. Just attacked me. No reason. Just after I'd had lunch with Isolda the other day. Got me down on the pavement. I didn't do nothing to him. He ripped my suit. I only just realised it was him.'

'You forgot to mention the four girls who kicked the shit out of you. Shortass.'

'What?' says Jennison. 'What's this? What girls?'

'I don't know what he's talking about, boss. He's crazy.'

Jennison looks incredulous and vibrates with rage. 'So, what, over a two day period, you've either seriously assaulted or killed *five* of my boys? Is that what I'm hearing here? Jesus Christ Almighty. And on top of that, you've been banging my fucking daughter! What – what the fuck sort of person are you, Beckett? Are you a fucking psychopath?'

Five? Is it really *five*? Footballer Dad, Blond Hair, Blue Suit, Black Suit and Shortass here. Yeah. It really is five. I can taste blood in my mouth.

'You're criminals,' I say. 'You're involved in bad *stuff*.

It's a high-risk occupation. You're putting people into unpredictable and dangerous situations all of the time. You're bound to get casualties. You and your guys are just not as good as you think you are. You're too dim.'

Jennison and Shortass stare in disbelief. Shortass's mouth is hanging open. His teeth are worse than I first thought. How could Isolda ever kiss this guy? Maybe they don't kiss. Has no one spoken to either of these two like this before? Has the risk element in what they do never occurred to them? Are they more stupid than I think they are? I pretend to have difficulty keeping my eyes open. I take a deep, laboured breath.

Jennison laughs, but it's loaded with bitterness and loathing. His breathing is ragged. I'm hoping he'll have a heart attack.

'God give me strength. Under other circumstances I might have offered you a job, Beckett. You've got balls even if you haven't got a brain.' He scratches his head. I'm worried about his wig.

'You're a major fucking pain, Sonny Jim. And now I'm going to have to go to all the trouble of finding a way of getting rid of you so Isolda doesn't realise what's happened. I hate having to lie to her and do stuff behind her back, but sometimes it's the only way.'

'I fully understand.'

'Where's Jackie's body? What did you do with him? What happened to him?'

'I can't remember.'

Shortass sees his chance to hit me again and attempts to grab it. 'Let me have a word with him, boss. I'll find out what he's done with poor old Jackie.'

'Did you hear that, Beckett?' says Jennison. 'Would you like Timmy to have a little word or two with you?'

'Do you think his vocabulary would be up to it?'

Before Jennison can think of a good repost or violent attack, his mobile goes off. I'm interested to note that his ring tone is *Surfin' Bird* by The Trashmen.

'What the fuck is it? *What?* Where? Is he alive? What's his name? OK. Bring him up to the house. I'll be over there in a minute.'

He clicks off and gives me a long, hard stare. 'Looks like the cavalry was arriving for you, Beckett. Too bad it didn't work.' He nods at Shortass. 'See if he's got a wallet.'

Shortass gives me an unnecessarily rough shakedown, finds my wallet in my back pocket and hands it to Jennison, who pulls everything out of it, chucking everything on the floor until he finds what he's looking for. He nods his head with some satisfaction.

'I knew it. I fucking knew it. I knew you wouldn't be able to do all of this on your own.'

I have no idea what he's talking about.

30

HE'S NOT WITH ME

The three of us leave Sara's new pad and crunch across the gravel back to the main house, Shortass still grabbing my arm. I fake a couple of stumbles on the way back, and have a genuine vomit just before we get to the front door. I don't know what's going on.

I'm pushed back into the living room. Jennison's mother is where we left her, but now she's leaning over an apparently unconscious Sara, and is carefully combing her hair. It's a creepy sight. Her breathing sounds laboured. I can hear a hissing sound coming from one of her oxygen cylinders, if oxygen is what's in there. It would be better if it was carbon monoxide.

Over by the window is Wide Chest, looking really pleased with himself, his piggy eyes wrinkling at the edges. At his feet is an unconscious male figure. Once glance at the red hair tells me who it is: Peter Dixon, private detective, matrimonial cases, corporate fraud and technical counter measures. There is red blood in the red hair.

I remember that his business card was still in my wallet. Now Jennison has got a link between us, no matter how tenuous. This may not be good news for Mr Peter Dixon. It may not be good news for me.

My feelings about his circumstances are ambivalent. Whoever tasked him with trailing me made a big mistake, but they couldn't have foreseen this outcome. If anything happens to him, his employers are going to think that I'm responsible. That may be to my advantage, it may not. This is not the first time that I've felt that a person or persons unknown are keeping an eye on me and I don't like it.

Jennison makes a little hand gesture to Wide Chest. This is his cue to start his story. He stands and talks like a policeman giving evidence in the dock and I wonder if he's ex-police like Blond Hair.

'I was in the grounds at the back having a fag, boss. Then there was a bit of a disturbance down by the fence, which backs onto the park. Birds flying up into the air an' all of that. I didn't think much of it, but walked down that way to have a look while I finished my fag. His majesty was just strolling about the place, like he didn't know where he was.'

Shortass pushes me down into my customary sofa. Jennison's mother turns away from Sara to stare at me. Her eyes bulge. Sara moans. I have to focus on getting her out of here.

Dixon is such an idiot. I warned him to keep away from me, but he couldn't leave it. I try to think how he ended up being here. He must have decided that it was still a worthwhile thing to keep tailing me. Maybe it was the money. Maybe it was misguided professionalism. Maybe he thought he was being a tough guy by ignoring me. Maybe he was afraid of whoever was employing him.

When he picked me up again, I don't know. I haven't felt his presence since I spoke to him outside that café. It's possible he was keeping a watch on Maccanti. He could have been sitting in a vehicle outside Maccanti, seen me and Isolda talking in the SUV and tailed us to this place without my noticing. He'd been lucky before, spotting me in Big Shots the other night. I start thinking about Thea. She certainly had a few surprises up her sleeve.

I feel annoyed I didn't notice him, but it's too late for that now. He must have seen the gate security, kept on driving, then discovered another way in. How did he know which house it was? Was he just lucky yet again? On the other hand, there aren't that many houses in this road. He may have tried a few before he turned up here. I can't imagine what he's going to say when he comes round.

Jennison and Shortass turn him over so he's lying on his back. He has a deep, nasty-looking gash on the side of his face. Jennison looks at Wide Chest for an explanation. Jennison's mother powers over for a closer look, hydraulics working overtime.

'Uh, I crept up behind him and whacked him over the head with Shirley here,' says Wide Chest proudly, pulling a SIG Sauer P226 DAK out of his inside pocket. Now where did he get that? It's a type of pistol used by several police forces in the UK. Maybe Jennison has contacts. It's always a risky endeavour, using a pistol like that as a bludgeon. It could go off.

'That didn't put him out, though,' continues Wide Chest. 'He turned around to try and hit me so I punched him in the face.' He giggles. Yes, *giggles*. 'That did the trick!'

'You did well,' says Jennison. 'Sit him up against the sofa, then give him a slap.'

Despite Dixon's bulk, Wide Chest manhandles him to

a sitting position as if he weighs nothing. He crouches down and slaps him across the face a couple of times. No response. He doesn't look fully unconscious to me and I wonder if he's faking it. Mummy takes her oxygen mask off.

'Squeeze his balls,' she croaks, in that strange, manly voice of hers.

Wide Chest looks dubious at first and glances at Jennison to see if this is a good idea. Jennison nods. Wide Chest crouches down, the fabric of his trousers straining against his enormous thighs. He bares his teeth, spreads Dixon's legs and squeezes his balls like he's trying to get every last drop of juice out of an orange. Dixon screams and his body bucks forward in agony. I'm not that sympathetic to his current plight, but I certainly felt *that*. Mrs Jennison's eyes crinkle with pleasure.

Now he's alert, Jennison slaps him about to get his full attention. 'We've got your mate and we've got you. You're totally fucked, my friend.'

Dixon looks confused. He moans. He grabs his balls with both hands. He rocks back and forth. He's sweating from the pain. He looks around the room, his eyes semi-focussed. He takes in Jennison and Jennison's mother, who peers at him and chortles nastily. He looks up at Shortass, who's sniggering, his little monkey face pinched and evil.

Dixon's eyes widen when he sees Sara in the see-through baby doll. He must wonder what the hell's going on here. Wide Chest returns to a standing position and the sudden movement makes Dixon flinch. Then he sees me and his confusion turns to panic. 'Tell them!'

Jennison looks at me. 'Tell them what? What's he talking about, Beckett? Come on. He's your bloody mate.

What's he talking about?'

Dixon's presence here is obvious to me, but a little too complicated to put into words for Jennison, at least in my present state. 'He's nothing to do with me.'

I suppose I should have said, 'He's nothing to do with you.' But it didn't occur to me. My vision got a little blurry. Just for a few seconds. It's better now.

'You had his business card in your wallet. What's the score? Did you hire another private eye to keep tabs on you in case you got into trouble? Or are you working together? Which is it? How many more of you are there? Is this what private detectives *do* nowadays? Hire other private detectives? Do *those* private detectives hire other bloody private detectives as well? Does it go on for fucking ever?'

He turns to Dixon. 'Come on, Mr bleedin' Dixon. Who are you working for?'

'I don't know,' says Dixon, without realising what a stupid reply that is. Jennison steps forward, swings his leg back and gives him an almighty kick in the face. It's the sort of kick you'd use if you were trying to punt a rugby ball over the other team's crossbar.

Dixon falls on his side. Blood pours from his mouth and spatters on the floor. They're going to have to give those terracotta tiles a good clean later on. 'Maybe that'll remind you, you pisser,' says Jennison, his face now warped by a callous sneer. When I first encountered him, I couldn't square his pension ad looks with the hammering nails thing, but I can now.

'I'm telling the truth,' mumbles Dixon, who's starting to look understandably worried. He's in a bad situation here. He has no friends.

Jennison thinks, quite reasonably, that Dixon is with

me. I gave Dixon a pretty strong warning about what would happen if I ever saw him again, even though it's probably clear to him that I'm currently in no shape to exact even the mildest retribution. He has no idea what's going on here. He's no danger to me but he's no help, either.

'How much do you know about what's been going on?' barks Jennison.

Dixon, of course, knows nothing, but Jennison won't believe that in a million years. He wants to hear something fantastic. He wants to hear some good news. He wants to hear that he's in the clear, that there are not dozens of people like Dixon floating about who know all about his business and what's been going on with Sara Holt; his little bit of fun for his daughter that had suddenly and unexpectedly turned bad.

Dixon isn't going to be able to tell him anything like that, but Jennison won't be happy until he hears it, even if it isn't true. He punches Dixon in the face a few times. This is such a sloppy technique. Jennison is far too emotional and stupid to be able to interrogate properly. Dixon spits blood and half a tooth comes out with it. Jennison turns to me.

'Who is this bloke? How many more are there?'

'There aren't any more. You're getting the wrong end of the stick.'

'The only stick you should be worrying about is the one with nails on I'll be shoving up your arse if you don't give me a straight answer. I'll fucking tear your guts down into a fucking bucket while you watch, you little fucking prick.'

Shortass stands behind my sofa. He grabs both of my shoulders to keep me up straight while I answer his boss, who I believe is getting a little stressed by everything, if truth be told.

I take a deep breath. I don't have the mental energy to lie or to use this to my advantage.

'OK. Listen. Someone hired this guy to follow me.' I clear my throat. 'He's been trailing me for a couple of days. It started before I even met Sara Holt. I caught him this morning and warned him off. Obviously, he couldn't or wouldn't take the hint and followed me here. I don't know how he found the house.

'I assume he must have seen us drive through the main gate and realised he couldn't follow, so he drove past and started looking for other ways in. I don't know what he did or what he's doing.' I take a deep breath and flop back into the softness of the sofa. That much talking has really taken it out of me and I feel a little faint. 'If I was him,' I say, 'I'd have checked every house off the private road until I found the SUV.'

'And then what?'

'Then he could put in his report that I'd come here with Isolda.'

'Why? Why would he be following *you*?'

'I really have no idea.' I allow myself another sigh. 'He was told by someone to keep tabs on me for five days and report back. He's telling the truth as far as not knowing who it was who hired him is concerned. Well, that's what he told me, anyway. I have no reason not to believe him. I don't know what's going on, to be perfectly honest. Can you stop asking me so many questions? I can't think straight. It's exhausting.'

He points at Sara, who is drifting in and out of consciousness. I'd almost forgotten about her and I'm a little worried about the effect the drug cocktail is having.

'So he knows nothing about what's been going on with the girl here.'

'The whore,' adds Jennison's mum usefully, her oxygen mask pulled briefly away from her face.

'Don't call her that, Mummy.' He has a little laugh to himself. 'I'm not paying for her. She's free.'

'What else am I meant to call her? That's what she is. She's just like all your other ones.'

'This is not the same, Mummy.'

'Her bastard of a father ruined your life and ruined mine, too. Do you think I wanted to look after your bloody daughter and your slut of a wife? I was sick. Looking after Dolly made me worse. It took years off my life. I've only got one lung. I've got pulmonary vascular disease. I've got Wolff Parkinson White syndrome. Your bloody painted slut wife committing suicide almost killed me. If she'd asked me I'd have saved her the trouble and stuck a knife in her slut back.'

Jennison looks dismayed. Shortass and Wide Chest look away, embarrassed.

'You were always weak, Tommy. You were a weak, crippled little shit. God cursed me from heaven the day you were born. I must have…'

Luckily, Mummy starts gasping, has to put the oxygen mask back on and the drivel stops. Jennison's attention is back on me again.

'So this bloke here knew nothing about me or what I'd been doing. He didn't even know I existed?'

I know I'm sighing too much, but I allow myself another one. 'He didn't know about you and he didn't know about Sara. In fact, *I* thought he was something to do with your lot. I had good reason to think he might be involved. But I asked him if the name Sara Holt meant anything and it didn't, and I believed him. This is something else. What it is, I don't know.'

I can see the cogs turning in Jennison's brain. 'But he knows about Sara now, doesn't he. Any report he writes about you, whoever the balls it's going to go to, is going to include this address and what happened here. It's going to include all the people here and what we've been talking about. He's seen the girl. He's seen me.'

'Well, I suppose so. I don't know. I don't really care.'

Dixon has been listening to all of this and is looking increasingly distressed. I can't imagine what he makes of it all. He starts talking. He's looking down, his attention on no one in particular. 'Listen to me,' he says, his voice shaking. 'I can keep my mouth shut about all of this. I don't know what the score is here and I don't care. I'm way out of my depth. I do divorce stuff usually. I had no idea that Beckett was a private detective until now. I didn't know what he was. He was just someone that someone else was interested in.'

Jennison doesn't like this for whatever reason. He's starting to lose his temper again. I just hope he doesn't get the hammer and nails out. 'I'll tell you what the fucking score is, you fucking dish of shit. The fucking score is you're in deep trouble. Who knows you've taken this job?'

'No one. I work alone. I don't discuss what I do with anyone. I never do. Client confidentiality.'

'So no one knows you're here and no one knows you followed Beckett here.'

'That's right. I didn't know I'd be coming here until I saw Beckett drive through those gates with the girl. I didn't know what this place was. It was just another thing that Beckett was doing; another place he was visiting.'

'And he doesn't employ you.'

'*Employ* me? Of course not.'

'And whoever does employ you didn't tell you why they wanted him followed. Is that right?'

'No. Yes. No.'

'You better not be lying to me.'

'I swear it. Everything I told you is the truth. No one knows I'm here. No one knows what I'm working on.'

'Where's your car?'

'I parked it by the entrance to the park that backs on to your property; the one near the tennis courts and the cherry trees.'

'Which entrance? The one a hundred yards down the road from the main gate into here?'

'Yes. Just a bit before the zebra crossing.'

'What sort of car is it? What's the registration?'

'It's a grey Audi A7 Sportback. Registration is PI 999.'

'Where's the keys?'

'In my pocket.'

Jennison nods to Shortass who strides over and takes some keys on a black Audi leather fob out of Dixon's front trouser pocket. He puts them in his own pocket.

'Is the car registered to you? Is it your car?'

'Yes. Yes it is.'

Jennison stares at Dixon and I can see the cogs turning again. He looks at Wide Chest and gives him a little smile.

'Kill him.'

Before Dixon realises what's happening, Wide Chest leans down and hooks a brawny arm around his neck. His weight and strength keep Dixon in place, who's still sitting down with his back against the sofa.

Wide Chest pushes him slightly to the side so he can

get his arm around his throat at a better angle. With a single jerk, he adjusts his position so his bicep is tight against the front of Dixon's windpipe. Then he just squats there, as if nothing is happening, his mouth slightly open.

It's happening for Dixon, though. He's kicking his legs back and forth, trying to get some leverage on the terracotta tiles so he can change his position and get out of this. His eyes are wide with panic. He knows this isn't a joke or a threat. He knows this is happening for real. Sometimes it looks as if he's trying to stand up, but this is impossible.

He's trying to speak, but can't manage it. Instead, he's making heaving, squeaking noises, as saliva bubbles from his mouth. Jennison's mother moves in closer to get a good view, while Jennison himself sits back down next to Sara, pulling her close to him and massaging her shoulders. She's awake now and stares at Wide Chest and Dixon. I can tell from her expression that she doesn't fully comprehend what's happening.

Dixon's face is red and his eyes are bulging. He's desperately trying to get away, change his position, anything to take the pressure off his throat. But it isn't working. He tries to grab Wide Chest's arm, but this is a total waste of time. Wide Chest is impassive: bored, even. This is just a chore for him. No. Not a chore. There's a look in his eyes that I missed. It's a quiet satisfaction. Whether he's getting off on this I can't tell. Perhaps it's the pleasure of practising a skill that he's very good at. Maybe he likes obeying and/or pleasing his boss. I don't know or care.

Jennison has started snogging Sara again, keeping one eye on Wide Chest's progress. He feels one of her breasts.

I realise that he can only do this while his mother's facing the other way. He must have a thing about his mother watching him groping a woman wearing a see-through baby doll. I know I do.

Mummy is right up close to Dixon. This is entertainment for her. She's enjoying herself. She caws away in that terrible voice, stamping her feet up and down on the wheelchair foot rest.

'Lovely. Lovely. Go on. Go on. Do it. Do it. Do it. You dirty bastard. Let him give you what's coming to you.' She smacks her lips. Drool pours out onto her lap. 'Go on. Go on. Squeeze the blooming life out of him. You filthy pig. Do it. Do it. Do it. Lovely.'

She spits on Dixon then she slaps the oxygen mask back on her face, her eyes fierce and unhinged. She's leaning forward. Her face is about a foot away from Dixon's. I'm watching this and I'm thinking, *what a way to go*.

To take my mind off things, I speculate about how I'd manage a straight choice between Klementina and Mrs Doroteia Vasconselos. It's difficult. Klementina, without doubt, has the sort of figure I like and had a healthy sexiness and hunger about her. But Doroteia exuded a sophisticated feral sexuality that would be intriguing to explore.

Also, the fact that she'd actually gone out for a walk with the express purpose of getting picked up or picking someone up for when her husband was away is pretty exciting. She and Klementina are such a contrasting pair that it's an almost impossible choice to make. I decide that if I survive this, I'll just have to have both of them.

Dixon's face is dark purple. He's struggling like the devil, but it's totally futile. Wide Chest's mind seems to be elsewhere. He's indifferent to what he'd doing like only a true psychopath can be. I wonder what he's thinking about. Girls? Why does he call his gun Shirley?

Sara pulls away from Jennison and starts to realise what's happening to Dixon. She looks horrified. Jennison gently brings her head back towards him so he can kiss her again and take her mind off things. She turns her face away like a child refusing bad-tasting medicine. The mask is off Jennison's mother's mouth again.

'Go on. Tighter. Tighter. Do it! Do it! Do it! You bastard! Look at him! Look at him! Lovely! Dirty! Dirty! Dirty!'

I take a professional look at Dixon's face. I would think he has less than a minute left. Shortass has a quick chuckle and speaks to Wide Chest in a friendly tone.

'Come on, Derek. You're slipping, mate!'

Wide Chest looks up and gives Shortass a quick matey grin. Then it's over for Dixon. Wide Chest releases him and he slumps forward, his head resting on his knees. I can see he's pissed himself.

'Yes! Yes! Yes! Yes! Lovely!' says Jennison's mum. She slaps her mask back on and reverses to where Jennison is sitting. The little motor sounds from her wheelchair are actually quite nice to listen to. Jennison lets go of Sara. Sara throws up on the floor. Jennison stands up.

'Right, boys. Thank you, Derek. Get him out of here. You know where to put him. We'll have a little meeting tomorrow and decide where to get rid of him. I'm too tired for it tonight. Timmy – go and find his car. Make sure he hasn't parked on a double yellow or something stupid like that. Make an appointment with Chandler's. Tell 'em you'll be there tomorrow with it. Get it crushed right down. I want it the size of an Oxo cube and I want it made into a key ring.'

Shortass laughs. 'Sure thing, boss.'

I have to admit, I was producing quite a lot of adrenalin during that little show. It seems to have made a difference. I'm feeling a lot more alert now than I was half an hour ago, even though I'm still getting the cold sweats and my mouth feels like I've been chewing cat litter.

Wide Chest effortlessly lifts Dixon up onto his shoulders and leaves the room. Jennison tells Shortass to tidy things up before he sorts the car out. He goes out of the room and returns a moment later with some cleaning things from the kitchen. There's a pool of blood and a puddle of urine where Dixon had been murdered and he gets to work on it quickly and efficiently.

I might get him to clean my flat when this is all over.

Jennison's mother mops drool and bits of food from her mouth with a tissue. She's a class act.

31

CORPSE SURFING

Sara is asleep now. I'm still rather worried about the effect that the drug cocktail has had on her. Maybe her constitution isn't up to it. Either that or she had a different dose or maybe even a different combination of drugs.

I can see Jennison staring at me. I think he suspects that I'm starting to recover. Some of the symptoms of that are hard to hide, like my conversation. It's hard to keep faking it when you start yapping away, because you can't remember how fluently you were speaking fifteen minutes earlier.

'I haven't decided what to do with you, Beckett,' he says. 'Your disposal has to be discreet and explainable, unlike your mate's there. It'll be awkward with Isolda around, so I can't exterminate you quite yet. Like I said, I don't want to hurt her. She's been through enough.'

'That guy Dixon wasn't my mate. I told you. I had no idea why he was tailing me.'

I'd almost forgotten about Isolda in all the excitement. Is she still having a bath? One thing's for sure: I'm not going to hang around here to find out what Jennison may or may not have in mind for me. I have one priority and that's getting Sara out of this hellhole.

As far as I can tell there are only the seven of us here;

me, Sara, Isolda, Jennison, Wide Chest, Shortass and Mummy. Wide Chest and Shortass are the biggest threats. One of them just killed a guy with his bare hands right in front of me. How the hell does Jennison get away with doing this sort of shit? The more I start shaking off the effects of the drugs, the more chilling and bizarre it all seems.

Dixon was an intruder on Jennison's property. Couldn't he have just called the police? Maybe that's the last thing he would ever do and that was just Dixon's bad luck. That has to be the reason. If Dixon was being questioned in a police interview room, God knows what he might say.

The police would want to know why he was there. He might tell them about me. The police might wonder what a private investigator was doing in Jennison's house. They'd check Jennison out. Dixon might remember that I'd mentioned the name Sara Holt. The police collate intelligence. The names Holt and Jennison might set alarm bells ringing on a computer somewhere, particularly when Sara has been reported missing.

Would Jennison know about this risk? He may not know the specifics but probably suspects. Yes – Dixon was a dead man as soon as he came over that fence.

'I can see from your expression you're coming back into the world, Mr Beckett. I'm going to have to store you away again, I'm afraid. I have a lot to deal with tonight. When I see you again, you'll be ready for a serious man-to-man chat with me and Timmy.'

'I can't wait.'

'Neither can Timmy, Mr Beckett, neither can Timmy.'

Shortass comes back into the room, angry as usual. Maybe he's been talking to Isolda. This must have been a dramatic couple of days for him. I know he wants to kill me but I can't get enthused about it.

'Timmy. I want you to take Miss Holt and put her in my bedroom. Put her on my bed. I think she needs to sleep her dosage off. I don't want her being like a bloody zombie all the time. I want to enjoy myself. I want you to tie her. I want her ankles tied and her wrists tied. I don't want her to do anything silly and I don't want her running out of here. Try not to cut off her circulation. I don't want her having gangrenous hands. I can't stand that on a woman. When you've finished, lock my bedroom door. The key's on the lintel. Give it to me when you're done.'

'Sure, boss.'

Shortass goes over to where Sara is sitting and hoists her off the sofa, hooking his big hands under her armpits. It's funny to see that she's actually taller than him. He scoops her up into his arms and carries her out of the room. Jennison watches as they both leave, a stupid smile on his face. Wide Chest returns and gives a thumbs-up sign to Jennison.

I let my mind go blank so I can listen to the noises of the house, in case it gives me a clue as to where Shortass is taking her. I hear him ascending some stairs. I hear his heavy tread directly above me. I hear it move to the right. Then it stops.

Jennison's mother seems to have nodded off. It's either that or she's died from overexcitement after watching a man being throttled at close quarters. I don't think it's her age; I think she's just not right in the head and never was. Jennison himself is looking tired. Not surprising; he's had a tough, stressful day ordering beatings and murders with interludes of self-pity. He looks at me, then he looks at Wide Chest.

'Have we still got those good handcuffs? The American ones?'

'Yeah. I'll go and get them.'

Wide Chest leaves the room. Jennison grins at me.

'I reckon if you weren't so fucked by what we put into you when you got here, I'd be in a pretty dangerous situation being alone with you, wouldn't I, Sonny Jim.'

'Yeah. Particularly with your withered arm.'

His eyes deaden again. 'I'd like to have a long, long chat with you. I reckon it'd be quite interesting. I'd also like to get you alone with just you, me and a cricket bat. I'm very, very upset with you.'

'But you're torn, aren't you,' I say. 'You'd like to kill me to get me out of the way and because of what I've done to your boys, but you think I have more to tell you and also you don't want to annoy Isolda. Or may I call her Dolly?'

He doesn't seem to be listening to me. 'I want to know where Jackie is. I want him to have a decent Christian burial.'

I can't stop myself. I laugh out loud. Jennison punches me in the face with a speed and power surprising for a man of his advancing years. That felt like it loosened a tooth and I can taste fresh blood in my mouth. Wide Chest returns with the cuffs.

'Get him on his feet,' says Jennison angrily, rubbing his hand.

Wide Chest helps me up to a standing position. I don't feel as dizzy from getting up as I expected to. I suddenly wonder how they knew to have that reception committee with the syringe ready when we got to the house. It didn't make sense.

Did Isolda say something coded to her father when

she rang him from the SUV? Was it something she said to George at the gate? She told him not to work too hard, as if it was a private joke. Perhaps it was that. Hardly matters now.

'Stick your hands out,' says Wide Chest. He's got a pair of American police handcuffs. They look new. Has Jennison got deals going with police forces all over the world to get his gear? He's just about to put them on my wrists when Jennison stops him.

'Put them on behind his back, Derek. We know he's a slippery customer. We don't want to give him any advantages.'

I turn around so I'm facing away from Wide Chest and feel the cuffs go on. He's clumsy and pushes too many ratchets in so it's painful and uncomfortable.

'That hurts,' I say.

'Good,' says Wide Chest, helpfully.

I hear him use the key to lock them. Well, that's two advantages that I might have had gone already. In an ideal world, he'd have cuffed my hands in front of me and not used the key. Oh well. I can already feel the numbness starting to kick in on my wrists.

'You know where to take him,' says Jennison.

Wide Chest nods, grabs my arm and marches me out of the house. It looks like I'm going to be slung in the dark place again. We walk across the gravel and then into the courtyard. It seems like an age ago I was in this place. Now I'm able to get a good look at it sober, I can't imagine what sort of purpose it had.

It's almost the same shape as an oast house, but not quite. Perhaps it was used for storage. Perhaps it was some sort of garage. Hard to tell. The no windows thing is baffling. Maybe Jennison had it converted so he could keep his prisoners in a state of disorientation while they were ripped to the tits on homemade drug cocktails. I hear it's quite the thing nowadays amongst the Kenwood cognoscenti.

It's quite a relief to feel the air on my face and I take a few deep breaths while I have the opportunity. Wide Chest's grip on my arm has slackened a little, but I won't be fast enough to take advantage of it. Not yet.

'Don't you think Timmy's a little too short and ugly to be going out with Isolda? I mean – she's beautiful, isn't she.'

'Shut up.'

'I thought *you'd* be more suitable for her. She goes for guys whose antennae aren't picking up all the channels.'

He stops and gives me a dead leg. That's probably the first one I've had since being in school. He opens the door to the dark place, shoves me inside and slams it shut. I land heavily on my chest and shoulder. Having the dead leg didn't help my balance, not to mention being handcuffed.

I stay where I am for a couple of minutes, trying to recover from all of my aches and pains. I do a quick inventory of my body. The most immediately painful thing is the dead leg, but that'll be gone in about five minutes. After that it's the pain of the too-tight cuffs on my wrists. The fall exacerbated that pain and I think one of my wrists might be bleeding.

My face is throbbing now; it feels hot, swollen and painful from the miscellaneous punches, kicks and slaps I received at the hands of Jennison, Shortass and Wide Chest. At least Jennison's mother didn't have a go – I don't think I could have stood the humiliation.

I know I'm not a hundred per cent, but I think I'm

over most of the immediate, harsh effects of my injection. I'm not hallucinating, I know who I am, I know approximately where I am, I know who all those people were and I know what I have to do. The only problem is, I'm imprisoned, totally helpless and can't use any of that knowledge to my advantage.

I spin myself around until I'm sitting up and then get myself onto my feet. The pain of the dead leg makes me grimace. I take another deep breath. The blackness in here is still as bad as it was before, so that can't have been one of the drug side effects. Then I sense something that I can't quite put my finger on. It's different in here. There's something not quite right about the atmosphere. I stand completely still, listening, but can't hear anything.

I try to picture the place in my head. There was the door, which only opened from the outside. When Wide Chest came to get me, there was a noise like sliding metal, which I heard again just now after he shoved me in. That means there's some sort of bar preventing anyone getting out of here. I don't think I saw it when I was outside just now, but it must be there.

For a second, earlier on, I saw a loft hatch door, dead in the centre of the room. But it was a couple of feet too high for me to be able to reach it. I can't stand here doing nothing all day, so I decide to take a walk around. Almost immediately, I'm flat on my face again.

I've tripped over something big on the floor. I landed on my chest and collarbone. I grit my teeth as I try to overcome the pain. I can hear my deep breathing, brought on by the shock. I'd like to see myself in a mirror, just to assess the damage.

I sit up and shake my head to clear it. I'm getting sick of this now. I kick in front of me to see what it was I tripped over. My foot makes contact with something soft and I get a chill in my stomach. I kick it again. And again. There's no doubt that it's a body.

I spin around, squat down and turn my back on it so I can check it out with my hands. I know it's almost certainly going to be Dixon, but I have to be sure.

I let my fingers wander up to the face and pat the side where Wide Chest punched him. I find that wide gash straight away, about four inches long and still wet with blood.

I place my fingers on the side of his neck, in case by some miracle he's not actually dead. There's no pulse, and he's still fairly warm, but he's definitely no longer in the land of the living.

OK. This is just a bit of a joke from Jennison and friends and designed to freak me out, no doubt. I have to think beyond that and see if I can use this to my advantage in some way.

I try to think about what he may have on his person that I can use. There were his car keys, but Shortass took those. What else? He certainly wouldn't carry any weapons and if he did they'd have been taken from him by now. I wonder what happened to my tactical pen. I think back to my meeting with him, if it can be called that.

It's going to be very difficult for me to search him comprehensively with these handcuffs on. I try to visualise him as he was this morning. He had a wallet. I made him show me his SIA licence. He took the wallet out of his jacket pocket and his keys fell out. Not his car keys; these were ordinary keys, house keys, with a cork from a wine bottle attached. And there were a few thin grey metal strips next to the keys. Burglar's tools.

I adjust my position and pat the jacket pocket nearest to me. Nothing. Did Shortass take these keys too? But then I feel something but I can't work out where it is in the geography of the jacket. Finally I find it. There's a low inside pocket on the right-hand side and there they are.

I fish them out and feel them carefully, trying to quell the elation I'm experiencing. Two Yale keys, a single mortice lock key, a smaller key and four slim metal strips of varying widths. I try to take one of the thinner ones off the key ring, but it's too fiddly so I give up.

Even though it's pitch black in here, I close my eyes to visualise what I'm about to do. I get one of the thinner metal strips in my fingers and feel along its length. It's about right; maybe two inches long and two tenths of an inch wide. The other keys hanging off it are a bit of a hindrance, but I'll have to work around that.

I sit up as straight as I can and feel the cuff on the left, giving myself a mental map of all its parts. I didn't get a good look at it in the house, but it's a basic design; there's the moveable single strand with ratchet teeth that fits into the static double strand. When it's closed on your wrists, there's a moveable serrated lever inside which locks the ratchet. This lever is moved out of the way when you use the key to open the cuffs.

What I have to do is to move the serrated lever out of the way using my thin metal strip instead of the key, which I don't have. It's a pretty simple mechanism to beat, but when you've been cuffed behind your back and you're in total darkness, this is easier said than done.

I have to position my wrist at an insane angle to get the metal strip into the double strand and I can feel the muscles in my hand cramping up.

It takes me six attempts before I get the strip in at the

correct angle. I'm aware that my teeth are chattering from all the adrenalin I'm producing. Still, adrenalin is good; it'll help to counteract the effects of the drugs a little more. That's my theory, anyway; a biochemist may disagree.

I now have to push the strip into the cuff so that it moves the internal serrated lever out of the way. I push it in a millimetre at a time. I'm afraid to do it any faster in case it bounces its way out or snaps.

Finally, I feel some resistance as the strip meets the first ratchet on the lever. The cramp in my hand is getting worse. I screw my eyes up tightly and concentrate on visualising what's going on in there. Finally, I'm able to push the strip in as far as it will go and can feel the lever move out of the way. I use my ring finger to tug the single strand and the cuff is off. I take a deep breath.

I bring my hand around to the front and give my freed wrist a quick rub before dealing with the other cuff. This only takes a couple of seconds. I put Dixon's keys and the cuffs in my pocket and progress to stage two.

It would seem that my only way out of this place is via the loft space. Of course, even if I manage to get up there it may not lead anywhere, but I have to give it a try.

From what I remember it was absolutely central in what seems to be a perfectly square room. Putting my hands out in front of me, I start walking until I reach a wall. I turn around until my back is against the wall and walk in as straight a line as I can manage, counting the number of steps I take until I reach the other side. It's twenty-eight steps.

Just to make sure, I do the same thing with the other two walls and it's still twenty-eight steps. Let's hope each of my steps is about the same length. From the wall to my left, I take fourteen steps, keeping my hand against the wall to avoid drift. Then I turn and take fourteen steps into the theoretical centre of the room and stop. If my calculations are correct, the loft hatch door should be directly above me.

I take Dixon's keys and the handcuffs out of my pocket and put them on the floor about a foot apart from each other. If I accidentally kick the keys across the room I'll have to start all over again, but it's unlikely I'll accidentally kick the handcuffs as well.

Now I have to find Dixon. I stand still and empty my mind. Even though he's dead, his mass and remaining temperature should give off small atmospheric hints as to where he's located. This may well be an unreliable technique, but if it works it'll save me some time.

After a minute or so, I decide he's roughly eight or nine paces from where I'm standing, about forty-five degrees to my right. I walk in this direction and trip over him almost immediately, after only four paces. Not perfectly accurate but not bad.

I pat my hands over his body, grab one of his forearms in both hands and drag him back to where I was standing. He's incredibly heavy. I realise where I am when I step on the handcuffs. By the time I stop, I'm panting and perspiring from the effort. I put the handcuffs and keys back in my pocket and start to manipulate his corpse.

Despite the pitch-blackness, I'm quickly able to familiarise myself with all his body parts and his clothing, terrible as I know that sounds. I grab the lapels of his jacket and hoist him up to a sitting position. As an experiment, I let him go to see what will happen. He falls onto his back.

I grab the back of his collar and hoist him up again. I move behind him and attempt to push his head in between his knees and get it to stay there. Unfortunately, he's got a bit of a gut and this is causing him to fall backwards towards me all of the time.

Still squatting behind him, I grab the back of his trousers and yank him up to a better position. I grab his hair and once again try to get his head where I want it. I need him bent double so I can use his corpse to stand on and get to that loft door. I don't want to have to break his spine to do this, but I will if I have to.

This time he almost stays where he is. It could be worse; at least he's got a few hours before rigor mortis sets in.

I'm going to have to keep him in position with the pressure and weight of my body and hope the loft door is where I think it is. I get him into position, holding his head down with my hand. I get a foot on his shoulders and put all of my weight on it, forcing him to stay where I want him. This only gives me a couple of extra feet, but it should be enough.

I quickly push myself up so I'm standing on his shoulders. He wobbles beneath me. It's like surfing; corpse surfing. I put my hands up and I feel the cold ceiling against them, but I can't feel the loft door. I don't think I can keep this up for long. Just as I'm seconds away from getting wiped out, I feel the edge of the wooden frame of the door. I was about three feet off.

I jump off Dixon just as he flops backwards and to the side. I drag him to where I think he needs to be and start the whole process over again. This time I'm a bit more confident and even though his body shifts to the left at one point I manage to stay balanced. I can't imagine what this must look like.

I hit the loft door with the ball of my hand and it flies open. It's on hinges, which are to my right. I grab the sides of the frame and pull myself up, leaving Dixon to fall away. I'm not up to this. I feel dizzy and my shoulders and arms blaze with pain.

Once I've hoisted myself up as far as my stomach, I stop for a moment, hanging there with my legs dangling down. Part of me wants to give up, but another part insists that I make the rest of the journey. With a huge effort, I use my elbows to drag myself into the loft area, turn around and close the door behind me.

I need a stiff drink.

32

EIGHT-INCH BLADE

It takes my eyes roughly ten seconds to get used to the darkness in here. It isn't as bad as downstairs. I can see my hand in front of my face, which is a start. What light there is, is coming from tiny gaps in between the tiles or slats or whatever the roof of this place is made up of.

I'm able to stand up without hitting my head on the ceiling. I take a few cautious steps, pressing my feet into the flooring as much as I dare. I don't want to end up surfing on Dixon's shoulders again.

There doesn't seem to be anything in here apart from dust. There's a vague smell of oil and pine, but that's about it. Now I have to get out of here without anyone noticing and without making any noise.

I walk to the rear so I'm as far away from the main house as I can get. I rub my hands across the wall. It's made up of rough-surfaced tiles, possibly fired clay, but they feel fragile, the sort that would noisily shatter into a million pieces upon hitting the ground, depending on how hard or soft the ground was. They seem to measure about six inches by twelve.

I put pressure on one of them with my fingertips. It doesn't move. I would imagine that they're hammered into place from the outside, or perhaps they've used clips.

They probably overlap and if the workmanship was good they're going to be difficult to remove.

There's only one thing for it. With my left hand I find what seems to be roughly the centre of one of the tiles. I clench my right hand into a fist, and with as much *ki* as I can manage, execute a hard, straight punch from just over a foot away.

Well, that hurt. I feel the impact point on the tile with my fingers. There's a fracture straight down the centre. OK. It just needs a little more force. I pull back my fist and whack it again. That time there is a little more give and I hear a loud crack. Have to be careful with the noise, but I doubt they'd have heard that from the house.

The tile is now in four pieces. I manage to pull it apart, carefully placing each piece by my feet. At last I can see outside. It's become moderately dark now, but there are external lights illuminating the grounds. All that's visible is a lawn and assorted shrubs in large pots.

I can see now that each tile is attached to a long strip of wood with small black metal clips. Slowly and quietly, I start to remove the clips, the wooden strips and the tiles until there's a huge hole in the side of the roof, big enough for me to get through.

I lean out and look down. It's difficult to see clearly, but I think it's just grass. This is good; it means I won't make any noise when I land. I think I'm about ten to twelve feet up. I close my eyes and visualise the jump. It'll take about two seconds to get to the ground. I intend to land about four feet away from the wall and attempt to do a forward breakfall to lessen the energy of the impact and hopefully remain undamaged. The last thing I want now is a sprained ankle or broken leg or both.

I can feel the wind on my face. I can smell lavender.

I'm aware that my pulse has increased, but that's understandable. No more pontificating. I'm in a hurry. I grab the tiles on each side and project myself forward into the darkness.

*

The moment I feel my feet make contact with the ground I roll forward to lessen the impact, much the same as if I'd come down by parachute or been thrown by a martial arts instructor. I take the breakfall down the length of my right arm and in a diagonal across my back until I'm up on my feet again. I manage to avoid grunting as the wind is knocked out of me.

I stay still and listen. No noise, no voices. All clear. I turn around slowly. I can see the house. I've got to get in there. I walk about fifteen feet to my right, to an area where the garden lights are not illuminating everything so strongly.

I wonder if Jennison has live-in staff. There was no evidence of this when I was in the house. If I was him, I'd just have people coming here at set hours during the day. I take a few steps towards the house until I can see the main entrance. This is lit up, as are most of the rooms on the ground floor.

It's been maybe fifteen minutes since I was inside. It's unlikely everyone is in the same place as they were when I left, but I can't worry about that.

Listening out for noises and movement, I make my way to what seems to be the rear of the house. I gulp some more fresh air into my lungs. I have to keep on my toes. There are aggressive crazy people in there with guns.

I can see a large kitchen, but there's no direct entrance

into it. I continue walking, keeping roughly twenty feet away and using the shadows to conceal my presence. There's a door to the far left of the kitchen. Not illuminated, but not open. I can't work out what it's for. Maybe it's a boot room of some sort. Well, I don't have time to speculate any further. I take a final look and listen and head toward it.

I crouch down and take Dixon's keys out of my pocket. There's a very faint sound of music coming from somewhere. I can't tell whether it's a stereo or the television.

This door has one lock. It's a silver knob lock. I'm amazed. Jennison should know better than this. He should have asked Shortass for advice. It's a fatal mistake to use these on outside doors. All a professional burglar would need would be a hammer. One hard strike and the whole thing's on the floor.

I don't have a hammer on me and besides, I can't afford the noise. I use one of Dixon's flat burglar tools and the thing is unlocked in fifteen seconds.

I open the door slowly, waiting for an alarm to go off. There's nothing. I push it open, step inside and close it quietly behind me. I'm in a small room filled with white goods. There's a washing machine, a spin dryer, a drying cabinet and a big freezer. There are shelves stacked with cloths and detergents and in the corner a whole area filled with mops, buckets and the like. The smell in here is harsh and acrid and I can feel my eyes burning. I recognise the yellow bucket that Shortass used to mop up Dixon's blood and urine.

I come out of this room into a section of hallway. I attempt to orientate myself. This is not exactly the back of the house. It was more to the left-hand side if we call the main entrance the front. That means to get to the living room, you'd have to turn right at this point and then take a left. The living room would then be straight ahead and at a right angle to the front door, looking out onto the lake, with the conservatory in the way.

Unfortunately, I can't see any way of getting up to the first floor to look for Sara. There must be only one staircase and I could see that from the living room. Besides, I'm not exactly sure what room she's in, only that it's above the living room and to the right, and that may not be altogether accurate.

I stand still and listen to the house noise. There's definitely a television on somewhere and it's downstairs. From the gunfire, I think it must be a film.

I zone that out and try to capture whatever else is around. The first thing I pick up on is the stridulous breathing of Jennison's mother, sucking the oxygen down. It's coming from my left-hand side, so she can't have moved since I left.

I can hear a male voice. I'm guessing that Jennison's still in there with her, possibly with Shortass in attendance. I have to remember that Isolda is somewhere in the house, and despite her entreaties to her father would almost certainly alert everyone if she spotted me wandering around unattended.

There are two fair sized rooms to my right. One of them is a large empty dining room and the other is some sort of general utility room, like a cross between a lounge, a diner and a games room. The door is partially closed. I can feel that there's somebody in there.

I walk up to the door as quietly as possible. It would be easier if this place was carpeted, but it's all terracotta tiles. Still, I'm wearing crêpe soles, so my walk is relatively silent and I'm pressing down firmly with each step I take to cut the noise out completely.

The door is about six inches open. Standing on the other side of the hallway, my back to a wall, I can see a bookshelf stacked with gardening books, a heavy-looking cast iron oven, the edge of a smoked glass dining table and a gigantic television screen, which is currently switched off.

On a table next to the television are two Xbox controllers, a white PS4 console and a stack of games. There's a small sink with a coffee percolator on a table next to it. I can somehow imagine Shortass and Wide Chest in here playing *Grand Theft Auto V* together until the early hours. There's also a transparent retro-looking cocktail cabinet full of drinks.

I hear someone cough, followed by a brief rustle of paper. It's Wide Chest, I just know it. I can smell his odour and I can feel his bad vibes. He's a physically strong murderous psychopath with a gun, so this has to be fast, silent and possibly lethal.

As soon as I open this door, he'll be on full alert and will let everyone else know that something's up. Then he'll probably try to subdue, maim or kill me. Maybe all three. I assume he's sitting at the smoked glass table. That would make him six or seven feet away from the door. For me to go in that room would be madness. I've got to bring him to me.

I cross over the hallway and stand flat against the wall, next to the section of door where the handle is. When he materialises in a moment, he'll have to grab the door handle on his side and pull it towards him. At that point, I'll have exactly one second in which to act. I just hope he doesn't come out with a gun in his hand; that would really make things a little difficult.

I hit the door just once with the back of my fist, loud enough to get his attention, quiet enough so nobody else hears it, fast enough so he didn't see me do it, but not so powerfully that it makes the door swing open. I'm so skilled that it surprises me sometimes, it really does.

I hear him sigh and put his newspaper down. 'Yeah, yeah,' he says. I wonder who he thinks it is?

The moment he opens the door, I swing around so we're face to face for a fraction of a second. The look he gives me is a stunned mix of astonishment and stupidity. I slap my hand on the side of his head and slam it sideways into the doorjamb, following this up with a head butt to his nose and a knife hand strike into the front of his throat, shattering the cartilage.

I push him back into the room and close the door quietly behind us. He falls heavily and I kick him as hard as I can in the balls while he's down. He attempts to say something, probably an objection of some sort, but it's difficult with a crushed throat, which is why I did it.

I reach into his pocket and pull out the P226, using it to pistol whip him into delirium, then a minute later cuff him to one of the legs of the oven. I check the gun over and it's fully loaded. I flick the safety off and shove it into my waistband. One down, four to go. Yes, I'm counting Jennison's mother.

I open the door, walk into the hallway and stand and listen. I can still hear a film that someone's watching, but can't quite place where it would be. There was a big television in the living room, so I guess it has to be coming from there.

To my left is a small toilet and next to that a room with more cleaning stuff. Almost opposite that is a kitchen. I can hear a kettle boiling, quiet piano music and someone moving around. I take the gun out of my waistband and point it towards the floor, gripping my right wrist with my left hand. If I remember correctly, the P226 takes a 9mm round. That would be bad enough in a real combat situation, but for close range shooting in a place like this it would be devastating.

I sidle along the wall, listening all the while. I don't think there's more than one person in there. When I'm three steps away from the door I can smell perfume; heady, musky, catches at the back of your throat. It's Isolda.

I take a deep breath and swing through the door, arms bent, holding the gun close to my body, index finger down the frame, both hands around the grip, thumbs meeting. She's got her back to me. She doesn't notice. Then I see she's caught my reflection in the window. She puts down the mug she was holding, fiddles around a bit and turns to face me, leaning back against the surface, hands behind her back, chest thrust forward.

She's wearing a black cotton t-shirt and baggy white jeans. She isn't wearing a bra. She sees where my eyes are going and smiles sweetly.

'Are you going to shoot me, Daniel?'

'Scream and you'll find out.'

I take a step back, close the door with my foot, then take a few steps to my right, still keeping the gun on her. She's still hot as hell but I don't trust her anymore. Maybe I never did. She pushes herself away from the surface and walks slowly towards me. I don't like it that she has her hands behind her back. It might be that it makes her breasts look more crudely provocative; it might be that she's hiding something.

'You've heard me scream before. I thought you liked it.'

'Shut up. Where is everybody?'

'I can't have you hurting Dad. It wouldn't be right. Not after all he's done for me.'

'He's abducted an innocent woman and just had a man killed, right there in your living room.'

She shrugs. 'He can't help himself. It's just business.'

'Bullshit. This isn't business, this is all about you. None of those things would have happened if it wasn't for you.'

Her eyes flash provocatively and she turns the flirtatiousness in her voice up to eleven on the dial.

'But I like those things, Daniel. I always have. I tried not to, but I failed. I liked hearing the stories about Dad that my grandmother told me. It sounded exciting. I liked hearing about Dad's friends. It was like Robin Hood and his Merry Men. Does that sound silly? It's why I've always gone for a certain sort of man. It's why I liked you. I could feel it in you straight away; that ruthlessness, that danger, that callousness. It's intoxicating. It makes me go a little crazy. I couldn't work you out, Daniel. I still can't. It's as if you're hiding something big about yourself, but that makes me even crazier. The fact that you won't let me in is a turn on.'

She's moving towards me, one slow step at a time.

'At the same time, I got a buzz from aiming a gun at you. I know that sounds mad. I like having power over other people. It doesn't matter how. It makes me feel powerful. It makes me feel good. I had power over Sara. She thought she was in charge, but really it was me. Put the gun down and we'll go and talk to Dad. He won't hurt you. I've told him not to. We can sort this out. Sara's not important. She never was. We mustn't be enemies, Daniel. We've got to be in this together, otherwise everything will fall apart. You don't want me to go to prison, do you?'

I don't say anything. I'm just waiting. She licks her lips. Her eyes are half-closed. She's panting.

'I'm on fire. You can tell, can't you, Daniel. You can tell I'm aching all over. You can tell I'm ready. I don't care that there are people here. That just makes it better. I know what you want. I can see it in your face. I can give it to you. You know I can. Put that gun away.'

'All I want is Sara and I want to get her out of this madhouse.'

She keeps walking towards me. She's smiling. Whatever she thinks she's going to do, it's not going to happen. I get a sudden shiver of fear mixed with desire. It's an interesting sensation.

'We could have been quite something together, Daniel.'

'I was saying that to Timmy. He wasn't so convinced.'

She smiles. 'I'm sure you can tell a lot of men have had me, but none of them were quite like you. I finally met someone who was as freaky as me. It was wild. It was immoral. I liked the taste of it.'

It's only a kitchen knife, but it has a nasty-looking eight-inch blade. She's no knife-fighter. She lifts it high above her head and strikes down, telegraphing wildly and aiming for my collarbone. Dropping the gun, I block it with my left hand while simultaneously striking her in the face with the edge of my right.

I grab her wrist and upper arm, twist my body hard to the right and bring her down, bent double, until I can walk across her and put her on the floor, bending her wrist back so she drops the knife. Well, that confirms it; the whole family is crazy. Yazmine's suicide was probably the only normal thing that ever happened in this house.

I pick up the gun and aim it at her head. She has a nose bleed. Despite the fact that she probably could and would have killed me, I still didn't like doing that to her. Guess I must be old-fashioned.

'Get up.'

There are tears in her eyes. 'I really did tell Dad not to hurt you or kill you. It wasn't all talk. What I said about us wasn't all talk, either.'

'Just most of it. Stop talking, Isolda, you're breaking my heart. And your dad's going to kill me anyway, if you're interested.'

'That's not true. He wouldn't. Not if I asked him not to.'

'He's just going to find a way of doing it so you don't find out. Do you really think I'm going to be allowed to go back out into the world when I know what's been going on here?'

'He might let you. If I say so.'

'None of you have thought this through properly. Do you think you can just go back to work tomorrow as if none of this has happened? This is serious stuff, Isolda; serious stuff perpetrated by stupid, arrogant people. Is anyone likely to be armed in there?'

'Not as far as I know.'

'You better be right.'

I grab her left arm to help her get on her feet. She scowls at me. We walk out of the kitchen and into the hallway. I'm keeping her two feet in front of me as we walk down towards the living room. The television sound gets louder. I can hear Jennison's mother's stilted breathing. I can hear Jennison talking to Shortass.

'It'll have to be both of them at the same time,' says Jennison. 'Dolly'll have to go back to work tomorrow and act normally. We'll do it when she's not here. You and Derek can get them in the Tourneo…'

'You sure?' says Shortass. 'That's new. What if we have to dump it?'

'No need. No one can link those two back to here. Only Dolly.'

I push Dolly into the room in front of me. With my left hand I hold the side of her neck to keep her steady and with my right aim the P226 at her temple.

'I hope you're not discussing getting rid of my body, gentlemen.'

'You're dead,' wheezes Mrs Jennison, enthusiastically.

Everyone here has something invested in Isolda and it allows me to control the room efficiently. None of them wants her brains over the wall, or at least I hope they don't.

Jennison is sitting on the sofa nearest me. He starts to get up, but I give him a look that tells him it's best if he doesn't. He's trembling with rage and is glaring at Shortass, willing him to do something.

Mrs Jennison has turned thirty degrees to look directly at me. It sounds as if someone has bet her she can't suck up all the oxygen in those cylinders in five minutes and she's desperate to prove them wrong.

But Shortass is quicker than I imagined. If I hadn't been pumped full of all those drugs, I'd have caught that slight movement and instantly blown his head off. But I've still not recovered and he managed to whip out a great-looking semi-automatic 9mm Luger, and is aiming it straight at the centre of my chest.

Death is The New Black

And now the dynamic of the situation has changed completely.

33

A REALLY SMART MOVE

'Right, you prick,' growls Shortass. 'Get that gun away from her head and throw it on the floor.'

'No.'

I keep my entire focus on Shortass. At the moment, he's the most important thing in the room. I'm watching for the miniscule body movements that'll tell me he's about to fire the gun. If that should happen, I'll have a third of a second in which to respond and put him down for good.

It's difficult in my present state, but I attempt to expand my consciousness into the whole room so that I'll sense any untoward movements or even malevolent thoughts from the others.

I don't know whether Isolda thinks I'd really shoot her in the head, but I can feel that she's frightened. It may not be me she's frightened of; it could be the whole situation, but I don't think she'll try anything physical. I try to block out her perfume. It doesn't work.

Jennison is fuming. He's the second most dangerous thing in the room. I don't think he's got a weapon. If he did, he'd probably have it aimed at me by now. I keep him in my peripheral vision, waiting for the smallest gesture. If he tries anything, my best bet would be to shoot him first and then attempt to shoot Shortass a fraction of a second later. My gun is already aimed in his direction, or I'd go for Shortass first. This is a difficult situation and I mustn't let my mind drift.

'Do something, Tommy, you faeces,' caws Mrs Jennison.

'Be quiet, Mummy.'

'Don't you tell me to be quiet. I sacrificed everything for you. I sacrificed my entire life.'

'Both of you shut up right now,' I say.

'If you harm a head on that girl's head, I'll *kill* you! Do you hear?' says Mrs Jennison. It's only now that I notice that she has no teeth and a slightly purple tongue. This outburst was too much for her and she slaps the mask back on her face and gulps down the O_2 once again.

'I'm not going to tell you again, prick,' says Shortass. 'Get the gun away from her head. Drop it on the floor. Kick it over to me.'

'You're about thirteen feet away. I'd never be able to kick it that far.'

'Don't get smart with me,' snarls Shortass, getting agitated. That's it, boy: keep the anger levels high.

Jennison moves forward. He has plans to get up.

'Stay where you are, Dad,' I say. 'You don't want your little girl to get hurt.'

'You come into *my* home and put a gun to my daughter's *head*? You are not going to believe what I am going to do to you, you bastard. I'm going to put Derek to work on you. We're going to make it last a long, long fucking time.'

'Derek's not very well. He's going to need a bit of surgery. Sorry about that.'

'You're lying.'

'You haven't realised it yet, Jennison, because you're

too thick. I'm *really* fuckin' bad news. Now sit back in that sofa and shut up.'

He flops back, momentarily defeated.

'Don't let him tell you what to do, Tommy. Don't be weak,' says Mrs Jennison. 'He's just a poof.'

Jennison says nothing. His mother puts her mask back on.

Shortass is wondering what to do next. He wants to shoot me, but he knows that could have catastrophic consequences. He's wondering if pulling the trigger now would be worth it. At least I'd be dead, but what if he missed? What if I wasn't killed immediately? What if I had time to shoot Isolda and then him? What would Jennison say or do if Isolda died because of his actions? I can see all of this in his eyes. He's tense. He's perspiring. This is all new to him.

Jennison, I don't have to worry about. He knows this is in the hands of Shortass and me, at least for the moment. He can only be a spectator until something fortuitous happens and it all starts going his way once more.

Then Isolda starts. Her voice is calm and assured.

'Shoot him, Timmy. Just pull the trigger. There's no way on earth he'll shoot me. I just know he won't.'

I tighten my grip on Isolda's neck. I look straight at Shortass and our eyes meet for a few seconds. Shortass holds my gaze and then looks away.

'You're wrong, Dolly. He'd do it. I can see it in his eyes.'

'You're the one that's wrong,' she says to him, contempt in her voice. 'Daniel and I have something special. We complement each other physically in a way that you and I never could. You're pathetic, Timmy.

You're barely a man. You're a sad, bullying little child.'

Bang.

I stopped blinking whenever a gun was fired long ago.

Isolda thought she was being crafty. She thought she'd enrage Shortass with her words and he'd shoot me. Instead he shot her.

This was a really smart move. I'm almost proud of him and not a little surprised. Isolda screams and instantly drops to the floor, removing my hostage advantage in one fell swoop. In that brief moment, I swing my gun around and aim it right between Shortass's eyes before he can get another shot off.

I glance quickly down at Isolda. There's a red patch of blood spreading across the white fabric of her jeans. It's a flesh wound in the upper thigh. It won't be fatal, but she'll need to get to a hospital pretty soon.

Not only did Shortass damage my room control prospects, but he also got back at her for what she's done to him by sleeping with me. Two birds with one stone, indeed.

Jennison jumps up to help his daughter and I let him do it. I take five steps to my right, keeping the gun on Shortass. He still aims his gun at my chest. We've got a bit of a standoff going on now, which is really irritating. I can feel my heart pounding.

'You are fucking finished,' barks Jennison at Shortass. 'You little fucking dwarf worm.' He undoes Isolda's jeans and gently pulls them down so he can look at the state of her thigh. Isolda jerks and moans as the fabric goes past the wound. There are tears streaming down her face. Despite everything, I want to go down there and help, but that's out of the question.

'Boss. Listen. It was the only way. As long as he had

the gun on Dolly there was nothing we could do! Once she were out of the picture…'

'Oh yeah and what are we going to do now? Call a bloody ambulance?'

Mrs Jennison powers over to where Isolda is lying. She takes her mask off. 'Stop making such a fuss, Dolly. It won't kill you. Get something on it, Tommy. Something to stop the bleeding until it clots.'

I take a quick look at Isolda. I'm pleased to see she's wearing a white thong. The wound is about two inches long. She's still sobbing. She lies on her side. The pain makes her vomit. She looks pale. Shortass is a good, accurate shot, if nothing else. Jennison produces a huge blue handkerchief and pushes it against Isolda's thigh. He looks up at me. 'This is your fault.'

'You're a dick, Jennison,' I reply. 'You've always been a dick. This is Isolda's fault and it's your fault.'

I still keep Shortass in my sights. I've got to get out this situation and find Sara. I need a miracle or something similar.

'You! Timmy!' shouts Mrs Jennison. 'Shoot him! Do it!'

'I can't, Ma,' says Timmy. 'He's got a gun aimed at my head.'

'You useless streak of horse piss.'

Jennison has tied what looks like a tea towel around Isolda's leg. Like the blue handkerchief, it quickly gets soaked with blood. He helps her to stand, then gets her onto the sofa, a few feet away from Mrs Jennison. Isolda doesn't look well; she's pale and has perspiration on her upper lip. She looks at me through heavy lids. I can't decipher the look. She still looks beautiful despite the gunshot wound and the vomiting.

I glance away from her. I'm still waiting for the slightest twitch from Shortass. I'm focussing on him so much I'm almost hallucinating. He's pale and shaking. He's not used to stress of this type. Jennison stands. He starts walking towards me.

'You can do what you like with that fucking gun. I'm coming for you, pretty boy.'

Despite the age and withered arm, Jennison is almost as tall as me and quite broad with it. He strides towards me. 'Kill him, Tommy,' screeches Mrs Jennison. I keep my gun trained on Shortass and my peripheral vision on Jennison. His right arm is stretching out to grab my left shoulder. Three seconds, two seconds, one second.

'Kill him, you useless berk.'

The instant before he makes contact, I put the gun in my left hand and use my right to grab Jennison's withered hand, crushing it in my grip. I whip his arm over my head, pulling him towards me.

I get him in between myself and Shortass and hit his shoulder hard with my gun hand, pushing him at high speed towards my diminutive new pal, who can't fire for fear of hitting his boss.

I have no idea what I'm doing, but whatever it is, it has to be done fast. Shortass looks confused. He waggles his gun around, trying to get a shot in before we reach him, but it's too risky. I wrench Jennison's wrist hard, using the pain this creates to control the direction in which he's going and ram him straight into Shortass. They both grunt with the impact.

While Shortass is coping with that, I elbow Jennison hard in the neck, following that up with a hammer fist to his solar plexus, which knocks him to the ground. Shortass looks dazed for a second, but soon recovers.

He still has the Luger in his hand. I grab the wrist holding the gun and pin it to the wall. I head-butt him, then punch him once, twice, three times in the gut. I notice he has hard abs. With his free hand, he grabs me behind the neck, pulling me towards him. I have no idea what he's trying to do.

I smash him in the jaw with my elbow and use the butt of the gun on his collarbone, hitting the wrong part so it just hurts him rather than breaks it. I can't do all of this while holding a weapon, so I shove it down my waistband while kneeing him in the balls. I have to get that Luger off him.

I can hear Jennison recovering, although groaning a little. Mrs Jennison swears and swears in that terrible, quacking voice. I pull Shortass's wrist back to beat it against the wall again, but the idiot pulls the trigger and gets a shot off. The noise is unbelievable at this range. I feel like I've been slapped in the face and I've got a deafening ringing in both ears.

I turn and elbow him in the face a few times. I see his jaw break. He grunts with the pain. I hold his gun hand in both of mine. Mrs Jennison is yelling something, but I can't make out the words. Is that Isolda screaming, too? Then another shot goes off. This one hits the floor tiles, ricochets upward and shatters one of the big mirrors on the wall. Ridiculously, I feel worried about the fish tank.

Jennison is getting to his feet. I hang on to Shortass's gun hand and try to break his arm at the elbow or lower down. I can feel that he's strong. I suddenly think of him climbing up the wall of Sara's flat. I think of him being in Sara's bedroom while she slept. Then I think of Sara. She's somewhere upstairs. I can't have her being shot by a stray bullet tearing through the ceiling.

My fingers are digging into his arm so deeply that they're drawing blood. He's much shorter than Blond Hair, but I'm going to attempt the same elbow break I did on him. His grip on the gun is phenomenal, but he'll have to let go when his elbow is cracked and shattered.

I turn so I have my back to him. I quickly slide down his body to adjust to his height. I have his forearm and wrist in both of my hands, twist them around and bring his arm down as hard as I can over my shoulder. Another ear splittingly loud shot goes off, followed by a blinding white light and a thundering explosion as the bullet rips through one of the oxygen tanks and the whole world comes to an end.

34

LAST SIGH

I don't think I was out for long. It just seemed like it. I may not have even lost consciousness. I wonder for a moment if I'm blind. I wonder if I'm somehow back in the dark room. My head feels as if it's been in a vice and there's a roaring in my ears.

A quick physical inventory: my back hurts, it feels like the little finger on my right hand is broken and I've got some sort of groin strain. There's a weight on my chest. I attempt to open my eyes but it's difficult. They sting as if they've been exposed to smoke. Now I can smell smoke. It's a bad, caustic smell. With difficulty I open my eyes, look down and see what the weight on my chest is. It's another human. It's Jennison and he's dead.

It all comes back fairly quickly, which is a relief; the bullet, the oxygen tank, the explosion. I push Jennison out of the way. He'd just got up when Shortass fired the shot that caused the explosion and his body must have protected me from the worst of it.

I manage to push him out of the way, stand and take a quick look at his carcass. It's difficult to assess the damage; the rear of his head is caved in by a huge lump of metal and his back and legs are soaked in blood, but I can't really see exactly what happened. Hardly matters, though.

Shortass is lying on his side. He's not dead, but his breathing doesn't sound good. No obvious damage that I can see, apart from his broken jaw and ruined arm, but he's bleeding heavily from somewhere else. I look for his gun, or even for the one I was using, but I can't see them anywhere.

The whole place is a mess; broken glass, broken furniture. I rub my fingers in my eyes to get some of the tears out of the way. As I'm doing this, I stumble over a brown furry cushion on the floor and see the P226. I pick it up and stick it in my waistband. I'll wipe it down and get rid of it later.

Jennison's mother's wheelchair is two separate lumps of twisted metal. I can only see her legs and wonder what happened to the rest of her. There's so much smoke in here that's it's difficult to make out anything, even if it's only several feet away. Then I look at the wall behind where she was sitting. It looks like someone has thrown four or five buckets of offal at it. And then the smell hits me; burnt flesh, faecal matter and God knows what else. Flames are starting at the bottom of one of the curtains.

And then I see Isolda.

She's still sitting where Jennison put her, the fabric that he wrapped around her thigh still soaked in her blood. She has a piece of silver shrapnel about six inches long embedded in her neck. There's no blood coming from the wound. There's another, larger piece of jagged metal in the side of her head, a little above the temple. Once again, there's barely a trickle of blood, though that's not necessarily a good thing.

She's still alive, but I don't think it'll be for long. Her

eyes flicker as she sees me and she smiles weakly. I sit down next to her and take her hand. It feels cold. Her breathing is rapid and her body twitches and jerks from time to time. Blood flows from her nostrils and her mouth. Her pulse is slow and her pupils are dilated.

'You're going to be OK.'

'I don't think so.'

Her voice sounds faint, as if it's painful to talk.

'Listen. You're going to be fine. We're going to get you to a hospital. They'll take care of you there.'

This is bullshit, of course, but there's nothing else I can tell her. Her hand squeezes mine. I feel a blast of hot air on my neck. The burning curtain behind me just got worse. This house will be a very dangerous place to be very soon. I can hear Shortass moaning. I'm wondering if anyone heard the explosion and has called the emergency services.

'You were so nice to me,' she whispers.

'I know.'

This makes her smile. 'Bastard.'

I push some hair away from her face and rub the side of my hand against her cheek. Still beautiful. There are tears in her eyes that weren't there a moment ago.

'Can you tell Sara…'

'I know. You don't have to say it.'

'Can you kiss me?'

I smile at her and lean forward. Just as my lips touch hers I feel a brief sigh escape from her mouth and I know she's gone.

I get up and head for Shortass. I don't know exactly what's wrong with him, but he looks in a bad way and his blood is spreading across the terracotta tiles; pints and pints of it. I gave him a hell of a beating, but I don't think it's much to do with that. Well, maybe a little.

I rifle through all his pockets until I find the keys for Dixon's Audi Sportback. His eyes open and he glares at me, sluggishly attempting to grab my arm. I bring my fist down hard on the base of his thumb and he lets go, slumping back against a chair.

The curtain that was burning has just made its neighbour do the same thing and now one of the sofas has caught fire. There's absolutely nothing I can do about this, so I don't even think about it. I feel sorry for the fish in the tank, though.

I run out into the hallway and head up the stairs. I don't know which room they put Sara in, but I bet it'll be the only locked one. I try three doors until I come to one which won't open. I take a step back, dig my left heel into the carpet and then give the door an almighty kick with my right, ten inches below the lock. The wood splinters immediately, but the lock holds. I give it another kick and I'm in.

Sara is lying on her side on the bed, her wrists and ankles tied with some sort of medium thickness pink nylon rope. She's not moving. I grab her shoulder, pull her onto her back and slap her face three or four times. What's going through my head as I see her lying there, ankles and wrists tied with pink rope, wearing a see-through purple baby doll, makes me doubt my suitability for this job or any other.

She opens her eyes and smiles when she realises it's me. She still looks out of it and her gaze is unfocussed. Shortass made a good job of the knots and I don't have the sort of fingernails that would easily prise them open. I rip out the drawers from the dressing table and quickly rifle through the contents looking for something sharp.

There's now a strong smell of smoke coming from downstairs.

I find a small black leather thing with a zip. I undo it and inside there's a man's manicure and grooming kit which includes small stainless steel scissors. Not ideal, but it'll have to do.

After a few frustrating, fiddly moments, I manage to hack and snip my way through the rope and pull Sara to her feet.

'Sara. Listen. Look at me. You're safe now. But we have to get out of here. You have to do as I say.'

She leans forward unsteadily, her eyes unfocussed, and puts her arms around my neck. 'When you kissed me on Baker Street I went weak at the knees.'

I rest my hands on her hips. 'Hey. Look. You're drugged. Snap out of it. You're a top designer. You don't say things like that to strangers. Now come on.'

I take her hand and half-drag her down the stairs. Before we get to the front door, I take a last look in the living room or whatever it is. It's full of flame. I can't see any of the bodies in there, which is probably just as well. I try not to think about the fish. I try not to think about Isolda.

I can't imagine how I'm going to get Sara to Dixon's car without carrying her and that's going to look conspicuous and memorable to anyone who's passing by or looking out of their window, particularly considering how she's dressed and how wiped out I must be looking.

I can hardly believe my eyes when I open the front door. The SUV is exactly where I left it, about seven yards away. I sit Sara down on the front step and run over to it. It's open and the keys are still in the ignition. Well why wouldn't they be? No one was going to steal this from outside Jennison's house and even if they did, it's a hire car. Besides, after Isolda and I arrived here, everyone was too busy with all the stuff they had to do to worry about it. I run back, lift up Sara and sling her over my shoulders in a fireman's lift, before dumping her in the passenger seat. She giggles like she's pissed.

There are no siren sounds. No crowds. Perhaps the explosion wasn't noticed. Perhaps it was noticed and ignored, who knows? I get Sara's seat belt on for her and turn the engine over. I'm rather relieved it works. There's a half tank of petrol.

It's dark now. It's a rather quiet, cool night, and I can smell honeysuckle in the air. I turn the heating up to full for Sara's sake, but open the window on the driver's side for mine. I'm still feeling drugged and need the stimulus. I take a deep breath. I look in the rear view mirror. I can see the flames have spread and are now behind the front door, but you wouldn't be able to see that from any of the other houses around here, not until it's too late.

I think of Wide Chest, still attached to the oven, frenzied, panicking, choking. Well, that's for you, Peter Dixon, you dumb shit. If they ever look into it, whoever sent Dixon after me will certainly have some food for thought.

I drive slowly down the road with the headlamps off, slowing down for each speed bump. As we approach the gate, I wonder if I've got any explaining/lying to do to George, but there's no one there and the lights are off in the gatehouse. When we're five feet away, the traffic barrier opens automatically and we pass through. They're plainly more concerned with people driving in than they are with people leaving. I can smell burning, but it's not the house. Not yet.

After ten minutes' driving, Sara seems to be recovering, if slowly. She puts her hand on my thigh and squeezes.

'How are you? Are you OK?' I say quietly.

'Your flat. These men came in. Two men. I didn't even hear them come in. Through the door, I mean. One was a big guy. Tiny, ugly, piggy eyes. He slapped me. I heard them walk over your noisy floor, but I thought it was you. I was half asleep. He slapped me so hard I hit my head against the wall. He made remarks about my body. He was leering at me then he slapped me again. He threatened me like it was a joke. He said he and his mates were going to…'

She starts crying, a hand covering her face.

I imagine Wide Chest trying to gnaw through his wrist like a wild animal as the flames engulf that kitchen, trying to get out of those cuffs before he's roasted. I feel nothing as I imagine his terror.

'They gave you some shit in your veins, Sara. Some drug cocktail. I had it too. But it'll wear off. I can tell it's wearing off already. Just breathe deeply and regularly.'

She ignores my excellent medical advice. 'I remember this nasty little guy. He had a syringe. He jabbed the needle in my forearm. It hurt. I had no idea what was going on. Then I woke up in that house. There was an old lady in a wheelchair. All those people. I didn't know them. I was frightened. I felt weird. I still feel weird.'

It only occurs to me now that Sara still doesn't know what the cause of all of this was, from the first street hassle to the blazing house. Isolda made herself scarce as soon as we arrived, so Sara would still not have made the connection.

'Is this going to go on and on until they kill me?' she

says, her voice a half sob. 'I don't know what I've done to these people. I don't know what I've done wrong.'

A cyclist pulls out in front of me. My reactions are so messed up that I almost hit him. He gives me the finger. I can't be bothered to give him a blast of the horn. I'm not sure where the horn is on this.

'It's not going to go on and on, Sara. It's finished now. All of the stuff that was happening to you; Isolda was behind it.'

She turns to look at me. '*What?*'

'It's a long story. She was getting resentful of your success. The two shows thing – Milan and New York – that was the last straw for her. She couldn't stand it. Her dad was some sort of career criminal. He offered to help her out. Put you off your stroke.

'He had these thugs working for him who did all the harassment, including breaking into your flat. They did it all in such a way that you wouldn't be believed when you told people about it.'

She looks out of the window for a few minutes.

'Can you pull over, please?'

'Sure.'

She gets out and throws up on the pavement. I ask if she needs help, but she waves me away. When she gets back in and we drive off, she's silent for a few more minutes. I'll let her do the talking for a while. If she asks about Isolda, I'll have to tell her.

'I can't believe it. I love Isolda. She's more than just someone who works for me. We're friends. I mean, I don't socialise that much, but I do go out with people from the company from time to time. How come I…I never got a *hint* of what you were saying? It's as if you're making it up for a joke.'

'She disguised it pretty well. She had to.'

She looks angry and chews at a fingernail. 'It's such a fucking betrayal. I just can't take it in. She would have benefited from it too! It's insane.'

'It's just one of those things. You never really know what people are thinking or what their motives are. You just have to assimilate it and move on.'

I should be a New Age psychiatrist.

'I don't understand, Daniel. I can see how being called *bitch* on the street and having your privacy violated could screw your work life up, but what about all of the other stuff? Didn't they go too far? Grabbing me on the street in broad daylight? Drugging me? Taking me to that place.' She starts sobbing violently, then looks down at what she's wearing, looking baffled, as if she's seeing the baby doll for the first time.

I put my hand on her knee. 'It's more complicated, Sara. Isolda's father was in prison for a long time. Sixteen years. He missed her growing up, his wife killed herself while he was away, his business, criminal and successful as it was, suffered and never really recovered.'

'But that's not *my* fault.'

'Wait. It only happened yesterday. Isolda had lunch with him. She just let something slip about you. Your original surname: MacQuoid.'

'What's that got to do with anything?'

'He made the connection. It was your father that put Isolda's dad in prison. He couldn't get to your dad or your mum, but he could sure as hell get to you. He wanted revenge. He felt he was owed something for all of those wasted years.

'I know it's ridiculous. He was going to make you into a sort of wife for himself. For 'wife' read 'permanently imprisoned and drugged sex slave'. That's what was going to happen to you.'

I have to pull over again. I'll have to save Isolda's death and Rachelle Beauchesne's coma for some time in the future when Sara and I have nothing to talk about.

*

I park the SUV in Tavistock Street, about one minute's walk away from my flat. My jacket was still in the back seat, so I drape it over Sara's shoulders and we head back along Wellington Street. Her unusual baby doll/leather jacket look attracts a little attention from the late crowds, but no one says anything once they've got a good look at me.

When we get inside, I sit her in front of the television, stick a nature programme on and make both of us some scrambled eggs, toast and coffee while I run her a bath.

While she soaks, I take a shower. I have a lot of things to think about, not least what the emergency services are going to make of what they find at the charred remains of Jennison's place; six dead, evidence of gunfire, not to mention Dixon, the only uncharred body on the scene.

A known criminal, his two henchmen, his mother, his daughter and a private investigator specialising in divorce cases, who parked his car half a mile away. One of the bodies handcuffed to an oven: I can't imagine the speculation.

The place will be covered in my and Sara's fingerprints, but she has no criminal record and I have no record full stop. The prints, if they manage to salvage any, could belong to anyone. I'm hoping they'll put it down to some type of gang warfare thing. After all, Jennison had quite a reputation in the old days and doubtless had/has a lot of enemies.

And now Sara. She's going to have to take some time off. I don't know how long. I don't know if she can recover what she'd intended to do with the shows in Milan and New York. I don't know how much she'll be traumatised by all of this. I don't know how much I should tell her about what went on while she was tied up on the bed.

The most logical route, as far as I can tell at the moment, would be for her story to end at the attempted kidnapping. She meets Rachelle Beauchesne. Rachelle is assaulted, Sara is dragged into an SUV and she somehow escaped when the SUV almost drove into another vehicle. The end. The only weak link in the story would be Eve Cook and I can take care of her.

Her friends at Maccanti would know all about me, as would Kimmons at her flat, but the story would end at the same point for them. For Melody, it would end when I had a row with Isolda and we stormed out of the building together. Whatever all the permutations and lies are, it's a big mess, and the only way to deal with something like this is to play it by ear and see how it all works out, knocking each police lead on the head as it materialises. Perhaps DS Bream can put in a good word for me.

Basically, I'm exhausted; I don't want to think about it and I wish it would all go away.

After her bath, Sara has perked up a little, although I did hear her being sick in the bathroom. I make us both a stiff drink and I tell her as gently as I can about Isolda and what happened at the house. I explain to her that neither of us is in the wrong, but it may not look like that to the police, should they wish to talk to her, particularly regarding my part in the whole thing, relatively innocent as it was (apart from a few minor indiscretions).

She understands and she wants to talk to the police herself. She wants the satisfaction of letting them know that they were condescending, sarcastic and apathetic towards her reporting of what turned out to be an extremely serious series of events that could have resulted in her permanent imprisonment, rape and even her eventual death.

It also resulted in the hell on earth of Jennison's place, which we only just managed to escape from with our lives. She wants to make a stink about it and she doesn't care who it hurts. Fair enough, I guess, as long as she keeps me out of the picture as much as is reasonably possible. As I said, I don't want to think about it anymore.

She sits close to me wearing another one of my sweatshirts and a pair of Rufskin running shorts. She stares blankly at the television screen and sips her vodka and tonic.

'Do you think I'll need therapy after this, Daniel?'

I almost laugh, then realise she's serious.

'I think you'll need to talk to someone. It won't all have hit you yet. You've had the trauma of weeks and weeks of harassment, then the abduction, then the drugging and all the rest of it. Any one of those things would be enough for one person.'

'I want to get on with things, you know? I want to put all of this behind me. It'll need a lot more work, but I think I can do it. I'll make Melody my MTA1 and she can look for a replacement for herself. She's got loads of contacts, she's always socialising with lots of people in the business. I reckon she could come up with half a dozen quality people in a matter of days.'

I suddenly think of Aziza. Her assessment of Sara's problem was about as incorrect as it could be. I think she owes me one for that. I go to the kitchen and make us another couple of drinks. I'm not sure whether either of us should be drinking alcohol after our recent drug intake, but sod it.

'There is someone I know who you could go and see. It's only about five minutes' walk from your offices. Wimpole Street.'

'Wimpole Street? Won't that be terribly expensive? Don't you have to book months in advance?'

'Not in this case. She's an old friend of mine. I'm sure I can persuade her to see you as soon as it's convenient for you and at a reduced rate. You could pop in for a chat during your lunch hours.'

Aziza will be fuming, particularly at the reduced rate, but she's sexy when she's fuming.

'She's a charming Egyptian woman. Her speciality is the type of thing you've had to deal with. I think you'll be comfortable with her.'

'Thank you.'

'You're welcome. I'll give her a call tomorrow.'

'It was the day before yesterday.'

'What was?'

'When we had that meeting in the Wallace Collection brasserie.'

God Almighty. Sixty hours ago. No wonder I feel so tired. I'm covered in aches and pains. I need to get a full check-up at some point in the near future. My little finger still throbs painfully and it's going a dark brown/green colour. I think I fractured it hitting Shortass.

'I'd like to go to bed now. Can I stay in your bed with you, please?'

'If you're sure you're OK with that.'

'I just need someone to hold me. I want to feel safe in case I wake up with nightmares. I doubt if either of us has the energy or inclination for anything else. I'm feeling rather delicate. Anyway, you're still working for me, remember?'

'Of course. It's just part of the service. Aftercare.'

We finish our drinks and five minutes later we're in my bedroom getting undressed. We're both too tired for our nakedness to bother us. It's a relief to actually lie down and feel the clean, soft cotton of a quilt against my skin. Sara lies on her side and I lie behind her, my arms naturally sliding around her waist. She's having difficulty getting comfortable and moves around a lot. It's very distracting. She turns on her back and looks at me. It's dark, but I can still make out the amber of her eyes. I run my hand gently down the side of her body and hear the tiniest of gasps.

'Actually,' she whispers, 'I'm not feeling *that* delicate.'

35

A DRIVE IN THE COUNTRYSIDE

By the time I'm heading towards Alaska Street the following day, it's close to lunchtime and I'm starting to feel hungry. Before I do anything about that, I have a little matter to attend to.

It's not especially warm, but it's a bright day and I can feel the sun on my face as I walk across the road from Waterloo Station and past The Wellington pub. As I walk down Alaska Street and turn the corner into Brad Street I can see Mr Ralph Blake, my eighty-something Italian car freak lock-up neighbour. I knew there'd be a good chance that he'd be around, though to be honest I was hoping that he wouldn't be.

He smiles and raises his hand when he sees me. 'Good morning, Mr O'Shaughnessy! Taking her out for a spin?'

'I thought I might put her through her paces in the countryside. Seems like it's going to be quite a nice day. How are you?'

'Fine, fine.'

He's attempting to get some greasy black muck off his hands with a red and white checked tea towel and not succeeding. He's wearing worn-out brown corduroy trousers, fluorescent yellow trainers and a white Nicki Minaj t-shirt, featuring the singer posing in what looks like a bikini with Pollock-style coloured paint splashes behind her. He sees I'm looking at it.

'My great-grandson got me this for Christmas a few years ago. Look at her, will you? That's what a woman's body *should* be like, not these stick-thin things you see everywhere wearing men's clothing. Great big full breasts, flat stomach, wide hips and a bloody big arse. That's what a real man wants, eh?'

I laugh. 'I can't argue with that.'

He looks at my face with concern. I have the beginnings of an impressive-looking black eye, almost certainly from Shortass's efforts last night or whenever it was. The rest of my face is dappled with grazes, smaller bruises and cuts.

'You look like you've been in the wars! Scrapping again?'

'Just trying to have a quiet drink. Fight between some lads broke out. You know what it's like.'

'Bloody idiots. I bet you gave them what for, though. You look the type.'

'Thank you.'

I grin and turn towards the door of my lock-up. I have to get Footballer Dad sorted and disappeared. Ralph is a pleasant enough chap, but I haven't got time for this today.

'Before you go, take a listen to this,' he says, continuing his hand cleaning efforts.

I can see his red Alfa Romeo Giulietta inside his lock-up which seems to have half its engine out and one of the doors off. The white Bugatti Veyron Vitesse is almost parked on the pavement with its bonnet open. He slams the bonnet shut, gets in the driver's seat and turns it over, hitting the accelerator. I still have a slight drug hangover and the roar of the engine make me feel like someone is trying to saw my head in half. He turns it off and gets out, grinning all over his face.

'Boosted it to 1200 bhp. Does 0 – 60 in 2.3 seconds now. Went out on the motorway a few nights ago. Two, three in the morning. Got it up to 250 mph for a few miles. Still not as it might be. Work in progress.'

If anyone else had told me that they'd been on a UK motorway doing 250 mph, I'd think they were lying or mad. Not him.

'You can give it a spin when it's fully sorted, if you like. See what you think. Second opinion and all that. Personally, I don't think the tyres on there are up to speeds like that. I can feel a bit of drag.'

I nod my head. 'Let me know when it's sorted. I'll see you later.'

'Wide hips and a bloody big arse,' he mumbles to himself, opening the bonnet of the Bugatti once more.

I press the codes into both keypads on my lock-up door and hear the inertia tube locks grind open. There's a cold blast of air as I go inside. I make sure I close the door before I switch the lights on. Footballer Dad is where I left him, lying on the floor to the left of the Maserati. I pull the blue cover off the car and unlock it.

The smell in here is still mainly petrol, oil and plastic; there's no odour coming from the corpse, nor should there be; it's only been here for about thirty-six hours and this place is always on the chilly side. I push it with my foot to see if the rigor mortis has gone and it has.

I open the door on the passenger side and pull the seat forward. There isn't much room in the back of these cars and it's a struggle to shove the body into the limited space. He's quite a heavy individual, but it's the cumbersomeness that's the problem, not the weight.

It takes me about fifteen to twenty minutes to get him in a position I'm happy with. Once that's sorted, I put the car cover over him and push the passenger seat back to its original place. I take a look through all of the windows and everything seems fine. It doesn't look like there's a body there, which is the main thing.

I drive down towards Guildford on the A3, being careful to keep under the speed limit, and stop off at a branch of B&Q to purchase a spade and a garden fork. I also get a sandwich and some chocolate milk from a machine there.

After a few miles, I turn off the main road and drive through the village of Thursley towards Frensham. This whole area is mainly pine forest wilderness and is described on the maps as an area of outstanding beauty.

Twenty minutes later, I turn off the main road onto a dirt track, continue for a mile and a half, then take a sharp right, eventually parking the car in the middle of a small grouping of Corsican pines where it can't be seen. I get out, drag Footballer Dad out of the car and put him on the ground.

I stand still and listen. I can only hear a few birds and a light wind in the trees. This is a fairly deserted, obscure and difficult-to-get-to area and isn't normally frequented by tourists, ramblers, dog walkers or whatever, but you always have to avoid getting cocky about being the only person somewhere. If *you're* there, there's a chance that someone else might be.

I haven't been here for a few years, but I can still remember the topography. I grab the garden tools in one hand and with a grunt, sling Footballer Dad over my shoulder.

It would be a lot easier to follow the paths to where

I'm going, but the risk is too high, so I keep to the thickly forested areas, despite the difficulties this creates.

I actually trip and fall at one point, Footballer Dad and the tools crashing to the ground with me. It was almost funny. I'm sure it'll be hilarious in a few months, maybe even side-splitting.

I'm going to be walking for just over an hour. The weight and awkwardness of carrying a body this far through troublesome terrain is exhausting and very uncomfortable. The leaf canopy makes it quite dark, which just adds to the problem. I try to convince myself that this is some sort of countryside gym workout or a cheery Outward Bound task.

By the time I arrive at my destination, I'm soaked with sweat and my left shoulder is absolutely killing me. My fingers are numb from gripping the spade and the garden fork. Still psyching myself into thinking of this as a workout, I put the corpse and tools on the floor, hang my t-shirt on the branch of a nearby tree and get down to digging Footballer Dad's grave.

In an hour it's complete. I jump down into it and only my head is above the surface of the ground, which'll do fine. It doesn't have to be too long; he's going to be in the foetal position. I take his clothes off, roll him into it, and get down in there with him to sort his position out.

When I get out again, I throw some assorted vegetation over him to help encourage anaerobic/aerobic bacteria and suddenly wonder if this is how the custom of throwing flowers or petals onto a coffin originated. It takes me fifteen minutes to fill in the grave and make a decent-sized mound.

I create a makeshift bag out of his jacket and roll the rest of his clothes into it. I'll dump this elsewhere; I don't want pieces of fabric turning up on the surface for the next six months, courtesy of the worm population.

I should have brought some tins of various animal repellent with me, but I'd have had problems carrying them. I'll just have to hope that whatever lives around here isn't that hungry or desperate. Five foot is a long way down for a small to medium sized mammal, anyway.

I cover the mound in some more vegetation and make my way back to the car. Just as I get in, it occurs to me that I have a loose end to deal with. I check my mobile. Amazingly, I have a signal. I give the Royal Free Hospital a call. Someone answers almost immediately.

'Emergency Department. How can I help you?'

Black Suit's name was Colin. Jackie Heath was his uncle. I assume his name is Colin Heath.

'Oh, hello. I'm just checking on my nephew who was brought in with a shoulder dislocation yesterday. His name is Colin Heath.'

'Are you a relative?'

God Almighty – I just said he was my nephew. 'Yes. I'm his uncle. My name's Jack Heath.'

'One moment, please. Colin Heath. OK. He's been admitted under Orthopaedics. I'll just put you through.'

'Thank you.'

I click off. That's all I need to know.

I make a couple more random stops to dump the tools, the clothes and the car cover and then I'm heading back to London.

When I get back to Exeter Street, I have a quick, hot shower and sit in the kitchen, drinking coffee and staring at the bars on the window. I ring Imperial China in Soho and book at table for two at eight o' clock this evening, then I give Klementina a call and tell her.

She sounds delighted. I'd forgotten how charming her accent sounded. We arrange to meet in the Slug and Lettuce in Lisle Street for cocktails at seven. I'm not that fussed about them myself, but Klementina seemed like a cocktails kind of girl and I want to make this a good evening for her.

One more call, then I'm going to have an hour's sleep. I call the Hotel Café Royal and get them to put me through to Mrs Doroteia Vasconselos in the Celestine Suite.

'I was disappointed that I did not see you yesterday afternoon, Mr Beckett.'

'My disappointment was greater, Mrs Vasconselos. How did your fitting at Rigby & Peller go?'

'Very enjoyable, thank you. The staff are so attentive, especially when you are spending a lot of money.'

'Did you get what you wanted?'

'I did. I found great satisfaction. I bought three balconette deep plunge brassieres and matching briefs. One of the brassieres was particularly charming; made from black corsetry lace. They described it as pure seduction. Almost see-through, I'm afraid to say. At first, they didn't think they had a double F cup in stock in that style, but they managed to find one eventually. I was so relieved.'

My mouth has gone dry. I swallow so I can continue speaking. 'Did you buy anything else?'

'I treated myself to a couple of new suspender belts, a garter belt and a rather lovely basque. They have so many elegant and alluring items. I find it hard to stop once I've started. I'm sure you have known many women who are like that.'

'Yes, I have.'

'We are so hard to satisfy.'

'But it's gratifying when total satisfaction is finally attained.'

'I agree. Though for some women, it can be very time-consuming to get to that point. The process can be quite strenuous and demanding.'

'It goes without saying that those demands would have to be met with vigour.'

'You're so right, Mr Beckett. Would you like to visit me here, say, tomorrow morning at eleven? I can show you the results of my fitting, if you are interested. I would appreciate your opinion, as a man.'

'I'd be delighted.'

'Tomorrow, then.'

'Tomorrow.'

I click off my mobile and take a deep breath. I just hope I'm up to giving her my best opinion after a night with Klementina.

As I'm making another espresso, I notice a bag near the coffee maker with the Royal Academy of Arts logo on it. I put my hand inside and pull out the Ken Howard blue crystal necklace that I'd bought for Isolda and forgotten to give to her. It's pretty. I put it back in the bag and drop it into the bin.

THE END

Books by Dominic Piper

Kiss Me When I'm Dead

Death is the New Black

Femme Fatale

Printed in Great Britain
by Amazon